CASSANDRA

IN

REVERSE

HOLLY SMALE

CASSANDRA

IN

REVERSE

 mira

ISBN-13: 978-0-7783-3453-8

Recycling programs
for this product may
not exist in your area.

Mira
22 Adelaide St. West, 41st Floor
Toronto, Ontario M5H 4E3, Canada
BookClubbish.com

Printed in U.S.A.

For my sister, Tara.

Always an army of two.

CASSANDRA

IN

REVERSE

When things go well, a shadow overturns it all.
When badly, a damp sponge wipes away the picture.

Aeschylus

WHERE DOES A STORY START?

It's a lie, the first page of a book, because it masquerades as a beginning. A *real* beginning—the opening of something—when what you're being offered is an arbitrary line in the sand. *This story starts here.* Pick a random event. Ignore whatever came before it or catch up later. Pretend the world stops when the book closes, or that a resolution isn't simply another random moment on a curated timeline.

But life isn't like that, so books are dishonest.

Maybe that's why humans like them.

And it's saying that kind of shit that gets me thrown out of the Fentiman Road Book Club.

Here are some other things I've been asked not to return to:
- The Blenheim Road Readers Group
- A large flat-share I briefly attempted in Walthamstow
- My last relationship
- My current job

The final two have been in quick succession. This morning, Will—my boyfriend of four months—kissed me, listed my virtues out of nowhere and concluded the pep talk by ending our relationship.

The job situation I found out about eighty seconds ago.

According to the flexing jaw and flared nostrils of my boss, I've yet to respond to this new information. He seems faint and muted, as if he's behind a pane of thick frosted glass. He also has a dried oat on his shirt collar but now doesn't seem the right time to point it out: he's married—his wife can do it later.

"Cassie," he says more loudly. "Did you hear me?"

Obviously I heard him or I'd still be giving a detailed report on the client meeting I just had, which is exactly what I was doing when he fired me.

"The issue isn't so much your work performance," he plows on gallantly. "Although, Christ knows, somebody who hates phone calls as much as you do shouldn't be working in public relations."

I nod: that's an accurate assessment.

"It's your *general demeanor* I can't have in this office. You are rude. Insubordinate. Arrogant, frankly. You are not a team player, and do you know what this office needs?"

"A better coffee machine."

"That's exactly the kind of bullshit I'm talking about."

I'd tell you my boss's name and give him a brief description, but judging by this conversation, he isn't going to be a prominent character for much longer.

"I've spoken to you about this on multiple occasions— Cassandra, look at me when I'm talking to you. Our highest-paying client just dropped us because of your quote, unquote *relentlessly grating behavior.* You are unlikable. That's the exact word they used. *Unlikable.* Public relations is a People Job. For People People."

Now, just hang on a minute.

"I'm a person," I object, lifting my chin and doing my best to stare directly into his pupils. "And, as far as I'm aware, being *likable* is irrelevant to my job description. It's certainly not in my contract, because I've checked."

My boss's nostrils flare into horsiness.

I rarely understand what another human is thinking, but I frequently feel it: a wave of emotion that pours out of them into me, like a teapot into a cup. While it fills me up, I have to work out what the hell it is, where it came from and what I'm supposed to do to stop it spilling everywhere.

Rage that doesn't feel like mine pulses through me: dark purple and red.

His colors are an invasion and I do not like it.

"Look," my boss concludes with a patient sigh that is nothing like the emotion bolting out of him. "This just isn't working out, Cassie, and on some level you must already know that. Maybe you should find something that is better suited to your... specific skill set."

That's essentially what Will told me this morning too. I don't know why they're both under the impression I must have seen the end coming when I very much did not.

"Your job has the word *relations* in it," my boss clarifies helpfully. "Perhaps you could find one that doesn't?"

Standing up, I clear my throat and look at my watch: it's not even Wednesday lunchtime yet.

Relationship: over.

Job: over.

"Well," I say calmly. "Fuck."

So that's where my story starts.

It could have started anywhere: I just had to pick a moment. It could have been waking up this morning to the sound of my flatmates screaming at each other, or eating my breakfast (porridge and banana, always), or making an elaborate gift for my first anniversary with Will (slightly preemptive).

It could have been the moment just before I met him, which would have been a more positive beginning. It could have been the day my parents died in a car accident, which would have been considerably less so.

But I chose here: kind of in the middle.

Thirty-one years into *my* story and a long time after the dramatic end of some others. Packing a cardboard box with very little, because it transpires the only thing on my desk that doesn't belong to the agency is a gifted coffee mug with a picture of a cartoon deer on it. I put it in the box anyway. There's no real way of knowing what's going to happen next, but I assume there will still be caffeine.

"Oh shit!" My colleague Sophie leans across our desks as I stick a wilting plant under my arm just to look like I'm not leaving another year of my life behind with literally nothing to show for it. "They haven't *fired* you? That's *awful*. I'm sure we will all miss you *so much*."

I genuinely have no idea if she means this or not. If she does, it's certainly unexpected: we've been sitting opposite each other since I got here and all I really know about her is that she's twenty-two years old and likes tuna sandwiches, typing aggressively and picking her nose as if none of us have peripheral vision.

"Will you?" I ask, genuinely curious. "Why?"

Sophie opens her mouth, shuts it again and goes back to smashing her keyboard as if she's playing whack-a-mole with her fingertips.

"Cassandra!" My boss appears in the doorway just as I start cleaning down my keyboard with one of my little antiseptic wipes. "What the hell are you doing? I didn't mean leave *right now*. Jesus on a yellow bicycle, what is wrong with you? I'd prefer you to work out your notice period, please."

"Oh." I look down at the box and my plant. I've packed now. "No, thank you."

Finished with cleaning, I sling my handbag over my shoulder and my coat over my arm, hold the box against my stomach, awkwardly hook the plant in the crook of my elbow and try to get the agency door open on my own. Then I hold it open with my knee while I look back, even though—much like Orpheus at the border of the Underworld—I know I shouldn't.

The office has never been this quiet.

Heads are conscientiously turned away from me, as if I'm a sudden bright light. There's a light patter of keyboards like pigeons walking on a roof (punctuated by the violent death stabs of Sophie), the radiator by the window is gurgling, the reception is blindingly gold-leafed and the watercooler drips. If I'm looking for something good to come out of today—and I think I probably should—it's that I won't have to hear *that* every second for the rest of my working life.

It's a productivity triumph. They should fire people for fundamental personality flaws more often.

The door slams behind me and I jump even though I'm the one who slammed it. Then my phone beeps, so I balance everything precariously on one knee and fumble for it. I try to avoid having unread notifications if I can. They make my bag feel heavy.

Dankworth please clean your shit up

I frown as I reply:

Which shit in particular

There's another beep.

Very funny. Keep the kitchen clear

It is a COMMUNAL SPACE.

It wasn't funny a couple of weeks ago when I came down for
a glass of water in the middle of the night and found Sal and
Derek having sex against the fridge.

Although perhaps that is the *definition* of communal.

Still frowning, I hit the button for the lift and mentally scour
the flat for what I've done wrong this time. I forgot to wash
my porridge bowl and spoon. There's also my favorite yellow
scarf on the floor and a purple jumper over the arm of the sofa.
This is my sixth flat-share in ten years and I'm starting to feel
like a snail: carrying my belongings around with me so I leave
no visible trace.

I send back:

OK.

My intestines are rapidly liquidizing, my cheeks are hot and a
bright pink rash I can't see is forming across my chest. Dull pain
wraps itself around my neck, like a scarf pulled tight.

It's fascinating how emotions can tie your life together.

One minute you're twelve, standing in the middle of a playground while people fight over who doesn't get you as a teammate. The next you're in your thirties, single and standing by
the lifts of an office you've just been fired from because nobody wants you as a teammate. Same sensations, different body.
Literally: my cells have cunningly replaced themselves at least
twice in the interim.

The office door swings open. "Cassandra?"

Ronald has worn the same thing—a navy cashmere jumper—
every day since he started working here a few months ago. It
smells really lovely, so I'm guessing there must be plural.

He walks toward me and I immediately panic. Now and then
I've caught him looking at me from the neighboring desk with

an incalculable expression on his face, and I have no idea what it could be. Lust? Repulsion? I've been scripting a response to the former for a month now, just in case.

I am honored by your romantic and/or sexual interest in me given that we've only exchanged perfunctory greetings, but I have a long-term boyfriend I am almost definitely in the process of falling in love with.

Well, that excuse isn't going to work anymore, is it.

Ronald clears his throat and runs a large hand over his buzz-cut Afro. "That's mine."

"Who?" I blink, disoriented by the grammar. "Me?"

"The plant." He points at the shrubbery now clutched under my sweaty armpit. "It's mine and I'd like to keep it."

Ah, the sweet, giddy flush of humiliation is now complete.

"Of course," I say stiffly. "Sorry, Ronald."

Ronald blinks and reaches out a hand; I move quickly away so his fingers won't touch mine, nearly dropping the pot in the process. It's the same fun little dance I do when I have to pay with cash at the supermarket checkout, which is why I always carry cards.

I get into the lift and press the button. Ronald now appears to be casually assessing me as if I'm a half-ripe avocado, so I stare at the floor until he reaches a conclusion.

"Bye," he says finally.

"Bye," I say as the lift doors slide shut.

And that's how my story starts.

With a novelty mug in a box, a full character assassination and the realization that when I leave a building I am missed considerably less than a half-dead rubber plant.

2

IT'S NOT ALL BAD.

At least tomorrow I won't be sitting in a loud office with a reception that looks like it's been licked by King Midas, listening to people who don't like me eat crisps, desperately hoping nobody calls for an Idea Hurricane, and pretending all the lies I'm being paid to tell don't make me want to rip my skin off with my fingernails.

Tomorrow will be a *good* day.

Obviously, the day after that I'll be sitting in my bank manager's office, breathing into a paper bag and begging him to extend my overdraft, so I should probably make the most of it.

"Cassandra?"

The lift doors slide open with a *ping* and I charge toward the exit, holding my cardboard box defensively out in front of me like some kind of Trojan shield.

"Miss Dankworth?" Credit to the receptionist: she isn't easily ignored. "Hang on a second—I've got Mr. Fawcett on line nine, and he says it's company policy to make sure you hand in your pass before you leave."

Cassandra Penelope Dankworth: that's my name. Thanks to my (dead) parents, I sound like a cross between a Greek heroine and a killer's basement.

"Can't stop," I manage. "In flight mode."

My heart is racing, my veins and pupils are dilating, my lungs are expanding and oxygen is racing to my brain in preparation for what it now assumes is imminent physical danger. Which is super handy if you need to run away from a rampaging woolly mammoth and not so handy if you're just trying to get out of an office block in central London without vomiting on your trainers.

Panicked, I body-slam the front door repeatedly until the receptionist takes pity on me and lets me out with a *click*.

Fresh air hits me in the face like a bright wall.

Eyes shut, I stand on the street for a few seconds and attempt to recalibrate. The insides of my eyelids are flickering—tiny warning flares sent up by dozens of sinking ships—and if I don't find a way to calm down immediately, *it* is going to happen, and nobody wants that: not here, not on a public pavement, not in central Soho surrounded by people eating eight-pound crayfish baguettes.

This is why Will keeps telling me to start yoga. But I just don't feel comfortable with that many simultaneous bottoms in the air.

"Excuse me." A woman in a viciously orange bomber jacket taps me lightly on the shoulder and I jump as if she just stabbed me with a cattle prod. "You're kind of blocking the entrance to the— Are you okay?"

I blink at her. "Banana muffin."

"I'm sorry?"

A giddy wave of relief. "I need a banana muffin."

With my cardboard box gripped tightly, I begin urgently

scurrying toward the tiny café on the corner. Banana muffins are comforting. Banana muffins are reassuring and familiar. Banana muffins don't wake up in the morning and tell you they care about you immensely but just don't see a future with you anymore.

The blue café doorbell tinkles behind me and it makes me briefly think of *It's a Wonderful Life*, which is a beautiful film about a much-loved man who has a positive impact on the world around him and which I, therefore, find difficult to relate to.

"Hello, young lady! Goodness, is it one o' clock already? Or are you early?"

I stare at the place where banana muffins should be.

"Oh!" The café owner smiles as if the whole world isn't now disintegrating beneath my feet. "I'm afraid we had a delivery issue this morning and they didn't have the banana ones you like so much, but we *do* have some delicious chocolate muffins and a lovely salted caramel, which I can personally attest is—"

"Banana," I insist, abruptly welling up.

"Not today," he clarifies gently. "Come in at your normal time tomorrow and I'll make sure I put a big one aside for you, okay?"

"But—" my grief feels overwhelming "—I won't be here tomorrow."

"Then why don't you take a seat for a minute and I'll see if I can find you something else instead?"

The old man points with concern at the green velvet chairs and a vivid memory flashes: Will, drinking a cappuccino and grinning at me with the sharpened mouth of a cat, lined with chocolate.

"Don't cry, sweetheart," the café man adds in alarm. "How about I put some banana muffins aside tomorrow so you can take extras home and freeze them?"

I'm never going to see Will again, am I?

That's the rule, right? They tell you they'll stay in touch, that you'll always be part of each other's lives, except it's just a script—a lie you're supposed to see through—but you believe them until they slowly stop answering your text messages and cat GIFs and one day you see them in Pizza Express with someone else and they pretend they can't see you even though you're waving as hard as you can.

I just didn't think it would happen with Will. Everything was going so well. I didn't get a chance to construct a suitable exit strategy from our relationship or plan a response to being dumped or properly rehearse how my heartbreak might feel in my head first.

I wasn't *prepared*.

"Hey," a woman in a big gray hat says as I stumble back out of the café door. "Wait just a—"

Everything is too far away and too close at the same time, too loud and also too quiet; a yellow door, an orange can, a blue sliver of sky, a dropped navy glove, the red ring around a street sign; a kaleidoscope turning.

A pigeon flaps violently and I put my hands over my face.

It's coming.

It's coming and without my banana muffin there is nothing I can do to stop it.

I need to get home *now*.

Struggling to breathe, I stagger round the corner into a sudden blast of noise so raw and so painful it takes a moment to establish that it's not coming from inside me.

"Fur's not fair! Fur's not fair! Fur's not fair!"

"Fashion has no compassion!" A woman with a purple bowl cut thrusts a leaflet at me. "A hundred million animals every year are raised and killed for their fur! They spend their lives in tiny cages before being viciously slaughtered so that humans can wear their skins!"

Blue-tinged magenta; cheese and onion breath. A surge of

hot electricity careers from one side of my head to the other. Cringing, I'm pushed into the sticky, bare flesh of a topless man.

"Minks are semiaquatic animals!" he shouts as I stare at his nipples. "They are biologically designed to hold their breath and so suffer horribly during the gassing process!"

"I—" I manage, tripping over a banner, and now I'm being swept down Regent Street like a paralyzed dolphin caught in a shoal of hundreds of bright, screaming, woolly-hatted fish with megaphones and whistles.

"FUR IS DEATH!"

"Fur is death!"

"FUR IS DEATH!"

Drums bang, purple smoke explodes, a car horn blasts, a child starts screaming and a dog barks. A sheet of pure sound passes through me and I start to pull apart on a cellular level, the way a glass shakes just before it shatters.

"Head-to-toe electrocution!" An old lady gets right in my face: pores like orange coral, emotions neon yellow. "Foxes get an electrode up their butts. Does that sound fun to you?"

I follow the direction of her eyes to the large furry tail clipped to the front of my handbag. Will teases me for being "such a child sometimes," but I like to hold on to it tightly when I'm on a busy train or someone gets too close to me in the post office queue. It's also clearly artificial: it's bright bloody *green*.

Which is what I open my mouth to politely explain when a spray of sticky liquid hits my face. It smells sour; tastes like ink and rotting Jelly Babies.

When I put my hand up, it comes away red.

Somebody starts wailing loudly.

And it's only as I start desperately clawing and elbowing my way out of the crowd that I realize the horrible monotone noise is coming out of me.

It's here.

It's here and I'm covered in (blood? Paint? Corn syrup?) and fireworks are exploding behind my eyelids and I'm *unlikable* and *relentlessly grating* and unemployed again and a siren goes off and a shop alarm shoots through my head and Will doesn't love me, couldn't love me, maybe there's nothing to love and there are no *fucking banana muffins anywhere*.

Openly sobbing now, I take the only option I have left. I find the nearest empty doorway, crouch in a small ball on the ground with my arms wrapped tightly around my head.

("Cassandra must stop reacting to stress like a hedgehog.")

And I wait for everything to go black.

IT'S ODD BEHAVIOR, I KNOW.

People have been telling me how weird I am since I was a small child, with varying degrees of anger and irritation. Over the years my "little episodes" have been put down to:

- Victorian-esque hysteria ("Get her some smelling salts")
- A dramatic disposition
- A desperate need for attention
- A pathological inclination toward ruining parties

All I know for sure is that as long as I can get somewhere dark and silent as soon as I feel one coming on, my "hissy fits" often recede just before peaking, like a sneeze or an orgasm.

And if I don't...

Let's just say a large proportion of my life is spent in constant fear that the next one will happen in a client meeting, in the middle of Zara on a Saturday afternoon or at somebody else's wedding. ("Cassandra must stop making everything about her.") My theory is that my brain is like a lazy IT department, and every time there's a problem with the electrics it just panics and pulls the plug out at the wall.

Switch her off, switch her back on again: see if that helps.

This must have been a particularly bad one; by the time I finally resurface, my limbs are covered in scratch marks, my body feels swollen—a balloon filled with water—and the street is dark and back to normal. The protest has gone.

Shivering, I look more closely at my wrist: so has my watch.

I look around: plus my box with my mug in it.

Nice one. Thanks, London.

Aching all over, I groggily attempt to rise like Aphrodite, except that instead of the Greek goddess of love and beauty, I'm obviously a snot-covered, unemployed woman in her early thirties, and instead of gracefully emerging from a seashell, I'm hanging sweatily on to the doorknob of a new establishment called Bar Humbug, attempting not to make eye contact with a judgmental binman.

On the upside, I feel infinitely calmer now.

You can say what you like about my brain—and a lot of people have done over the decades—but it certainly knows how to return to factory settings.

"HELLO? WHO IS IT?"

I wish my flatmates would stop yelling this every time I open the front door: I'm the only other person who lives here.

"Cassandra," I say, locking it behind me.

After careful consideration, I splurged on an Uber back to my flat in Brixton instead of attempting to navigate public transport as I normally would. Now may not be the time to start splashing cash around, but it's also not the time to be half a kilometer underground with a brain that feels like over-milked mashed potato.

"Oh." Sal appears in the kitchen doorway wearing a pair of

bright pink cropped shorts and casually props one foot on the other toned leg like a ridiculously beautiful flamingo. "It's you."

"WHO?" Derek shouts again from the living room.

"Cassandra," Sal calls back with a deliberate note of disappointment, eyeing me suspiciously as if I've just broken in. "We're waiting for the takeaway guy."

"Do they have a key now too, then?" I put my bag down and take my trainers off.

"Ha. Always so unbearably witty."

Salini Malhotra is a smidgen shorter than me—"tall for a girl" (generally only an observation made by short men)—and has glowing skin, full lips and the kind of cheekbones I can only assume were carved by Zeus himself. Derek Miller is her boyfriend and similarly attractive, if you like men who leave used teeth-whitening strips and blond beard shavings all over the bathroom, which I do not.

I've lived here for about six months now, and my flatmate is still scanning my features as if she's going to be asked to draw them at some point in the future.

"Oh!" I say, suddenly remembering the fake blood from the protest and realizing I must look like I've been casually caught in a meat grinder and forgotten to mention it. "I'm not hurt—don't worry."

"I'm not going to," Sal sighs tiredly, unhooking her leg and turning to forage in one of the cupboards for a glass. "You seem fully capable of looking after yourself, Cassandra."

I watch her for a few seconds. The color coming out of her isn't quite anger, but it's definitely in the same family: a blue-red, like the shade of an expensive designer lipstick I've been told I can't wear because it clashes with my hair. I can feel the intensity of her emotion tickling the edges of my skin, trying to get in. Not quite anger, more than resentment, too bright to be disgust…

"Derek," she calls to the living room. "Your *other* girlfriend is here. Aren't you going to come and say hello?"

Whatever it is, Sal clearly hasn't forgiven me yet. There are also a few splashes of vomit yellow shooting out of her, but that makes no sense and I'm tired, so I must be reading it wrong.

"Be nice, babe," Derek admonishes, ambling into the room with the blank smile of a toothpaste model and staring at her bottom. "She screwed up. We all do it sometimes. Try to let it go while we're all living under the same roof, yeah?"

Then he slowly wraps a long arm around her and pulls her toward him for a kiss in a gesture that reminds me a lot of an elephant eating a peanut.

"Fine," Sal sniffs, watching me warily over his shoulder as if I'm a gas canister placed next to an open flame and should be monitored at all times in case I take the whole house down. "Sorry. I just think it might be easier for all of us if we had the place to ourselves again. It's not really big enough for three people. Plus, she's in her thirties. Surely she wants a place of her own by now?"

As if I'm sitting on a deposit for a beautiful flat in Primrose Hill but have instead decided to take their tiny box room in Brixton for the sheer pleasure of watching them grope each other by the tea bags.

"You're both twenty-nine," I point out shortly.

"Everyone knows thirty is the cutoff point before flat-sharing with someone you're not screwing is just a bit sad." Sal peels herself away from Derek and narrows dark brown eyes in my direction as if trying to find somewhere to put me, like an awkwardly shaped piece of Tupperware. "Why don't you just move in with the lawyer you're dating? Get out of this little *rut* you're clearly in."

My stomach contracts as if whacked by a netball: a sensation I haven't felt for quite some time but which is carved deeply into my muscle memory.

On the contrary, I am currently rut-less.

"Will isn't a lawyer," I say. "He's a wildlife cameraman."

I'm about to triumphantly add that he's not dating me any-more, actually, before realizing this might not be the slam dunk I'm looking for.

"Just leave it now," Derek says firmly, bopping Sal affec-tionately on the nose. "I mean it. We said we'd give Cassie as much time as she needs to find somewhere else to live, and we're going to do that. We're not dicks."

"I'm looking," I say. "Really."

By "looking" I mean: opening Gumtree twice, examining the kind of studios I can afford, deciding that the devil I know at least has hot water on tap and no shower cubicle literally touching my bed, and firmly closing my laptop again. Maybe if I hide in my room long enough, they'll forget all the drama of a few months ago and we can go back to normal.

With "normal" being us having absolutely nothing in com-mon and some passive-aggressive comments about my sarto-rial choices.

It still beats whatever the hell *this* is.

"I'll look harder," I mumble, looking around the kitchen with a frown. Something feels wrong. It smells…different. They got fish and chips last night, and normally the smell of beer-battered death festers for days, but it's already gone. The yellow scarf is hanging back on its hook, and when I turn toward the sofa, my purple jumper has disappeared.

Shit. In all the fun of today, I forgot about the texts.

"I apologize for leaving my porridge out," I offer formally, turning toward the sink. "I'll wash it up now."

Except that's gone too.

"Did we get a cleaner?" My hedgehog bowl is neatly posi-tioned back in my minuscule cupboard (the only kitchen space they offered me and which I have to organize daily like a game of *Tetris* to stop it all falling out). "Because I'm not sure I can… chip in toward that just now."

"What?" Sal turns on the television loudly.

"Never mind," I sigh. I'd tell you what I did to destroy yet another cohabiting situation, but I've already lived through the humiliation once. All you need to know is it was a misunderstanding, not one of my prouder moments and I don't really blame Sal for treating me like novelty wallpaper that seemed like a good idea at the time but is now proving inordinately difficult to get rid of.

"Oh!" she yells as I head up the stairs to my tiny bedroom. "You got another bloody letter, Cassandra! I put it outside your door again, but can you do your own admin going forward, please? I am not your personal bloody secretary."

Blinking, I pick up the envelope leaning against my door like a drunk middle-aged man at a bar. The handwriting is so familiar—*Cass*—and a queasy sensation ripples through me; I close my eyes briefly until it's gone.

I got a letter yesterday too. This is getting really out of hand.

Ripping it in half, I open the door and throw it in my wastepaper basket again: I've no intention of reading or answering this one either. Then I close the door quietly, flop backward on my small double bed and stare blankly at the ceiling. It *is* a nice little room and I don't want to leave just yet if I can possibly avoid it. Yes, it was originally a bathroom and it's so small I have to hang my large collection of clothes on open racks and shelves next to a remaining chipped sink, which is visually distressing even if I organize them all by color and texture (which I obviously do).

But it's also clean, cheap and perfectly symmetrical, which is a rare combination in London. It has no apparent mold or bloodstains and does have a real window, which is an improvement on five of the eight other places I looked at. The sun comes in just before work in the morning, and—if you fall asleep at a specific angle—sometimes you wake up with a warm, happy yellow stripe of it lining your eyelids.

Very occasionally, that exact spot also happens to coincide with Will's bare chest, which means if I position myself carefully, I get to wake up to the sound of his heartbeat too.

Got to, past tense, no longer relevant.

Fuck.

Grabbing my phone, I smash out a text before pride or self-respect can stop me:

Are we absolutely sure we've made the right decision?

I quite like the dignified way I've shifted to plural pronouns, thereby implying we had equal input into the situation when we absolutely did not.

Then I press SEND, hold my breath and try not to count.

Forty-eight seconds later:

Yeah! It's going to be great. You'll see!

I blink at my screen.

Uh.

"Great" is not the word I'd use, Will.

Another *beep.*

**You and your thesaurus brain. ;)
Prodigious. Stupendous. Life-changing.
Best decision ever. Better?**

Not really, no. People ask what's "wrong" with me all the time, but now and then I wonder if I'm actually the problem. That is the most inappropriate winky face I have ever seen.

Jaw gritted, I write back:

Glad you're happy.

Then I throw my phone to the end of my bed.

Four months.

I spent four months of my life with a man who is now apparently celebrating the end of our relationship as if it's the World Cup final. And I should have seen it coming: that's what's so embarrassing. Will is a handsome thirty-four-year-old man with a serious, nearly-got-married relationship under his belt; I'm still collecting our used cinema tickets and keeping count of exactly how many dates we've been on. Last night was number twenty-six, which I still think deserves a *little* more respect when over than "best decision ever," thank you very much.

To clarify, I'm not *always* the one being dumped.

You might think that's the case, but out of twenty-three temporary partners, I'd say it's about 55 to 60 percent me doing the dumping. Dating and relationships are super exhausting, even if the other person really wants to be in it. Which, as he has just made extremely clear, Will absolutely does not.

Suddenly drowsy, I climb under the duvet and pull it over my head so it forms a little private fort. My blond hair crackles with static, puffs out like dandelion seeds and then immediately sticks to my face. Brushing it away, I yawn and close my eyes. This always happens. Too much emotion in one go and my brain experiences a power surge and sends me to sleep to preserve battery. Inconvenient when you're at, say, your parents' funeral, but not so bad when you're already in bed and you don't have that much left to stay awake for.

I'm nearly unconscious again when the doorbell rings.

Behind my eyelids, a bright flash of neon blue.

"For the love of— CASSANDRA! IT'S FOR YOU. Where the bloody hell is this takeaway? Are they catching it themselves? I am sodding emancipated."

Confused—I'm still too sleepy to work out if Sal means *ema-*

ciated or if her father has stopped paying the mortgage—I droop out of bed and pull on my old, bright yellow dressing gown over the top of my work clothes. It's been a long day and everything hurts. I need all the extra fluff I can get.

Pulling the hood up and hearing my hair crackle again, I step into the hallway.

"Hey, chick." Will grins.

4

WELL, THIS IS UNEXPECTED.

"Get it?" Will adds after six long seconds of me staring silently at him. "Because you're all fluffy like a baby chicken? And also you're a woman, so it's a playful nod toward an outdated and misogynist terminology I would never use in earnest?"

I open my mouth.

Admittedly, I've never had a real long-term relationship before—at four months, Will is my Personal Best—but is it standard practice to turn up at your ex's house on the evening you dumped them and comment on their loungewear?

"Did work run late?" Will glances at the time on his phone. "Are you dressed underneath, Cass? Because we need to leave now if we want to make it."

In shock, I peel open my yellow dressing gown to reveal a dark navy jumpsuit like the world's least sexy poultry-themed stripper. Another bolt of confusion: Wednesday's work jumpsuit

is black. I must have been so upset by our breakup this morning I went ahead and donned the wrong one.

"You look perfect." Will grins. "Grab your trainers."

And I know at this point I should probably ask a few perti-
nent questions—any questions at all would be good—but Will
just said I look perfect, which is nice to hear, so I nod and obediently grab my trainers.

Maybe he's here for a debrief.

Maybe this is what happens after twenty-six dates: you don't
just end a relationship one morning with a kiss and a series of
compliments and then never speak again. You come back later
for a formal termination meeting so you can discuss it all in-
depth, break it down into bullet points and make a list of exactly where it all went wrong. Because I have to be honest: I
thought about it all morning and I have no bloody idea.

"Hi." Will smiles as I step out of the front door, leaning forward and gently pecking my cheek.

I stare at him. "Hi."

That feels inappropriate too: surely he gave up the right to
casually put his lips on me this morning? A familiar whiff of
too-strong black coffee—I miss him already and he's literally
touching me—and Will strides down the path with me following, still staring. His walk was one of the first things I noticed
when we met. It's both intrepid and jaunty, like Odysseus in
charge of his ship. There's something generally solid and daunt-
less about Will—he's an oak tree of a man—and that's a *very*
attractive quality for someone who feels flimsy and daunted
90 percent of the time.

What the hell is going on? In fairness, I didn't check my
emails at all today: maybe the missing contextual information
I need is sitting in my inbox.

I'm also desperately trying to identify any colors or emotions,
but there's nothing there. Whatever Will is feeling, it's either not
very strong or he's hiding it from me. He's very, very good at

that. It's one of the reasons our breakup came out of nowhere. I didn't see anything at all until the last minute.

"Remind me where we're going?" I ask.

A tiny burst of hope: maybe he's *not* here for an End of Relationship Interview after all. Maybe he's here for Constructive Feedback we can dissect, process and work on together. Maybe I can convince him to re-contract despite his doubts about me, like a desperate mobile-phone salesperson.

Will lifts his eyebrows. "If It Ain't Baroque."

"What?" I abruptly stop walking. *"Why?"*

"Because it's an excellent pun, Cassandra. And a unique culinary experience. It's a three-minute walk away and I'm starving. Also, I booked it weeks ago. It's in the diary."

Will constantly travels the world for work, so what we lack in employment-life synergy, we make up for with very clearly outlined weekly schedules and emailed itineraries I send him every Sunday evening.

"Okay, it's just…" I frown. "Never mind."

It just seems a little cruel, that's all. Will is normally so thoughtful and sensitive… *Unless* this is all part of a plan? A romantic gesture, designed to smooth things over so we can seamlessly recommence date twenty-seven?

And frankly, I can't wait that long.

I'm not going to sit down in an eighteenth-century-themed pop-up restaurant and pretend to read a menu I already know by heart and fake-smile at a waitress with lipstick on her lace collar just to find out if I'm single or not.

"Will," I say, grabbing for his hand and awkwardly clutching his fingertips instead. "About this morning—"

"Shit." One color flickers, but it's too faint and too fast for me to tell what it is. "I totally forgot about that. I was just stressed, waiting for my next assignment to come through. Work's been a bit thin on the ground recently. I'm so sorry, Cass. I can be such a grumpy asshole."

And there it is: everything I've ever wanted since approximately ten past eight this morning.

My joy feels visceral, like an egg breaking.

It wasn't a *breakup*; it was a misunderstanding—conflicting views, a normal part of a healthy relationship!—and I massively overreacted. ("Cassandra has an unpleasant tendency to catastrophize.") The fact that I still don't understand what happened seems largely irrelevant as long as it's fixed.

"Don't apologize." I beam, squeezing his hand. "I'm sure it was my fault too, whatever it was. I'm sorry. It's forgotten. Never to be mentioned again."

Overwhelmed with happiness, I'm unsure what comes next. On one level, this is an epic romantic reunion that requires unbridled passion, and on another, we're standing in the middle of the road being beeped at by a white van. I lean up to kiss Will on the lips. He jerks his head toward me like a turkey, then tugs me across the road.

"Let's not get run over this evening, hey?" His voice is buoyant but stiff at the same time, like a floating log. "I really want the Chicken Fricassee with Goosed-berries and Giblets, which is another reason I'm glad you took off that yellow fluff. I'd have felt like I was sitting opposite an ingredient."

Brixton at night is busy and loud, but there's an appealing Dionysian quality to it. A richness to the colors, a thickness to the air. It's raw meat and incense and chiffon and bin juice and purple and cinnamon and lamb and cigarettes, which often suffocates me, but tonight—feeling like this, holding Will's hand—it's warm and enveloping, like marinating in something delicious.

"Again?" I carefully adjust our entwined fingers so mine are on top. "Wasn't it gross enough the first time? Just how good are inner organs, anyway?"

We stand behind another couple outside the refitted metal cargo container as a girl wearing a long red velvet skirt from

Whistles and a brocade apron ticks off names on a clipboard. (I recognize the skirt from the Christmas season three years ago.)

"No idea," Will says. "Never had it."

"Welcome to If It Ain't Baroque!" The girl smiles at us with red lipstick and she's wearing the same shirt as yesterday too: there's a tiny smudge of pale pink lipstick on the elaborate collar. What else isn't she keeping clean? "We hope to give you an unforgettable comestible experience tonight. Name?"

"Cassandra Dankworth."

"Baker."

"Oh," I say with a small snort. "You mean for the booking. I thought maybe you just meant generally."

Luckily nobody heard: Will is looking at his phone and the girl with the historically inauthentic costume is already leading us through the twenty-foot box to our round mahogany stools. It's a very strange place. Combining corrugated steel with flocked wallpaper, fake duck heads and carved gold chairs is a courageous—and, some might argue, unsuccessful—decision.

But Will clearly likes it, so I'm happy.

On the upside, it isn't often you hear the word *comestible* two nights running.

"Didn't you have the fricassee last night?" We delicately perch like sparrows, facing the wall, and look at the menus. "Remember? We talked about how mace the spice comes from the outer shell of the nutmeg, but mace the *weapon* is capsaicinoid-based and named after the bludgeoning stick from ancient Greece, and only one of them should be sprinkled on chicken?"

Admittedly, all of that conversation came from me.

Will nods, still staring at his phone screen, so I take another look around the restaurant while I wait for him to reengage. I wonder what was shipped in here originally. Cereal? Soap? Books? If the latter, I would argue that turning it into this place was a downgrade.

"What are you talking about, Cass?" My boyfriend finally looks up. "We didn't come here last night."

"Umm." I blink. "Yes, we did."

"No, we didn't." Will sweetly pours me water from the jug before I knock it over both of us again. "I was in the studio all night, panic-editing some film."

"Wrong." I look around and point. "We sat right *there*. You ordered the Fricassee with Goosed-berries and I ordered the Beet Root Pan Cakes—four words—and then I got upset because you put your spoon in my cream puff."

"Nope." Will laughs. "Although that *does* sound a lot like something you'd do."

"You'd licked it! You put your saliva in my pudding!"

"We have sex, Cass." He smiles and looks down at the menu. "I frequently put my spoon in your cream p—"

"Will," I interrupt quickly before the waitress hears and assumes we are something casual and short-term, which we are demonstrably not. "They are *tangibly* different situations. We also kiss, but it doesn't mean I get to spit in your mouth while you're asleep."

He laughs. "*Do* you spit in my mouth when I'm asleep?"

"No," I say hotly, "because it's about *consent*."

I did memorize the menu of this place in detail *and* google photos of it in preparation *and* ring the restaurant to ask for vegetarian options *and* do a dry run of the location on the way to work *and* peer through the window, so there's a very solid chance I've researched myself into a bunch of fake memories again.

Plus, we have arguments about Will's disgusting hygiene habits a lot: he has zero food boundaries.

"Fine." I relent, picking up a roll of "wite bred" even though I'm pretty sure that's not how it was spelled in the eighteenth century either. "You win. I think maybe I'm just really tired. It's been a very…confusing day."

Under the bar top, Will gently puts a hand on my thigh. Not for the sexy reason you might think: my right foot is repeatedly kicking the corrugated wall so hard it sounds like a tin drum and our neighbors keep glaring at us.

With effort, I squeeze my hands together and focus on that pressure instead.

Will's eyes are soft. Too soft. "What happened?"

I flush and look away. "Well..."

"Hello, our valued patrons!" Lipstick and Lace Girl is back. "Are you ready to Baroque and Roll? Drinks? Can I suggest a couple of glasses of Puss and Mew?"

"Just regular red wine, please," Will says with the kind of authority that comes right from the base of your soul, like the garlic and onions in a homemade soup. "The chicken for me, and...did you say you wanted the beetroot pancakes, Cass?"

"I didn't say I wanted it," I mumble, hungrily stuffing a bread roll into my mouth and suddenly realizing I forgot to eat today. "I said it's the only thing on the entire menu that doesn't contain internal organs."

"You're funny!" The waitress scribbles in her notepad and I'm not sure if she's written that down too, like a therapist. "Have you guys had a good day so far?"

And they're off: chatting about the weather, which inexplicably leads to how long the restaurant has been open and what profits are like around here and whether they're thinking of eventually setting up a permanent base, while I study the menu as if it's *The Iliad*. How do people do this? How do total strangers weave conversation back and forth like this without tying themselves up in knots? How do they know what to say next? More importantly, *why*? It's like watching a musical where they all break into the same dance without rehearsing it first: totally inexplicable.

The waitress finally leaves with our order and I feel Will assessing me.

"Cassie," he says quietly.

I look up. "Yes?"

"You realize we were just talking, right?"

Now I'm really confused. "Yes."

"So what's with the face?"

"The face? Which face? *My* face?" I pick up a knife and hold it up, but it's too deliberately tarnished to see anything. Embarrassed, I start frantically rubbing at the dried fake blood from the protest. "*Will*, why didn't you say something?"

"Why didn't I say something about what?" Will puts his hand on my bouncing leg again. "What's going on? Talk to me, Cass. You're all over the place this evening."

I breathe out slowly. Oh, not much going on, Will. Just dumped myself, went into unnecessary mourning, got fired, stole a plant, had the plant taken back off me again, cried over a muffin, got covered in blood and imploded in the doorway of a Dickens pun. None of which makes me sound like a woman you want to hold on to permanently and I've only just got you back.

"I'm fine," I say, smiling widely. "Thank you for asking. How are you?"

"I'm excellent." Will looks up as our food arrives looking— a very real bolt of confusion—*exactly* like I knew it would, despite the lack of photographic evidence. "I'm brilliant, actually. I just got some great news, but…"

My boyfriend looks at his maced chicken, then back at me, then back at his chicken. I suddenly sense a torrent of colors: a strange mix I can't untangle, like a ball of different-colored wools. There's something new in his eyes too, but I can't read that either.

"So I just got offered an assignment in India." Will reaches for his wine and takes a way-too-big mouthful. "To shoot a documentary on pangolins. I'm leaving on Saturday, for a month."

What in the love of basic narrative continuity is going on?

"Yes." I frown, putting my fork down. "I know."

5

SCIENTISTS DON'T KNOW WHAT déjà vu is.

Is it a memory formed so quickly we remember an event even as we experience it? An electrical malfunction that fires both the "now" and the "past" parts of the brain simultaneously? A skipped neurological pathway? A wormhole, a religious experience, a glitch in the matrix? It's unclear, but as Will launches into a monologue I've already heard, eats a meal he's already eaten and sips wine he's already sipped in a themed restaurant I am now positive we've already been to, the back of my neck prickles.

"Cassie."

A bottle smashes behind the tiny bar, and a mobile phone rings with a film soundtrack I've heard before.

"Cassie."

The front door slams and the water jug—

"Cassandra, will you please put bloody Google down for a second? I am trying to talk to you."

Blinking, I look up from the Wikipedia entry on déjà vu.

"Look at me," Will says, gently taking my phone out of my

hands and putting it on the table. "I know this might be a bit of a surprise, but it's a really great project and I've been away for work before, so there's no reason we can't—"

"When did you find out? How long have you known?"

Will frowns. "About 5:00 p.m. Why?"

I continue to stare at my untouched pancakes. We haven't spoken since I left for work this morning, which means there are only two possibilities: either my boyfriend is gaslighting me to the rafters, or a key wire in my brain has dislodged itself. Glancing up quickly, I study Will's face. It doesn't *look* or *feel* like he's lying, but I'm too disoriented now to work out whether the emotions I'm sensing are his or mine.

One of us has gone insane. Judging by today, it's me.

"I don't feel good," I say abruptly, standing up and knocking over the flaming *water jug.* "I think I'll go home now, please."

Lap dripping, I lurch from the table. Whatever it is, I cannot risk another meltdown: not here, not now, not in front of the loveliest man I have ever dated. Two in a day would be unprecedented, but maybe I hit my head. Maybe I'm experiencing some kind of time-delay concussion. Maybe all my carefully arranged neurons have been mixed up, like the tiles in a Scrabble bag.

"Really?" Will grabs a handful of sopping napkins, looks with longing at his meal and back at me, clearly torn. "Right now? Can't we discuss this while we eat?"

A distinctive shriek of laughter from the red-haired woman behind me and I remember that laugh, I *do*, or at least it *feels* like I do.

"I'm leaving," I reiterate firmly. "Now."

"Then I'll come with you." Will grabs a bread roll and stands up. "I didn't think you'd react like this, Cass, or I wouldn't have just thrown it out there like that. It's an amazing opportunity and I thought you'd be happy for me."

Except I'm pretty sure that last time I *was*. I showed him an interactive map of India on my phone and excitedly monologued about the pangolin with my mouth full. I did an impression of the subservient way they hold their little hands together like underpaid butlers, and Will laughed until post-dessert coffee came out of his nose.

Except apparently that didn't happen, which means something in my brain is moving either too fast or too slow and it's a big problem, like a car in the wrong lane. All at once the shipping container feels way too contained. Holding my breath, I stagger out of the entrance and stand in the busy street with my eyes shut, holding my thumbs tightly and trying not to feel completely terrified.

Breathe, Cassandra. Breathe.

But not too fast or you'll black out again.

"Cass?" Will emerges behind me a few minutes later. "I've paid, but they can't doggie-bag the food. Apparently, the eighteenth century wasn't made to go. What on earth is going on? This behavior is eccentric, even for you."

Breathe. Breathe. Breathe…

Cautiously, I open one eye and then another.

It's gone. As fast as it came, the déjà vu has disappeared. Everything is back to normal, my synapses have adjusted, the world is no longer warping and I'm going to pretend Will didn't just say that last sentence.

"Allergy?" I attempt faintly.

"You didn't eat anything." My boyfriend sounds tired, as if having dinner with me is like climbing a mountain in inappropriate footwear. "But let's just go back to yours. We can talk about it there."

We don't speak the whole way back, and with every step, my glitch feels more surreal, the way a dream slowly drains away when you open your eyes. I repeatedly glance at Will, but he's not looking at me. His jaw is set. We're holding hands, but his hand feels wooden. Not real. A fake hand. As if I'm romancing Pinocchio.

All the way home something lime-colored is arching out of him, and I know most people think green is jealousy, but it's not: not this time, anyway.

It feels like a decision is being made.

"I'm really sorry," I say for the fifth time, removing my navy work jumpsuit and hanging it up carefully before remembering I might as well throw it on the floor or into a furnace: I won't be needing it next week either way. "I don't know why I behaved like that."

"It's fine." Will unzips his jeans and climbs into my bed. "Honestly."

Which is a problem because people only say that when they want you to know they're lying. Gingerly, as if my boyfriend is a tiger, I climb under the duvet and stare at him. Are we going to have sex tonight? It's difficult to tell. On one hand, it might break the tension, but on the other, I'm not entirely sure the right tone has been set.

After a few seconds, Will grabs a book out of his bag—some kind of biography of David Attenborough, a bit on the nose—so I obediently take my cue and grab my book too (*The Penelopiad*). I could always take off my bra and see if that has any kind of impact on the atmosphere.

"You know, Cassie," Will says after a silence, putting his book down, "if you're upset about something, you can talk to me about it. I need to know. Don't just run out in the middle of dinner without any explanation like that. That's not how adult relationships work."

I flinch. "Okay."

"It's my job. I take what I'm offered. I don't get to choose where I go and when."

"I know." A pause. "It was the beginning, though."

"What?"

"It was the beginning of dinner. Our food had just arrived, so I don't think that counts as the middle. If you count the waiting time, maybe we were a sixth of the way through, a fifth maybe, but it really would depend on if we'd had dessert too."

When what I want to say is: *please don't leave me again.*

"Right." Will peels off his black socks, one by one, and lobs them across the room. I watch them glide through the air. It doesn't *feel* like a sexual advance, but he's getting increasingly naked, so I could be wrong. "My point is that you have to try to communicate a little better. Open up a bit more. You can't just close down and run away every time you get upset about something."

Actually, my go-to alternative is to silently freeze like a wide-eyed rabbit, and historically that goes down even worse.

"Okay."

"Okay?" Will rolls toward me and props his chin on his hairy arm. "And on the back of this agreement, there's nothing you want to say? Nothing you want to share with me?"

His face is so beautiful, like a landscape. His nose is slightly wonky and big, his left canine is snaggled, there are two small moles on his cheek and there's a patch where his stubble shadow doesn't grow as evenly. But it's somewhere I know: they're landmarks I want to draw a map from and return to whenever I can.

"I like your face," I contribute desperately.

"That's not what I meant." Will sighs with a huge yawn, kissing my forehead and turning off the bedside light even though it's only nine thirty in the evening.

I lie stiffly on my back with my arms by my sides and stare in confusion at the dark ceiling, accurately scattered with the glow-in-the-dark stars I bought online and spent days configuring. What *did* he mean? What does he want me to share with him? What was the correct response? I wish people would just tell me what it is I need to say to make them happy with me instead of constantly expecting me to guess.

"So," I venture eventually. "Are we going to have sex tonight, do you think?"

Apparently not: Will's already asleep.

A heartbeat; a stripe of warm yellow light. The dull hum of fighting flatmates, like a nest of pissy wasps under the floorboards.

Disoriented, I open my eyes.

At some point last night I must have rearranged myself, because I'm now lying on Will's chest and he's staring down at me. Again. Is he going to study me first thing every morning now? I'm not sure I like it very much. It makes me feel like I'm both hanging up in the Tate and being peered at under a rock, like a wood louse.

"I like your face too," he says, leaning down to kiss the top of my head like I'm a kid on their first day of school. "That's what I should have said last night. You have an extraordinarily beautiful face, Cassandra Penelope Dankworth."

I unstick my mouth with a *clack*. "Huh?"

"And you're so thoughtful." He smiles. "When I lost my favorite glove on that Antarctic shoot, you found an identical pair and saved one in case I did it again. Remember?"

Of course I remember: it was three weeks ago. Confused, I scrabble to sit upright. I'm beautiful? Thoughtful? Good at glove shopping?

What the hell is—

"And you're sweet," Will continues in a rush, clutching at my hand. "I know a lot of people don't see it, but I do. You're whip-smart and so gloriously weird. I genuinely love hanging out with you."

I lean against the cold wall and stare in alarm at Will's face. He has the distant, affectionate and scripted expression of a man giving a eulogy, as if my boyfriend has woken me in the middle of a speech at my own damn funeral.

"I need you to know that," he continues, his voice becoming gravelly, like a car in a driveway. "I need you to know how highly I think of you, Cassandra. I think the world of you."

No.

No no. No no no no—

And as a lifelong atheist, I do not say this lightly, but:

"Oh my fucking God." Scrabbling, I grab a secret Pegasus T-shirt from down the side of the bed and pull it over my head so I'm not sitting here, being rejected, with no top on. "Will, are you doing it again?"

"Am I...doing what again?"

"Dumping me. Are you waking me up and saying lovely things about me that you clearly don't mean so that you can casually segue into *breaking up with me* again?"

Will winces. "But I do mean them."

"Focus on the relevant question, please."

A pause; then: "Yes."

"This can't be happening." With zero grace, I roll out of bed and start circling the tiny room in my knickers. "What is wrong with you, Will? That's not a rhetorical question. I'd like a clinical report that I can print out and hand to all your future partners, because this is unacceptable."

"Cassandra..." Will runs his hands through his neat, no-sex hair. "I woke up in the middle of the night and couldn't sleep. It's been on my mind for the last few weeks and I thought maybe we could tackle it when I got back from my trip, but we've only been together four months and I'm just not sure—"

My insides are starting to hammer. I feel sick. At least he's not blindsiding me like yesterday. Yesterday, I beamed at him mid-dumping and said, "I love that we're starting the day with this kind of positive morning report now! When you're done, can I do one for you?"

There needs to be a word for both heartbroken *and* humiliated. Heartiliated, maybe.

"Don't do that," I say quickly. "Don't *only four months* me. Four months is how long Persephone lives with Hades in the Underworld and it's long enough to turn the entire world to winter. Four months is not nothing."

"Wasn't that six months?" Will says, frowning.

"Seriously? That's what you're going to focus on now? It depends on the bloody source, Will. It's still a significant amount of time."

"You're right. Dick move. I'm sorry."

My eyes are wet, and my hands are shaking, but at least this time I appear to be physically capable of speaking and moving. Last time I went full Frozen Rabbit and stared at Will in unblinking silence until he gave me a tentative hug, told me he'd always want me in his life and left with one black sock still in my wastepaper basket.

"But *why*?" I manage this time.

"I don't know." There are so many colors pouring out of Will right now—he's a human prism, spinning in the window—but the one I'm going to find hard to forget is the pale blue of *relief*. "I can't quite put my finger on it, Cass. It's just that—"

"You care about me so much but you don't think you can love me? Not in the way you want to love someone? Not in the way you're waiting to love someone?"

"Ouch." Will winces. "That sounded a lot better in my head."

And yet he said it last time too. My throat is tightening again. It's so incredibly cruel. I'm not being dumped because I did something wrong, or said something wrong: I'm being dumped because I *am* wrong. Because Will is hoping someone *less* wrong is just around the corner.

I'm breathing so hard now I sound like a dehumidifier.

He can't leave it like that; not again.

"I need a better reason this time." Remaining self-respect: officially zero. "Give me details, Will. Point me in the right direction. Because it's not normal to be thirty-one years old and have literally nobody. It's not normal to have never had a romantic relationship go past four months. Which means that logically, statistically, it has to be me, so I need to know. What is it that's so unlovable about me? Give me something tangible to work on. Please."

And I know it's humiliating—I know you're supposed to act like the one that "got away" (even while you're in the process of being consciously lobbed back in)—but I did that last time and learned nothing, so what else do I have to lose? In the last twenty-four hours, I've already lost everything.

Will tries awkwardly to wrap his arms around me, but now his touch hurts me and I push him away.

"There's nothing wrong with you, Cassie," he lies gently.

"That's very evidently not true."

"It's not *you*. It's just…" Will looks desperately around the room. "There's something…missing. I don't know what it is. A connection? It's just something I need from a relationship that isn't quite…here."

When what he means is: there's something missing *in me*.

I watch as Will guiltily pulls on his jeans, picks up one sock and continues desperately searching for the other (I don't have the heart to tell him it's sitting in my wastepaper basket again). In one way or another, this is what my relationships always boil down to: a failure to "connect," as if I'm a broken piece of Lego that no other bits of Lego can click on to.

"Cass," Will says, pulling on his T-shirt, "I want to talk about this more. I do. I want to keep you in my life if I possibly can. But can we do it later? Maybe this evening? We overslept and I'm meeting the pangolin people in Clerkenwell at ten."

"Sure," I say flatly, giving up and sitting on the end of my bed like a plonked doll. "We can talk about it later. Let's just keep doing this, Will. Every morning you can dump me, and every night you can come back and pretend nothing happened. Over and over and over and—"

I freeze.

I am motionless, fixed, suspended in the sky. Then, with a sudden rush, it feels like I'm falling: Icarus plummeting toward the sea with hot, molten wings; Daedalus, watching him. In slow motion, I cross the room and pick up my watch from my bedside table. For a few seconds, I stare at it. Faded blue strap, decade-old leather fraying, tiny gold second hand moving.

Ears numb, I turn it over:

"Time, as it grows old, teaches all things."

—*Mum and Dad x*

A sudden memory: unwrapping the curled green ribbon from the box, warmth of restaurant candles, the whole family laughing because I said it looked like my parents were claiming an Aeschylus quote for themselves.

"What's going on?" Will asks as I carefully slide it on and fasten it in its normal hole. My eyes abruptly fill. I thought my watch was gone. I thought it was stolen when I blacked out in central London. I thought I'd never see my sixteenth-birthday gift from my parents ever again. The pressure around my wrist feels familiar and reassuring; something loose inside me settles.

"I lost this," I say quietly, wiping my eyes and looking around as the room starts to warp. "Yesterday. But now it's...back again."

Almost as if it never left.

Almost as if it wasn't yesterday.

"Stop lying to me!" The kitchen door slams into the wall. "I saw the shitting text message pop up on your screen!"

"Sal," Derek whimpers outside my room. "I was just being—"

"If you say *friendly* again, I will rip your dick off and use it as dental floss," I whisper as a series of tiny, imaginary cold fingertips run up and down my spine.

"If you say *friendly* again," Sal bellows a fraction of a moment later, "I will rip your dick off and use it as dental floss!"

My bedroom smells of death and potatoes.

"Fish and chips."

"Yeah." Will nods, now visibly confused. "Your flatmates are delivery-food aficionados."

World contorting as if I'm locked inside a telescope, I stare down at my watch again.

"It's Wednesday again," I say calmly. "Isn't it."

What's strange is that small changes upset me immensely and always have done. A tree trimmed outside my house, the reorganization of a supermarket aisle, a new haircut, an updated app format. I cried for hours when they "new and improved" the recipe for the mashed potato I eat every Monday night.

But the big stuff?

The deaths, the tragedies, the life-changing shifts that rock everyone else to their core? That's when I'm cool, calm and collected. It's why I had to give three speeches at my own parents' funeral, and also—I'm assuming—why I heard my great-uncle Joseph call me an "empty robot" under his breath when I sat back down again.

I don't understand it, but there's just something in me that knows how to stand still when the earth shatters.

"Yes," Will confirms. "It's Wednesday. What—"

"And we've never done any of this before," I continue, staring at the line of light piercing the curtains: the same bounce of dust particles as yesterday. "We've never eaten in that awful themed restaurant before. You've never taken a job with pangolins before. You've never dumped me before."

"Of course not." Will looks untethered for the first time since I've known him. "Why would I break up with anyone repeatedly, Cass? This is distressing enough once."

With an almost hypnotically Zen-like sense of calm, I walk over to the wastepaper basket and tip it up. There should be two black socks in there, and there's only one. There should also be two identical ripped pink envelopes in there, and there aren't. There's just one, with the curly handwritten word *Cass*, torn in half.

I went to work yesterday in a black jumpsuit; I came home in a navy one.

And now I'm not falling anymore; I know.

My phone rings.

"Hello?" I say in a flat voice. "Cassandra speaking."

"Don't you flaming *hello Cassandra speaking* me," my boss screams melodiously down the phone. "It's nine thirty-five in the morning—why the *balls* aren't you at work?"

6

IT'S COMPLETELY IMPOSSIBLE.

There's no other way to put it: I am Psyche, arranging her seeds into piles; I am Heracles, slaying the Nemean lion; I am Theseus, navigating a labyrinth designed to be lost in. I am doing what is not supposed to be possible, and yet it appears that I am doing it anyway.

But I tell Will we can talk about it later.

Even though—as I climb into yet another Uber—I'm no longer sure there's going to *be* one.

"There she is! How *are* you, sweetheart?"

My boss is standing in reception, so it might be time to describe him now: a portly man in his late forties called Barry Fawcett, with the belligerent, farty air of a bulldog (even though everyone knows that bulldogs are friendly, so this is an unfair comparison). He has also never—not in the entire ten months and three days I've been working here—called me *sweetheart*, so I can infer from this abrupt shift in vocabulary that he's very angry indeed.

"How am I?" I say blankly. "Stuck in a time loop, Barry. Cheating the laws of time and space, but unable to elaborate further at this point."

With a surreal sensation, I turn toward my clients.

Jack Burbank is the CEO of a "men's boutique skin-care company"—tall, chiseled, blond hair like a Ken doll with highlights. Gareth Wilson (head of marketing) is similar but slightly less tall, less chiseled and less blond, like they ran out of Jacks but kept drawing them anyway.

"How's your mum, Cassandra?" Jack leans forward and gently rubs the top of my arm as if he's spicing up a chicken breast. "Barry was just explaining that she's ill, which is why you're an hour and a half late for our important meeting today. Something about an immovable hospital visit?"

Why does sympathy always involve *so* much touching?

"My mother is dead, Jack." I step out of his reach. "Has been for a decade, so whatever you've been told was a tasteless lie, I'm afraid."

Gareth and Jack glance at each other.

"Well." Barry clears his throat: the vivid purple is starting to prickle again. "I must have got it mixed up, Cassandra. Your grandmother, perhaps?"

"Also deceased," I inform him. "I have no close family or friends, and you should probably know that already, Barry, given that my emergency contact is my hairdresser."

On one level, I'm freaking out. I've already had this exact meeting. Gareth and Jack were wearing precisely the same clothes they are wearing now; I updated them on the terrible campaign results; they said *wow* and then went into Barry's office—and I should *not* know this, because that's just not how time or knowledge or days of the week or meetings work. Admittedly, I'm not a scientist, but I feel like that's basic entry-level physics.

But, on another level, there's a lot to be said for repetition, and I think I might actually understand what's going on around me for the first time in my entire life. It's not an entirely unpleasant sensation. Maybe this is how other people feel all the time; some of us just need a dress rehearsal first.

While my clients process this information, I look curiously around the office. The watercooler is still dripping, bagels are paused—hanging in midair while my colleagues watch the drama play out—and the radiator continues to gurgle. Sophie's fluffy ginger head pops up briefly over her computer screen like a gopher and disappears again.

"Well." Barry scratches one of his jowls so it sways dramatically. "That's... Perhaps we should just start the meeting?"

"Tell him," I say, turning abruptly to Gareth and Jack.

"Sorry?"

"Tell him that you've replaced this agency already. Tell him that you're firing us today and you were going to whether I was late or not."

Another glance. "We don't know what you're—"

"They don't like me." I turn to Barry. "They're unhappy with the way I've handled their product launch, but mostly they don't like me as a human, so they're firing us. I am *relentlessly grating. Unlikable.* Have I remembered the phrasing correctly?"

Jack's face becomes enjoyably blotchy. "I haven't said that."

"You will," I inform him, looking at my watch. "In about ten minutes. Then I say I don't really like you that much either and then you leave and I get fired because Barry has *absolutely had it with my shitty attitude.*"

There's joy in irony and I was named after Cassandra, the mythological Trojan priestess who was cursed by a sexually thwarted Apollo to see the future but never be believed. A strange legacy for any parent to give a tiny baby, but thirty-one years later, it seems I *finally* know more than anyone else in the room.

"Is this true?" Barry stops fawning. "Are you firing us?"

"Umm." Jack scratches a well-moisturized throat and glances around the office. My colleagues are now watching us intently, having completely abandoned pretending not to. "We've ultimately decided to take SharkSkin in…another creative direction."

"A direction further away from this agency," I clarify helpfully. "Toward another, different agency."

"Implied," sighs Jack. "But yes."

Without further ado, I pick up the empty cardboard box from behind the gold reception. Last time Jack and Gareth had gone before Barry called me into his office: I'm not sure I want to voluntarily wait for him to insult me again.

Unless…

"Before I leave," I say, because this is potentially a huge wasted opportunity, "do you think you could tell me why you don't like me?"

Jack and Gareth stare. "Sorry?"

"It would be helpful if you could just outline the basics." I grab a pen from the top of the reception desk and prepare to make notes on the box. "Details would be particularly well received."

"*Cassandra,*" Barry hisses.

"I'm not being sarcastic," I say earnestly.

Obviously I've *felt* Jack's discomfort around me for months now. It's a sticky, burnt-orange wriggliness, and not unlike the internal squirm you feel when you see a flattened squirrel on the road. Frankly, it's hard to focus on creative ways to sell moisturizer when you're being forced to feel like roadkill for hours a day. But I also don't know what's going to happen next: whether I'm going to be repeating today again or whether this is just a small blip in my chronology, a scratch in the record of my life, a track played twice in a row.

Either way, this seems like useful information to have.

"Well," Jack snaps through paper-white teeth, "I'd say it's mostly doing weird shit like this."

I look down. "Oh."

"Cassandra," Barry says in a low, aggressive voice. "Can I speak to you in my office, please? Now?"

"No, thank you," I say firmly. "Your constructive feedback has already been extremely thorough."

With the office still watching, I carry the box to my desk.

"You know," I hear Jack say not very quietly to Barry, "I'm all for equal opportunities and box-ticking and disability acts and shit, but I feel like you should have told us Cassandra was on the spectrum *before* we signed with you."

I briefly picture myself sliding down an iridescent rainbow.

It seems unlikely that's what they mean.

"Oh shit." Sophie leans across her desk toward me with wide blue eyes, like a small, sarcastic doll. "They haven't *fired* you? That's *awful*. I'm sure we will all miss you *so much*."

"You don't have to keep saying that," I tell her tiredly.

Assessing my desk, I automatically pick up my mug and put it in my cardboard box, turn off my computer and reach for the keyboard wipes, and inexplicably this is what does it, this is what finally tips me over the edge: the moist antibacterial cloth is what sends me spiraling into an existential crisis, because am I *actually time traveling right now*? Breathing faster, I stagger toward the exit. You know what? This shouldn't be happening to me. I'm not trained. I'm not a horologist or a physicist, I'm a mediocre PR account manager, and I've already been told I have a loose grip on reality without *this* shit.

Panicking, I start pushing at the pull door.

Because it's finally starting to hit me: if today keeps looping, this is going to be my life now. I'm going to be eating Beet Root Pan Cakes (four words) forever. I'm going to be informed about the considerable environmental significance of pangolins forever. I'm going to be woken up by my boyfriend, dumped, ripped apart by my boss and fired, forever.

I'm going to be told I'm unlikable and unlovable, over and over again, and there'll be nothing I can do about it, because even with infinite chances you can't make someone like you or love you in less than twenty-four hours. There's a solid chance I could be stuck in the third-worst day of my life for the rest of eternity, much like Prometheus: chained to a rock, doomed to have my liver pecked out by eagles every single day, then waiting for it to grow back every night so it can happen again. Except, instead of eagles, it's other humans, and instead of beaks, it's hurtful words, and instead of liver, it's *my entire fucking identity.*

So while I'm not averse to repetition—I take enormous pleasure and comfort in it—of all the days to repeat, I would not have picked *this* one.

"Cassandra!" Barry appears in his office doorway. "What the hell are you doing? I didn't mean leave *right now.* Jesus on a yellow bicycle, what is wrong with you? I'd prefer you to work out your notice period, please."

Unless—

With a sharp turn, I charge back toward my desk. Because if I've learned anything from Greek mythology—and I've learned everything—it's that our fates may be spun, measured and cut, but they can also be altered. In all the stories, time after time, humans and demigods defy the Moirai and take their destinies back from the gods on their terms.

I am stealing this bloody rubber plant.

Ensuring that Ronald is focused on his spreadsheet—headphones on, the only person in the office not now watching me with their mouth open—I grab the clay pot firmly with both hands and run back through the agency door.

Go go go *go*—

My phone beeps:

Dankworth please clean your shit up

Hitting the lift button, I hold my breath and count: five, four, three, two—

The office door swings open.

"Cassandra?" Ronald has the same incalculable expression on his face, and no no *no*, this doesn't bode well for me and my pecked-out liver at all.

He clears his throat. "That's mine."

I can't do this.

I cannot.

I refuse to.

I'm point-blank stating right now that I will not be participating in a repeat of this *bloody awful day* again.

"The plant." Ronald points at the shrubbery. "It's mine and I'd like to keep it."

"Of course," I say flatly. "Sorry."

Ronald reaches out a hand and I move quickly away so his fingers won't touch mine, except this time I don't move quite fast enough: his fingertips graze mine, pain shoots through my entire body, and I instinctively flinch and pull away. We watch as the rubber plant somersaults through the air and hits the ground. Pot broken. Leaves snapped. Dirt everywhere.

"Oh, thank the gods," I say, putting a hand over my face.

"Did you...mean to do that?" Ronald says, crouching on the floor and staring sadly at the carnage.

"No," I say, suddenly dizzy with relief.

Because if things can be broken, then things can be changed; and if things can be changed, then it stands to good and logical reason that they can also be fixed.

That's all I need to know.

7

THE LIFT PINGS OPEN.

"Cassandra? Miss Dankworth? Hang on a second—I've got Mr. Fawcett on line nine, and—"

"Can't stop," I say, racing past her. "No time."

Or way too much of it: at this point, it's difficult to tell. All I know for sure is I need to rerun exactly what happened last time. That's how you replicate an experiment, right? You repeat the conditions as closely as possible. Although, if I'd known I'd end up with this kind of undocumented ability, I'd have paid a lot more attention in GCSE physics, purchased my own Bunsen burner.

Panicked, I body-slam the exit repeatedly because I still do not know how to open doors. The receptionist lets me out with a sigh and a *click*.

Breathing slowly, I stand on the street.

What was my next move? I remember pretty much everything that has ever happened to me as if it's still happening: my memories are so accurate and so vivid I can watch them like films whenever I want to, searching for details like a detective. Unfortunately, I was so overwhelmed yesterday, the image is blurry, as if somebody has rubbed olive oil all over the screen.

"Excuse me." The woman in the orange bomber jacket taps me lightly on the shoulder and I jump yet again. "You're kind of blocking the entrance to the— Are you okay?"

I blink at her. "Banana muffin."

"I'm sorry?"

A giddy wave of relief. "I need a banana muffin."

With my cardboard box gripped tightly, I charge with growing excitement toward the café. Banana muffins are comforting. Banana muffins are reassuring and familiar. Banana muffins might be part of a fundamental glitch in the universe that allows me to travel through time and space, according to my now spurious calculations.

The café doorbell tinkles behind me, and this time I think of *Peter Pan* and how fairies die unless you believe in them. Maybe this is just how magic works: like a melodramatic and attention-seeking Tinker Bell, you have to clap for it as hard as you can or it simply can't be bothered to keep going.

"Hello, young lady! Goodness, is it one o'clock already? Or are you early?"

I stare at the place where banana muffins should be.

"Oh!" The café owner smiles. "I'm afraid we had a—"

"—delivery issue," I fill in for him. "No banana today, but you do have some delicious chocolate muffins and a lovely salted caramel, which you can personally attest is an adjective I'll never know because I interrupted."

He stares. "'Delicious.' I was going to say 'delicious.'"

"Thank you," I say gratefully. "I'm sure they are."

Turning round, I charge back out of the café before realizing I must have missed a step. Scanning my memories, I check the street. The girl with the hat is nowhere to be seen—I must be a little early—so I wait until I see her in the distance, head down, looking at her phone. That's probably close enough. Checking the street—yellow door, orange can, a blue sliver of sky, dropped navy glove, red ring around a street sign—I wait a few seconds for another pigeon to flap aggressively, which it does.

I flinch again: fucking pigeons.

"Fur's not fair! Fur's not fair! Fur's not fair!"

Increasingly emotional, I take a deep breath and run as fast as I can around the corner into Regent Street: straight into the heart of the protest. And even though I know it's coming, even though I'm here on purpose, it still hurts as if every cell in my body has been filled with gasoline and promptly set on fire.

"Fashion has no compassion!" The woman with the purple bowl cut thrusts the same leaflet at me. "A hundred million animals every year—"

I shut my eyes at her closeness: every part of me is now folding inward like a paper airplane.

"Minks are semiaquatic! They—"

Breathe, Cassie. Breathe.

But I can't: the noise, the crowds, the flares, the colors, the alarms, the whistles, all at once it feels like I'm a million mouths and none of them can speak but all of them are screaming and I'm being swept away again, down the road, carried in the madness and the chaos like a stick in a flooding human river.

"FUR IS DEATH!"

"Fur is death!"

"FUR IS DEATH!"

The invisible scarf is tightening again.

"Head-to-toe electrocution! Foxes get an electrode up their butts. Does that sound fun to you?"

The lights behind my eyelids are flashing.

Just in time, I remember to put my hands in front of my face a second before the red liquid hits me, but it's still sticky, it's still smelly, it's still revolting, I still don't want it on my skin, and I start crying again even though I knew this was coming, even though I chose to let it happen, even though I *wanted* it to happen.

Desperately, I search the names of the buildings.

I'm nearly there: I can feel it.

With a shudder of reprieve, I claw and elbow my way out of the crowd toward Bar Humbug, then huddle in the doorway with my arms tightly wrapped over my head. The world starts to flicker in and out, like the waves of darkness that hit just before you disappear every night. It's coming again and I don't know what's going to happen, I don't know if this is going to work, I don't understand what it is or *how* it is, and frankly, I'm no longer sure it matters.

All I know is I'm not doing this day again.

Because, as horrible as it is, it's also kind of tempting to stick here, in this nothing of a Wednesday: settling into the sameness the way I've settled into my grubby little Brixton bedroom. There's an appeal to the repetition of it, no matter how terrible. I could make this day comfortable and stay, nestled into the monotony and familiarity, content in the knowledge that nothing will ever surprise or shock me again. Zoning out, the way I can listen to the same song on a loop a hundred times until I can't hear it anymore, until I don't realize it's still playing.

Until I don't even notice that it hasn't moved on.

But I'm not going to.

I had a plan for my life—laminated and stuck to my bedroom wall—and this wasn't it. I never intended to end up thirty-one years old, unloved, unemployed and alone, covered in fake blood and curled up in a tight ball on the pavement. At some point in my past something went wrong, so if there's even a chance I can do it all over again—throw out this life like a first pancake and make another, better one—I have to at least try, don't I?

According to Sophocles, "time calls only once, and that determines all." But what if it doesn't? What if time calls again and again? What if it doesn't get the message, doesn't give up, doesn't let go? What if it's calling me from the point where it all went wrong, pulling me back there to do it again?

Because if the first page of a book is a lie and all we have are lines drawn in the sand, then that makes time the wave that erases them all.

I'm going to start my story from the beginning.

FIRST, THOUGH, I'LL NEED to control time.

It can't just be rocking up without warning and then pulling me through the cosmos whenever it bloody feels like it. After all, I've spent my entire life carefully regulating my environment and everything in it. Temperature. Light. Noise. Food. Textures. Routines. Rules. Emotions. People, especially when they're running in school corridors. I shape the world into one I can fit into more comfortably, and then ensure nobody touches it or messes it up.

So I'm going to be completely honest here.

Making sure that time behaves properly feels like a skill that is *very* much in my wheelhouse.

Cautiously, I open one eye.

When am I?

The *where* is immediately apparent: I'm still curled in a ball inside a doorway on Regent Street, my arms wrapped tightly around my head. Cautiously, I unravel and look down, searching for clues. My watch is still around my wrist, which suggests I have neither looped again nor been stolen from; it also suggests it's just after 1:00 p.m., which is handy.

Groggily, I assess my hair—still a bob, although I haven't changed my hair since I was eight, so this proves nothing—and then my hands: adult, which is a relief. Being a teenager is not an experience I particularly want to repeat. With a dazed pat, I look down: work jumpsuit. This is a little disappointing, although I'm not exactly sure why I thought I'd be given a makeover midair, like a kind of space Kylie.

I peer down the road: the protest has gone again.

Evaluating the evidence, it appears that I have moved through time but not through space; I cannot alter my geographical location, or get dressed using my new powers (unfortunate). Is this specific location some kind of magic portal or are my new powers portable? It's unclear, so that will obviously have to be investigated further.

Full of burgeoning hope, I rise from the (cigarette) ashes.

And that's when I see it: the Bar Humbug sign, swinging smugly over my head. It opened about six months ago. I remember because they handed me a shot of vodka at lunchtime, which felt both generous and also highly inappropriate.

Then I peer more closely at my jumpsuit: it's still black.

Fuck.

All the evidence *also* points to the fact that I've just been curled up in a ball on the pavement for just over fifty minutes, going nowhere. Yet I find myself inexplicably shocked. Indignant, actually. In mere hours, I haven't just adjusted to my ability to defy the laws of physics, I now feel entitled to it. As if not being able to move through time whenever I feel like it is some kind of human rights violation.

Devastated, I wipe my hands on my thighs.

So—that obviously didn't work.

The problem is that I know exactly *where* I want to go (or, more specifically, *when*). There are a million possible moments I would probably return to and change if I could: tiny decisions that have quietly carved my life in the wrong direction, like water running over a rock. Things I shouldn't have said. Things I shouldn't have done. Passive-aggressive messages I shouldn't have left stuck to the front of communal fridges.

But all potential paths lead back to one place, one time, one event.

The moment where my life broke.

Where maybe I broke with it.

So now I know where I'm ideally headed, all I've really got to do is work out the *mechanism* of how to get there. Do I have to fully melt down before time travel is triggered? Is the hedgehog position a requisite? Sobbing uncontrollably? Being covered in blood? If I have to black out *every* time I want to go anywhere, this is going to get unnecessarily dramatic and also a bit grubby.

Thinking hard, I pull myself to my feet and begin wandering toward Oxford Street: automatically slotting back into my daily ritual like a plastic horse on a merry-go-round. Cheese sandwich on a bench at twelve thirty. Banana muffin and latte at one. Then twenty minutes of wandering around clothes shops in a daze, mindlessly pawing at fabrics and either wincing or kneading them with my eyes shut like a blissed-out cat. Memorizing every item until I can cite them to strangers years later ("Skirt, Mango, spring 2016"). Which would be quite an impressive party trick, I suppose, if I ever went to parties.

Obviously, I need to make a proper plan.

No more of this impulsive nonsense: I need to get the right books, spend a few days on Google, maybe email a few relevant scientists. I've already traveled through time once, so I'm positive I can do it again. I just need to figure out *how*, potentially via some kind of intricate spreadsheet.

More optimistic now, I step toward the electric doors to Zara. There's always a fun little dance while I wait for the glass doors to either fail to open or slam shut while I'm halfway through. As always, I put one anxious hand in the air and slowly wave it backward and forward, like a nervous chameleon getting ready to move onto a new leaf. The doors slide open with a *whoosh*, and a man strides straight past me: headphones on, head down, engrossed in his phone.

"Will?"

Stunned, I stare after him as he begins awkwardly attempting to stuff a brown paper bag into his satchel. I'm now desperately trying to switch focus. It feels like years ago already. Will. Breakup. This morning. Wait. Did he…just dump me and head straight to Zara Man for a natty wardrobe update? Also, didn't he tell me mere hours ago that he had a meeting in Clerkenwell? Did he just *lie* to me?

My cheeks flare. Of course he did, Cassandra. History has repeatedly established that what a man says directly after he dumps you is literally whatever will get him away from you fastest.

I'll sort out time travel later: an ex-boyfriend waits for no woman.

"Will!" I say, impulsively running after him. This is almost definitely the last chance I have to talk to Will about our relationship. From experience, the further away from the breakup itself, the less likely people are to want to discuss it in detail and the more likely they'll just go ahead and change their phone number instead.

Adjusting his backpack, Will heads toward the tube stairs and I speed up: I don't want our final ever conversation to happen surrounded by the scent of a million body fluids that don't belong to either of us.

"Will," I say, lightly touching his arm.

He turns around and pulls his headphones down, and his

face is so lovely, something inside me crumbles like a piece of stale fairground fudge.

"Can we talk?" I focus instead on the bobbled green neckline of his jumper. "Just for a second?" Better adjust his expectations. "Ninety seconds, actually. Sixty seconds if I speak very fast."

"Umm." Will hesitates, then nods. "Sure."

"Here goes." I breathe out with control as if I'm playing the flute. "So I've been thinking over what you said about *sharing* and *opening up*, and you're right. I don't. I find it incredibly hard. Painful. And when I *do* open up, I share way too much because I'm not sure where the line is. You know, that socially appropriate line between good share and bad share. I can't see it. There's all this *truth*, gallons and gallons of it, but how much do people want? Fifty percent truth? Ninety percent? Just a trickle? None at all? Nobody ever clarifies, so I'm constantly getting it wrong."

Will opens his mouth and I crash on regardless.

"And then I share too much or not enough, and people get angry, or irritated, or uncomfortable, or bored, or hurt. It's confusing, and it makes me very anxious. But you asked me to *share* and *open up*, so here goes."

I suck in the deepest breath I can find, like a free diver.

"I time traveled. Or...I *think* I time traveled. You broke up with me, twice. I got fired, twice. There were no banana muffins. None. And when I realized what was going on, I tried to control it. I thought maybe I could go back to the day my parents died and try to save them. Which is ridiculous, right? As if I'm Heracles, charging into the Underworld and grabbing Alcestis. But that's what you're supposed to do with magical power, isn't it? You're supposed to do something extraordinary for the people you love."

I'd tell you what Will's reaction is, but I've yet to look up.

"And it wasn't entirely altruistic," I admit quickly. "I think maybe losing my parents so suddenly...sent my life in the wrong direction. I guess I hoped maybe I could put everything back on track. Try again, somehow. But *mainly* I just wanted to see my mum and dad because I still miss them so badly."

Will's jumper is very bobbly: he needs one of those little combs.

"Anyway." I breathe out. "It didn't work, obviously, because who the hell actually thinks they can *time travel*? So clearly I've lost my mind. Which has probably been on the cards for quite some time, as I'm sure you'll agree. And I don't expect you to believe this, or even care, given that we've broken up, but I needed to tell someone, and frankly, you're all I have."

The accuracy of this statement brings me crashing to a halt.

Will is all I have. My ex-boyfriend of not quite four months is *all I have*. And this is exactly why you shouldn't chase people down in the street without a script: you end up realizing devastating shit like that.

"Anyway," I conclude flatly. "I shared. It's your turn to talk now. Go."

There's a silence, and—as the silence stretches, melted and stringy—all at once, I sense Will's colors. They are nothing like I've ever seen coming out of him before. They're strange and mismatched, like a cake made with ingredients that taste out of balance. Confusion, which is to be expected. A little sadness, maybe. Pity, granted. But…something that looks and feels a lot like…*fear*?

With a deep breath, I finally look up and—

"I am so sorry." Will smiles. He has the voice of a man picking up a broken bird. "But I don't know who you are."

The ground pivots.

"Don't feel embarrassed," he adds gently. "It happens a lot. I look exactly like eighty percent of the men on Tinder."

Stomach folding, I check the street again. Superimposed on top of thirty minutes ago, I now realize the images look nothing alike. Nobody is wearing a jacket; the air is golden. The shops have different window displays. The trees have more leaves. Will's hair is half an inch shorter, and his beard is neatly trimmed. Even his khaki backpack is…not revolting. He clearly hasn't taken it on a shoot to Antarctica and left it near some penguins yet. I was so busy focusing on what was going on inside my head that I completely forgot to notice anything around me.

I wish I could say that's unusual, but it's really, really not.

"Anyway," Will says politely, taking a step away. "Good luck. I'm so sorry to hear about your parents, and I hope you find the person you're looking for."

He turns his back on me, and never mind the fact that I just chronologically hopped about again: this is clearly my first meeting with Will and I just told him I'm his insane time-traveling ex-girlfriend who doesn't have any friends.

This isn't a meet-cute. It's a meet-*horrifying*.

"Wait!" I say, chasing down the stairs after him. "What day is it?"

"Wednesday," Will says over his shoulder.

My brain is furiously clutching at information as it plummets, a bit like Alice in Wonderland, falling through books and random maps. That makes sense: hence my black jumpsuit. I know it's the same year, based on the newly decorated Bar Humbug, so—

"And the date?"

"The sixth of June."

"But today is our anniversary!" I declare before I can stop myself, and yeah, I think that does it.

"Bloody hell," Will mumbles, jumping the remaining stairs and slamming his Oyster card down on the barrier as if it's the only thing stopping me from chasing him like Cerberus the three-headed dog. I consider myself a relatively intelligent person, but I'm obviously kidding myself, because it's only *now* occurring to me that I could have just checked all that information on my phone.

Kicking myself, I climb slowly back up the stairs to Oxford Street while I process what just happened, shoulder blades pulled tightly together like tiny wings to make sure I don't touch anything sticky. Suffice to say, that could have gone better. In fact, in the history of romantic first meetings, I can't think of many worse. Oedipus and Jocasta, maybe.

But…it also *worked*.

Somehow, I moved through time again. I changed something, undid something: drew a different line in the sand. Not for the better, admittedly, but it's a start, right? Although—given the pretty established laws of alternate universes and branches of reality—I'm starting to suspect it might be different sand entirely.

Which means I have one option left.

Smoothing my hair, I walk back to the doorway of Bar Humbug, clear my throat, crouch down in a tight ball on the ground and close my eyes.

I'll just have to try again.

9

"EXCUSE ME."

I squeeze my eyelids together.

"Excuse me. Lady."

Frustrated, I lift my head and flinch as the manager of Bar Humbug looms toward me again: blue eyes narrowed, clean-shaven, breath warm and minty and infinitely too close.

"Are you okay?" His pores are large and he has a ripe white-head on the end of his nose, perched like a tiny hat. "Do I need to call someone for you? I can see you're having a crisis or what-ever, but you've been down there for quite a while now, and no offense, but you're putting off potential customers."

Just past his shoulder, three defeated-looking people with terrible posture are standing on the pavement. One of them is unblinkingly eating a sandwich and staring at me as if I'm one of those painted Yodas that hover in Covent Garden.

"Not that I blame you," the manager adds with a smile. "Hump day. Oof. No fun for anyone. But this is a new bar and we're going for a more upscale, less panic-attack-on-the-pavement vibe."

I check my watch again. Forty minutes.

I've been crouched in this doorway like a self-appointed snail for nearly three-quarters of an hour and the furthest back I can get is 1:02 p.m. on Wednesday, the sixth of June, which is the day I met Will. I've tried everything I can think of. I've moved to a different bar doorway and then back again. I've tried chanting and singing. I've attempted (and failed) to cry. I've given passing out again my best shot. I've curled in a ball, lain down flat, stood up. I've scratched my legs and rocked. I've even attempted overwhelming myself on purpose by standing next to a builder drilling a hole in the pavement, and it had absolutely zero impact.

Apparently all I actually need to do is close my eyes, focus hard on when I want to be and open them again. That's it. Time travel: nailed. Except I've tried seventeen times now, and I can't get back any further than this specific moment. Frankly, it's less time *travel* and more of a time tweak. An imperceptible trim. The horological equivalent of what I ask my hairdresser for every six weeks.

All I want is to use my new powers to go back a decade and stop my parents from getting in the car. Hop back quickly and tell them to get a train instead. Stop them being late because Dad pulled over to buy me congratulatory roses. Ask them not to take a small country road and stick to the motorway. Hell, maybe I just won't graduate at all. That way they won't be killed on their way to the ceremony and (bonus) I won't have to get up on a bright stage and smile at people I don't even recognize because I so rarely turned up to lectures: they were far too noisy and crowded.

But the universe isn't even faintly interested in this story. Instead, it would quite like me to stay stuck here: gazing into the eyes of a strange man who keeps telling me I'm unwanted and asking me to leave.

Which appears to be quite the reoccurring pattern.

"I'm sorry," I say yet again, finally giving up and struggling to my feet. I need to start working on my thigh strength: getting up from the ground should not be this consistently difficult.

"No worries." The manager tilts his head to the side for the seventeenth time. "Why don't you come inside for a drink? I'm sure we can send you back to work feeling a lot more relaxed."

On the upside, I guess at least I do now have a job to return to.

"No, thank you," I say politely. "I don't think midday intoxication is going to make traveling through time any less confusing."

Or any less tiring. It turns out rewinding your own life is both physically and mentally exhausting, a bit like changing all your bedding.

I have now reached two possible conclusions:

a) I don't have the power to go back further than four months, and/or
b) This is a significant date, beyond which I am unable to move.

There's a good chance I'm simply not strong enough.

Or that this is some kind of horological safety catch. Cassandra is brand-new at time travel and doesn't seem to be naturally gifted: let's make sure she doesn't accidentally destroy the entire planet and everyone on it. The universe is stepping in to limit the damage I can do. You get four months, Cassie, and that's it. No saving your parents for you. Frankly, we cannot trust you with that kind of responsibility. Baby time wheels for Cassandra Dankworth it is.

Which is devastating, obviously, but also not miles away from what I've already been told at multiple jobs: I rarely get the key for the stationery cupboard.

Wiping my face, I breathe out slowly and try to acclimatize to the overwhelming disappointment. I have failed to control all of time and I need to be gracious in defeat. There's no point sulking about it. I don't want the universe thinking I'm ungrateful or spoiled and taking my new powers back off me again. Frankly, I'll take whatever I'm given. I can move about in small hops, and that's enough. *Today* matters—that's what the cosmos is trying to tell me—and four months is still enough to make a real change to my life.

And if that's the case…

Well, I may not be the best person at reading between the lines—frankly, I struggle to draw the right conclusion when the information is written directly on them—but it's pretty clear exactly what I'm being directed toward.

Or, more importantly, *who*.

To: Barry Fawcett
From: Cassandra Dankworth

Sorry but feeling strange today so taking the afternoon off.

Cassandra.

Having now thoroughly checked my phone, it seems that everything is precisely as it was four months ago: calendar, diary, emails, texts or sobering lack thereof. Time has simply reset. This means—if my memory serves correctly, which it always does—I'm just about to go into an "Idea Hurricane" at work in which somebody suggests putting dogs in capes and everybody claps for no reason.

If I can't use my new prophetic ability to get out of things like that, I don't see any remaining point to this gift at all.

Twenty seconds later:

To: Cassandra Dankworth
From: Barry Fawcett

We've spoken before about your email etiquette,
Cassandra. Please note your tone. No, you can't have
the afternoon off for "feeling strange." Are you sick or
are you not sick? I saw you eating a cheese sandwich
fifteen minutes ago.
    Unless you are physically ill, please return to the
office after your lunch break.

Barry

    I could just email back, but this also seems like an opportunity to practice a little traveling within the set time boundaries I've apparently been given. Closing my eyes, I focus on the moment just before I sent my email.
    Then I open them again and carefully check my Sent folder: my email is gone.
    Undone, as if it never happened. Result.
    Thinking hard, I write:

To: Barry Fawcett
From: Cassandra Dankworth

Dear Barry,

Hello, how are you? Well, I hope. :)
    Isn't it nice weather today! So sunny! ;)
    You have a three-hour brainstorm scheduled for
after lunch and I won't be attending. They are not my
clients, I have nothing of value to add and frankly you
will be paying me for doing absolutely nothing. I do

not feel comfortable about this so I have decided to take half a day's owed holiday instead.

I hope it goes well! :)

Cassandra xxxxxx

Apparently the trick is to write what you actually want to say and then go back in afterward and surround it with irrelevant niceties and emojis just to make it harder to find, the way you bury a sweet in a pile of flour and force children at birthday parties to sift for it with their faces.

But tone: dutifully amended.

Pleased with how this is already going, I turn my phone off and pop it in my bag. I now have a few hours to make sure I'm exactly where I'm supposed to be, at exactly the time I'm supposed to be there. This seems important. After all, much like Andromeda—tied to her rock—who knows the difference a minute could make? What if Perseus had taken a different route, or Pegasus had flown too slowly? What if the sea monster Cetus had risen just a moment earlier, or Medusa's head had gotten stuck in the bag?

Time is the invisible thread that weaves our stories together.

And sixty seconds can change everything.

The café bell tinkles. I look up just in time to see an elegant old lady walk in wearing a beautiful tartan flat cap that I immediately covet. She assesses the room and greedily eyes the big green velvet chair opposite me.

Feeling like a criminal, I plop my bag on it.

I've been here more than an hour already, illogically camping out like someone waiting outside a store for the release of a new iPhone when they know they could just order it online. In my original timeline, I'd only just arrived at the café—flattened by the brainstorm, hoping to delay a return to the flat—but it's just too risky.

Without being too dramatic, an old lady could have sat down on the wrong chair and ruined my entire life.

Relieved, I watch as she takes one by the window.

"Another coffee?" The waitress hovers next to me like a monochrome hummingbird and I can *feel* the blue impatience pouring out of her. In my defense, the café is not *that* busy. In her defense, I've been picking at the same banana muffin and sipping the dregs of a cold coffee now for seventy-five minutes.

"Mint tea, please." I finger my watch again. "Thank you."

Where is Will? Did I get the time wrong? I spent a few hours preparing for this moment, hunting through secondhand shops for a new vintage outfit, getting uncomfortably changed in a toilet cubicle and then furtively applying tester makeup in Boots, but now I'm starting to worry I've ruined everything already. What if I've knocked everything off course? What if the amazing blue tulle dress I'm now wearing is the thing that changes the universe? What if my black jumpsuit is actually the most attractive thing about me? More importantly, what if, by applying for reasons of hygiene only the makeup colors that haven't been tested yet, I've made myself look like a drunk butterfly?

I'm just rifling through my bag for something to either con-firm or refute this hypothesis when the door tinkles again and my skin fills with warm light, like a dark room with the cur-tain tugged open.

From under my eyelashes, I watch as Will approaches the counter.

I study him as he orders a cappuccino with extra chocolate and beams casually at the waitress, then bends down and delib-erates between the baked goods, even though I already know he'll pick a Black Forest cupcake. I watch him as he waits for his coffee, hands slung in his pockets with his thumbs on the seams, illogically scanning the menu on the wall even though he's already ordered. I watch him straighten his posture and press the little dark curl down on his neck, the exact lock of hair that tickles my nose when I lean up against his warm back in the morning.

And I'm suddenly certain: this is now how I want to spend my time.

Correction: my times.

Because Will isn't just any old boyfriend to me, one of the twenty-three men I've briefly dated over the last decade: another name on a double-sided A4 list of Simons and Patricks and Sams and Joes. He's not disposable, a paper-plate human, one I can throw away and replace with an identical version when we're done.

And I can't keep being told, over and over again, that something about me is shaped wrong, unable to fit others, incapable of "connecting," like a jigsaw piece with the edges sanded down.

("Cassandra does not play well with others.")

All I want is enough time to try.

Breath held, I watch as Will picks up his coffee and cupcake and—

Shit.

With lightning reflexes I didn't even know I had, I grab my handbag off the chair and plop it on the floor next to me. Then I blow gently on my mint tea, pick up my book and wait as patiently as I can while Will quickly scans the café for a seat: assessing, deliberating, discarding. Our first meeting was perfect—it needs no alteration and no editing—and I can suddenly feel the monster rising, the water roaring, the horse soaring, the sword swinging: our story, starting again.

Except, this time, I'll find a way to reach across the gap.

Will walks toward me.

"Hi there." He smiles, exactly as he did the first time round. "Do you mind if I sit with you?"

10

"SURE."

That's all I have to say. It's not Euripides—I'm not winning any competitions—but it worked last time: got the right man in the right seat at the right time. But I can't do it. My lips are stuck together, my tongue is limp; the muscles in my throat click uselessly, like an engine trying to start. I feel like the Minotaur: part human, with the head of an animal that cannot speak, desperately trying to communicate.

Horrified, I stare at Will with circular bull eyes.

"No problem." He smiles after what feels like an eternity but is actually eight seconds. "Sorry to bother you. I'll sit somewhere else."

Which he does, and our love story is promptly over.

The end.

So I try again. Licking my lips, I close my eyes and focus as hard as I can on the moment just before I screwed everything up. When I open them, Will is standing over me again, smiling.

Abrupt joy rushes through me.

This is—by far—the best unasked-for gift I have ever been given.

"Yes," I say in relief.

"No problem." Will dips his head slightly. "Sorry to bother you. I'll sit somewhere else."

I blink, trying to understand what just—

"No!" I shout urgently as he walks away. "No! I meant no, I don't mind! Come back! Please sit with me!"

But he's gone—*very* gone—and our story is done.

Which is fine: I'll just try again.

"Hi there." Will smiles as I wait with my carefully prepared word held in my mouth like a hard-boiled sweet. "Do you—"

"No," I say urgently, then realize I've just jumped my cue.

He sits somewhere else.

Again.

My panicked face rejects Will for me.

Again.

He hesitates a fraction too long, and a woman with banana bread veers around him, nabbing the chair.

Again.

I can't look at him, so he apologizes and sits somewhere else.

Again.

★ ★ ★

My limbs are in the wrong order: I am a plastic Halloween skeleton, put together by a small child. I try to rearrange— an elbow, an ankle, a femur, a coccyx—but now my fingers are twitching, one at a time, as if I'm playing invisible scales on the world's tiniest piano. Sure sure sure, all I need to say is sure sure *sure*, but the word *sure* no longer exists, it's a made-up word, and I've ruined it, I've ruined everything again, why can't I get anything—

"Hi there." Will smiles. "Do you— Oh my God, are you okay?"

I've just burst into tears.

Conclusion: I cannot do this. It doesn't matter how many times I hop back in time, or how simple this process is supposed to be. It doesn't matter that our original meet-cute was flawless and I just need to repeat it, or that all I've got to do is *get this man to bloody sit down.*

The harder I try, the farther away from me Will moves.

At one point, the look I give him from across the room is so intense, so accidentally hostile, he simply asks for a take-out cup and leaves. I'd naively assumed that this first meeting would be easy. Put two people who find each other attractive back in the same place at the same time in the same controlled environment and you'll get the same results, right?

But apparently time doesn't work like that.

It sets us up together, over and over again—like a DJ at a college disco when the slow songs come on—and then I step in like a taciturn headmistress and ruin it before the dance even starts. Time is so incredibly *fragile.* It's like tissue paper, like gossamer, like a spider's web in the corner of a kitchen cupboard. One wrong move, a little bit of pressure, the head of a broom, and the narrative disintegrates.

And one thing is becoming abundantly clear: it is *me.* I am no longer able to pretend that I am not the problem here. I cannot delude myself into thinking that I am the victim, the undeserving casualty of bad romantic luck, the poor princess tied to a rock in chains against her will.

I am making the rock, over and over again; they are *my chains*.

Thanks to my new gift, I am literally watching myself repel my future boyfriend away from me over and over again, and it's making me wonder just how many people I've done this to in my life already, without even realizing it. How many people have I repelled with the wrong word in the wrong tone at the wrong time, with a hostile or blank facial expression, an inability to make eye contact? How many people were supposed to be in my life before I accidentally sent them spiraling away?

And it's this realization—that it's my problem, and therefore one that I can solve—that snaps me out of it.

I am getting my first date with Will again if it kills me.

Which—given how many banana muffins I've eaten in a row and how exhausted I am now—it might feasibly do.

This time, I manage to rewind a little further.

I give myself a few minutes of preparatory pep talk—you are Hippolyta, Queen of the Amazons—tuck my bob neatly behind my ears, apply some lip gloss, brush the muffin crumbs from where they're sitting in a neat little line in my cleavage like they're waiting for the post office to open.

Then I jump up and switch seats, taking the one opposite me instead.

A relieved stillness rushes through me, the way my leg feels when it finally stops bouncing up and down. Sometimes all I need is the shock of change to break me out of a loop of my own creation.

I look at my fingers: my tiny imaginary piano has gone. I can do this. I've done it successfully once before, so logically I can do it again. Will fancies me from the moment he sees me:

I know he does—he's told me. *This is going to work.* I'd say it's destiny, but if the last forty minutes have taught me anything, it's that fate is an entirely made-up human construct, like weddings, gender reveals and birthday parties.

The doorbell rings. Will enters, orders his coffee; selects his cupcake; gazes at the menu; turns around, deliberates and—

"Hi there." He points at the chair that used to be mine. "Do you mind if I sit with you?"

"Go ahead." I nod calmly, barely glancing up.

Will sits down and pulls out his battered old laptop, and I have to resist a sudden, overwhelming urge to warn him that he's going to spill an entire mug of black coffee on it in about three weeks' time and lose a lot of very important files. Although he'll also take this disaster in his stride so beautifully, and with such great humor and graciousness, it'll make me fall for him just a little bit more.

Conscientiously, I return to fake-reading my book.

That sense of déjà vu is back: a familiar clatter of cups behind the counter, a door being slammed, the delivery of my mint tea, a baby starting to cry. It's all exactly as it was the first time again, as if time has a preferred route—a mild-voiced but bossy GPS—and our detour is now over. All I have to do is exactly what I did the first time round, which means that in five, four, three, two, one—

"Wow." Will looks up from his computer. "That's quite some book for a Wednesday evening."

With a delay to suggest I'm engrossed, I look up. "Is it?"

"*The Iliad*?" Will grins widely, and I notice the sweet gap between his front teeth, just as I did the first time round. "That's more Thursday or Friday reading material, surely."

"Not at all." I smile back. "I try to save later in the week for other books written by a member of the Simpson family."

"I've heard Bart's version of *King Lear* is extraordinary."

"Not a patch on *Paradise Lost* by Maggie."

We both laugh and I feel it: something warm and rosy and pink, reaching across the table between us like fingertips. Apparently the obscene strength of my long-term memory is "kind of creepy"—and the weakness of my short-term memory "extremely irritating"—but I am abruptly grateful for the ability to remember this entire conversation, word for word.

It means I have a preapproved script to follow: one I already know works.

"You've traveled a lot," I say, precisely on cue.

Will looks up again in surprise, so I point at the battered stickers plastered all over his doomed laptop. Thailand. Australia. The Philippines. Iceland. I did make this observation last time too, but I feel a lot more confident in the assertion now I know the story behind every single one of them.

"Not really." Will beams, and something in my stomach abruptly glows. "I just like pretty and painfully stylish strangers in coffee shops to think I do. Sadly, my *I'm A Very Interesting Person* sticker fell off last week."

I stare at him with round eyes.

Umm, he was supposed to say, *I have, yes, mostly for work, what about you?* And then I say, *No, actually, I haven't left England for a decade*, and he says, *Oh, that's such a shame, why not?* and I say, *I've had nobody to go with and also the sun gives me painful hives* and immediately regret it.

I cannot believe Will Baker has gone off script already.

"I…" What sticker? What's he talking about? "Me? Am I the pretty stranger?"

"Yes." Will scratches his head. "Sorry. That was a joke, and also a desperate attempt to flirt with you. I've been out of the dating game quite a while. Can you tell?"

"Yes," I confirm. "That was bloody awful."

Will bursts out laughing and I feel my entire body relax in relief.

"Can I start again?" He assesses me with a slightly different expression on his face, but I have absolutely no idea what it could be. "My official answer is yes, I travel a lot. Mostly for work. What about you?"

"Umm." I decide to correct this thread immediately. "Not so much. My job is…mainly London-centric."

"What do you do? Is it around here?"

"A PR agency just around the corner. What about you?"

I don't think we talk enough, as a species, about how ridiculously difficult it is to make basic conversation. People act like it should be fun, but it isn't. It's like playing tennis, and you have to stay permanently perched on the balls of your feet just to work out where the ball is coming from and where it's supposed to go next. Is it their turn? My turn? Will I get there fast enough? Have I missed my shot? Did I just interrupt theirs? Am I hogging the ball? Is this a gentle back-and-forth rally, just to waste time, or would they prefer one of us to just smack it into the corner?

It's exhausting even when I don't know all the answers already.

"Nope." Will bites into his cupcake and the cherry drops on the floor. "Ah, sod it. That was the best bit." He picks it up and pops it in his mouth, and I guess his food hygiene habits haven't improved in this strand of the universe either. "I have a client based in Soho, but my studio is actually in Clerkenwell. I'm having to buy T-shirts on the run because I don't have time to do laundry."

Will grabs his khaki satchel and pulls out the paper Zara bag from earlier.

Blimey: he didn't do this last time either.

"Why am I showing a stranger with clearly amazing fashion

sense the rubbish clothes I just bought?" He grimaces. "Sorry again. It's been a long week."

"I want to see them." I'm weirdly touched by the casual domesticity of this gesture: the incredible intimacy of it, as if somehow we are already a couple and he genuinely cares what I think. "Show me."

It's becoming rapidly clear that I can stick to the script as much as I like, but Will isn't going to. He functions on an almost entirely ad hoc, momentary basis, saying and doing what he feels at any given moment, with no respect at all for the pencil drafts of his alternative existences.

This is going to be a lot trickier than I originally thought.

"You're going to rue the day you let me sit opposite you." Will reaches into the bag and pulls out blue, red and black T-shirts. "They're just plain, but this one's got a little logo, so..."

I start laughing in earnest now, because I've been teasing him about this T-shirt for months: he wears it when he "doesn't think he'll be taking off his jumper," yet inevitably ends up taking off his jumper.

"Turn it over."

Will does as he's told and stares in horror at the giant Mickey Mouse emblazoned proudly across the back. "Oh, for the love of— Why would they put that on an adult man's T-shirt? I can't wear that now, can I?"

"Yet something tells me you will," I accurately predict.

"Yeah, I totally will," he admits with a dry laugh, looking delighted. "You got me in one. Shit. No wonder I'm still single."

No wonder I'm still single.

And, just like that, we're back to the original script. Will dropped that information and left it sitting there like gum the first time round too: knowing it would stick. Except last time, I wasn't sure what it meant. Was he hitting on me? Alerting me to his dating availability? Was it simply an exchange of irrelevant data, the way conversation so often is? What if he was generally commiserating with me on his marital status because I looked like a person used to being alone for long periods of time too?

Last time, this one sentence sent me into a spiral of anxiety and embarrassment and white-hot confusion.

This time, I can feel the meaning: wedged in my shoe.

"Well," I say, finally making direct eye contact with an almost Herculean strength, like lifting a boar above my head. "Now you know, maybe you can work out why I'm still single too."

Will grins widely, meeting my eyes, and I cannot believe how much easier flirting is when you've already rehearsed it once before.

"Well, why don't we—"

His phone starts ringing at exactly the right time and a spoon behind me clinks and a bag hits the floor and it's happening again, just as it did in our original timeline. We're back on the same path again. Maybe destiny isn't such a stupid human concept after all.

"Hold that thought," Will tells me a second time, picking up his phone.

Behind the counter, the coffee machine hisses and bright yellow runs through me in a line, like a trickle of paint. I know what's going to happen next, because it already has. For possibly the first time in three decades, I'm not weighed down by trying to read someone's colors and their facial expression and their body language and their tone and their words and also look out for jokes and sarcasm and flirting and secret insults and what is implied and what is left unspoken and somehow simultaneously filter out the chatter around me and the milk frother and the sensation of the chair under my bum and the movement of my fingers and position of my own feet and the breeze on my face and the sound of the doorbell ringing and the sound of my own heart and breath and the muscles in my own face.

For just a few seconds of my life I get to just be present, and it is *joyful*.

Will glances at me, frowns and mouths *you okay?*

I smile and nod.

"Right now?" Will rolls his eyes at me and I dutifully copy him and roll mine back. "Okay. Just in a café. Be there in five."

Will puts his phone away and stands up, grabbing his ancient laptop off the top of the coffee table, and I know I shouldn't touch anything on this timeline, shouldn't be screwing around, this thread is so delicate, so fragile, so easy to—

"Back up," I blurt.

Will pauses in packing away his laptop. "Sorry?"

"Back up." I point to his computer. "Your files. Back them up. Onto a hard drive or a cloud or a stick or whatever." He frowns, so I quickly add: "I just have this…thing. Where I re-mind people to back up their laptops regularly. So just…back up. That's all I'm saying. Okay?"

It's a bit of a romance killer, but I couldn't just sit there and let him lose important files with the knowledge I have: it would be entirely unethical.

"I never back up." Will smiles. "So thanks for the reminder."

I nod as he zips up his bag, watching his face closely, wait-ing to see what will happen now. Have I knocked everything off track again? We're back to the unknown, to people-reading and desperate guessing; to a constant state of confusion, where every social interaction is a bewildering smorgasbord of clues that never quite add up. I guess I'll just have to take my mo-ments of predictable, familiar bliss when they come.

So, I urge him silently, *I don't suppose you'd fancy hanging out again, would you? We could grab a drink, maybe?*

"So…" Will slings his bag across his shoulders. "I don't sup-pose you'd fancy hanging out again, would you? We could grab a drink, maybe?"

I may not be able to read Will's colors, but I can certainly read mine.

"I would like that," I say as casually as I can while the air around me suddenly fills with gold and pink. "I'm Cassie."

"Hi, Cassie," my future boyfriend says. "I'm Will."

11

THE TITAN EOS HAS a really unfair reputation.

Essentially the Bridget Jones of Greek mythology, the rosy-fingered bringer of dawn is known for two things: opening the gates every morning so her brother Helios can drive the sun across the sky, and being cursed by Aphrodite with a really shit love life for all eternity. So, while most of Olympus is indulging in endless torrid love affairs and pairing up like penguins, the immortal Titan Eos dates, and fails, and dates, and fails. She's the original rom-com heroine: forever focused on finding love, wearing shades of pink, seen by all the other gods as a bit of a desperate loser.

But, of all the goddesses, I think Eos is the most powerful.

Love is a courageous thing to pursue, and to me Eos represents hope, and resilience, and light in the darkest hour. She represents the strength to keep trying, even when you know you're doomed. She represents new beginnings and refusing to accept defeat. She also represents the ability to change your husband into a cicada when he gets very old and kind of annoying.

What could possibly be more inspiring than that?

★ ★ ★

"Hello?" I open the front door. "Is anybody in?"

I vibrated with happiness all the way home, and now I need to go and lie down: all this joy is making me a little nauseous.

"Hey hey." Sal wanders into the hallway and looks me up and down, wiping flour off her eyebrow. "Wow. Look at you. That *dress* is off the charts."

There's something missing in my flatmate's eyes and it takes a full three seconds to work out what it is. In all the excitement of restarting my life with Will, I'd totally forgotten that I've simultaneously restarted *everything*. We're now four months ago, back at ground zero: The Time Before.

The relief is so intense, I almost fall asleep on the spot.

"Off the charts which end?" I check. "Good end or bad end?"

"Good." Sal laughs. "Very, very good."

"In that case, do you want it?"

My love for my new blue dress abruptly died on the way home, when I realized that the material feels like sandpaper and the neckline is suffocating and the elastic around each giant sleeve grips like hands and the *waistline*—ugh. A waistline must either be secured very tightly with a wide belt—holding my body together—or left completely loose, but it cannot just linger, touching me whenever it feels like it. Within a twenty-minute tube journey I went from being extremely pleased with my new purchase to wanting to set it on ceremonial fire and throw its ashes out at Vauxhall.

Which, for the record, is *precisely* why I only wear five of the exact same jumpsuit in specific daily colors for work. I don't have the space for a tactile- and decision-based roller coaster every day while also trying to hold on to my job.

"What?" Sal blinks. "You're giving me a brand-new dress? Right now."

"Okay." A little surprised, I reach behind me and start tugging at the zip. "Don't you want me to dry-clean it first?"

"Right now *question mark*, Cassie," Sal clarifies with a tiny smile. "I'm not asking you to strip down in the middle of the hallway."

Embarrassed, I stop unzipping. "Ah. Of course."

"Do you want dinner?" Sal wipes her hands on her apron and I abruptly remember that this was the three-week stretch where she decided to train as a chef. Before that it was a masseur, and next it will be a bedroom-based YouTuber. It didn't go well. Maybe I should warn her. "I've made a... Well. I'm not really sure what it is, to be honest. It was supposed to be a lasagna, but I didn't arrange the pasta properly and now it's kind of goop in sheets."

"Dead animals," I point out. "Also, it's Wednesday."

"You can just say *no, thank you, Salini*," she sighs lightly, flour on the end of her nose. "You know, without the I'm-going-to-vomit face."

In bare feet, Sal wanders back into the kitchen and I follow, feeling ashamed of myself. I should have said yes, or at least offered to share the garlic bread, but Wednesday is Veggie Chili Day. I have quite enough change to deal with right now—given that I'm busy editing the entire universe—without screwing around with my weekly menu too.

I stick my dinner in the microwave, then freeze as Derek struts into the room wearing a vest with little pre-ripped holes in it. With the consciously mischievous air of a self-appointed Pan, he pinches grated cheese from a plate, gets slapped by Sal and immediately circles back round to do it again.

"'Sup, Cassandra." He grins, licking his tanned fingers. "That's a very *dramatic* outfit for midweek. I thought you were all about the rompers. And don't worry, by the way. I've got a takeaway app ready to go. My girl is a bit of a wizard in the kitchen, by which I mean she magically turns edible ingredients into shit you can't eat."

"Bugger off," Sal says amicably. "I'm trying to expand my

culinary repertoire—much to my mother's dismay. And ignore him, Cassie. That dress is epic. Never take fashion advice from a man who habitually wears a deep V-neck."

Derek pulls a face at me behind her back and I don't know what the face is or why he's pulling it at me or what face I'm supposed to pull back or what it all means, so I panic, stare at the floor and go red instead. There's a long silence while I desperately search for something friendly and flatmatey to say, to make sure our entire relationship doesn't fall off a cliff like it did last time.

"Did you both…have a day?" I attempt with difficulty. "That was nice? Participating in your…respective professions?"

They both turn simultaneously to stare at me and I flush further.

How was your day?

How bloody hard is it to say *how was your day?* and just leave it there?

"Did we have a day that was nice, participating in our respective professions?" Derek laughs. "Sal? Did we?" He turns back to me, and I prepare myself for evisceration. "Is English your first language, Cassie? It's cool if it's not, but we can help you if you need extra lessons."

"Yes," I confirm bleakly. "English is my only language, apart from an amateur splash of ancient Greek."

Although I can certainly see why my proficiency might be in question. Sometimes I stop understanding basic words, or how to use them, and get mixed up for no reason. I recently referred to my phone as "my banana" and Will laughed so loudly three pigeons flew away simultaneously.

"So actually I've just realized," I say formally, taking a few steps backward and staring at the top of the kitchen cabinets, "I've…got an important thing. To do. In my bedroom. Alone. Have a nice evening. Goodbye."

"Cassie," Sal says in frustration as I bolt out of the room.

"He was just teasing. Please don't take it— *Stop eating the shitting cheese, Derek. It's to sprinkle on shitting top. Nigella Lawson doesn't have to put up with this kind of disrespect.*"

"I don't think you should say the word *shit* so much when you're talking about our dinner," Derek objects, and Sal laughs loudly.

"Valid," she agrees warmly behind me, and I hear a loud kiss. My stomach suddenly hurts a bit. It's funny how living in a house with other people in it feels infinitely lonelier than living completely alone.

Slipping off my shoes and leaving them lined up on the rack in the hallway—they're the only shoes on there, the rest are piled on the floor, which leaves me questioning why we even have a rack—I make my way up the stairs to my room, unzipping as I go. As soon as the door is closed, I rip the blue dress off and lob it violently across the room, then pull on my yellow dressing gown and feel immediately calmer. It smells like me. It *feels* like me. Softness settles on my skin and I can see Mum: fluffing the duvet on top of me while I lie rigidly on the bed, giggling with my eyes closed. It was so delicious and made me so happy, she did it every single night, even though I'm now realizing her arms must have ached with the weight of it.

I still miss it, so much. I've tried to fluff my own duvet and dive under it at the last moment, but honestly, it just doesn't have the same impact.

Smiling slightly, I glance around the room. Every cell in my body is slowly unfurling, as if I'm covered in leaves: as if I'm a plant taken out of a pot and put back in the ground.

My bedroom is back to normal again. Will ran out so quickly after both our breakups—aka this morning, aka yesterday morning, aka four months in the future—and I was too distressed to make the bed and open the curtains or remove his one dirty sock from my wastepaper basket.

Now time has done it for me, like an invisible Mary Poppins.

My bed is smooth, perfect, made with the specific soft, fresh white bedding I stock up on and keep stored in the cupboard. The curtains are billowing gently and the sun is lighting up the eyes on my little blue owl toy. My soft green blanket is folded perfectly, and my books are arranged in size, then color, then in order of how much I like them. My beautiful—mainly vintage— clothes are all arranged chromatically, like a rainbow, and my shelves have all my ornaments on them, strategically arranged and carefully dusted every Sunday evening: a bust of Athena, a tiny gold miniature of Medusa, an Aphrodite pendant, a little jeweled peacock that is Hera's favorite.

Honestly, I think I can take changing the universe in my stride as long as nobody screws with my bedroom.

Feeling peaceful now, I turn my music to a looped piano track and feel every note: running along my shoulder blades, down my vertebrae, across my thighs and into my feet, a moving wave of bliss. The wrong noises hurt me—pinching, punching, scraping—but the opposite is true too: a shifting kind of sweetness in every organ. I don't think I could give up one if it meant losing the other; not—in fairness—that anyone is giving me the option.

Smiling, I light a candle—feel the crackle in my ears and the glow in the small of my back—then wander around my bedroom, touching everything with my fingers and making a list of whatever time has erased. A specific book about Medea. A rare pair of thin gold hoop earrings that don't tug at my earlobes. An extraordinary green silk jacket that feels like a nectarine and makes me think of a specific oak tree at the bottom of the garden where I grew up.

Satisfied, I fill my watering can from my sink and wander round to check how time travel has affected all my plants. They're a little smaller—as is to be expected—but they seem content. Happy. There's Melpomene—a philodendron—which thrives in the dark just like the goddess of tragedy, as does my bird of paradise, Urania (the Muse of astronomy). Terpsichore (the goddess of dance) is a fern that rustles when the window is open, and Aphrodite is the string of hearts hanging by my bed. My snake plant is obviously called Medusa, my pothos is called Pothos (son of Eros), and I'd go on, but at this point people normally ask me not to.

"Arachne?" I lean toward my spider plant. "What's up? You're looking a little sad. Hot? Cold? Too much sun? Tell me what you need. You're not thirsty, so don't give me that—you get watered on Tuesdays."

"Hey, Cassie?" A soft knock on my door. "Are you on the phone?"

"Umm." The alternative is a conversation with vegetation, so… "Yes. Hang on. Let me just say goodbye. Yup. Yup. Uh-huh. Sure. That's so interesting. Speak to you later. Bye."

Flushing, I put the watering can down and grab the blue tulle ruffles from the floor.

Then I open the bedroom door and thrust it forward.

"Here you go. It doesn't smell."

"Cool." Salini laughs and takes it out of my hands. "Cheers."

"Actually, it might smell." I take it off her again. "And be a bit damp. I'm really sorry. I can dry-clean it. It's just…" The tube was crowded and a man touched me and I yelped like a stepped-on dog and everyone stared at me and I literally *felt* the sweat break out beneath my underwire. "I sweat profusely."

"The best girls do." Sal grins, carefully taking the outfit back again. "This is an amazing dress, Cassie, and it's so generous of you. No need to apologize. You're a strange one, sometimes."

She says it mildly—almost affectionately—but it's still weird how people observe things like that as if it's news to me; as if my *strangeness* wasn't one of the first things I ever learned about myself.

"Also, you forgot your dinner." Sal hands me my steaming

chili on a plate; she's popped some garlic bread and grated cheese on top. "So I thought I'd bring it up for you. Here you go."

I am so unbelievably moved by this gesture I'm not sure what to do with it.

"Thank you." I take the plate, feeling abruptly weepy. "I don't really like the garlic bread touching the chili, though. It goes soggy."

I take the garlic bread off and hand it back, so it doesn't get wasted.

"Noted." Sal's nostrils twitch again, and she shoves the bread in her mouth, then reaches into her apron pocket and pulls out an envelope. "I nearly forgot, Cassie. This arrived this morning for you. Smells of…" She sniffs it experimentally. "Roses?"

"Pomegranate," I say flatly, taking it off her.

"I didn't even know people still bought scented stationery." Sal leans against the doorway, hip resting on the door frame. "Or wrote letters, for that matter. It's so old-school. Looks like a lot of effort's been put into it. Long-lost love?"

"Not lost enough," I say, lobbing it on the bed. "Clearly."

The handwritten word *Cass* feels like it's pulsing in neon letters. The envelope is lying quietly but dangerously on my duvet cover as if it's an ancient grenade still with the potential to take down a whole building. My stomach twists painfully. I keep moving house, but they always find me. This is the first of what is about to be four handwritten letters to this address and it just feels like a waste of stamps, calligraphy ink and rain-forest materials. They write apologies; I don't read them or reply. My response is unchanging and incredibly easy to predict: you'd think they'd have worked it out by now.

When I finally turn back, Sal is still standing in my doorway—apparently waiting for something, but I don't know what.

"Is there anything I can help you with, Salini?"

"Oh!" Sal blinks three times and finishes the soggy garlic bread. "No. I just thought we might… Never mind. Cheese to sprinkle. Lasagna to burn. Boyfriend to make live in the garden and so on."

Sticking her hands in her apron pockets, Sal jumps back down the stairs to the kitchen two at a time—extremely dangerous with no hands, very maverick of her—and I think I may have put the emphasis of that sentence in the wrong place.

"Is there anything *I* can help *you* with?" I murmur furiously. "For fuck's sake, Cassandra."

Closing my door again, I cautiously pick up the envelope again and sniff it. I suddenly feel sick, woozy, light-headed, overwhelmed. A million memories are now pushing at the back of my brain all at once and I can feel myself standing rigidly with my full weight against the door so they can't get in.

The letters always smell of pomegranates: the fruit of the dead.

As I've touched on before, Hades kidnapped Persephone and took her to the Underworld, then used pomegranate seeds to trick her into staying in hell for six months of the year (or four, depending on who's telling the story, thank you, *Will*). It's a very specific scent: tart and rich and immediately easy to identify. I just cannot for the life of me work out exactly what it's supposed to *mean*, sprayed all over our correspondence. I suppose I could just open the letter and find out, but that's obviously what people who write letters want: I will not be manipulated that easily.

All I know for sure is that I don't want it in my space; the emotions it brings with it are not invited.

Jaw clenched, I walk over to the wastepaper basket and peek inside it, just to double-check. It's empty. No black socks, no unread letters. Will has never been here, he's never dumped me here, he's never woken up and kissed me and left me here. That bit of my history has yet to be written. Right now, it's just an empty wastepaper basket with any number of future contents possible, and maybe—if I'm really careful, if I play my cards right—some of them don't have to happen at all.

Firmly, I rip the envelope in half and throw it in the bin again.

And maybe some of them do.

12

BY THE NEXT MORNING, I have a full plan.

Flying by the seat of your pants is a massively overrated aviation term, in my opinion. People act like it's an interesting personality trait, but there's a reason we have maps, and guidelines, and approved airline routes, and it's to make sure that—much like Douglas Corrigan, the American pilot for whom the phrase was first coined—we don't plan to fly from Brooklyn to California and somehow end up in Dublin.

Thanks to the gift of time travel, it seems that I now have four whole months to save my relationship, my living situation and my career. And I'm going to do whatever it takes to get there. As long as I can work out roughly where I went wrong the first time round, I should end up in a much happier place.

Or, at the very least, on the right bloody continent.

"Cassandra!" A pause. "Where the hell has Cassandra gone now?"

I'm in the office toilet, hiding.

Which is less a part of The Plan and more a realization that I may have screwed up The Plan already and it's only nine thirty in the morning. The first thing I saw when I arrived at work was a handwritten orange note stuck to my computer monitor—from Barry, asking to see me—and despite being a fully grown adult, I feel exactly like I've been called to see the headmaster for a detention. I'm assuming, anyway. It never happened at school; I was an excellent student.

Quickly, I blast the tap and run my hands under it.

Then I exit the bathroom, shaking them to suggest that I have just been urinating for thirty-five minutes and not staring blankly at the monkeys in the wallpaper, wondering whether a jungle might be a less confusing environment.

"Bloody hell, woman," Barry snaps. "Use a hand dryer."

"No, thank you," I say politely, wiping my hands on my pink Thursday jumpsuit and regretting it immediately. "Harvard University found two hundred and fifty-four colonies of bacteria growing in hand dryers, and they are unnecessarily loud. How may I help you today?"

Barry smiles. "Did you have a nice holiday yesterday?"

"Yes, I did," I say with considerable relief. "Thank you so much for asking."

"I'm being sarcastic, Cassandra." The smile on Barry's face disappears and he abruptly resembles corned beef. "I am really starting to lose my patience with your attitude now. Your email yesterday was frankly unacceptable. You can't just ditch work for the afternoon whenever you feel like it, no matter how many vacation days you've stored up. And don't think I haven't noticed how many Idea Hurricanes you have now excused yourself from, Cassandra. They are *requisite*. That means *not optional*. Frankly, I don't give a toss how you feel about them personally. They are a part of this agency's *ethos*, an Opportunity to Effectively Ideate Together and Touch Base on What Makes Our Clients Tick in a Big Picture kind of way, and you *will attend*."

I am certain that Barry has a list of corporate jargon stuck to his wall that he studies on a daily basis, because I've heard humans talk before and this isn't it.

"But—"

"It's on the website," my boss cuts in, much more loudly. "In animated neon lettering I paid an embarrassing amount of money for. The official agency ethos is not Collectively Pooling Our Creative Resources, Everyone but Cassandra Dankworth, Who Thinks She's Too Flaming Good for Them."

"But that's not what I said," I object in genuine surprise. "I simply pointed out that you would be paying me for doing no work, which seems very unethical. It feels like stealing from the company."

"Cassandra—"

"*Nobody* does anything." I hold out my hands as a desperate plea for just a little bit of rational thinking. "It's not just me. It's a three-hour session of talking about their private lives and eating biscuits. Half of that particular one was spent discussing who hooked up with whom on the last Away Day. I just don't think it's an efficient use of our resources, and it makes me extremely uncomfortable."

I'm now becoming slowly aware that the entire agency has gone silent and they have swiveled in their chairs to look at me.

I can feel my whole body fold inward, like a piece of origami.

"I don't understand," I finish desperately, trying to keep my voice low so my colleagues can't hear it. "I'm just being honest, Barry. I saved you and our clients money and myself time. That's a good thing, isn't it?"

"I give up." Barry sighs through gritted teeth, turning back toward his little glass box in the corner. "It's like talking to a brick wall. Attend Idea Hurricanes. No more impromptu afternoons off. Or it'll be a mute point, Cassandra, because the rest of your PR career will be one long holiday."

"Moot," I say automatically.

"What?"

"Moot. You said 'mute.' They're two different words."

"For fuck's sake, Cassandra," Barry sighs, closing his door behind him.

Clearing my throat, I go back to my desk and awkwardly arrange everything into straight lines until I can feel the glares from my colleagues slowly move away from the center of my forehead. I can see waves of sticky orange resentment seeping out of them like Fanta spills, trickling across the open-plan office, but I'm not entirely sure I understand why. They know I'm not lying. For our last brainstorm, seven of them brought beers and popcorn.

Everything is suddenly too bright, too loud, too close, the air is starting to hurt my skin, so I quickly grab my noise-canceling headphones, pop them over my head, pick up my pen and focus on remembering everything I can about my first solo meeting with SharkSkin. We've only just won the contract, and the brand hasn't launched; Jack doesn't despise me yet. He doesn't *like* me—there's definitely discomfort there—but it hasn't quite hardened into the shriveling, withering sensation it eventually turns into.

As I write, the fizzing in my chest slowly starts to settle.

My plan is going to work. I can do this—I know I can. I can adjust my future. With the lessons I have learned over the last few months, I must be able to find a way to fix the career I accidentally obliterated the last t—

My neck prickles and I look up in irritation.

The top half of Sophie's face is moving, but I have literally no idea how long she's been talking to me. It could be minutes, could be hours. I could have been sitting here for six years with my body growing into my office chair, and frankly, when I'm this focused, I still wouldn't have noticed. With a painful wrench—like being dragged by my hair out of a big well—I tug my headphones down.

"What?"

"—canes?" Sophie punctuates her keyboard with one jubilant finger. "I think they're actually really helpful. Yesterday Grace thought of *dogs in capes*, and isn't that just so original? I don't know if they're going to use it, but it was a lot of fun. Teamwork is *super* important in a job like this."

I stare at her. Sarcasm? "Mmm."

With a sense of relief, I go back to my work, but Sophie's eyes are on me again; I lift one headphone.

"—brand," she continues blithely. "It's *so* fun. I'd love to work with such a challenging client and come up with something that might impress them."

"Sure," I say, waiting with the headphone held in the air to see if she's done yet.

Nope. She's still talking.

"But I've been put on this stupid travel company and they're happy with everything," she sighs. "Like, stop sending me to swanky hotels in exotic places all the time, you know? So annoying. I just want to stay in London. Hahaha."

I glance in irritation at my watch: Jack and Gareth will be here any moment and, from what I remember of this meeting, I'm going to need every single second of mental preparation to stop myself accidentally driving my career into a wall again.

"Sophie," I say as politely as I can, "when my headphones are on, it's a pretty clear visual indication that I do not wish to engage in pointless chitchat."

"Oh," she says, smile disappearing. "Sorry."

"SharkSkin are here," the receptionist announces, and with a suddenly dry mouth, I hang my headphones back on their little hook and grab my file. Everything around me is turning up, as if a switch is being steadily twisted: ceiling lights, coffee smells, the little noises of my colleagues bumping hellishly against each other like a band full of ten-year-olds on recorders.

Pinching my nose, I stand and walk toward the agency doors.

Be *likable*, Cassandra. Be *non-grating*. Remember that social hierarchy exists and stop telling people senior to you that their ideas are total shit. Just in time, I remember to force my face into a dimpled smile, even though it feels like pulling toffee with my hands.

"Miss Cassandra Dankworth!" Jack grabs both my hands. "What a pleasure. I cannot wait to get started on this product launch. It's going to be genre-defining—I can feel it in my bones."

Smile stiffening, I try to abandon my body like a ghost and count quietly in my head because it just seems easier than screaming *STOP BLOODY TOUCHING MY SKIN, YOU ARE HURTING ME* and then dealing with the consequences.

One, two, three, four—thank fuck, he's finally let go.

"Hi, Cassandra." Gareth smiles, trying to find a better grip on a massive cardboard box. "Nice to see you."

"Nice to see you too," I lie, glancing at what's in his hands as if I'm Pandora and all of mankind's eternal doom is about to be released. "Follow me to the…meeting room, please."

I refuse to call the Ideas Brewery by its official title: frankly, it's an offense to both ideas and breweries everywhere. Barry had a "heavy hand" in its creation, and it's essentially a torture chamber built by toddlers. There are flashing neon signs, swings and bouncy balls instead of chairs, bright jars of jelly beans, gold ladders that go nowhere, an inexplicable fake fountain that gurgles in a strangely non-regular pattern, plastic green grass instead of a carpet and a neon climbing wall that nobody has climbed in the entire time I've been here because we're not geckos.

The room is also positioned very strategically so that Barry can see straight inside it without physically moving from his desk. As we enter a hellscape Hades would be proud of, I'm trying very hard not to notice him sending me a message with his eyes. I have no idea what it is, but if it was that important, I'll assume he'd have communicated it by email.

"Very cool." Jack nods appreciatively, gazing round while grabbing three jelly beans and shoving them in his mouth. "I will say your boss certainly knows how to make work feel like play."

"Yes," I agree flatly. "You wouldn't believe the amount of people in here who pick their nose and then fiddle with the confectionery. It's an absolute caper."

Jack stops chewing and spits a jelly bean onto the table.

I probably shouldn't have said that.

"Right," Gareth says, putting the box down. "Cassandra, am I correct in thinking we'll have a larger team? It won't be just you?"

"Correct," I confirm, perching delicately on a red ball. I chose a swing last time and nearly face-planted a cactus. "I'll be putting the team together this week."

I'll choose Anya with the lip piercing and Miyuki with the waist-length pink hair, they'll spend their entire time flirting in the kitchen and it'll be an unprecedented disaster that seals my fate as a future waitress.

"This is my passion project," Jack explains again proudly, choosing a blue ball with the confidence of a child who knows exactly what toy he likes and has zero intention of sharing it. "Bit of background on me—spent years building a portfolio in the finance sector, a bit of property too, up north, nice and cheap, and now I'm ready to try something creative. Something with a bit of flair."

I nod. Be *likable*, Cassandra. Be a *People Person*. Don't just ignore him and open your file like you did last time.

"That is a very interesting origin story," I say formally. "Thank you so much for sharing it with me."

Out of the corner of my eye, I'm warily watching Gareth start opening the box, and here's an interesting fact: the legendary

Pandora's box was never actually a box. It was a mistranslated enormous clay jar, a punishment from Zeus because Prometheus gifted humans fire and thus a calculated way to destroy us all.

Something tells me this one has the power to do it all over again.

"SharkSkin is going to be industry-changing," Jack continues expansively, holding his palms upward as if he's presenting the ceiling for analysis. "A brand-new way of looking at men's skin care. This is about *self-love*. There's all this constant chat about women loving themselves, but who says men can't love themselves too? Don't real men deserve to look after our skin as well?"

I physically feel my face drop, so I consciously tug it back into a sweet smile and watch as Gareth dutifully starts pulling items out of the box. Greed. Envy. Illness. Pain. Disease. Misery. Death.

Only joking. It's a few branded jars of face cream.

"Sure," I say as my throat starts tightening. "Although men have demonstrably been using skin care for thousands and thousands of years already, in multiple ancient cultures all over the world." I cough. *Unlikable. Grating.* "But I see what you mean. What a fascinating question to explore further with the public."

"So these are the prototypes," Gareth says, laying them all out on the table. "Ready to hit the stores in a couple of weeks. As you can see, they all have a shark on them." He lifts one eyebrow. "Lots and lots and *lots* of sharks."

I stare at the packaging in horror. I'm not sure why, but I think I'd been desperately hanging on to some futile hope that by traveling through time, I might have somehow ended up in a thread of the universe where SharkSkin wasn't yellow and blue stripes with orange lids and a leaping shark drawn jumping across the front, flecks of blood spinning out of its mouth. I don't know who the designer is, but they've clearly never been to either an optician or an aquarium.

"Sharks are the ultimate masculine animals," Jack asserts and pushes one toward me. "This is the day moisturizer, Cassandra, which will be our lead launch. Go ahead and smell it."

"No, thank you," I say politely.

"Go on." He nudges it closer. "Smell it."

I push it away. "I don't really need to."

"Smell the cream, Cassandra," Jack says in a much sharper voice. "I don't want a PR who isn't *fully invested*. It's algae-based, you know. Lots of antioxidants. I think you'll be impressed."

Holding my breath—there's no getting around it—I pick up a jar and slowly untwist the lid. I've had a problem with scent since I was a baby. Anything too rich, too powerful, too meaty, immediately sets off a vicious gag reflex. ("Cassandra must stop being so dramatic at lunchtime.") I have to pull my jumper over my nose and mouth every time I walk past a butcher's shop or I vomit on the curb outside the roast-beef-sandwich queue.

But this is my job. My future. My destiny.

Come on, Cassandra. You can do this.

You have been granted the gift of both hindsight and prophecy, and all you need to do in return is...not what you did four months ago. Literally anything other than what you did four months ago is fine. Bending down, I inhale cautiously. It's a surreal yet extremely potent combination of mold and petrol and mint and a faint whiff of inexplicable pork sausage, and I immediately start gagging.

My mouth fills with water, my throat closes.

No no no no no—

"Fuck me," I say as my words tumble out in a rush, a punishment from the gods. "That is absolutely disgusting."

YEAH, I DID IT AGAIN.

Now and then, time likes to replicate situations *exactly*.

"Excuse me?" Jack snarls as I put a hand over my mouth and try to push the words back in. "*What* did you just say?"

I can feel my brain scrabbling urgently at the inside of my head like a trapped gerbil, attempting to find a way out, but there isn't one. I know, because I've spent the last four months trying.

"Sorry," I sigh, closing my eyes.

Let's try that again.

"Sharks are the ultimate masculine animals," Jack says, pushing one toward me. "This is the day moisturizer, Cassandra, which will be our lead launch. Go ahead and smell it."

"I said no," I say, screwing the lid back on.

"Excuse—"

"And the fact that you think *masculinity* is epitomized by

cold-blooded predators says a lot about modern society, don't you think?"

Sorry, but it needed to be said.

Undo.

"Go ahead and smell it," Jack says, and I snap on my prettiest Lego smile and pick up the moisturizer.

"Gosh," I say, holding my breath. "That's powerful stuff."

"Yes." Jack nods, finally satisfied. "I wanted something instantly identifiable. That's *SharkSkin*, I want people to say."

"Oh, they will," I confirm.

In a matter of weeks, SharkSkin will become synonymous with a scent that makes dogs hurl, along with a misogynistic PR campaign that not only fails to sell product, but will make me personally—as the brand manager—look like a woman who hates women, and skin, and sharks, thus ending my career in an impressively three-dimensional fashion.

Silently, Gareth lines up bottles on the table, all of which have our leaping, open-mouthed ambassador plastered all over them. It feels like unfair representation. Sharks are generally very peaceful: I'm sure there are plenty of times they just swim around, not covered in blood, chilling out with their mouths closed.

"There's going to be an entire range," Gareth states in a strange voice, and I study his face, but I can't for the life of me work out what expression is on it. Embarrassment? Indigestion? They look so similar. "Face wash. Serum. Vitamin C. Sun cream. Body lotion. Toothpaste, eventually, but we're still... working on the formula."

"It'll be done soon," Jack contributes proudly. "Testers don't seem to want to put it in their mouths."

Gareth makes a weird choking noise and rubs his nose.

"The thing is—" I swallow, but there's no way around this: I can muck around with time as much as I like, but I still have to keep trying to nudge this meeting in a different direction or I'm going to end up in exactly the same place again. "Are we all definitely set on SharkSkin as a brand name?"

Jack stares at my leg: I didn't even realize it was bouncing.

"It's just that shark's skin is made up of layers of sharp dermal denticles," I explain, pressing my right leg with my hand until the bouncing neatly transfers to the left instead. "Each has a vascular pulp section, a middle made of dentine and an outer layer of enamel."

My client continues to study me blankly.

"Teeth," I clarify quickly, pushing my research forward across the table so he can see the diagrams I printed out for visual impact. "A shark is literally covered all over in thousands of *living teeth* and I worry that this isn't what humans look to emulate with their skin-care regime."

"The name stays," Jack snaps. "Next."

"Okay." I start quickly rifling through my file, even though I know exactly what the next response will be too. "So I guess the next question is what demographic we're targeting, because—"

"Men," Jack says. "Next."

"Gendered skin care is a little outda—"

"So here's the campaign." Jack leans back and props his hands behind his head—while simultaneously balancing on a ball, which is actually quite impressive. "'Skin Care With Bite, For Real Men.'"

I close my eyes. It's the same. Somehow, in a completely different strand of the universe with an infinite number of ideas to choose from, Jack's gone ahead and picked the same shit catchphrase that's going to lose me my job again.

"It won't work," I say flatly.

"But I think it will."

"It won't."

"I'm pretty sure it will."

"I am *telling you*, Jack." My voice is definitely *grating* now, but there's no getting around it. "I have seen exactly what will happen if we go down this path, and it will be a disaster. Nobody will cover it. Nobody will buy it. We'll be laughed at by everyone. *Everyone.*"

Jack scowls. "So you can see the future now, can you?"

"Yes," I say sharply. "And we will fail."

My client stares at me, and with a deep breath I lift my eyeballs and stare back at him: feeling a bit like Patroclus on the beaches of Troy, holding my sword aloft, pretending to be Achilles and waiting to be fatally run through with a spear.

"Your job," Jack says, and it's exactly what happened last time, right down to the crimped edges of his voice, "is to support *my* business plan, Miss Dankworth, which *I* am paying for. With *my* private funds. Am I perfectly clear? *Not* to give me this negative, defeatist attitude and arrogantly assume you know better than I do."

Don't do it, Cassandra. Please don't do it.

Just tell Jack he's a visionary and a genius—a Daedalus of creative ingenuity, a Circe of chemical construction—because the only logical way to save your job now is to make sure he likes you. Except I can't. Lying makes me feel sick, and I've never been able to fake humility. ("Cassandra has no respect for authority.") Just as before, I feel a familiar, electric ripple of rage: this time definitely mine, mustard yellow. Because why should I have to pretend? Why should I have to stroke this man's inflated ego, especially when now I *know* I'm right?

"My job," I say, smiling tightly with all the remaining energy I can muster, "is to successfully launch your brand. If you want to sell a lot of product, you'll need to appeal to a much wider demographic than men who personally identify with sea life."

Jack lifts his chin and there it is again: the squelchy, resentful sensation that will follow me from now until the moment of my unemployment. He dislikes me, and it starts precisely here.

But I refuse to go back in time to change it. I refuse to exhaust myself, just to let him defeat me without a fight.

Instead, I harden my gaze: if he wants *arrogance*, he's got it.

"Skin Care With Bite," Jack asserts again, "For Real Men. That's the campaign, Cassandra, and it is your job to *make it work*."

I nod, jaw tight. "Understood."

"Coverage in ten pieces of mainstream media," he adds firmly. "That's what Barry promised us when we signed with your agency. Ten pieces, including national radio. Not including regional."

Not going to happen. "Fine."

We're going to get one local Norfolk hit and the seventy-six-year-old presenter will mistakenly tell everyone the moisturizer contains actual shark and we'll get a tirade of hate mail from animal activists and horrified children.

"Great," Jack says, looking past me and brightening up at my boss, now lingering outside. I'd turn around too, but I can't or I'll fall off my ball. "I'll look forward to being kept up to date, on a daily basis." Sometimes on a minutely basis, if I remember correctly. "Thank you, *Cassandra*."

Jack says my name with just enough emphasis to make it sound unfashionable and outdated, then leaves the room while I carefully bounce up and down a few times, preparing to stand up as if I'm on a space hopper. I can't believe it. That meeting went almost *exactly* the same as it did originally. I've got literally all of time on my side—an eternity of do-overs—and I haven't fixed anything at all.

"He's just really invested," Gareth says awkwardly, putting the bottles neatly back in the box. "Jack's not a bad guy. I've—"

"Known him since you were at school," I say tiredly. "Yes, I know."

"Yeah." Gareth frowns and studies me. "I guess Jack told you at the pitch meeting. There's a lot of—"

"Pressure on him to get this right." I roll to my feet. "There's a lot of pressure on me too, you know. My whole career depends on it."

"Right." I can feel Gareth's eyes on me as I gather my totally unused file of ideas. I might as well have brought in a year's worth of the *Beano.* "And exactly how certain are you that this strategy won't work?"

"A hundred percent."

Maybe I should just cut my losses and leave my job now, before I have to listen to jokes about having *bitten off more than I can chew* for the rest of my PR career. Except…if I mess with this strand of history, who knows the impact it will have on all the others? What about Will? What about my flatmates? What about the rest of my plans? I suddenly feel like Theseus, carefully unraveling his red thread around the labyrinth so he knows how to get back out again when it's all over.

I can't risk cutting the thread and doing it all in the dark.

"If you can think of a way around this," Gareth says as we walk back into the main office, "call—"

"You directly." I nod flatly, holding out my hand for his business card. "Got it."

Gareth stares at me for a few seconds.

"You'll do what you can to help," I prompt, wiggling my fingers. "If I can think of any way around it, I must let you know."

Except I won't, because I don't have the faintest idea of what to do next. I'm not a good account manager at the best of times, and now I've been painted into a corner that I am simply not creative enough to get back out of. I've tried before, and I've failed. I'll just get impatient and try to tiptoe directly out of the room, ending up with thick white emulsion all over my socks and footprints all over the house.

"Gaz, are you coming or what?" Jack says, poking his head back around the agency door. "We're going for—"

"Sushi," I finish, even though the irony is lost on him.

Gareth frowns at me for a few seconds—thrown by my creepy

omniscience—then hands me his business card and disappears. With a small sigh, I search the office for Anya and Miyuki, but they're already giggling next to the photocopying machine. Apparently they're having a not very secret but extremely passionate affair that everyone in the office knows about but me, and it will become a running colleague joke that I don't figure it out for another seven weeks.

Carrying my folder in my arms, I return to my desk.

"Fun?" Sophie smirks.

"No," I say flatly, pulling on my headphones and glancing at the empty desk next to me with a sudden sense of foreboding. No Ronald. No rubber plant. Except on some level I'm watching for them, waiting for them, and it suddenly hits me that I'm allowing my life to fall back into exactly the same shape it was the first time round: gravitating toward familiarity and repetition, the way I always do. Encouraging the sameness, because even when it's awful, I still like it more than change. Slipping back into time as if it's an old pair of comfy slippers I refuse to throw away, even though they're not even that comfortable anymore and my toes are sticking out and getting cold.

And this wasn't the point of what it is I'm trying to do.

I'm supposed to be taking risks, making *changes*, and if I don't—if I simply wrap myself in the comfort of a timeline I already know—I'll just end up where I was at the beginning, and I'll have wasted my time.

Worse: I'll have wasted all of them.

Swallowing, I get out my phone.

Hi Will. It's Cassie. Would you like a drink sometime?

In my original timeline, Will texted me first. I waited, and checked my phone fifteen times an hour, and then I assumed

I'd read the entire situation wrong and gave up. Except maybe that was the start of our failure to *connect*: me, failing to take the initiative. Me, being too cautious, lacking spontaneity or impulsivity. Me, reading things wrong and processing the world fifty times too slow.

Maybe love prefers to be eaten warm, like biscuits out of the oven.

My phone *pings*.

I'd love a drink! You free tonight? Xx

And obviously my answer is *no*. My answer is: I have never in my entire life been *free tonight*, because if we haven't arranged it days in advance and I haven't spent the day mentally preparing myself for social interaction, I am not coming.

Your poorly arranged plans are of no interest to me.

Except, last time *all* my dates with Will were subjected to my schedules and itineraries—a color-coordinated calendar, shared across emails—and now I'm starting to wonder if that doesn't rip the romance out of a blossoming relationship somewhat. From a boyfriend's perspective, I can see it might be difficult to *connect* with a woman who needs advance warning in writing before any interaction can take place, like applying to the council to build an extension.

Icarus may have ignored warnings and flown too close to the sun—culminating in a flaming, drowning ball of feathers— but at least he leaped. I'd have been stuck in that Cretan tower forever: planning flight paths, double-checking the fortnight's weather conditions and laminating blueprints.

It's time to be brave, so this time I type:

Sure thing! Where? Xx

14

I SPEND THE REST of the day on Google.

With one work document open so I can flick to it whenever Barry walks past, I search for answers the way I always do: not in the fundamentally biased advice of nearby loved ones—largely because I don't actually have any—but in the reassuringly objective words of billions of people I have never met and don't particularly want to meet.

That kind of collective impartiality results in data I can really trust.

Swiveling my screen so nobody can see it, I type:

How Do I Connect

There's a lot of information about hooking up my phone to my TV, so I try again.

How Do I Connect With Humans

Now I sound like an alien, so I try a third time:

How Do I Connect With Other People

And...jackpot.

Within 0.66 seconds there are 11,560,000,000 results, which is comforting. I am clearly not the only person who finds bonding difficult. In fact, with those stats I'd argue that the real mystery is whether there is anyone left who doesn't.

With a pad and a pen, I make a neat list, highlight the important bits and pop it in my bag: if I need a prompt I can always pretend I'm looking for a lipstick. The clock hits five and—slightly self-consciously—I run a hand through the front of my hair, undo a top button on my jumpsuit and attempt to make myself look like a sexy, desirable human woman who hasn't spent the entire day researching the fundamentals of basic communication.

"Date?" Sophie asks as I turn my computer off.

"Seventh of June," I reply, slinging my bag over my shoulder, and I'm three floors down before I realize what she meant.

According to the internet, you are supposed to start a date by *Smiling With Your Whole Heart*, which would be tricky even if it wasn't literally impossible: my face doesn't really move much, no matter how I feel. Happiness and sadness and anger and period pain all look much the same for Cassandra Penelope Dankworth; I am a remarkably consistent creature, and will probably age quite well.

But the moment I see Will, I still feel my face stretch into a wide, genuine smile; maybe because he's beaming at me too.

"Hello." Will leans forward to kiss my cheek. "Are they closed?"

He smells so calm, of something foresty and cool, and I quickly have to remind myself that this is our first date, we're not actually four months into a relationship, we haven't had sex yet and I'm definitely not allowed to wrap my arms and legs around him like Scylla and drag him to the bottom of the ocean.

"No." I put my tissue back in my bag and move away from the little keyhole I rubbed in the pub window so I could see inside. "I just wanted to see what it looked like before I went in. I've never been here before."

By moving the date forward, I've also somehow changed the venue. Our first date was brunch this Saturday, but now it's Thursday evening we're in a pub. I'm feeling lost, and slightly wishing I'd spent thirty fewer minutes looking up *How to Bond Better* and a little more time looking up exactly where I would be attempting it.

"Me neither." Will smiles, throwing all his weight against the heavy wooden door. "My work colleague said it would be nice and quiet, though. So I guess it'll be an adventure for both of us!"

Will's positivity is one of my favorite things about him. I love the way he makes everything feel exciting. It doesn't matter if it's a trip to a DIY shop to pick up grout whitener or a five-day trek across the Andes to find spectacled bears, Will approaches life like it's the start of the Odyssey and he can't wait to get cracking. I suddenly feel quite proud. I guess trying out a brand-new pub without researching it in detail first is a bit like meeting him halfway. I am truly trying to *Compromise*, just like the bossy random strangers online told me to.

"Where works?" Will gestures around the room with a gracious hand. "You pick. I'll go grab us some drinks. What would you like?"

Scanning as fast as I can, I attempt to assess every potential spot.

One table is too close to the front door (disruptive), another too close to the toilet (smelly); one is far too near a group of loud, braying men in suits (noisy, smelly, disruptive and also really irritating). One table faces the window (bright) and I take strongly against one because of the shape of the chairs (Gothic, prone to collecting dirt). I frown. Everything is a little bit…scabby. Sticky. At times like this, I can see both why I was nicknamed Goldilocks at school and also why it wasn't a term of affection. ("Cassandra must stop being such a fusspot.")

"There," I decide, pointing to a dank corner.

"Then I'll grab a candle too," Will responds cheerfully. "So we can actually see each other's faces. What would you like?"

"Hang on." I sit down at my chosen table, then realize there's an air vent blowing straight down on top of me. "Sorry, I'm going to have to choose again."

Standing up, I hover for a few seconds around each available table like a bee collecting nectar. One seems good but on further investigation is too near a fridge, and I can feel the low drone of it like a finger running down the back of my neck. I won't be able to focus on a single word Will says, and *Listen Properly* is very high on the list currently sitting in my handbag.

"Cassandra?" Will says, watching me with a small smile. "Drink?"

"Oh." I choose a table and sit down. "Red wine, please."

Luckily, I made that decision years ago: partly so at least one element of social activity would always be reliably consistent, and also to make the entire process a little bit simpler. Will grins, nods and strides over to the bar, so I make the most of his absence to double-check the list. Most of it is self-explanatory: normal human rules. Smile. Listen. Ask questions. Don't talk about yourself all the time. Make eye contact. Don't act as if you know everything. Don't correct people with a very apparent sense of satisfaction. Focus. Be open. Give compliments. Remember what they've told you.

Some of which comes naturally to me, and some of which does not.

Which probably explains an awful lot.

"So." Will returns with his beer and my wine, and puts them on the table with such enthusiasm that he immediately ruins the only nonsticky table in the building. "I'm chuffed you texted, Cassie. I spent the entire morning thinking about you, and working out how long before I could ask you out while striking the right balance between keen and cool. I'd decided two days, so you beat me to it."

My face fills with heat and I'm so delighted I beam at the table.

One sip in, and I've already improved things.

"You may also be pleased to hear that I backed up all my files." Will swigs from his pint with an air of triumph. "Went straight home last night, backed them all up, felt a sense of inner peace and tranquility I genuinely thought was a myth, so thank you."

I smile—feeling quite altruistic—then realize I'm staring at my wine.

Every single list, without fail, includes *Make Eye Contact*: apparently there have been copious studies done about the importance of eyeball-to-eyeball connection. Which is unfortunate, because the sensation of knitting needles being stabbed through my pupils to the back of my brain somewhat reduces my ability to feel sexy or romantic.

With immense effort, I lift my eyes and stare at Will.

The moment our eyes connect, there's an intense rush of warmth, intimacy, bonding—it's working!—but the longer I hold it, the more intense and painful it becomes. How long is right? It feels a bit like offering to hold a baby and then realizing you have no idea when to hand it back again without being rude.

Eight seconds. Ten seconds. Twelve seconds.

Will clears his throat and looks away, and I think it's just gone from romantic to serial killer in fifteen seconds.

I look down. Stupid internet. "So, what do you do for work?"

"I film animals." Will grins and leans on the table with both his elbows; his entire body is suddenly surrounded by bright yellow, the color of a Post-it. This always happens when he talks about his job. His enthusiasm for his career is so thorough, so undiluted, it reads as just one, pure color. "I've wanted to do it ever since I was a kid. I saved up all my Christmas money for three years, bought my first camera at nine, took wobbly film of a squirrel in a garden. Although I'm still waiting for the footage to be accepted by the people at BAFTA."

I laugh, even though I know he hasn't actually submitted it yet.

"That's very impressive dedication," I agree, drinking my wine. "At nine I was still convinced I was going to be an international pilot."

"Presumably you're not?"

"No. Turns out I am petrified of flying. Discovered it at ten and changed my destiny accordingly. Did you know the word *petrified* actually comes from the ancient Greek word *petra*, which means *rock*? I found out on an easyJet flight to Athens. Literally solidified. I had to be physically picked up by my dad and carried off into baggage reclaim like a piece of marble."

I can still feel the texture of my father's slightly scratchy blue jumper, smell his sage-and-salt smell, sense the cheek stubble as he kissed the top of my head with so much love I could feel it in my toes. It's as if it's still happening: as if I'm still being carried across Gatwick Airport in his arms.

My eyes fill slightly and then I look up and meet Will's gaze. He smiles so warmly, I feel myself smiling back: memory neatly secured back in its box.

You know what? This actually *is* easier.

On our original first date, I was far too nervous to look at Will for more than half a second at a time. Now I know him better, it doesn't hurt nearly as much. I'm not as scared; I know this information about him already. There's a firm base of knowledge to rely upon and reference, which means I can relax slightly.

Also, I'm not spending 90 percent of my energy either trying to *look* like I'm listening or *actually* listening.

I can do one or the other, but not both simultaneously: I'm not a magician.

"So PR wasn't your lifelong childhood dream, then?"

"Sure." I grimace and tap the coaster up and down repeatedly. "Scribbling press releases around pictures of unicorns, pretending to call journalists with a yogurt pot. No. I left school and…" I take a deep, brave breath: decide to be *open*. "I'm a lot like my mum—pretty much identical, actually—and I think everyone just expected me to follow her into academia. She was very well-known, in her field. But I was eighteen and I didn't want to always be in her shadow, or feel like I didn't have my own path, wasn't my own person, so I specifically went in the opposite direction. It didn't really matter *what* direction at the time, as long as it was different. So I picked Media and Communications out of the brochure by closing my eyes and opening it on any random page. Not one of my most insightful moves, as it turns out."

"Very brave, though," Will chuckles.

"That's just a word people use for decisions that are poorly thought through." I grin wryly. "Plus, I ended up living back at home and commuting anyway, so it was an empty gesture of independence."

Let's just say that university, much like school—involving crowds, noise, social events, group feeding, itineraries that nobody ever seems to respect properly—wasn't a habitat I was naturally suited to.

"I did the exact opposite," Will laughs, swigging from his beer. "I picked a course in cinematography that was as far away as physically possible from where I grew up. Literally got a map, drew a line. Four hundred and fifty miles."

"Edinburgh is that far from Bournemouth?" I say without thinking.

Silence, then: "Sorry?"

Will's voice has sharpened, his eyes are startled, and nobody warns you what it's like to romance as a prophet: you become the creepiest date on the planet. I promised myself no time travel this evening—a traditional date, no meddling with the universe—but I cannot let that mistake stand: I sound absolutely crazy.

Carefully, I close my eyes.

"Literally got a map, drew a line. Four hundred and fifty miles."

"Which is from where to where, exactly?"

"Edinburgh to Bournemouth," Will confirms, and I feel a familiar rush of happiness: nailed it. "A nice eight-hour drive between me and my massive, noisy family, who I love dearly but needed a break from when I hit eighteen."

I think I got away with that, but I'm going to have to be a *lot* more careful going forward. I cannot reveal how much I already know about Will, which is going to be extremely difficult. I really like loudly knowing all the answers to everything: it's one of the least "likable" things about me.

"And do you live alone?" I attempt to look curious: as if I don't know he has a tiny one-bedroom flat in Finsbury Park. "Or with friends?"

"Alone." Will pauses, scratches his nose, laughs loudly. "I was about to describe myself as a lone wolf, and then realized that's not true at all. I love being surrounded by people. It just sounds a little bit sexier than me walking around in my boxers, drinking out of bowls and using a fork to make my coffee."

"Strange that it's always carnivores that are allowed to be alone without being judged, isn't it?" I think about it. "Do you think that's a masculinity thing? Eagles. Wolves. So unfair. Like, *solitary gerbil* doesn't really have the same ring to it."

"Very true. I'm just an isolated hamster."

"A singular rabbit."

"An unaccompanied goat," Will laughs, scratching the top of his left ear. "You make an excellent point. Basically, I broke up with my ex nearly a year ago, and when she moved out I just got too busy to find a new place to live." He shakes his head. "I'm doing it again. I didn't get too busy—I got too *lazy.*"

Her name was Rosie and Will is literally the least lazy person I've ever met: he's the kind of person who finds something fun to do while the kettle is boiling. By comparison, I'm basically a mushroom.

"And you?" He leans forward toward me, across the table, and it takes all the control I have not to abruptly reach out and touch his hands. *Control yourself, Cassandra.* "Do you live alone?"

"I wish I did," I sigh. "I live with a couple, Sal and Derek, although maybe not for much longer."

Honestly, I'm still trying to work out the timings.

"That can't be much fun." Will grimaces in sympathy. "Have you been single a long time? Because living with a couple right under your nose like that can't be particularly easy."

I take a moment to work out how to respond to this honestly.

Not that long, Will. Actually, we broke up yesterday—which is in about four months—and spoiler alert: it was you!

"Not so long," I admit carefully. "It's relatively recent."

"I'm sorry," Will says in a low voice, and it really sounds like he is, which is nice. "Are you okay about it?"

I think about this question for a few seconds. Apparently, to *connect* you need to be vulnerable and open, and—as I've mentioned—that is something I historically struggle with. I like to keep myself contained, like a suitcase: easily zipped up so it can be removed at any given moment. But that strategy hasn't worked out so well for me thus far, so maybe something needs to change.

"Yes." I nod. "I think…I had some important lessons to learn. Still to learn, probably. I'm not very good at…sharing. At all."

It's curious: I can feel my brain sifting carefully through the last four months as if I'm panning for gold, looking for nuggets of relevant information. Is this it? Is that what I did wrong? How many times did Will ask me to *share* with him? To be *open* with him? Quickly, I scan my memories and count. Nine times. The last time was about four sentences before he dumped me. Twice, on two consecutive days.

I think maybe the epic mystery of my breakup with Will has just been solved.

"Sharing?" He frowns slightly. "Like…sharing food?"

"Oh, hell no." I inadvertently make my Vomit Face. "I never share food. Gross. So unhygienic. You want food, you order it. Don't just go around sticking your spoon in my cream puff."

Will laughs loudly, and this time it *definitely* sounds like I meant sexually.

"No spoon in your cream puff." He nods. "Noted."

We smile at each other, and I feel something inside me *click*.

"So go on, then, Cassandra." Will leans across the table and the edges of his fingers just touch the edges of mine. I feel a tingle all the way through my body, like a shock of lightning. "Share something with me that nobody knows. Anything. Doesn't matter how big or how small. Prove the idiot wrong."

I think for a few seconds about what I can safely tell Will.

I've never been in love.

Not really. Not fully. With him is by far the closest I've ever been.

And I'm really scared that I'm not capable of it, not built for it, not destined for it—that I don't know what true love means, or feels like, and I never will—which means that I am, actually, broken.

"I keep a color chart with me at all times." I pull my hand away, reach into my handbag, pull out a piece of cardboard and put it on the table. "There's one next to my bed, and one in my bag, and one in my drawer at work, and one in the loo, and a couple of spares in case they get damaged. I literally go nowhere without one."

Will picks it off the table and studies it. "Like...paint chips?"

"Yes." I nod. "I find it very hard to...understand emotions. I read them like colors. I *feel* them like colors. I see and feel sounds as colors and lights and sensations too, especially when it's dark, but that's more literal. Physical. Like fireworks and fingertips. This is a little harder to explain. It's like my brain can't really work out what emotion it's sensing, so it turns it into a color instead of a word. Not just mine. Everyone's."

"And is it the same color every time?" Will's eyebrows shoot upward, then wrinkle together like a bird landing. "Like, red is anger, blue is sadness, yellow is happy, that kind of thing?"

"I *wish*." I shake my head. "That would make it a whole lot easier. Then I could just translate it, and eventually I guess I'd learn how to be fluent. No. Sadly, the colors are different, every time. It's always new, so I'm constantly starting from scratch."

"Wow," Will says, handing my color chart back. "That's..."

"Weird." I breathe out. "I know. But paint colors help ground me, give me something solid to reference, and that makes me happy. It works the other way round too. All I have to do is look at a color and I feel a really powerful emotion. Like, all the way through my body, even though I can't quite tell what it is. I get *so* much joy from these chips of paints. It's like...an encyclopedia of feelings."

I put my little battered chart back in my bag and breathe out.

I never told Will that the first time.

Actually, I've never told any date that before. I tend to do a quick whip-round before they come to my house: unstick the charts from the walls, tuck them inside a book, make sure they don't spot my bath-time reading stuck to a tile. Nothing hits the spot quite like an hour in blisteringly hot water, staring at an exquisite rosemary green, but I do not feel comfortable telling another human that when they're considering having sex with me.

"Should I be worried?" Will says after a pause, finishing his drink.

Something inside me punctures.

"About me?" I nod. "Probably. You certainly wouldn't be the first."

"No." Will grins and stands up. "Should I be worried about this ass of an ex-boyfriend? Because I think you're awesome, Cassandra. And I don't want to spend more time thinking you're *more* awesome, only to find out some dude who doesn't appreciate you properly is lurking just around the corner."

In Greek mythology, Iris is the goddess of rainbows: the human personification of the spectrum, who uses the symbol of the rainbow to link the gods to humanity, sky to earth. And as I sit in that grotty little pub and look up at Will's lovely face, that's suddenly exactly how I feel.

As if I have every single color possible inside me too.

"No," I say quietly. "He's in the past."

"Good." Will leans down to kiss me and I didn't see it coming and it's soft and slow and hours sooner than expected and it wraps around us both like a bright orange cat. "Same again?"

I close my eyes.

"Good." Will leans down to kiss me and I lean into it, enjoy it, try to bookmark the memory so I can return to it whenever I want to. "Same again?"

I smile, nod. "Yes, please."

Because Will *is* in the past.

He's just in the present, and maybe the future now too.

15

WHAT TO DO WITH all this happiness?

I am Psyche, gazing at winged Eros; I am Hero, united with Leander. I am Eurydice, watching Orpheus from an olive tree. And okay, all these romances went pretty badly wrong, but that's not really the point I'm trying to make.

I bet they still felt amazing at the beginning.

"Cassandra! This isn't your normal day!"

Beaming at the floor, I hold out my open handbag and desperately wish I'd removed the inexplicably unwrapped tampon, now flinging itself around in there like a toddler on a dance floor.

"Are you okay?" My bag gets scanned and handed back. "We normally set our clock by you. Saturday, 11:00 a.m. That's Cassandra Time. Every single week, without fail. Here comes Cassandra. It's Friday today, isn't it?"

"I reckon it must be Saturday." The other security guard grins and quickly swipes the sensor down the green jacket I repurchased on my way here, worn on top of my white Friday jumpsuit. "I'm much more inclined to believe that Cassandra is right and the British Museum is wrong."

"Too right," the other one laughs. "Let them know. Cassandra is in control of time this week—Saturday it is."

I continue to beam happily, still staring at the floor.

Little do they know that I haven't actually been here for nearly four months. I got caught up in the exotic novelty of Having a Relationship—sex, wandering through Borough Market, eating pizza, browsing Sainsbury's, much of which, I'm now realizing, involves food—and clearly something had to give. Apparently, waking up at the same time every weekend to go to the same place to look at the same artifacts and read the same signs and eat the same sandwich from the same café is simply not as appealing to brand-new boyfriends as it is to me.

But the internet has made it very clear—*To Connect to Others, You Must First Connect to Yourself*—and this is the place in London where I feel most like me. Although, honestly, I think me and myself are already pretty well connected: we spend an awful lot of quality time together.

"You should check out the new exhibition on Peru," the security guard calls as I shoulder my handbag and charge toward the entrance. "Gold llamas and everything—it's going to blow your mind!"

"Will do!" I lie cheerfully, because I don't come here to have my mind blown.

I come here to fit the pieces of my mind back together again.

A dozen schoolchildren race past me, screaming and squawking like tiny neon parrots, so I pull green foam earplugs out of my bag—chosen to match my outfit—and stick them firmly in my ears. I know history belongs to all of us, but I really wish there were allocated hours where some of us could enjoy it in peace, like adult lanes at a swimming pool. Little people are so *loud*. Carried on the newly insulated roar of my own breathing, I move up the stone stairs, into the hall with stars on the ceiling, past the Posh Gift Shop (birthday purchases only) and into the Great Court.

Just as I do every time, I stand neatly on top of the engraved Tennyson quote and tilt my head backward so I can stare upward at a gray sky, split into perfect triangles behind the huge glass dome: contained, structured, the entire universe beautifully organized, like a well-ordered fridge. Intense happiness wraps around me; familiarity pulled tight, like a much-loved blanket.

My phone *pings*.

To: Cassandra Dankworth
From: Barry Fawcett

You have got to be kidding me.
   Where are you? I thought I made myself
abundantly clear yesterday. Have you just skipped
out on ANOTHER Idea Hurricane?

Happiness faltering a little, I type back:

To: Barry Fawcett
From: Cassandra Dankworth

Dear Barry,
I am in the British Museum. It's only open between
ten and five, and I find having a job gets in the way
of visiting hours.
   I have been to this particular brainstorm, and
this is how it goes:

-Relevant ideas are put forward and immediately
rejected
-Everyone discusses the upcoming Away Day
-They then reminisce about a past Away Day
-A large box of doughnuts is eaten

-Anton ignores everyone's input and goes ahead with the precise client strategy he already had before the meeting.

It's a waste of time, and I say this as someone who has plenty of it.

Cassandra

A few seconds, then:

To: Cassandra Dankworth
From: Barry Fawcett

Come and see me first thing on Monday morning.

And I'm fired again, obviously.

Except, it doesn't matter, does it? When I woke up this morning, it suddenly occurred to me that I'm not using my new-found abilities to their full capacity. I can travel through time, which means I can draw the day in pencil and then simply erase it when it's done. I can have a holiday whenever I feel like it.

Which is quite a weird sensation for someone who hasn't taken an actual holiday or gone anywhere in eleven years. The last time I went abroad was for a week to Crete with my mum; I can still taste the black olives, smell the coconut in her sunscreen and feel the sunburn on the tips of my ears.

Pushing the memory away, I start to race through Egypt.

What else could I do with this new gift? I could steal an ancient artifact. I could knock over a priceless statue. I could strip naked in the middle of the atrium and sprint through the Anthropology Library with my socks tucked on my ears like a spaniel. I could do anything, go anywhere, be anyone, try on a million different lifetimes that don't quite fit and discard them on the floor, as if they're pairs of jeans.

The only problem is: I don't really want to.

For starters, it sounds destructive, energy-consuming and exhausting. Also, I *know* who I am: I've been trying to be like everybody else for the last thirty-one years. If it was possible, I think I'd have done it already.

Much more importantly, I don't know how time travel *works*. I've had a quick look through some books—both fictional and theoretical—but nobody can agree. Am I *erasing* time? Is it disappearing completely, a wet sponge across a board, or can you still see where the chalk lines were when the water fully dries? How strong is the butterfly effect? What happens to everyone else when I create a new timeline? Are they deleted too? That's terrifying—surely no sane universe would give me that kind of power—in which case are there *multiple* timelines? Do I simply create alternative existences that carry on when I'm gone?

In which case, am I just leaving other Cassandras to clean up my mess?

How many versions of me are roaming around, hating me for it?

Either way, I think I'm going to play it safe. Which is probably no surprise to anyone. If the universe wanted somebody capable of fully exploring the furthest limits of time travel, it probably wouldn't have picked me: a woman who has eaten the exact same breakfast every morning since she was six. All I can do is try not to hurt anyone, remember that my actions may have consequences even if I'm not there to experience them, and assume this gift will be taken away from me again at any given moment, like the water pistol my parents bought me when I was ten and immediately regretted.

In short, no stealing the Rosetta Stone for me.

As always, I pause at the guardian of Room 23.

Crouching Venus is much as she has been for two thousand years: naked, hunched over, surprised midbathing and desperately attempting to hide from us, the creepy voyeurs. It's both classic—a weaving together of fiction and reality, transforming the audience into part of the art—and also weirdly modern. Like an ancient version of that dream where you suddenly realize you're in a supermarket with absolutely no clothes on. As always, I have to fight the urge to hand her a towel.

My phone *pings*.

Hey! Just wanted to see if you're free tomorrow?
Brunch? :)
What you up to?
Will x

The world tips slightly, then rebalances.

This is exactly the text Will sent me on Friday the first time round, almost as if our first date last night never happened. Somehow, we've slipped back into the original timeline anyway. As if time, much like me, gets very upset when you try to alter its plans without plenty of warning. Which I can't complain about, given how I react to an undelivered banana muffin.

It's a weird sensation, though. Now I know Will, this reads like a different text message. I can see the formality, the earnest smiley face, the careful spacing. There's even an intentional grammatical error, to impart a casual, breezy tone. He hasn't casually slipped into a total failure to use accurate punctuation quite yet: that starts in about three weeks.

My chest suddenly feels warm, as if I'm holding a hot-water bottle.

Smiling, I type:

Yes, I'm free! I'd love brunch!
I've got a hangover so I've bunked off work and I'm at
the British Museum, staring at naked people. :)
Cassie x

SEND.

Texting is so hard to get right—too long, too short, too keen, too cold, very inappropriate, Cassandra what is wrong with you I'm at a christening—and I can't read the tone, so, for safety, I've learned to copy whatever I've just been sent as if it's a handy template. If they use a smiley and one kiss, I use a smiley and one kiss. Do they like exclamation marks? Me too. Ten minutes between texts? Ten minutes, *to the second*. Do they use incorrect grammar? I don't do that—I'm not a monster— but I might abbreviate slightly to match.

Except—much like the giant gold-and-ivory statue of Athena stolen from the Parthenon—this day is destined to be dismantled and removed from history, so I guess it doesn't matter *what* I write.

It is unnervingly, giddily liberating.

My phone *pings*.

Last time I was there they made me put my clothes back on. No fair. :(

I laugh.

Did you know why the penises are so tiny on Greek statues? The ancient Greeks considered small dicks beautiful because they associated masculinity with intelligence and control, rather than with lust and sex. Big penises therefore symbolized a lack of masculinity, or the depravity and silliness of satyrs and fools, whereas little, flaccid penises on a rippling body meant the ideal Greek man or god. Fascinating, right?

Sadly it means a lot of them have snapped off as a result. >_<

Normally I'm careful to truncate my monologues—whittling them down until they're no longer "speeches"—but this time I don't bother because I don't have to and Will's response is immediate.

I was born in the wrong millennium. Although at least my nose would have survived, right? ;)

"Excuse me," a voice says as I erupt into giggles like a five-year-old just handed their first Valentine's card. "If you're just going to stare at your phone, could you move so I can see the statue, please?"

I look up in surprise into the disintegrated crotch of Apollo.

"Sorry," I mumble, gliding off again. I've been here literally hundreds of times, and *never* has everything felt quite so naked. Suddenly, it's no longer a building filled with fascinating ancient history. It's a room packed full of bums, boobs, penises, chests and vaginas covered in a whisper of scarf or a well-placed instrument, like a massive group orgy of beautiful people that accidentally invited Medusa.

Honestly, I have never been quite so turned on by metamorphic rock.

Peering closer at a bust, I smile and take a photo.

Underneath, I write:

Has anyone ever told you that you look a bit like the philosopher and teacher Epikouros?

Beep.

Every day. Epikouros this. Epikouros that. He's hot though so I'm taking notes. I need to work on curling my beard.

Beaming, I type back:

And your wavy bowl cut.

Beep.

I just can't get the tiny rollers to hold. :(

I giggle again: this is the most successful flirting I've ever done.

I'm not quite sure where the natural end is, though, and historically I tend to somewhat overplay my hand, so I decide to stop before I get carried away and Will starts simply responding with "ha."

Beaming with triumph, I put my phone away and drift happily past the (headless) lion and the three (headless) Nereids to Room 18: the so-called Elgin Marbles. Then I slowly follow the carvings around the room in the route I always take: left to right. The frieze originally ran round the Parthenon, and broke all contemporary rules. Instead of carvings depicting gods and goddesses, it showed normal Athenians: men on horseback, women strolling, a few casually seated individuals who don't seem to understand the point of a procession.

It doesn't matter how often I come here, I fall in love with ancient Greece a little more every time. It's so vivid, so alive. So weird and imaginative and strangely detailed. Even with key body parts missing, these feel like real people with real stories: lines drawn in marble instead of sand.

Working clockwise, I linger for a few minutes—as I always do—at the South Metopes, which depict the epic battle between the centaurs and the Lapiths. They're square stones, almost three-dimensional, and they remind me a little of Batman cartoons: here a punch, there a slap, *pow, crack, bam.*

Then I reach the East Pediment and my heart rate speeds up.

I can only assume that the giddy, breathless way I feel about these statues is how normal humans feel about spotting a gath-

ering of A-list movie stars in the local Starbucks. There's Helios, god of the sun, riding his horses into the day, and his sister
Selene, goddess of the moon, riding hers away. Heracles is there
with his famed Nemean lion skin, right next to Demeter, the
goddess of the harvest, and her daughter Persephone, split goddess of spring and queen of the Underworld. Aphrodite and her
mother, the Titan Dione, are elegantly draped across a chair,
positioned next to the handsome sky father, king god and original fuckboy, Zeus.

And at the very center is Athena, the guardian of Athens
and the birthday girl around whom they've all gathered. It's the
beautiful, the immortal and the divine, casually hanging out
together as if they're on a yacht in Cannes. I cannot understand
why there aren't glossy magazines detailing the goings-on, outfits and gossip of each of the Greek deities instead: that would
be something I'd collect the *hell* out of.

I'm just peering more closely at the exquisite folds in Aphrodite's
marble dress—she might be the most beautiful goddess, but I'm not
a fan, I blame her for the entire Troy debacle—when my hairline
suddenly prickles, as if I've touched something electric.

Frowning, I turn around and study the room carefully.

An old man is leaning on his walking stick; a lady is carrying a baby in a sling like a broken arm; a small boy is screaming
at his harassed father: *"Pig! I want to see pig!"* There's a student,
sketching in a red notepad; a slightly paunchy man in a tight
gray suit, making a business call on his phone so that his voice
bounces straight off the marble like a rubber ball.

My stomach abruptly folds in half.

And a young woman of twenty-nine years old, arms crossed,
staring at one of the Metopes: a Lapith, kneeing a centaur neatly
in the balls. Her jacket is long and gray and her hair is dark and
cropped—the backs of her ears stick out a little—and I can't see
her full face but I know it's her like I know I'm me and some-

thing in me unravels, as if the red string I've been holding on
to so tightly has abruptly rolled away.

"Daddy, why is that lady hiding?" A boy points a grubby finger in my face. His shrill little voice cuts through my earplugs
like a machete through marshmallow. "Is she playing hide-and-
seek? *You* said we can't do that here."

Flustered, I peer over the top of the huge pediment I now
inexplicably find myself crouched behind: how much time did
I undo this time?

The room is empty again, but I am not.

Something has exploded inside me, the way the Ottomans
accidentally blew up the Parthenon in the 1600s. All the tiny
pieces of myself I brought here to reassemble have scattered and
I don't know how to retrieve them. This museum was my safe
space, the one place I didn't think she'd be, and I don't know
where to go now. This is what happens when you store gun-
powder where it shouldn't be stored: one wrong move and the
damage is extensive.

I cannot just carry on with my day, as if I'm not in ruins.

Lights beginning to flicker, I uncurl like a wood louse and
walk with dignity toward the exit: my own breath in my ears,
the colors around me starting to separate like ink and oil. How
did she find me here? Was it a coincidence, or did she hunt me
down? Either way, this place is no longer safe. It's not a place
I can rest anymore. There are too many emotions, hidden inside. It feels like somewhere that could detonate at any given
moment.

Outside, I take out my earplugs and lean against the museum wall.

I am full of dust and noise.

Getting my phone out, I type her number from memory
and write:

I'm sorry too

I stare at it for a few seconds, debating the consequences.

There aren't any. I don't want to unlock that box; I don't want to let out everything inside it. It must be kept away from me, at all costs. But if there's ever a moment to send a text you know you're immediately going to regret, it's probably the moment just before you potentially delete the entire universe.

Swallowing, I press SEND and close my eyes.

When I open them again the text has gone and the sky is pink and the day has started again.

16

YOU'VE PROBABLY HEARD THE story of Sisyphus.

A famously clever man, when Thanatos (Death) came to collect him, Sisyphus convinced him to chain himself up instead. With Death thus trapped in his house and unable to do his job, everybody on earth stopped dying. When war became pointless, a furious Ares released Death himself and sent Sisyphus to Zeus for bad behavior. As punishment for daring to outwit a god, Sisyphus was forced to push an enormous boulder up a hill. Every time it got near the top, the boulder would roll back down again and he'd have to start from the beginning.

Over and over and over again, for all eternity.

And I have clearly made someone very angry indeed, because this is now exactly what happens to Friday.

I fall asleep on the tube and end up in Walthamstow. *Undo.*

I make it to work and send a press release with my client's website spelled wrong to fifty journalists. *Undo.*

I drop a full bowl of porridge on my keyboard. *Undo.*

I save a budgetary report to a folder in the morning that by the afternoon I can't for the life of me find again. *Undo.*

I leave my bag full of highly confidential client information in the café while I'm buying my banana muffin. *Undo.*

I kick a watercooler in frustration and accidentally break it. *Undo.*

I accidentally swear at Barry. *Undo.*

By 11:00 a.m., I have been fired three times and I've broken at least three pieces of office equipment, cursed at two colleagues, eaten four banana muffins and five cheese sandwiches, had twelve cups of coffee and am no longer capable of keeping track of what has been done and what has been undone. All I know for sure is that this Friday is lasting forever, and obviously I say that every Friday, but for the first time in my life I mean it literally.

"Cassandra!" Barry yells. "Where the hell is Cassandra Dankworth?"

Exhausted, I stare down at my body: genuinely concerned for a moment that all of my messing around with time has also erased *me.*

"I'm standing right here," I say from directly behind him.

"Oh. Well, there's no need to sneak around like that." My boss turns round and glares at me, florid as a runner. "I don't want to hear any more ridiculous excuses for why you can't attend this Idea Hurricane, Cassie."

"I don't have any excuses," I admit. "I've used them all up."

This is my fourth identical brainstorm and I'm starting to feel caught in time, as if I'm in a rotating Debenhams door. Dizzy, I glance up at the clock. Every single time, Barry yells "Cassandra! Where the hell is Cassandra Dankworth?" and thirty seconds later, Anton says:

"Idea Hurricane!"

Right on time, he stands up and claps his hands together like a PE teacher. "See you in three! There will be doughnuts!"

And Grace says: "The glazed ones?"

And Amir says: "I like the éclair-doughnut hybrids. Who brings them in? Does anyone know? I want to get some for my girlfriend."

It's like being stuck in the most boring play ever written, except nobody will let me nap and all the fire exits are locked.

"Cass—"

"Yes, I'll make notes." Without thinking, I nudge the waste-paper basket slightly to the left just as a balled-up piece of paper comes flying through the air behind me; I refuse to pick it up from the floor one more time. It hits the middle of the bin with a satisfying rattle. Then I pick up my pen and notepad—doodled and undoodled and doodled again like some kind of cosmic Etch A Sketch—and grab the chair from behind my desk.

Ignoring my colleagues, I roll it noisily through the office.

"Don't mind me," I say, pushing it into the meeting room and finding a place at the darkest end of the room. This is my fourth session, and if anyone thinks I'm sitting on a ball or a swing yet again, they've lost their minds. I simply do not have the core strength for this kind of nonsense.

As the room steadily fills with people and snacks, I put my sunglasses on: the light has become unbearable. Then I lean over the table, prop my chin on my arms and do my best to pass out with my eyes open. Just before Sophie perches next to me, I roll away slightly so her shoulder doesn't keep bumping into mine. When I'm tired, even the faintest touch feels like a brick through a window.

"Right." Anton pauses, glances at my sunglasses and clearly decides it's not worth a commentary. "Thanks for coming, everyone! Help yourself to snacks and bed in. We could be here for some time."

He can say that again: I'm still grappling with the concept of time itself, but I can say with some certainty this meeting is going to take up at least half of it.

Sunny sunny sunny, I doodle idly in my notepad.

"Our client is Original Sun," Anton continues expansively, leaning on the meeting table with the gravitas, confidence and poise of a man who has never been dumped while naked. "Which as you can probably tell is a luxury self-tanning brand. We're looking for a mantra that really encapsulates everything we're trying to represent. Think glamor. Think sophistication. Think that straight-from-the-beach feel and sand beneath your toes. Let's Hurricane!"

We all simultaneously flinch. "Let's Hurricane" is what Barry wants us to say before every brainstorm—it's an agency branding thing, apparently—but Anton seems to be the only one who wouldn't rather rip off his toenails with a staple remover. It works: he gets a promotion in about nine weeks' time.

"How about Sunny Sunny Sunny?" Miyuki suggests, eating candy floss, and I write *What UV Is What You Get*. "Or What UV Is What You Get?"

"Been There, Sun That," I mutter under my breath, because one really big perk of knowing everything is that I get to be right a lot.

A dude at the other end of the table shouts, "Been There, Sun That!" and Sophie turns to stare at me like a tiny owl.

My phone buzzes, so I pull it out under the desk:

Hey! Just wanted to see if you're free tomorrow?
Brunch? :)
What you up to?
Will x

With as little movement as I can manage, I type:

Yes, I'm free! I'd love b

"No phones, please!" Anton smiles fiercely at me until I put mine back in my pocket. "The outside world is not allowed in the Ideas Brewery! We're trying to create a fully immersive creative experience here!" He pauses so everyone can absorb his marketing superbrain. "Also, great ideas, everyone, but I don't think they're *quite* on-brand. Puns aren't really the *pinnacle* of sophistication. We're looking for something a little more nuanced. So let's keep thinking!"

Original Sun is very obviously a pun, but when I pointed it out in the last full cycle, Anton moved the doughnuts away from me. Instead, I write *Text Will back* on my notepad. Our communications are starting to blur into one.

"Oh my *gosh*," Jessica interrupts, and that's it: brainstorm over. "Guys, we've got, like, three weeks left until our company Away Day and Barry left the organization to me again this year, so I've had the *literal best idea ever*." She looks triumphant about her misuse of figurative language. "I was thinking...wait for it—"

"Don't go paintballing," I interrupt without thinking.

"Cass-an-der-a." Jessica swivels on her ball to stare at me. "What the hell is *wrong* with you? Why are you always *like* this?"

You know what? I was going to tell her that Amir is going to get shot in the bollocks and sent to hospital squealing like a mating fox and Grace will drink so many shots that she vomits into her own handbag and Anya + Miyuki have a giant fight outside McDonald's and Barry is furious at our "unprofessionalism" and it goes down in history as the worst-planned Away Day our agency has ever had, but with the way Jessica just added a vowel to my name, I don't think she deserves my warning anymore.

"Has anyone been to that new bar around the corner?" Grace twists her swing from side to side, gazing at the ceiling. "I've heard they've got this shot called Sex with an Alligator, which is raspberry liqueur, melon liqueur, sweet and sour and Jägermeister, and if you *really* want to amp it up you can add some absinthe."

At least this meeting has clarified why her vomit was bright green.

"I've had the Leg Spreader," Anya chips in. "Can't remember what's in it, but it sure worked hahaha."

Miyuki kicks her under the table yet again and nope nope nope, I cannot do this, I will not, I categorically refuse to spend any more of my time listening to this: I don't care how much of it I have, it's still not enough.

"What about the Puss—"

"Does anyone have any ideas for a moisturizer brand?" I abruptly sit forward. "Sorry to commandeer this meeting, but this isn't the place to discuss private lives and I feel like our time could be put to more efficient use."

Everyone stops chattering and slowly turns to look at me.

I'd name them all for you, but I'm going to be completely honest here: at this point, they are basically a Greek chorus. Faceless, noisy and popping up at irritating moments to interrupt my plot.

"I have a new client," I say, glancing desperately at my watch. By my calculations, I have about four minutes before Barry turns up to "see how things are going" and congratulate Anton on being "such a team player," so I need to work fast. "I'm really struggling. They're called SharkSkin, their packaging is so ugly and they want to run a skin-care campaign 'for *real* men.' It's not going to work, the client will blame me and I'm starting to panic. Can anyone help me?"

I can't read each of their facial expressions, but I can say for certain: combined, the colors are not pretty. Not that I can really blame them. I guess that's what happens when you treat individuals like an ensemble, which I'm fully aware I do and it's another massive flaw in my character.

"Please?" I suddenly remember to add. "I forgot to say 'please.'"

"Hey hey." Anton's smile is searing, like a steak held to a hot plate. "Totally get it, Cassandra, we've all been there! Difficult clients are the worst. But—correct me if I'm wrong—this isn't your meeting. If you want your own Idea Hurricane, you've got to write it down on the blackboard wall outside the day before."

"I know that," I admit. "But I don't have time."

I mean, I *do* have time, but there is absolutely no way I am going back and undoing my amazing first date with Will just so I can write *SharkSkin* on a wall in chalk. All I need is one faintly acceptable idea. It doesn't need to be genius, and it doesn't need to be award-winning. It just needs to get more results than *zero*.

"At least the name is on point." Jessica beams from where she's arching her back on her ball like a large cat. "SharkSkin? That's not going to need changing."

"Really?" I blink at her, genuinely surprised. "Is it good?"

"No," she laughs, and I realize this is her revenge for the paintballing revelation. "I'm being sarcastic. It's shit. Obviously."

"Great," I say sharply, glancing at my watch again. Three minutes. "Thanks for that, Jessica. Now I'm being sarcastic too, in case it wasn't clear. It's too late to change either the name or the packaging, so does anyone have an idea that doesn't come with a large salted side of sneering and derision?"

Silence. Then a faint mumble comes from my right shoulder.

I turn to look at Sophie. "Sorry?"

"My boyfriend." She clears her throat, flushes and rallies bravely. "He uses my products. I spend all this money on skin care, and he steals it. We have *so* many fights about it, because I'm, like, fine with sharing, obviously, and I love him, so it's not a problem, but he lies about it and it's not a little purchase. I'm only a junior account exec and he earns way more than me, so he should honestly just buy his own."

Brain clunking in incredibly slow circles—which is about as fast as my PR brain gets—I turn to the rest of the company.

"Who here has used skin care they didn't actually pay for?"

A few hands go up, then a few more, and within minutes

almost every hand in the room is in the air. Apparently, my colleagues have stolen from their partners, their siblings, their flatmates, their parents, their friends, their children, each other. I am genuinely shocked. It's not just dishonest and unhygienic: Is this how other people live? Just weaving seamlessly in and out of each other's lives and beauty products, with no barriers between them at all? Meanwhile, I carry my skin care in and out of the bathroom with me every day in a little net bag, like oranges.

I clear my throat. I suddenly feel unbearably alone.

"It drives me mad," Miyuki says, turning to look pointedly at Anya. "Absolutely crazy. They use your expensive stuff and you get the zits?"

Anya winks subtly at her; another pang of loneliness rips through me.

"Right." I try to drag myself back to the topic at hand; Barry is about to appear at the window and I'm out of time. I'm officially not allowed to steal any more of it. "That could work. There's a whole host of randomly allocated awareness days we could try and pin it to—"

"You could hide it," Sophie says from my shoulder.

"What?"

"You could hide the moisturizer. If it's that ugly, you might as well have fun with it, right? Stash it all over the country, run a competition to find it, see if the public can hide it too. Then you could run a story with research about how many people steal other people's skin care, and the mantra could be Skin Care You'll Want to…"

"…Hide," I finish in amazement as Barry comes in through the door.

Sophie beams at me—no apparent snark that I can detect—and now I can see more than just the top half of her face, I'm extremely worried I've been reading her tone completely wrong since the moment I started here.

"Umm, Barry?" Anton's mouth stretches around his entire head like a pair of sports sunglasses. "I don't mean to be a party pooper or anything, but I think it's my duty to let you know that Cassandra just hijacked my meeting. Like, I booked this room *weeks* ago. It seems unfair. She rarely attends or makes an effort and then she comes in and takes over, and it just seems very arrogant."

"Like she thinks she's the most important person in the room," Jessica chips in helpfully. "I mean, she's wearing sunglasses *inside*. And always these colored jumpsuits, like she thinks she's a celebrity. Which is crazy because she's barely an account manager and she's, like, in her late thirties."

"I'm thirty-one," I correct sharply. "You're head of Human Resources. You should probably know that."

Barry folds his arms and looks at me and I think I'm about to be fired again.

Four times in one day: impressive by any standards.

"Sorry. Again." Then I turn to Sophie. "Thank you."

She opens her mouth, and I close my eyes.

Undo.

"Hey," Anya says as we all file out of the meeting room, fifth brainstorm finally—thank Zeus and all of Olympia—over forever. "Cassie. Did you say that you wanted to brief me and Miyuki on SharkSkin after lunch?"

Yawning, I pause from pushing my wheelie chair back to my desk.

By my rough calculations, I've now been awake more than thirty-eight hours, and every cell in my body feels like it's been stitched together with dental floss. I can't remember if I've eaten on this round, or hydrated, or have been to the toilet. I've also briefed both Anya and Miyuki in detail three times now, but obviously they don't remember any of it. You'd think all the rabid flirting would have left some kind of mark on their sub-consciousness, but apparently it's evaporated.

"No," I say smoothly. "Thank you."

"But—"

"No, Anya. I've chosen a different team."

With a faint, irritating sensation that I've forgotten some-thing, I return to my desk and watch Sophie stick a finger ten-tatively up her nose. Narrowing my eyes, I watch more intently. There's a tiny sparkly stud in her right nostril that I've never noticed before, and it suddenly occurs to me that maybe she's not consuming her own body mucus: she's just rotating the stud.

"Sophie." I sit down. "Would you like to be on the SharkSkin campaign?"

"Really?" Her eyes become spherical. "Oh my goodness, *yes, please*. I've been hinting for *weeks*, Cassie, but I didn't think you'd got it. I was like, I think I'm just annoying her. I actually said to my boyfriend last night, I think Cassandra definitely doesn't like me. He was like, she sounds like a bit of a bitch, so don't worry about it, but I said you're not, you're just super-smart and laser-focused, and I was right!"

Well, that's embarrassing. Hints received: literally none at all.

Her boyfriend may have a point.

"Sophie," I say abruptly, frowning as a thought occurs to me, "if I was to, just for instance, be abruptly fired in the mid-dle of the office without warning, how would you respond to this news?"

Sophie thinks about it carefully, as if it's a completely normal question to ask your colleague on a Friday afternoon. "I think I'd probably say, 'Oh shit! They haven't *fired* you? That's *awful*. I'm sure we will all miss you *so much*.'"

Yup: there's no sarcasm. She absolutely means it.

"I'm so sorry," I say.

"What for?"

"Nothing." I smile at her. "Glad to have you on board."

17

I ALWAYS WAIT WITH my whole body.

It's a three-dimensional physical experience: me, suspended in time as if hanging from space by my knicker elastic. Everything warps—gets stretched out and transparent like cling film pulled tight—until I start to feel time filling every organ.

On Saturday morning, I begin waiting for my second date with Will the moment I open my eyes. I wait for him while I swing my feet out of bed and wiggle my toes in my fluffy rug; I wait while I shrug on my chick dressing gown and check that nobody else is up. I wait while I shuffle sleepily to the quiet kitchen, and I wait while I make myself coffee and banana porridge. I wait while I clean it up, while I shower, wash my hair, dry it, style it; I wait while I carefully apply my weekend makeup. I wait while I select my outfit, a floral silk T-shirt and gold high-waisted trousers, because that's what I wore to brunch with Will the first time: he said I looked *phenomenal* and ideally I would like him to say it again.

I wait while I get on the train and sit there, curiously watching my immobile face in the window reflection, and I wait while I walk slowly to the brunch café.

I wait while I choose exactly the same red booth seat.

I wait and I wait and I wait until time stops and every cell of me begins to feel tired and bleached, as if I was once drawn in bright color and waiting has faded me into pastels, like bright sunlight.

With just ten minutes to go before Will arrives, I remember to hop up and look at the blackboard menu on the wall. I didn't like what I had last time at all—the strawberries on my pancakes were mushy; I had to pick them all off and fold them in a napkin when Will was in the toilet—so if nothing else, I'd like to use my time-travel skills to select a less high-maintenance breakfast.

Still waiting, I stare at the board and assess my options.

Brunch is a particularly dangerous meal for me: one wrong move, and the morning is totally ruined. Bananas are usually safe, but I've been known to involuntarily spit a squishy one onto a restaurant table, so it's still a risk. Bacon and sausage are stylized corpses, so that's an immediate rejection. Egg is the slimy period of a chicken, so nope. I don't like anything too crunchy, or too slippery, or too fluffy, or too wet, or too dry, and I don't like my foods touching each other, so it's normally a rush to separate them when they get here. I can sometimes get away with a pancake as long as the syrup comes on the side, but avocado on toast is a full liability: if it's brown, or stringy, or slimy, or has simply been sitting on top of the toast for more than two minutes, it doesn't even get touched.

The guilt I feel about the money I spend on food I haven't actually eaten is overwhelming: it's definitely more than on rent.

I'm just contemplating dry toast, jam in a pot—three options, so I can examine the frogspawn quality of each flavor—when I feel sharp pain running down the whole right side of my body. Frowning, I turn slightly. An older lady with gray hair in a neat bun is standing right next to me, also staring at the menu. And I mean *right* next to me. She's not touching, but she's so close her personal gravitational field feels like it's made out of hot needles.

Politely, I clear my throat, step slightly away and try to re-focus on the menu.

She moves toward me to get a better look at it too.

I step away, a little more purposefully.

She moves toward me.

Shooting her a furious glance, I take a dramatically big step to the right and try to stay calm while my throat begins to close in panic. I can *feel* her body heat. The tiny space between us is starting to crackle. My entire body now hurts. Why do people always do this? What is *wrong* with them? I can't buy a cheese sandwich in Sainsbury's without a total stranger standing so close I can smell what they use as shower gel.

As if tied to me by a string, the woman moves closer to me yet *again* and I promptly lose my shit.

"Could you please get away from me?"

"*Excuse* me?" She bristles like an offended porcupine. "*What* did you just say to me, young lady?"

"I said could you get away from me and give me space?" The air crunches. "I was here first. There is absolutely no need to stand this close to me. Wait your turn. You are being incred-ibly invasive."

The woman inhales loudly through wide nostrils and the air is suddenly full of red and black dots, like scattered fruit gums.

"How *very* rude you are," she sniffs. "*Outrageous* behavior."

She stomps back to her little booth, where a distinguished-looking man is waiting—probably her husband; they match like socks—and says something in a low voice until they both turn to glare at me as if they believe the combined power of their eyes is going to pick me up and carry me through the window. I clear my throat and look away, feeling their eyes on my skin like insects. It's genuinely bewildering. She hurts me, yet when I ask her to stop, I get insulted? Where is the logic, I ask you?

At least time is nearly up now, so I make my final choice—pancakes, plain, low-risk option—and sit back down to finish waiting.

Thirty seconds to go. Twenty-nine. Twenty-eight, twenty-seven...

Adrenaline starts to race.

Twenty-four, twenty-three, twenty-two...

I'm someone who, being told a package will arrive at some point between two and three, starts waiting by the door at 9:00 a.m. like an anxious poodle, whining every time they hear a car.

Eighteen, seventeen, sixteen...

It's like I have my very own standby mode and I can't do anything else until it's been turned off again; one phone call can wipe out an entire weekend.

Twelve, eleven, ten, nine, eight, seven, six, five, four, three, two...

Will's not here.

He's not here, he's running late, and the second he's officially late, time starts to warp again. I don't feel suspended anymore. I'm not just dangling: I feel tugged, as if someone has slipped millions of tiny hooks under my skin and now they're silently ripping me apart.

One, two, three, four, five, six...

He wasn't late for our first brunch, was he? No, he was six minutes early. I remember distinctly, because Will only started being consistently late after date six. It started with a minute or two here or there, and it eventually got to a point where it was regularly thirty minutes, punctuated with apologetic and detailed text updates on his whereabouts. As if I wasn't just sitting wherever we were supposed to meet, casually stretched across time like a pig on a meat hook.

When it hits five minutes, I start to hyperventilate.

By ten, I'm in tears.

By twenty minutes late, my brain is starting to pulse in and out like a jellyfish, there's unbearable pressure behind my eyes, everything is starting to spin slightly and I think I'm about to pop and coat the brunch place with a thin, shiny layer of Cassandra Dankworth. The lady and her husband are staring at me again, so I follow their eyes and become vaguely aware that I'm rocking in my seat and clawing at my forearms with my nails, just to release some of the time trapped inside me.

Unable to handle it any longer, I grab my phone:

Where are you? :)

In my defense, I normally say nothing at all.

I've learned my lesson the hardest possible way, so I now prefer to sit and be quietly tortured, then passive-aggressively say *oh, there you are* with a tight smile when whoever it is finally rocks up, but honestly, if this relationship is going to work long-term, then Will's going to need to meet me in the middle. Or at least be *consistently* late, so I can plan around it.

My phone beeps:

In bed. ;)

Another rush of woozy anger, like hot mustard.

You haven't even left yet?

My eyes are prickling.

????

Stay calm, stay calm, stay—

You know, Will, when you waste my time like this it's

really disrespectful. It's like you think your time is more valuable than mine. It is not. You need to start being where you say you're going to be, exactly when you say you're going to be there. Just because I have plenty of time doesn't mean I want to spend it waiting for you. Thank you.
Cassandra.

Okay, I've really lost my temper now: you can tell because I've slipped into old-lady's-complaint-letter-to-a-newspaper format.

My phone beeps:

What the hell are you talking about?
Waiting for me where?

Confused, I blink at my phone screen.

Then I plummet, hard.

With mounting terror, I scroll quickly through my messages, looking for the conversation we had yesterday about brunch. We had it, over and over again. We arranged to meet here, just as we did for our original first date, *six times*.

Except the conversation is gone.

Which means— Oh my God.

I wrote *Text Will back* on my notepad, then deleted it with my time Etch A Sketch and forgot to remind myself again in the narrative I left behind. I didn't text him back. Will isn't late: I never arranged this date with him in the first place. I left him hanging, then yelled at him in writing, and it's starting to really hit me now that continuity is becoming a massive problem.

Will has been late *dozens* of times: it seems unfair that the one time I kick off I'm in the wrong bloody universe.

Quickly, I text back:

Sorry! That was meant for someone else! Hahaha.

Just in case any fragment of this terrible thread gets left behind. Then I close my eyes.

When I open them again, I'm standing by the menu. The gray-haired woman takes a step toward me, and I abruptly turn around and walk back to my booth: I think that's enough aggression for one day, Cassandra.

Quickly, I text:

Hey! I'm so sorry for the delay! Work is crazy. I'd love brunch! How about we hang out tomorrow instead? Cxx

I refuse to do Friday again: not even if Will was Odysseus himself.

An immediate beep.

No worries! That would be great!
Sunday is my favorite day anyway.
Let's do something fun. :) Wx

Fun? Fuck. Now it looks like I have to upgrade our brunch date to something more exciting and romantic, just to apologize for being a bitch in a version of the universe Will doesn't even remember.

I'll think of something super fun—leave it to me! Meet at 10? :) Cx

Beep.

Perfect! Wx

Relieved, I stand up and look at my watch. It's nearly midday now, which means our *second* second date starts in roughly twenty-two hours. That's—I quickly calculate—nearly 80,000 seconds of stretching myself across time like a clothesline between two garden fences.

I think I deserve every single one of them.

And I go home to wait.

18

"GOOD MORNING!" WILL WALKS toward me, grinning like a handsome salamander. "You look disarmingly beautiful today, Cassie."

I bloody should: I've had nearly an entire weekend to prepare.

"Thank you," I say as he leans in to kiss my cheek and his facial hair scores my skin. I bought yet another vintage dress—pale yellow lace—so that I'd be starting today without any old memories attached to me (apart from those I'm subliminally absorbing from its previous owners). You'd think I'd be bothered by wearing secondhand clothes, but—contrarily—I find it strangely comforting. "So do you."

"Excellent." Will laughs and twirls in a bizarrely hot way. "Disarmingly beautiful is the look I was going for this morning. I toyed with endearingly ravishing, but sadly that particular shirt was in the wash."

I laugh, enjoying myself already. "Combined with your beguilingly pretty trousers, I see."

"Naturally." He flourishes. "What else, for our second date?"

We both beam at each other and I feel a turquoise-colored sweetness ripple down the back of my neck.

"So what's the plan?" Will stares around King's Cross train station, then stretches with his fingers spread out wide like a cat in the sun. "I'm feeling full of beans today, Cassie. I'm actually glad we didn't do brunch yesterday, because I was so tired after editing all week I stayed in bed for most of it, eating pizza out of a box balanced delicately on my chest."

I smile and try to ignore a cold flicker of horror at all those spiky crumbs lost in the crevices of his duvet cover.

"Actually—" I reach into my bag "—the plan is right here."

Triumphantly, I hold out an A4 piece of paper printed on both sides with bullet-pointed suggestions, all approaching "fun" from a variety of angles. There's the physical activity kind of fun, the silly kind of fun, the eating kind of fun, the alcohol kind of fun, the mentally challenging kind of fun. We may not have time for all of it, but I've put it all in the most convenient order, just in case.

There's even space in the itinerary for the impromptu kind of fun—I know how much Will enjoys that—but I don't think we'll get round to it. Honestly, there's just no real way of knowing how long spontaneity will take.

"Blimey," Will says, taking it out of my hands. "Cassandra, this is really something."

I study his face carefully. "Something...good?"

"Oh, yes." He grins widely. "I've never been on a date before with someone who has thought it all out so carefully ahead of time. I'm really touched. No last-minute-panic cinema for us."

I relax slightly. This bodes well for all our future dates too; next time maybe I'll crack out the laminating machine.

"Hang on." Will skims the document again. "I'm seeing a bit of a theme. Picnic in the Botanic Gardens. Bike riding. Punting. Treasure hunt. Pub. Look at colleges. Eat fudge. Either we're going to Cambridge, or King's Cross has really changed over the last few months."

Something in my stomach flaps like a pigeon.

"We're going to Cambridge. Is that okay?" I clear my throat and can't quite meet his eyes in case he spots something in them I'm not ready to share. "It's really sunny today, so I thought it might be fun to do something a little less...urban."

"Absolutely!" Will rubs his hands together, which is an endearing little gesture he always makes when he's preparing for a big adventure: it looks a lot less villainous than it sounds on paper. "I love it! I've not been there for years and years."

"No." I smile faintly and study the timetable boards. "Me neither."

Everything is precisely as I remember it.

Which is probably not surprising for a university founded in 1209—they're not big on change here either—but it's both reassuring and discombobulating. As soon we emerge from the train station, I start to feel...a lot. I can't unpick it—there's roughly six colors happening at once—but it's painfully intense. Confusing. Everywhere I look, memories are layered on top of each other, like sheets of Sal's lasagna: separate but also stuck together in one big lump.

We've spent the entire journey chatting about Will's family dramas—they are legion—so my abrupt silence does not go unnoticed.

"Everything okay?" Will frowns at me. "Cassie?"

In the sunshine I can see my dad waiting for me in the car after I was dropped off from a school trip: squishing his face up against the window to make me laugh. I can see my mum by the turnstiles, fumbling through her velvet pockets for train tickets she always managed to lose before we got on an actual train.

Actually, that's not accurate. I can see *all* the times they were here.

Hundreds and hundreds of times: each crossing over and through each other like holograms, shining in every direction I look.

"Absolutely." I shake myself and smile at Will. "I was just trying to remember our first date activity, that's all."

Pulling the plan out again, I pretend to stare at it while I regroup.

Focus, Cassie. Put it all back in the right box and slot it neatly back in the brain cupboard. At least I already know what we're doing first: punting. I've seen all the films; they do it in Venice. I know the cinematic value and the impact it has on couples. We will drift silently down the river, staring into each other's eyes and holding hands, and at some point in our future we'll go, "Remember when we fell in love while we were punting?" and our eyes will get misty at how incredibly romantic it was.

Admittedly, romance is yet *another* arbitrary human construct I don't entirely grasp, but I remain hopeful that if I stick to the rules I might one day understand it a bit better. It mostly seems to consist of doing nice things with people you'd like to see naked, but I'm clearly missing something.

"Punting?" I suggest as we stroll toward town. "Then bike ride and picnic?"

"Great," Will says breezily, taking everything in his stride, as usual. "I've never done it before, so this is exciting. Did I see fudge on the list? Because I fancy grabbing some of that on the way too."

I glance at him adoringly, then away again before he sees it. Never have I known a human who adapts to any environment so quickly or with so little fuss: he's like one of those glorious trees that grows in between the cracks of a cement pavement.

"Of course." I can feel his excitement in me too. "And then maybe—"

Will has just slipped his hand into mine. It's large and warm and slightly grainy like wood, and I suddenly realize this is the first time we've held hands in this version of time, and it *feels* like the first.

I'm so overwhelmed, I can't speak.

After a few moments of my pointed silence, Will clears his throat and reaches for his sunglasses as an excuse to drop hands again.

Fuck.

"Did I see fudge on the list?" Will smiles at me. "Because I fancy grabbing some of that on the way too."

"Of course." I wait for his hand to slip into mine and focus on attempting to talk at the same time, like some kind of magical multitasking juggler. "And then maybe we can wander around a few of the colleges?"

"Absolutely. Any in particular?"

"Emmanuel," I say way too quickly. "Or…you know. Whichever. I'm easy."

Hand—finally—in hand, Will and I wander through the cobbled streets of Cambridge town center toward the old colleges, stacked like ornate cakes against the river. All the colors are starting to bubble again—now I can see my parents taking me to buy new school shoes, books, a sandwich, all happening at once—so I focus hard on the pressure of my fingers intertwined with Will's instead.

"What's up, *dock*!" A very young man in too-tight shorts, a waistcoat and a straw boater approaches as we hit the river, far too enthusiastically. "Welcome to *Pun*-ting! An extra-*oar*-dinary experience, where we take the *oar*-deal out of punting! *Canoe* think of a better way to spend your time?"

Will and I glance at each other; our nostrils flare.

"*Oar*-kward!" the poor university student chuckles with an air of financial desperation. "Excuse me *barging* in, but tell me exactly *yacht* you want and I can get you there *schooner* or later."

Okay, I may not know much about romance, but I don't think

it involves sitting on a floating bit of wood while a twenty-year-old art history undergraduate makes faintly boat-related puns at us for the next forty minutes.

Our entire relationship appears to be haunted by wordplay.

"You know what?" Will looks at me and lifts his eyebrows. "How about we hire one and punt it ourselves? I think I could do with the exercise."

"That is a *ferry* bad idea." The student grins. "*Knot* on my watch!"

"What do you think?" Will turns to me. "Cassie?"

I study the elements of his face, trying desperately to work out what he's thinking. There's something in his eyes. A small flare in his nostrils. A subtle change in the line of his mouth and eyebrows. With growing panic, I assess the clues, stick them together, compare them to similar expressions from the past and fumble for the message he's trying to send me. I think it might be: *We're not getting on that bloody boat.*

"Sounds good to me?" I guess tentatively.

Will grins at me, obviously delighted that we're on the same page, and I feel a bolt of triumph: smashed it.

"No, seriously." The poor boy drops his sales pitch. "That's a really terrible idea, guys. Like, punting's deceptively hard. If you've not done it before, you're going to regret it. I promise you."

I stare at him in surprise: he abruptly sounds a lot like Tiresias, muttering his dark prophecies from the Underworld.

"We'll be okay," Will says cheerfully, squeezing my hand.

Giddy with the conspiracy of it—look at us, reading each other's thoughts with simply the power of our facial muscles and eyebrow hairs—Will and I wander toward the self-drive punts, or whatever they're called.

"Boat?" the guy barks, and this is a bit more like it.

"Yup." Will pays and we clamber on. "Any tips?"

"Yeah." The boatman laughs. "Don't fall in."

"Right. Cheers." Experimentally, Will grabs his pole and staggers to the front of the boat. It suits him. He looks like he was born to be there. "How are you doing, Cassie? Comfortable?"

I glance stiffly over the edge. Of course I am not comfortable.

I'm sitting on what appears to be an elaborately fashioned plank, inches away from green water with duck crap floating in it. I'm wearing the worst possible outfit for this venture, and I've had to sit on my bag and tuck my dress around me like a lacy burrito. As I look up and down the river, I can't help but notice that all the other couples are sitting side by side, smiling in the sunshine, and we're the only two idiots who decided to Do It Ourselves. This is what happens when you decide to wing it without a proper conversation: you make poorly considered decisions like this one.

"Yup," I lie tightly. "Supercomfortable."

"Then off we go!" Popping his sunglasses on with a disturbing wobble, Will pushes firmly away from the bank and I feel the boat tip underneath us. "Which way do you want to go first?"

I look desperately back at solid ground. "Don't mind."

"Let's try this way, then."

Looking suddenly far too sturdy—this can't be equal weight distribution—Will begins to punt away down the river and fear rapidly mounts. It's so dirty. Filthy. And not in the apparently sexy way. How am I supposed to feel romantic when I'm seconds away from being covered in the feces of mallards?

"Whoops," Will laughs as we smash into another boat, coming in the opposite direction. "It's like bumper cars! Afternoon, guys!"

Another couple smile and wave at us, looking blissfully stable.

With a tiny squeak, I hold on to the sides.

"Isn't it lovely here?" Will is very clearly in his element. "Look at those buildings! So beautiful. Which one did Darwin go to, do you reckon? I love Darwin. He's my favorite old dude with a beard."

"*Christ,*" I mutter as the boat wobbles yet again.

"Sorry?" Will continues shoving his long stick into the mud and propelling us pretty much nowhere. "Didn't quite catch that."

"Christ's College," I say, raising my now squeaky voice. I try not to look at a memory of my father, waving at me from the bridge. "Darwin went to Christ's College, as well as John Milton the poet and Robert Oppenheimer, father of the atomic bomb. Could we go a little more slowly, do you think?"

The boat has now run into the opposite bank with a loud *crunch.*

We pitch to the left and I squeak again, this time a lot more loudly. I have officially changed my mind about punting. This was a terrible idea, and about as romantic—and hygienic—as eating the same strand of spaghetti and then offering them the rest with the end of your nose.

"Sure!" Will tries to push us away, to no avail. "You know, that guy was right. This is a lot harder than it looks."

"So maybe we should get out." Really panicking now, I begin shuffling down the boat toward him. I've lost all sense of reason and rational thinking: I just want this to stop. "Maybe I can help you, or we can drag the boat back from the sides."

"Cassie, please don't—"

I instinctively shuffle forward a bit more; Will loses his balance and drops the pole. The boat suddenly swings out toward the center of the river, the world rotates on its axis and I don't need to be a seer or prophet to know what's going to bloody happen next.

"Bugger," I hear as the universe tips over.

And in we both go.

Will is laughing loudly; I am not.

"Well," he chuckles, wiping his eyes, swimming to the boat

and clinging on to the side. "I'm guessing that wasn't part of the plan, was it?"

My throat is tightening; my eyes are filling up.

I'm wet and I'm dirty and I'm cold and there's duck shit in my hair and my new dress is permanently ruined and I'm going to be wet and dirty and cold and faintly green for the rest of the day because I didn't bring a change of clothes, and I'm trying *really* hard to be cool with this, to brush it off, laugh about it, find some kind of silver lining, but all the other punters are laughing at us and it's not funny and my father is gone and there's *duck shit in my hair* and I'm dirty, I'm dirty, I am so bloody *dirty*.

"Cassie?" Will reaches out a hand as I attempt to kick my feet and panic sends me under again. "God, can you swim? I should have checked."

With my mouth open, I involuntarily take a gulp of dirty water, then start crying, which means more open mouth and more dirty water and more duck shit, and I go under the water again, choking and gulping, and I see Will's horrified face and this isn't romantic, this isn't connecting, and I think I just saw a dead rat and I think I've just ruined *everything*.

Desperate, I close my eyes.

"Everything okay?" Will frowns at me. "Cassie?"

"Absolutely." Amazed, I look down at myself—dry, clean, not sobbing—and honestly, time travel is the best present ever. It's like a massive fluffy towel, handed to me by the universe. "I was just trying to remember our first date activity, that's all."

I take another look at the plan.

"Not punting," I say firmly. "I don't like punting. Picnic?"

"Oh," Will says with a faint air of surprise. "Sure. Did I see fudge on the list? Because I fancy grabbing some of that on the way too."

★ ★ ★

We get the fudge again, plus sandwiches, Pimm's in cans, crisps.

Feeling hopeful all over again, I wander with Will to the *side* of the river this time and together we watch the punters, slowly gliding up and down, laughing and kissing. I feel a sharp pang of isolation: I guess I can add that specific romantic scene to the list of things I'm permanently shut out of.

"This is so nice." Will returns from the ice-cream van and hands me a Mister Whippy, then lies next to me so he can lick his. "I travel abroad so much, sometimes I forget that this country is also full of amazing adventures."

Licking my ice cream too, I try to lean back just like him. "Yes."

Will's brown eyes are suddenly trained on me.

Stiffening, I stay as still as I can and attempt to look like a person who cannot feel themselves being studied like a bug in a jar. I'm being a normal human, right? This *is* how people sit, isn't it? Am I jittering, rocking, bouncing, clawing? Has Will noticed that I'm just copying his body language and facial expressions, or is he thinking how pretty I look in the sun? Does he like me, or is he faintly creeped out by me? Is he interested, or bored? Is he considering kissing me, or wondering why I look like I've only been given this body recently and still have no idea how to drive it?

("Cassandra seems to believe she might be an alien.")

It's all a complete mystery.

All I know is the longer he studies me, the more confused I become. Also, the sheer effort of not accidentally playing piano fingers on my ice cream is exhausting: it feels like I'm fighting the Colchian dragon and hoping nobody will notice.

"You have ice cream on your chin," Will laughs finally, reaching toward me and wiping it with his shirt collar. "Like a little goat."

Before I can react, he leans in and kisses me, softly.

With my eyes closed, I tilt into the kiss and suddenly feel a flash of his colors like a red apple: round and sweet with flashes of green. All at once, I feel my entire body relax. As if his colors are now mine too.

I also feel ice cream dripping down my hand.

Now there's a tongue on my face.

"Oh, hello." Will laughs as we break abruptly apart and a large black dog lunges for my ice cream. "Where did you come from?"

I reel away: my Mister Whippy has gone all down my front, and I watch in mounting horror as the dog spins in a circle, knocks the Pimm's over my skirt, eats my cheese sandwich, steps in the grape box and sticks his nose in my bag, all in approximately three seconds flat.

"Basil!" A cut-glass male voice behind us. "Basil! Naughty boy! Come here!"

Will laughs again as the dog bounces away.

"Little bugger," he says amenably, grabbing a few napkins and trying to mop up the damage, which is clearly unmoppable. "Cassie, do you want my sandwich instead? I can just fill up on the fudge. Let's be honest—I was going to do that anyway."

Starting to hyperventilate again, I stare down at myself. I'm covered in long black hairs and ice cream and orange stains and I'm sticky and dirty and I still don't have a change of clothes and I cannot believe this has happened again and before I can stop myself I jump up, turning to face the owner of the dog as my brain starts to audibly slam the inside of my head like a woodpecker.

Don't do it, Cassie. Don't do it. You're not a milk monitor anymore. Don't do it, not in front of Will, not when everything is going so—

"Can you not read the sign?" I point at it. "It says Keep Your Dog on a Leash."

"I'm so sorry." The owner grimaces. "I took him off for just a—"

"There are *rules*," I snap, brain slamming again. "There are *rules* for a reason. Why do you think rules apply to everyone else but not to you?"

"Cassie..." Will starts next to me. "Don't—"

"WHY CAN'T EVERYONE JUST FOLLOW THE BLOODY RULES," I bellow, starting to cry again.

The dog owner scuttles away, clearly terrified, and as the fog clears, I turn back and see Will's face. The happy apple color is totally gone. He looks absolutely appalled—wondering what kind of maniac he just bought an ice cream—and I feel the horror in myself: now it's mine too.

"Oh my God," I whisper as my rage subsides and is replaced by a wave of nausea. "I am so sorry, Will. I don't know what came over me."

I do know what came over me. It's exactly what always comes over me when someone breaks rules, no matter how totally arbitrary they seem to be. Something in my brain snaps, and I detonate like a hand grenade. Which is incredibly hypocritical, given how happy I am to ignore rules if I don't personally agree with them.

So I think the more appropriate question is: What the hell is wrong with me?

"Cassandra—" Will says slowly, and I close my eyes.

"Everything okay?" Will frowns at me. "Cassie?"

"Absolutely." I swallow, now absolutely exhausted. "I was just trying to remember our first date activity, that's all."

I peer down at the plan.

"Why don't we start with a treasure hunt?"

19

NOW, *THIS* IS A BIT more like it.

Grabbing fudge for the third time, Will and I stand together in
the sunshine and chew, heads bent over our little treasure map.
Every now and then, I glance up to check if there's any lingering memory of the last two failed date attempts on Will's face,
but there doesn't seem to be.

I can tell from the fact he still seems to quite like me.

Which is good, because—after my shocking behavior over
the last few hours—I'm not sure I do. In ancient Greek theater,
the actors all wore thick masks that served a number of pur-
poses. They had different identities, which allowed the actors
to switch roles and genders easily, and exaggerated expressions
that allowed the audience to clearly see what emotion they were
portraying from a distance. The masks also served the incredibly clever purpose of projecting the actor's voice into the au-
ditorium, thus allowing them to be heard by everyone.

Most of the time, it feels like I'm wearing a mask too.

As if the real Cassandra is hiding underneath, staring through two big eyeholes, wondering which mask she's supposed to use at any given moment and if she's managed to pick up the right one. Trapped and unable to breathe. Pretending to be someone else, all the time. Watching from a distance. Terrified of what will happen when the mask falls off and reveals the actor underneath.

Which is pretty depressing, so I try to focus again on my romantic date.

At least this time I'm playing to my strengths. You can say what you like about my character profile—and many people do—but I am at least a woman who knows how to answer questions competitively, tick off boxes and win an arbitrary prize for being right.

"'Pirates have hidden their loot in a box somewhere in Cambridge,'" Will reads chirpily as I read next to him, my right shoulder zinging against his left. "'It is *your duty as detectives* to solve the clues and unearth these buried treasures.'" He chuckles. "They're clearly not very clever pirates. We're seriously inland. It's at least ninety minutes' drive to the nearest ocean."

I smile, already engrossed with the first question.

This is going to be a real test of my willpower. It's extremely tempting to use time travel to find out all the answers and then hop back and solve them all immediately, thus both winning and impressing Will with my cleverness, which is—I'll be honest— my natural instinct. It would also be cheating and deeply unethical, and I suspect the Laws of Romance forbid it too.

Luckily, I don't think I'll need to: I already know the first answer.

THIS MAN HAS BECOME A FABLE
FOR BEING SOLID AND HIGHLY UNSTABLE.
BUT DON'T WORRY, HE'LL NEVER FALL DOWN—
FOR IN HIS HANDS IS...

Will frowns. "Any idea?"

I bite my bottom lip and try to look like I'm actually thinking about it. Of course I have an idea; it's a riddle for six-year-olds.

"The leg of a table." I turn sharply and start heading toward the right college. "It's a statue of Henry VIII, who was the founder of Trinity. Students stole the scepter out of his hand and replaced it with a wooden table leg. It's still up there."

"Blimey." Will hops to catch up with me. "How did you know that?"

"Beginner's luck," I say with a small shrug.

Together we reach the statue and stand for a few minutes, marveling at the incredible architecture of the college itself. It really is magnificent—detailed, slightly wizened, like the face of a beautiful old man. My throat is tight again, and a hot flush is climbing my throat. I really, *really* love that it says Stay Off the Grass, and people actually do as they're told. This is my kind of place.

"Right." Will studies the statue for a date and enters that into the app. "We've got our next clue."

THIS ANCIENT HERBIVORE EATS
A MINUTE AT A TIME
AND SO THE WORLD PASSES

I have to at least *look* like I'm thinking about this one.

"Huh," I say, scratching my chin. "How very challenging."

"Wait!" Will bounces up and down, and I can feel his amber excitement in my whole body. "Ancient herbivore! Could it be a grasshopper? They belong to the oldest group of chewing herbivores on the planet. I shot an insect documentary years ago, and I still remember that fact."

I laugh and turn in the right direction for our next stop. "You're right. It's the Corpus Chronophage on Bene't Street.

A gold clock with a grasshopper that bites the time as it goes round, installed by Stephen Hawking."

"Cassie. Wait." Will pulls my hand and I stop. "Have you done this treasure hunt before?"

"No," I say truthfully.

"So…how do you know all the answers already?"

Because I know every single stone and pebble of this city; because Cambridge is engraved inside me, written on the core of who I am like a defaced tree trunk.

"I grew up here," I say, flushing. "Sorry, I should probably have said."

"You *grew up* here?" Will looks amazed. "Why didn't you mention it?"

"I…" I'm embarrassed now. "I haven't been back in a really, really long time. A decade, actually. My mum was a professor here. Emmanuel College."

"Wow." Will thinks about this. "Was. She's not anymore?"

"No," I say simply. "She died in a car crash with my dad ten years ago and I haven't returned since the funeral."

My throat is shutting again; my eyes are stinging. Why did I choose to come back today, of all days? Why did I think it would be romantic to add a good dose of grief to my date plans? Why did I think any of my memories would have faded at all, when they never really do? At least it slightly explains my hysterical outbursts: I'm already teetering on the edge of every possible emotion.

It's been a whole decade, and the grasshopper has eaten no time at all.

"Cassie." Will holds my other hand. "I am so sorry. When you mentioned her in the pub… I had no idea."

Before I can reply with an offhand, dismissive comment, he's wrapped his arms around me and buried me in a hug. I feel myself instinctively resist for a second, then realize it feels lovely and simply breathe out and sink into the rare human contact. I never told Will any of this the first time round. I didn't tell him about Cambridge; I didn't tell him about my parents; I didn't tell him that I ran away and never came back. I didn't tell him anything at all.

For a full minute, I simply let myself be held.

"Do you want to talk about it?" Will pulls away and holds my face in his hands, like a precious ostrich egg. "I've still got both my parents, so I can't even imagine a life without them. It must be so hard."

I swallow and the world wobbles, then clears; my cheek is wet.

When was the last time someone asked if I wanted to talk about it? Really talk about it? When did another person notice that I was in pain? I feel a wave of something so intense my brain rotates, but I don't know quite what it is. Gratitude? Love? It's so hard to tell the difference: the colors are so similar.

"No," I say, wiping my face. "I think I'd prefer to do the treasure hunt, if that's okay. Just don't be mad if I get all the answers right. My parents were massive dorks and they really loved all this stuff."

Will laughs and kisses my forehead. "Then I shall follow your lead."

I feel another wave of love, or something very much like it.

"So…" Focusing, I stare at our next clue. "How quickly do you want me to get them right? I know them immediately, so do you want me to pretend I don't for a bit to make it more fun?"

TAKE A BEAT TO LOOK AT THE STREET
WHAT A TREAT
TO SEE JUST THE SOLES OF HIS…

Will grins and slips his hand in mine. "Unleash your powers."

"Feet," I say as his kindness spreads through my fingers and up my arm, into my chest. "It's the Antony Gormley statue on the Downing Site. There's a full cast-iron man statue, buried in the ground so you can only see the bottoms of his feet. It's fascinating, because you can take your socks off and stand on top of it. You become connected to the statue, somehow. Like you're joined through the earth."

"I love it," Will says, putting his arm around me. "Let's go see that."

And I think: I'm pretty sure I love you too.

We wander the streets together, and for the first time in years, I stop struggling against my memories and simply let them launch out of my skin, like a projector. Translucent, they fill the air around me, playing simultaneously.

I see and feel and smell my mum everywhere. Sitting on the floor of the academic bookshop, wearing huge headphones, grinning with a poppy seed from the bagel she ate every single morning stuck between her teeth. The regular tap of her thumb against my hand as she held it, or the way she turned off all the overhead lights of every room we went into even if there were people already in there. I can feel the soft pink silk lining of her favorite jacket on my fingers, the smooth texture of her auburn fringe on my cheek when she kissed me; I smell the butterscotch syrup on her breath, dripped at 9:00 a.m. on the dot into her coffee. I see Dad too. Adjusting his black-rimmed glasses as we walk toward Emma College, chattering with the porter, hiding behind one of the ivy-clad walls to surprise me, naming all the plants. I see the tilt of his head when he put on a tie, and how he made conversation seem so easy.

Somehow, I wander through a now that is also a then: peering through the college window into Mum's old office and watching a thousand smaller versions of myself grow steadily larger. Hiding under her desk. Sniffing her fountain pens. Running my hands along the spines of her alphabetized books while she forgot I was there for hours at a time. Except I didn't mind,

even if it meant no lunch that day. Because I could lose myself the same way, just like her, and as I watched her eyes glaze
and her face slacken and her cheeks glow, I felt happy for her:
knowing she was somewhere beautiful and safe and joyful,
where nobody could reach her. Knowing that I had my own
quiet, joyful places inside myself I could disappear to as well.

And I can't help wishing again that I hadn't spent the last
five years of my time with her pulling so violently in the opposite direction.

Ludicrously trying to pretend that we were oh so different.

That we weren't, in our essence, the same.

Intermittently chatting, Will and I walk through the gardens that Dad helped grow, and I see two dark shapes running,
giggling; my father crushing a lavender stem between his fingers and holding it to our noses. I smell its purpleness all over
again, warm and opaque. I see us all in the restaurant we went
to every single Friday night, and the layers of time are still there,
still separate, still goopy: a joke on top of an argument on top
of a bored silence on top of Mum sending the same meal back
five times until it came back just right and everybody laughing.

And I miss them in every part of me, but I don't feel sad or
lost, the way I assumed that I would.

I feel dark, glossy green, like the underside of a leaf.

I feel the color of being home.

Eventually, Will and I get ice cream again. I don't drop it on
myself; Pimm's stays off my dress; dogs stay on their leads, as
they've been told to. Encouraged, I bravely gather my inner
resources and force myself onto the student's boat; Will and
I giggle together and kiss as he puns his way along the Cam.

By the time we return to London, I am giddy and primrose.

It's tricky to identify my emotions, but—as I scan my body
for sensations—I'm pretty sure it's happiness, shining in a bright
pastel thread. And yes, I've obviously cheated. Every now and

then today, I've used time travel to experience the best bits of our date more than once. Twice. Sometimes three or four times. A specific look in Will's eyes, a smile, a laugh; a finger gently lifting my chin. I can't stop time—I've tried, and that's out of my power—but I can certainly loop it and stretch it as much as I like, which is very nearly the same thing.

So I do: just to spend a little longer, in this day, with Will.

"I've had the best time," he says when we reach King's Cross, tipsy and with sunburnt noses. "Thank you."

Will kisses me and I kiss him back vigorously, resisting repeating it forever.

"I kind of don't want it to end yet." Will scratches his head. "If you felt like...extending the date a bit longer?"

I blink at him. "What do you mean?"

Does he know? Has Will inexplicably guessed that I've been extending it in tiny little rollbacks all day already?

"Do you want to come back to mine?" Will laughs. "That wasn't a very subtle way of putting it. Sorry."

"Oh!" Relieved, I think about it. "No, I don't think so."

"Shit." He flinches. "Did I just blow it? Is it too soon? I shouldn't have asked."

"No! That's not what I mean!" How do I put it? "It's just... I don't think we're supposed to have sex yet."

We don't have sex for another two weeks, according to our first timeline. And while it was lovely, and I obviously want to, I'm also a little worried about what will happen if we screw with that part of our chronology. It could send everything careering into total chaos, and it's going so well.

Also, the internet very clearly says three dates minimum is Sexy Time, and this is only our second: I will ignore their anonymous advice at my peril.

"Next time?" I say hopefully.

"Of course." Will kisses me again. "Next time, Cassandra."

I AM HERMES, WITH wings on my feet.

As I reach the bottom of my road in Brixton, I can't be entirely sure how I got here: whether I walked back, or caught a train, or hovered three inches above the ground, balanced on my flip-flops. All I know for sure is that I've done the right thing. This second date beats our *other* second date in every possible way, and my brilliant plan is absolutely working.

Will and I feel infinitely closer and more *connected* already.

My phone beeps:

We never collected our prize! Xx

I laugh, still feeling drunk on him (and Pimm's).

I guess we'll have to go back and do the whole treasure hunt again! xx

Beep.

I'm going to be SO good at it the second time round.
xx

I grin and type back:

Practice makes perf

"Cassandra."
I stiffen; from Hermes to Galatea in two seconds flat.
"Cassandra."
Marble, I fall out of the air.
"Cassandra."
Frozen, I lift my eyes.
"Cass." A young woman stands up from my front doorstep, where she's been crouched: folded inward on herself, like a rosebud. "If you're not going to read any of my letters, you need to talk to me. So here I am."

I am made of solid quartz and all I can think is: *that hat.*

She's wearing a hat, wide-brimmed, gray, and I know that hat. I have seen that hat before. Unable to move, I open my recent memories and rifle through them, searching for this hat as if it's a joker in a pack of cards. I find it, almost immediately. This hat—and the woman inside it—was in the café in my original timeline. I bumped into her, and she tried to talk to me. *Hey, wait just a—* But I didn't see her face. I was too overwhelmed. I then waited for her to arrive in my second loop, without realizing who it was. She was in the British Museum when I would have been at work in the first timeline, and now she's on my doorstep when I was originally at the cinema on my own.

How many other parts of this story has this woman been hiding in?

It suddenly feels as if time is revealing her to me, like an ancient statue hidden under shifting sand. Or, more specifically, like the head of Hermes found under a shopping center during routine sewage works.

"Cass," she says when I don't respond, approaching me slowly with one hand held out as if I'm a temperamental horse and she's my patient trainer. "Can you hear me, or have you already shut down?"

Her face is so young and so old at the same time: layered like tracing paper.

"Don't bolt. Hear me out, okay? Five minutes. That's all I need."

Her hair was never this short, it's the haircut of someone who knows their face doesn't need softening, and everything is suddenly starting to saturate: pink flowers, red front door, green weeds, blue sky, I'm steeped in color like a tea bag and they run into each other and hurt my eyes and the volume turns up, sears my skin, prickles my spine, and it's too much, it's too much, it's too bright, too loud, too big, and I cannot, I cannot, I—

You're a monster.

Desperately, I close my eyes and hold my thumbs.

"What are you doing?" Her voice gets closer. "Oh my God, Cass, are you *literally* shutting me out now? There's avoidant behavior and then there's just physically closing your eyes while I'm talking to you."

Honestly, I'm not sure exactly what it is I'm trying to do now.

All I know is I have to go.

"Come on, Sandy-pants." She uses my old nickname, laughter lifting her voice like a hot-air balloon. "You're thirty-one years old. You can't just stand in your own front garden with your eyes shut—it's patently ridiculous. We need to talk, Cass. This has gone on long enough now. I've sent you so many letters and tried to respect your space, but honestly, you've taken the piss with it, so now I'm not leaving here again until this is sorted. You can't just keep running away from me."

I squeeze my eyelids a little more tightly.

You're a monster you're a monster you're a monster you're a—

I've only managed to travel through time before—never through space—but I suddenly don't just need to leave now: I need to leave *here* too. It's a familiar, primal sensation: powerful and uncontrollable, like thirst or hunger. As if I'm struggling against a hand holding me underwater. I have a sudden flashback of sprinting across the school playground to hide in one of the bushes, every other lunchtime.

You're a m—

With everything I have, I focus a little harder and the lights start to flicker.

"Cassandra," she says gently. "Please. Just open your—"

"Do you want to come back to mine?" Will laughs. "That wasn't a very subtle way of putting it. Sorry."

I gather the pieces of myself back together and open my eyes.

"Yes," I say. "Please."

21

SO, THIS IS NEW.

"Just chuck your jacket anywhere," Will says, wedging his front door open with an alarming amount of effort. "Make yourself at home."

Yup, that will categorically not be happening.

Half-full mugs are propped on every surface; the floor is strewn with papers and books and unopened bills; abandoned T-shirts and jumpers and boxers sit exactly where they were dropped, as if humans spontaneously evaporated while still wearing them. Plates with dried baked beans and rigid crusts of toast are piled high on the dining-room table, half-hidden under a laptop and a microphone and wires and a watch and a bottle of unopened water.

Glancing to my left, I spy a tiny, grotty kitchen with absolutely no visible surface area and quickly glance away again. I don't need to see the future to know that I will not be *making myself at home* here without a mop, industrial-strength bleach and a large black bin bag.

Maybe some petrol and a lighter so I can set it all on fire afterward.

"It's a bit of a mess," Will understates cheerfully, picking up a sleeping bag and lobbing it into a corner with no discernible embarrassment whatsoever. "Sorry. I still haven't unpacked from my last job and it's kind of a tip."

Will has clearly never been to a recycling center, because they are *significantly* better organized than this. The invisible scarf is wrapping itself around my throat again, and it had only just started to unravel.

So much mess. So much dirt. So much inaudible *noise*.

My throat makes an embarrassing little quacking noise, like a baby duck, so I quickly turn it into a cough, wrap my arms around my stomach and attempt my childhood trick of detaching myself from my own skin like a popped balloon inside papier-mâché: shrinking so I can get away without actually going anywhere. Then I feel my brain follow suit. Quietly, it slips into the room at the back of my head, closes the door and stares through the window.

Four months.

Will and I dated for *four months*, and the two times I visited him here, it was spotless. Although I'm now starting to realize it had the surprised, lemony scent of a place that isn't on close regular terms with antibacterial spray. Truthfully, I've also never stayed overnight here before. I made plenty of excuses—I live closer to both our offices, my flatmates need me to stay in for a package, I am making a slow-cooker casserole I need to check regularly, which defeats the entire point of a slow cooker—but the truth is that I just can't sleep anywhere that isn't my own bed.

Somehow, I thought coming home with him tonight would kill two birds with one sex stone: helping us to *connect* while also giving me an alternative sleeping arrangement, away from my own house.

I'm now seriously doubting my stupidly flawed logic.

"There you are! Were you a good girl today?" Will's voice behind me is strangely high and musical. "Did you behave yourself?"

"Umm." I am physically incapable of moving my eyes from a red-wine spill on the carpet. Why would you drop a glass of wine and simply leave it there to marinate? How is it not all he can see? "Yes. I guess so."

My hand suddenly feels wet and I squeak as something large and cream and fluffy begins to scrabble at my stomach. Horrified, I push it away and begin to urgently swipe at the network of gross little hairs now coating my yellow dress. Again. Apparently they are capable of firmly attaching to me, but not to the animal they came from, which hints at poor design.

"Sorry!" Will laughs. "I should have warned you. You like dogs, right?"

Breathing quickly, I stare at whatever breed this is—miniature polar bear?—and fight an anxious roar at the base of my throat. *Another* dog? Is there no space on this planet free of canines? Somehow, I manage to swallow my cry of distress. I'm not sure that curling up in a ball and screaming GET IT THE HELL AWAY FROM ME is going to make my connection with Will stronger.

"Of course," I say, forcing a smile. "Everyone likes dogs, right?"

To clarify: I do *like* dogs. Dogs have an openhearted, affectionate and demonstrative quality I cannot relate to at all, but which I respect immensely. I just don't want them anywhere near me, with their wet, smelly tongues and their hot, meaty breath and their filthy paws and their constant provision of bodily excretions. I like them like I like children: far away, behind a soundproof barrier.

"Her name is Lion," Will explains as the dog scampers back

and gazes up at him with an open adoration that I recognize in myself. "Short for Dandelion, because of the white fluff that blows literally everywhere."

I clear my throat. "I didn't know you owned a dog."

I'm starting to spin out. How the hell has this happened? Where has Will been hiding a dog for over twenty-six dates? Is she a *secret* dog? Oh my God: have I screwed with the universe to such an extent now that I have somehow *made an entire dog from scratch*?

"Oh, I don't!" Will scratches the dog's head; another billow of eiderdown drifts into the corners of the living room. "Or not really, anyway. I used to share her with my ex, Rosie, but when we broke up last summer, she got full custody. Except she's gone on holiday, so she needed me to take care of the Lion for a few days and I couldn't say no, could I?" His voice is high and tender again; he bends down, cups Lion's face and kisses the end of her nose like a Jane Austen hero at the end of a book. "I didn't get to keep you because I travel too much, don't I? Yes, I do. I do!"

I'm now extremely relieved he wasn't using that voice to talk to me.

"Oh," I say, a little less confused. "I see."

Was the dog always here? She must have been. I just didn't know about it because yesterday was our first date, so I guess he didn't mention it. Although—looking back—it does also explain the state of his jumper.

The dog races back over to me and I can feel Will watching me more closely now. Pet owners always do this. They behave as if your reaction to an animal accurately measures your empathy and compassion levels, like the little sticks you hold in your urine to test for ketones or pregnancy. She's an adorable dog. She is. Her little black eyes and nose are floating in her white fluffy face like three neat fingerprints. I just don't want to touch her or vice versa.

My neck is starting to feel hot and prickly—I'm about to cry—but I didn't come this bloody far and traverse the entire universe to fall at the pet hurdle.

"Hello," I say, tapping the dog's nose with one finger. "It's nice to meet you."

"So polite and respectful," Will laughs, leaning forward to quickly peck my lips. "Let me quickly feed her and I'm all yours, Cassie. Make yourself comfortable. I'll be back in a tick."

I wait until he's gone to scour my mouth aggressively on my jumper sleeve: the thing he kissed before me has almost definitely been up another dog's butt.

Then I stand stiffly in the middle of the living room.

How do I make myself comfortable when I can't touch anything? Where am I supposed to put myself—stand on one leg in the corner of the room like a flamingo? My entire body is locked and rigid, so I desperately give myself a little shake, try to limber myself up. Do a little dance. Attempt to turn my body language into that of a woman keen on imminent sexy times, when all I can think about is that blue T-shirt on the floor.

I quickly pick it up and fold it on the table: that's better.

Will returns, beaming, and I suddenly see the tiniest flicker of a color I didn't expect. Dark gray, almost slate. What is it? It feels a little like resentment. Who is it coming from, him or me? All I know is I am *consistently* being told that I am oblivious to the emotions and feelings of those around me—even though I'm trying my absolute hardest—yet nobody seems to notice them when they're mine.

"Hi." Will smiles, pulling me toward him for another kiss.

"Hi," I say automatically, closing my eyes.

Kissing is so weird: we're literally testing each other out to see if there's a fit, trying on genes as if they're jeans. Exchanging the chemicals in our saliva, swapping bacteria, stimulating oxytocin and dopamine to make us bond, and all so that we can eventually mate with the ultimate productivity and produce the offspring most likely to survive and it's supposed to be sexy and romantic and sometimes it *is*, but right now, watching from a distance with my brain locked at the back of my head, it just feels like one of the weirdest things humans have chosen to do.

Somebody else's saliva is in my mouth, I'm swallowing spit that doesn't belong to me, and how is this *ever* something I voluntarily allow to happen?

"Umm." I pull away. "Please can we watch a film?"

"Oh!" Will blinks. "Yes! Of course!"

We both instinctively turn to look at the sofa—coated with a thin yet clearly visible layer of fluff, like a duckling—and Will *finally* sees what I'm seeing.

"Shit." He winces. "It's really quite grotty in here, isn't it. I'm so sorry, Cassandra. What must you be thinking? I didn't expect you to come back tonight and I only returned from a shoot last week, so I've been buried at the studio. It's not normally like this, I swear."

That is very clearly a lie, but I feel myself soften anyway.

I'm being completely unreasonable. He's tired and busy, and the flat isn't *that* bad. My horror of dirt and mess and dogs and lateness is a *me* problem. I see no reason why other people should have to live according to my personal eccentricities, and I'm certainly not going to judge Will because he doesn't. Frankly, I'm way too busy judging myself. Not everyone spends their spare time arranging their ornaments into nice straight lines and wiping down the woodwork.

"Don't apologize," I say, leaning up to kiss Will again.

As our lips press together—as his hand slips around my back and tugs me against him and the other hand touches my cheek and electricity flows straight into my brain—something in me abruptly fires up with a growl like a gas oven and suddenly all the grossness is gone: kissing makes sense again.

"Do you have another television?" I ask when we finally break away to breathe. "Like, in the bedroom?"

He does: it's a big flat-screen he edits on, right next to his bed.

"Great minds." Will laughs and kisses me again. "I was *just* thinking of asking if you'd like to see it. Wink wink, come see my massive TV, it's huge and lights up, and so on."

Taking my hand, he leads me with a cute little happy bop to the tiny room tucked behind his kitchen and—as he leans into the door—I feel all the wing muscles in my shoulders abruptly decompress and unravel. The bedroom is clean, tidy; it smells of lemon and fig. I'm suddenly feeling a *lot* more amorous.

Nothing says Sexy Time quite like freshly washed bedding.

"So." Will lets go of my hand and grabs the remote control from his bedside table. "What do you fancy? Are you into old movies, by any chance? *Rear Window*? *Casablanca*? *An American in Paris*? *Psycho*? Shit, not *Psycho*. What an entirely inappropriate suggestion. Get it together, Will."

My heart abruptly swells: Will's monologuing because he's nervous, which happens to me all the time, but almost never happens to him.

Now I finally feel "at home."

"*Rear Window*," I say firmly, because last time we watched this it inexplicably led to the best sex of my entire life. "Did you know Hitchcock constructed the entire apartment block on the Paramount Studios block? And the ballerina lived in her studio the entire time of shooting?"

Will gives me a funny look. "I *did* know that, yes."

"I love the way it's all set in one room." I climb onto the bed and perch against the wall. "We're watching them, watching others, who are watching telly, which could be us, so it's like a hall of mirrors. Never-ending voyeurism. Even the sound is diegetic, which means—"

"It all comes from within the world of the movie," Will finishes in delight. "Do you like old films too?"

"I didn't used to," I confess carefully. "But my ex got me into them."

"Sounds like my kind of guy." Will launches himself onto the bed next to me with an enthusiastic bounce and turns on the film. "Old movies are a bit of a passion of mine as well."

I smile. "What a crazy coincidence."

Technically the last time I had sex with Will was less than a week ago, but I feel strangely nervous. It doesn't feel like it was in this lifetime, and—it suddenly occurs to me—that might be because it wasn't. I've deleted our entire sexual history and now I have to type it all back in again from scratch. While I remember his body, his smells, his taste, the memories feel stored away, so they also feel unknown again, to be explored from the beginning.

Rear Window starts, but every cell is now focused on Will.

What's his body language? Unclear. How close is he sitting to me? Half a meter. How regularly is he breathing? Normal rate. How far is his hand from touching mine? I look down: five centimeters. Is he trying to send me…invisible sex vibes? I strain to check for them. No idea. There are no discernible colors—extremely frustrating—but there *must* be other measurable ways to tell if someone would like sex or not. The human race wouldn't have progressed much if everyone was just taken by complete surprise, every single time.

Will moves a fraction and my heart hops—sex now?

Nope, he was sitting on the remote control.

"Did you know that Hitchcock directed from inside Jimmy's room?" I can't bear the tension any longer, or the possibility that there isn't any tension at all and I haven't noticed. "The actors in the buildings opposite had earpieces so they could hear him."

"I did not know that," Will lies, and I know this for sure because he's the one who told me. "Interesting."

I glance at his face, but I can't read his expression either.

This is ridiculous. Admittedly I'm the one who asked to watch a film, but how do I now convey that I no longer want to actually watch a film? How do people go from not-sex to sex?

One minute you're watching Grace Kelly hit on Jimmy Stewart with a bewildering lack of success and the next you would quite like to physically slot your organs together like a pair of dovetail joints in a wooden table: there's no natural segue to this process that I can see.

Maybe I should just ask him politely for sex, like ordering a sandwich.

Get it out in the open: check whether we're now planning to have sex this evening at all, specify my preferences and then confirm *when* and *how* this process will start so I can mentally prepare myself. Although I did this last time too, and from memory it was the last thing I said before he dumped me.

"So," I say hesitantly. "Do you think—"

Will slips his hand into mine and nudges the side of my nose with his nose, and I don't know if that was a Start of Sex nudge or a Please Stop Talking the Film Is Starting nudge, so I hold my breath and wait to see what's going to happen next. He shifts almost imperceptibly toward me. He moves his hand. He looks at my face. I quickly try to cover my bases by looking interested in the film but at the same time also open to the possibility of not watching it.

Finally, Will reaches a hand up, tilts my face gently toward his and studies me, his face peach and wobbly in the Hitchcock light. Eye contact really does take on a whole new sensation when your eyeballs are nearly rubbing.

Embarrassed and dizzy, I suddenly remember to start breathing again.

Through my nose, in case my breath smells.

"You're so incredibly striking, Cassie." Will softly traces my lips and chin with his finger, as if he's drawing them. "Beautiful, but unusual. There's something feline about you, soft but distant at the same time. Up close, your eyes even have tiny flecks of yellow in them. It's not a face that's easy to forget."

"You'd be surprised," I admit. "I ran into an old flatmate a few months ago and they called me Cathy."

Will laughs loudly and pinches my chin between his fingers.

"Not easy for *me* to forget, then. Not that I've tried. I've thought about you constantly since we met. You know, I was meant to be getting a takeaway coffee."

"When?" I scrabble for the connection. "Now? Aren't they shut?"

"I mean, the day I met you in the café." He laughs again. "I'm attempting to confess, Cassie. I was *meant* to be getting a takeaway coffee. I was late to meet a client. But I saw you, immersed in your funny ancient book, in that puffy blue dress, caring not a fig about everyone staring, and I thought, bloody hell. She's really something. So instead of leaving, I got a cupcake, then pretended to study the menu, then pretended to look for a seat, then pretended to pick one opposite you, then pretended to get my laptop out as if I was going to actually work. It was all a big performance. I thought maybe you could tell."

I stare at Will in amazement. Not only did I completely miss all of that the first time round, I somehow missed it nine times after that too. Also, people were staring at me? Apparently, I missed that too.

"I could not tell," I confirm, genuinely bewildered. "Gosh."

"Gosh indeed," Will laughs. "And all I can say is, I am *very* glad it worked, because you are *just* as interesting as your face."

My eyes suddenly well up: I think I do love him.

Like really, almost definitely, but I can't tell him quite yet, not on our second date. I'm not a total idiot: it'll end everything.

Will leans forward and kisses my nose again, then my cheek, my eyelid, my eyebrow and my mouth, and *this* is why we kiss. Kissing is the sex prelude, the preparatory trumpet, and everything starts to feel warm and bright and peach and giddy, and when Will abruptly stops, I mewl in frustration, as if I dropped a bottle of milk.

"Why did we stop?"

"I just wanted to check you're okay." Will studies my face and I'm so flushed and turned on I have no idea what it's saying. "I am, but it's only our second date, Cassie. We don't know each other that well, after all. There's no rush."

"Yes, I'd like sex now, please," I manage, because we *do* know each other that well, or at least I know him, and suddenly it feels like all our twenty-eight dates leading up to now have just been a dress rehearsal for the real love story, the real romance, which is happening *now*. "Also, it's not our second date. Not really."

Will frowns. "It's not?"

"No." I lean in to kiss him again and I can feel his breath move in my throat. "I moved my bag."

He pulls away. "You moved your bag?"

"Yes. I moved my bag so you could sit with me. I saw you and I liked you, so I made sure you could choose to sit with me if you wanted to. We both intentionally picked our meeting, so I think it makes *that* our first date."

"You moved your bag, huh." Will thinks about this for a few seconds, then grins the widest I've ever seen him grin and moves his big warm hands to the base of my spine. "In that case, I reckon you're right. This is date three."

"Date three." I nod vehemently. "The internet says we're good to go."

"Well, if the internet says so," Will laughs, picking me up and swinging me round on his bed in a way that makes my brain fold inward like a paper fan. "Then, Cassandra, *go* we shall."

22

SO WE WENT.

And I have to be honest: it was a lot like going nowhere at all.

"Well."

"Well," I agree as we both stare at the ceiling. "That was…"

"Great!" Will nods. "It was great. Really, really great."

I am almost completely certain that if you say *great* three times in a row, it immediately cancels itself out. Zeus once had sex with Danae in the form of golden rain pouring through a subterranean chamber, and I'm pretty sure it was still more impactful than what just happened between me and Will.

"Mmm." I nod too. "Really great."

It was not great. It wasn't even fine. It was like we were playing totally different sports on the same field at the same time. Foreheads banged; arms tangled; noses crunched. At one point, I smashed my elbow against the wall and squealed with pain; Will got stuck in his jumper and when I amorously tugged at it I nearly popped his head right off. Neither of us knew where to look and focused on the headboard. Will eventually climaxed in a flat, relieved kind of way—as if he'd just done a week's laundry and now didn't need to think about it again for a while—while I was so far away from it I might as well have been standing by the washing machine with him, separating out my whites.

And the whole way through, we could hear Dandelion: whining and pawing outside the bedroom door, as if she wanted to save her beloved from whatever horror was clearly going on in here.

To be frank, I'm not entirely sure I blame her: I kind of wish she had.

"We can do better," I say into the silence. "I *know* we can."

I know this for certain because we already have.

"It was good!" Will rolls toward me and taps me with a tired, floppy hand, as if I'm a light he's trying to turn on in the middle of the night. "And the first time is always a bit awkward, right?"

Except our real first time wasn't awkward at *all*.

It wasn't perfect, but at least we were playing the same flaming game. I can't help wondering if somewhere out there, another version of Will and Cassandra are having cosmos-shattering sex, right at this very moment. There is no excuse for what just happened, and I obviously can't just leave it like that. *Extremely awkward and makes things uncomfortable* might be written on all my Work Assessments, but I'm not having it written on my sexual performance too.

"Let's go again," I say, closing my eyes.

Undo.

"So is this good?"

"Mmm-hmm."

"What about this? Is it good if I do this?"

"Mmm-hmm."

"And what about if I…?"

"It's all good," Will says, reaching up to touch my sweaty

face. "Maybe we…could leave the constructive feedback until afterward?"

I flush and stop moving, feeling a lot like I do after most of our Away Days: as if there's a Comment Box and I've put in way too many comments.

"Sure. I'm sorry."

"Don't say sorry. I'm sorry. I shouldn't have said that."

"It's fine. I'm sorry. Sorry for saying sorry."

"Sorry."

We both gallantly attempt to continue, but it becomes rapidly clear that we've both logged off as if it's 5:00 p.m. and we've just simultaneously closed down our computers and picked up our coats.

"Quick break?" Will asks hopefully as I roll off.

For the love of—

Undo.

The third time, we've just started when there's a loud *bang* and Dandelion catapults herself across the room, jumping on both of us and barking at me.

Undo.

Fourth time: Will tentatively asks midway if I've fallen asleep.

Undo.

I contribute with far too much energy to compensate and Will asks if I'm okay in a way that suggests I might not be okay.

Undo.

On our sixth attempt, everything seems to be going better.

I don't interrogate him for information; Will's nose doesn't jab my eyeball; nobody apologizes; the dog doesn't get involved. I'm exhausted, because honestly I'm just not athletic enough for this quantity of sex, but I experience a last-minute surge of energy, like a runner at a finish line hoping for snacks and a shower.

"Well," Will says breathlessly, staring at the ceiling.

"Well," I agree, wiping my forehead. "That was great. Thank you very much."

Silence.

Then: "You're welcome?"

And I'm all for good manners, but I think I just accidentally thanked Will for sex like I'm getting off the 196 bus from Elephant and Castle.

Embarrassed, I hold my hand up and attempt to high-five him. Will did this after the first *real* time we had sex and there was something so sweet and team-like about it. It made me so happy. Like we'd won something together. Like we'd be winning a lot of things, going forward. Like it wouldn't even matter if we occasionally lost.

Will blinks at my hand for a couple of seconds and for inexplicable reasons it doesn't work when I do it. When I make this gesture it no longer looks playful and charming: I look like a kid who just did their first roly-poly.

"FUCK!" I scream at the ceiling.

Undo.

Just before the seventh attempt, I silently appeal to Aphrodite and all of the Erotes: Eros, Pothos, Anteros, Pan, literally any god or deity that might have any link to sex or lust at all. Desperate, I briefly switch to Roman, just because they always seem a little more aggressively sexual: Voluptas, Aurora, Cupid, Suadela, Venus. I even momentarily call on Qadesh, the Middle Eastern goddess of sacred ecstasy.

It finally works: we both orgasm, albeit nowhere near together.

I'll take the win where I can.

"Well," Will says when we pull apart, wrapping his arms

around my waist and immediately pulling me back toward him. We stick together with a small sucking sound and I hate it, but apparently you have to wait at least twenty seconds before peeling yourself off someone who's just been inside you, otherwise you risk coming across as rude. "That was…"

I wait anxiously for feedback with bated breath.

"Amazing," he concludes, wiping his forearm across his damp forehead. "No awkward first-time sex for us, Cassie. We smashed it!"

Will holds his hand up for a high five and I stare at it in irritation for a few moments. It's cute again. Seriously, how come it's adorable when he does it and creepy/childish when it's me?

"Yay for us," I yawn, tapping it.

Waves of blackness are starting to slip over my head and somewhere in the distance Grace Kelly finally gets her man to love her for what feels like the trillionth time and the credits begin to roll. Although I can't help wondering if she should have had to try so hard in the first place: she's Grace bloody Kelly.

As sleep tugs at my pores, the entire area where Will is touching me suddenly starts to prickle, burn, feel unbearable, trapped, claustrophobic, and that's it, time's up, sex is done, no more touching me, please.

As politely as I can, I peel myself off him and shuffle away across the bed, one limb at a time, like a crab.

"Hey." Will shuffles after me. "Want to go again?"

"Absolutely not," I say, and pass straight out.

A square, suspended in the air; a line of light; lemons. A dark shadow on the door; blue flickers; something heavy on my legs and material that feels bobbled, confusing, rough, and I can't breathe, I can't breathe, I can't—

Terrified, I lurch to sitting. Where am I?

Disoriented, I concentrate as hard as I can and try to process the new data while my heart bangs into my fingertips. The square is a window. The line of light is a hallway. The smell is laundry detergent and the shadow is a dressing gown. The blue is a TV screen saver. The lump is white, a sleeping dog, and I'm… in a bedroom. In a bedroom that isn't mine. In…Will's house?

"Will?" My voice wobbles. "Is that you?"

"Mmm-hmm." A hand pats my face. "Sssssshhhh. Gosleep."

Heart still racing, I lie back stiffly.

This room has the wrong smell, the wrong light, the wrong door, the wrong window. Everything is wrong. Different. My ornaments aren't here, my books aren't here, my lamp isn't here, my plants and owl toy aren't here; the bathroom's in the wrong place and if I get up the carpet will feel different under my toes and the sink will be in a different place and the mattress doesn't feel like my mattress and the duvet is the wrong weight and the pillow is scrunchy and the curtains are the wrong color and I don't like it I don't like it I—

I sit bolt upright again. "I want to go home."

Will stirs. "Hmm?"

My voice is tight. "I want to go home."

"You want to—" Will wakes up properly now and struggles onto his elbow, blinking at me in the fish screen-saver light. "You want to go home? Cassie, are you okay? Are you sleep-talking? What's happening?"

"I want to go home," I say more insistently.

"Cassie." He turns on the light. "Shit. What's going on? Talk to me."

"I want to go *home*." Panic is rising, choking, my eyeballs are jittering, my thumbs are held. The room's all wrong, it's wrong, it's wrong; I wrap my arms around my knees under the duvet and rock, seeking a pattern, a familiarity I can hide in, but I can't find one, there's dog hair on the duvet, dog hair on me, the light is wrong, it's in the wrong place and—"I want to go home, I want to go home, I want to go home, I want to go home, I want to go home, I want to go home, I—"

I'm looping, trapped: a bumblebee against glass.

"Whoa." Will gently brushes the hair out of my face and wipes my eyes. "Ssshhhh. Don't cry, Cassie. Of course you can go home. But can you please tell me why? Did I do something wrong? Can I try to fix it?"

He moves to wrap his arms around me and I jerk away.

"I want to go home," I cry desperately.

Will pulls away, and as I sob into my knees, I can feel the colors spinning out of me: shame, confusion, fear, guilt, distress, pain, humiliation, all the many, many bloody reasons that *I do not stay at other people's houses.*

Like a tide receding, I gradually feel my sobs start to quieten, my body still.

And as my own colors fade, I can suddenly see Will's.

He's looking at me as if he went to bed with Lamia, the beautiful Libyan queen, and woke up with Lamia, the disfigured demon who ate little children. And it doesn't matter that it wasn't her fault. Lamia transformed into something unrecognizable, so that's how everyone saw her. It always happens. Always. Little by little, something inside me comes to the surface and drives everyone away.

I have to undo this.

I cannot let Will look at me as if I'm someone else.

When I open my eyes, Will is fast asleep.

I watch him for a few minutes: studying the lovely lines of his resting, slightly dribbling face. He looks so peaceful. So happy. So completely unaware that in another timeline, in another universe, he's about to be woken up by a woman he's just had sex with for the first time, bawling and begging for home like a tiny child at their very first sleepover.

("Cassandra can be worryingly immature and childish.")

With a bolt of overwhelming sadness, I lean over and stroke Will's cheek.

"Mmm-hmm." He pats my face. "Sssssshhhh. Gosleep."

Because it's only *now* starting to hit me that what I'm doing might not be…right. Good. Ethical. Am I *manipulating* Will? Am I simply using time travel to control him? Am I using my prophetic skills for evil, like Ouranos, the sky grandfather who learned that his children would one day overthrow him and so immediately ate them?

Now the sadness is shifting, changing, but I can't tell into what.

("Cassandra can be incredibly selfish.")

Am I just bad?

("Cassandra is prone to self-absorption.")

Is this why I'm alone?

("Cassandra is a difficult person to warm to.")

Because all I know is that I want to be with Will, I want to love him, I want him to love me—I think maybe he *could*—but he chose not to. In another version of this universe, he made a conscious decision not to be with me.

Twice.

And I'm trying to make him be with me anyway.

"Will?" I say as my throat abruptly closes. "I'm so sorry."

He stirs. "Mmm?"

"Nothing."

Stiff as a board, I lie back in the bed with my arms by my sides, which is how I really sleep when I'm not pretending to look bendy and casual: like a vampire, but without a pillow. And as I lie there, touching nothing and nobody—a jigsaw piece with the edges sanded down—I suddenly realize: I'm not traveling through time to undo the things I've done wrong or the decisions I've made.

I am trying to undo myself.

23

I AM ALSO NOT using time travel properly.

Stiff as a celery stick, I lie wide awake until 7:00 a.m.—just in case the humiliation happens again—then make Will a cup of coffee, kiss his cheek gently, leave the mug on his bedside table and make my way back to my house to get ready for work. Even in my tiredness, I cannot help but feel that somewhere out there is a brilliant scientist who would be saving the world with these abilities, or at the very least carrying a spare change of clothes.

"Well, well, well."

Exhausted, I shut the door of the Brixton flat behind me, hang my bag on its little hook and wonder who says *well, well, well* other than cartoon villains with their fingertips pressed together. The trains were packed, people kept touching me, so I instinctively kept rewinding thirty seconds just to get away from them without making a fuss, and it effectively doubled my journey time. Now I can move through space too, I probably need to work out how to navigate London without using the Underground at all. Technically, I could just go back to the last time I was in a specific place, but I can't figure out how to do that without erasing everything that's happened in the interim.

"Good mor—" I turn round. "Oh, fuck me."

Derek is leaning against the kitchen door frame, eating a bowl of cereal. The only thing separating him from a naked statue of Apollo is a tiny pair of blue Y-fronts and the absence of a laurel wreath or a lyre.

"Looks like somebody already has." He grins, shoveling more Coco Pops into his mouth. "Where have you been, you dirty little stop-out? Don't stare at my penis, Cassie. It's generally considered poor form."

Flushing, I drag my eyes away and stare at the ceiling pendant.

"Must have been a good night," Derek continues, and his eyes feel like fingertips. *Crunch. Crunch.* "I didn't know you had it in you, Cassandra. Although it looks like you did. More than once, judging by the state of your hair."

I open my mouth in shock and shut it again.

"Hey." He chuckles lightly as I quickly do up the button of my denim jacket. *Crunch.* "I'm just joking, Dankworth. Banter, you know? You don't need to look *quite* so appalled. I'm not a *predator* or anything. I'm just playing around."

Breathing out, I try my hardest to make eye contact.

My pupils briefly connect with Derek's and—with an almost audible *crack*—unbearable pain shoots through them to the back of my head, then bounces down into the rest of my body like a pinball: ricocheting off every single organ on its way down.

Nope. Can't do it. I'd rather shoot myself in the head.

Defeated, I look away again.

"Umm." I take a small step forward. "I need to get changed for work."

Derek laughs but remains blocking the doorway, so I calculate my next move. My bedroom is on the other side of him, so I'm going to have to get past him somehow, like Oedipus and the goddamn Sphinx. Holding my breath, I carefully manage to inch past him by doing a three-point turn, as if I'm trying to maneuver a sofa.

"Do I make you nervous, Cassie?" Derek follows me into the kitchen.

Yes. "No."

"I don't mean to, you know." He sits down at the kitchen table with bulging golden thighs, grabs a cup of coffee and smiles. "I just want you to be comfortable here, Cassandra. My *casa* is your *casa*, after all."

If that was true, I wouldn't only have one shelf of the fridge and he'd be wearing clothes.

I continue to politely shuffle away. "Mmm-hmm."

"So, who *is* this man you're seeing?" Derek pulls another chair out and gestures toward it chummily. "Do I know him?"

I look desperately at the chair, then at the escape route to my room.

All I want is a coffee, a shower, a change of clothes—maybe stare at a few calming colors for ten minutes so I can decompress—but if I'm unfriendly to Derek now, I'm going to send things spinning off in the wrong direction again. And, somewhat unfairly, if I'm *too* friendly to Derek, it's also going to go spinning off. So I have to find somewhere in between. A safe place of friendliness, somewhere in the middle. I don't want to move again; I am so sick of packing boxes.

Maybe I can use this conversation to my advantage?

"No." I perch on the chair delicately. "You don't know him."

"So what's his name? Occupation? Age?" Derek sits back and I cannot help noticing that his abdomen is shiny. What has he been rubbing it with? Margarine? "And how long has this hot new romance been going on? It's not...what's his name, is it?"

"Ted," I guess. "No, that was over six weeks ago."

Over isn't exactly the right word to use when it was never technically *on*, but I'm not sure what else to call two dates with an accountant who asks if you think his calves are sexy before pulling up his trousers and propping his leg up on the restaurant table.

To reassure myself, I glance up at the clock: still on time to get to work.

"So this is…?"

"Will Baker. Cameraman. Thirty-four. Two, I mean three dates."

I can feel Derek's eyes on me and I need to look at him before my physical inability to do that is eventually used against me. Holding my breath, I count—one, two, three, four, five—then lift my eyeballs and try to keep them up as if I'm Atlas, holding the sky above my head.

Hold it. Hold it. Hold—

"Well," Derek says as I breathe out and drop my gaze on the floor, slightly dizzy with exertion. "Will Baker the cameraman is a very lucky guy, that's for sure. You're quite the catch, if I do say so, Cassandra Dankworth."

My blood freezes.

"Nope," I say, trying to stand up. "Thanks. Bye."

Except now I'm frozen again.

This can't be happening. This whole thread can't be starting again, already. We're *way* ahead of schedule. Weeks and weeks ahead. How did I get here so quickly? This must be my cosmic punishment for screwing with the timeline: You want to speed things up, Cassandra? Feeling a bit impatient? Don't want to let things play out organically? Here you go, buddy. See how you like this.

But I'm not ready; I haven't planned what I'm going to do about Derek and Sal, or how I'm going to respond this time. I haven't written a script, or rehearsed it in my head, or written down possible alternative outcomes.

I am not *prepared*.

Unable to move, I sit and stare at the floor.

Unless…

If I don't come home today, Derek and I won't have this conversation, our relationship won't start to tip dangerously in the wrong direction; I'll be safe again.

"Hey," Derek says, standing up as I close my eyes tightly. "Cassandra, don't freak out. I was just being frien—"

24

"—DLY WITH ALL THE MOST *influential* bloggers. I've made a list for the short leads—we're too late for the longs, obviously, but we can always try in a few months if we want to hit the Christmas pages. I'm thinking of tailoring each box, running a prize, and obviously I've set up the socials. I've worked out a great hashtag, and also the press release, which I just printed out—and that's here."

I blink at the A4 paper, abruptly plopped on my desk.

"This is just the beginning," Sophie continues, beaming at me. "But I've got a uni buddy who's really prominent online, so she's going to help us kick things off. What do you think generally of memes?"

I didn't time travel, by the way.

Or I did, but only just enough to skip returning home and instead simply stay on the train to work. It just *seems* like I time traveled because I haven't listened to a single word Sophie has said.

It's not her fault: public relations is just really, really boring.

"I have no thoughts at all about memes. Ever." I frown distractedly. "When did that plant get here?"

"Over the weekend, I guess?" My colleague switches topic
with the grace and elegance of a swallow. "I think someone
new must be starting soon."

I stare at the rubber plant in amazement. Ronald.

It's so strange, watching time line everything up like dom-
inoes and then knock them down in order, one by one. The
plant is here, which means Ronald should follow it next—I
scan my internal diary—Monday. Although why he decided
to send it ahead with a few boxes of files and his own personal
office chair is a mystery: maybe he likes to signal his arrival,
like Zeus with his thunderbolts.

Speaking of thunderbolts... I grab my phone:

Sorry for running out this morning; you looked so
peaceful, I didn't want to wake you up! I've got a big
week at work and had to get here early.

Thank you for such a lovely day yesterday, and an
even better night. See you soon, I hope. ;) xx

A few seconds later, a beep:

Good morning! I can't remember the last time I slept
that well. I had a great time too. :) Shall we do something later in the week? Wx

Giddy with prophetic knowledge, I type:

Yes, please! I would love that. Cx

I already know our next date will be this Friday.

We will go for a curry and Will chooses one so spicy he starts
choking and laughing and crying simultaneously and is forced

to drink water out of the table vase, but I think it's only gallant to let him find this out for himself.

"Boyfriend?" Sophie asks as I sigh happily and put my phone away.

"Not quite yet." I feel a fierce rush of excitement. "He's going to refer to me as his girlfriend for the first time in just over a fortnight. A waiter asks what kind of wine we'd like, and he pointedly says he'll have whatever his girlfriend wants."

It is, hands down, one of the most triumphant moments of my life.

Sophie blinks. "Oh."

"I'd imagine," I add quickly as the office door opens.

Exactly on time, Barry walks in and begins perusing the office in portly circles, like a tiny Henry VIII arriving at court. He does this every Monday. You can sense him coming from fifteen meters away, just from all the hastily closed social media pages. Sophie grimaces at me and scurries back to her desk to await whatever horrors he's constructed to "boost morale" this time.

"Knock knock," Barry says, pausing behind her with his mug of tea.

"Who's there?"

"Interrupting cow."

"Interrupting c—"

"Moo!" Barry pats her shoulder. "We have fun, don't we?"

Sophie's giggle sounds almost real—impressive—and I watch warily as Barry smugly parades round the desk toward me with both his hands grasped around his tea mug like a fortune teller with her crystal ball. I do not like Monday mornings. Last time my boss targeted me with a "joke," I stared at him until he explained it three times and walked away, grumbling loudly about the importance of a sense of humor.

"Cassandra." Barry pauses at my desk. "What on earth are you wearing?"

I look down in surprise. "Sex knickers that haven't been

changed in roughly sixty hours" seems an inappropriate an-swer. "A yellow lace dress. Nude bra and pants. Gold sandals. A denim jacket, but I was about to take that off."

"I wasn't asking for a list of everything you're wearing, Cassie," Barry sighs, rolling his eyes at Sophie as if I can't see it. "What I *mean* is, it's Monday. You should be wearing a green jumpsuit, no? Sort of leaf-colored. Or is it moss?"

I stare at him, amazed. "Huh?"

"Emerald." Miyuki pauses by the desk, eating peanut butter on toast. "Monday is emerald jumpsuit day. Tuesday is black. Wednesday is navy."

"No, *Tuesday* is navy," Anya chips in from just behind her. "Wednesday is the black jumpsuit. It gets confusing."

"And Thursday is pink and Friday is white!" Sophie bounces in excitement on her chair like a ginger puppy. "Cassandra has allocated jumpsuits like other people have Days of the Week knickers."

"Except nobody wears *them* on the right day," Grace inter-jects from across the room. "Ever. Right?"

"Right!" Sophie nods. "But I bet Cassie would. Wouldn't you, Cassie?"

I blink at my work colleagues. I don't know exactly how to feel: touched that they've noticed my work-attire schedule, embarrassed that I'm now very clearly wearing yesterday's sex clothes or horrified at the way this topic has veered into hor-ribly unprofessional territory so quickly.

"Can we stop talking about my underwear at work, please?"

I'd also point out that I'm not a six-year-old girl, but Barry has just moved his hands slightly and I can now see the picture on his mug: a cartoon deer, jumping away from an arrow. It's so old the entire image is faded and scratched, but you can still see the words *Did You Myth Me?* scrawled underneath.

A flicker of white electricity runs quickly from one side of my head to the other, as if I've been struck by Zeus himself.

Stay calm, Cassandra. Remember, you're at work. Stay humble and respectful and professional and—

"Barry." My voice is tight. "Is that my mug?"

"Oh." My boss studies it with infuriating nonchalance. "I don't know. Is it?"

"I will rephrase for clarity." Breathing hard, I lurch to my feet. Electricity runs between my ears again, and I feel my brain sizzle. "That is *my mug*, Barry. Why are you drinking out of *my mug*?"

My breath is coming hard and fast now: a steam train at full pelt.

The entire office has now gone silent, but I don't care, I will rip the world apart, I will turn them to stone, that is *my* mug, it lives on *my* desk, it belongs to *me*, everyone knows that, it comes with me everywhere and how *dare* he—

"OH MY GOD," I yell as Barry inexplicably goes to take another sip. "GET YOUR LIPS OFF MY FUCKING MUG!"

Bursting into flames, I rip it out of his hands and cradle it like a furious mama bear with her tiny cub. Hot tea goes all over my hands and chest but I barely feel it. Is my mug okay? Is it ruined forever? Can I wash it with toilet bleach? Will I ever be able to look at it again without thinking of Barry?

"Umm," Sophie says nervously over the top of our computers. "I think we have a new cleaner, Cassie. She moved all the mugs from our desks to the kitchen. So maybe that's why there was a bit of a mix-up?"

Anger sizzling, I spin to look around the office. Every single face is turned toward me and the color they're producing as a group is extremely unpleasant: a kind of sludgy, icky brown.

At times like this, I can totally see why I'm so unlikable.

I'm not a big fan of me right now either.

"Oh," I say. "I see."

"Let's have a chat in my office, shall we?" Barry says sharply, and yeah, this particular firing is definitely my fault.

★ ★ ★

"—think someone new must be start—"

"Hold that thought," I tell Sophie, jumping up and running to the kitchen.

I get there just in time. My boss is casually perusing the open cabinet—a king surveying his kingdom—and I have to fight yet another identical flicker of white-hot rage: you want tea, buy your own bloody mug, *Barry*.

"Whoops," I say, taking my mug out of his hand. "How did that get in there?"

Then I run back to my desk and put it safely in a drawer.

"Sorry," I say in relief to Sophie. "Where were we?"

The first time I lived this week, I spent most of it in the toilets.

While I think everyone can agree I'm not a PR star, Selling-In is where I really do the opposite of shine. I have a long list of journalists I'm expected to speak to and convince to run my story. This takes at least an hour per phone call: three minutes to talk to them, and fifty-seven minutes to stare weepily at the script I've typed up and stuck to my computer. I slur and I stammer, my phone feels like a hand grenade that could go off at any moment, and after every call I have to lock myself in the loo to either cry or experience some lava-hot anxiety diarrhea.

If I'm really lucky, this gets pointed out loudly by one of my colleagues.

Little by little, I fall apart.

By the middle of a Selling-In week, everything hurts all the time: light, sound, smell, temperature, the texture of my own clothes on my skin. I cower in dark corners when everyone else is in meetings. I stop being able to use public transport. I stop being able to eat or sleep. Eventually, I stop being able to speak at all. By the weekend, I am so sick I have to spend it in bed, just like I did after a full week of school.

So when Barry accused me of *not being a People Person*, he wasn't wrong.

Sometimes I barely feel like a person, singular.

This time, Sophie watches me make my first call—"H-h-h-h-hi, th-th-this is C-C-C—"—and leans over her computer.

"Hey, Cassandra. Would you mind terribly if *I* make all the phone calls?"

I stare at her. "Uh?"

"It's just I *really* love talking to journalists." She twiddles with a lock of her chaotic red hair, blue eyes even larger than normal. "I'm building connections that will last my whole career, right? So you'd be doing me a *huge* favor. I'll do the talking, and you do the emailing. Deal?"

I stare at her for a few seconds. "B-but B-Barry won't let me."

"Barry doesn't need to know." Sophie shrugs easily. "He comes into the office, does his little walk around, you pick up the phone and make a pretend phone call. Okay? Problem solved."

It takes me at least fifteen seconds to work out what she's doing and—when it finally clicks—I feel my chin crumple and I have to swivel away and pretend to be abruptly fascinated by the watercooler.

I love her.

I love her with every cell in my strangely sensitive body. Every single mean thing I have ever thought about Sophie I now officially retract: the way she slams her keyboard with her fingers is *perfection*.

"Okay," I manage, straightening my face and swiveling back. "I guess I could go with that plan. If it would help you, obviously."

"Oh, it would." She nods vigorously. "We're a team, right?"

At the word *team*, my chin abruptly crumples again and my bottom lip pops out. What the hell is wrong with me? I'm nearly a decade older than this girl. Why does it feel like she's somehow mothering *me*?

I swivel away, straighten my face, then swivel back.

"Yes, Sophie. We're a team."

By Wednesday, I have spoken to literally nobody and it is *glorious*. Every now and then, I take off my noise-canceling headphones just to witness Sophie chat happily away to strangers. No script. No stammering. No sweating or crying or running desperately to the toilet. It is truly a marvel, like watching Bellerophon slay the Chimera.

Admittedly, we do *very nearly* get caught by Barry.

"Hello," I say to the speaking clock. Every hour or so, I make a fake call just so one of my colleagues doesn't dob me in. "This is Cassandra Dankworth, calling from Force It PR." Sophie widens her huge eyes at me, so I smile and widen mine back. I have no idea what we're communicating to each other, but it is *so* lovely to be included. "I was just wondering if you received the press release about SharkSkin? Oh, you did? You'll run it? Cool. Bye now."

"Fawcett," Barry says as I put the phone down.

Jumping six inches, I swivel toward him. "Uh—"

"My name is Barry Fawcett." He scowls at me with his little bulldog face. "Fawcett PR. Can you say *Fawcett* for me?"

"Fawcett."

"Because it sounds a lot like you are saying *Force It PR*, Cassandra, and that is extremely not funny."

Busted. I totally was. "Sorry, sir."

"Don't let it happen again." Barry walks off in a huff and apparently Sophie's straining baby blues meant *Barry is standing directly behind you*, except they look a lot like *how's it going?* and also *it's nearly lunchtime* and also *this journalist is boring*, so how am I supposed to tell the difference?

We're just giggling about it when my phone beeps:

Still up for tonight? W xx

I stop giggling. Tonight?

"Hey." I lean up so I can see over my computer. "It is Wednesday, right?"

"Yup." Sophie nods with admirable certainty. "Sure is."

I check my jumpsuit again (black), then double-check my calendar—we're definitely midweek—and I am now extremely confused. Our curry date is on Friday. Will hasn't technically asked me yet, but that's okay: he asks tomorrow morning. I remember it very clearly because I was starting to panic that our date hadn't gone as well as I'd thought. We've exchanged a few texts over the last day and a half, but I'm almost certain there's been nothing at all about tonight.

Disoriented, I scroll through our texts to look for clues.

Panic starts to mount.

Where have all our texts gone this time?

And it's only as I scroll back with increasing freneticism that I suddenly realize: I've been tweaking time over the last two days. Not a *lot*—a burnt piece of toast, forgotten house keys, last night I fell asleep during a TV show and decided to just erase time instead of looking for the remote control—so I didn't give it much thought. But perhaps I should have, because have I accidentally erased my texts with Will again?

Quickly, I type:

Of course! Remind me again what we're doing? C xx

A few minutes later:

The exhibition. I asked if you might be up for it?

Shit. We did talk about it, on our train journey home from Cambridge. I've just forgotten because I didn't go on this date in the original timeline. I was stuck at work until 10:00 p.m., entering my campaign failure into a spreadsheet and using up all the toilet roll.

"Sophie?" I look up abruptly. "Do you think we're doing okay?"

"Oh, yes," she confirms calmly, studying her screen and rotating her nose stud. "Should all be good. Campaign's going to be fine. I wouldn't worry."

She says this as if public relations is both easy and quite a lot of fun, which is frankly bewildering.

Relieved, I type:

Of course! Your friend's exhibition!
Can't wait! Confirm location?

Then I glance at my watch, stand up and grab my green velvet jacket.

I'm suddenly really excited.

Admittedly, I'd ideally prefer a lot more time to mentally prepare and do the necessary research, but this also means I get to see Will again a whole two days early. We might be able to squeeze in *two* dates before the weekend, where previously there was only one. I've also recovered from my moral and ethical dilemma now: I was exhausted and postcoital, it was the middle of the night, and everyone knows epiphanies when you've just orgasmed don't count.

My phone beeps with an attached location.

Great! See you in a bit! X

Beaming, I grab my bag and charge toward the door.

"Hey, Cassie?" Sophie looks up with her phone propped under her chin and puts her hand over the receiver. "There's a call for you. Do you want to take it?"

I hesitate, stomach flipping, before remembering our genius

plan. This is possibly the best PR career move of my entire life. I may never have to actually talk to a journalist ever again.

"No, thank you." I wink. "Take a message and I'll *email* them back tomorrow."

"Sure thing." Sophie smiles. "Going somewhere nice?"

"Just some animal photography exhibition in Shoreditch," I say, straightening my jumpsuit collar, and I can literally *hear* the coupled-up smugness in my voice. I've heard it before in others, so many times, but never before in me. It's delicious. No wonder people seem to enjoy rolling around in the smugness quite so much. "Then maybe out to dinner, I don't know."

Okay, now I'm just showing off. Strange how much easier it is to "open up" and "share" when the answer isn't *Going home to rearrange my books into chromatic order and then maybe sitting on my bed on my own, looking at paint chips.*

"Sounds lovely." Sophie beams. "You can tell me all about it tomorrow!"

I glance at Ronald's rubber plant, suddenly triumphant: I no longer feel quite as replaceable as I once did.

"Yes." I nod. "I think maybe I will."

25

I'M EARLY FOR OUR brand-new date, so I invest my time wisely.

This mainly consists of walking up and down the pavement outside, googling photographs of what it might look like inside and also trying to see through the window so I can prepare myself, mentally. When that doesn't work, I resort to lingering by the front door and popping my head round every time anyone walks in or out, like a giant game of *Mole Attack*.

There's still no sign of Will—he appears to be late, and thus it begins—so at six o'clock to the second, I venture inside.

If I were a god, this is close to what Olympus would look like. The room is a large, perfect square, and everything is spotless; the walls are white, the wood floors gleam, the lights are dim. From the ceiling beams hang hundreds of tiny fairy lights, giving the room the magical quality of a Christmas bauble, and real plants are scattered everywhere. Piano music plays, soft seats lie waiting, and there are four enormous white Greek-style pillars to make me feel even more at home.

Honestly, the only thing that ruins it is the fact that there are other humans in here, enjoying it all too.

On the upside, at least there are no small children.

Increasingly curious, I approach one of the photographs. It's a gazelle, kicking a lioness in the stomach: the lioness is suspended in the air, shocked by the sheer audacity. Frowning, I move to the left. The second photo is a polar bear, peering at an iceberg through an abandoned camera lens. The third is a small gray owl, slipping off a branch. I peer a little more closely and my nostrils flare. I recognize that expression: it's exactly how I look every time I fall off a ball in the middle of a meeting.

Hang on. Are all these photos meant to be *funny*?

A waiter approaches. "Mini quiche?"

"Is this a comedy exhibition?" I glance around again: people are chuckling and shaking their heads. There's a monkey smacking himself in the face, and a seal waving; a giraffe photo-bombing an antelope. Evidence is certainly mounting. "Are these photos supposed to be hilarious?"

"Oh." The waiter laughs. "Yeah. Obviously. Have you seen the one with the squirrel playing a flower like a flute? Tiny burger?"

I blink at the non sequitur, then glance at the tray he's holding. As a general rule, I do not eat food that has been perambulated in public for hours like a grubby child around a park. Although I'm enormously grateful to the waiter. Thank goodness I found out the tone of this exhibition *before* Will arrived and I tried to earnestly analyze them all: that could have been *really* embarrassing.

Focusing harder now, I reject the miniature junk food and move to carefully assess a large brown bear sitting in a hammock. I suppose it's funny because it wasn't built for him but he's using it anyway? Because we're projecting human behavior onto an animal? I mainly feel sorry for him: he's just trying to enjoy his hammock, and next thing he knows, there's a human taking a photo so other humans can stand around and laugh at him for it.

I'm just moving on to a chipmunk scaring an eagle—that's not funny at all, I bet it doesn't end well—when I hear a familiar chuckle.

Frowning, I spin round and search the huge room again.

There's another loud laugh, and I narrow my eyes: from just behind one of the huge white pillars, I spot a shoulder that looks suspiciously like a shoulder I've recently seen naked. Its owner laughs again and confirms my suspicion. Will. Has he been here the entire time? How did I not sense it? Even more surprisingly, does that mean he actually got here *earlier than me*?

Blimey. Maybe I'm traveling through time purely so that Will can finally learn to actually keep to it.

With a rush of giddy turquoise sweetness, I stride toward him.

Beaming, I veer round the corner.

My brain buckles.

"Cassie!" Will turns to me with a wide smile, then leans forward and kisses my cheek. He smells oaky and fernlike; his color is pale moss. "There you are! When did you get here? You should have texted! Isn't this exhibition brilliant? I was just chatting to—"

"Diana."

"Diana! What an excellent name!" The waiter approaches Will with mini quiches and Will grabs six with—as usual—no consideration at all for hygiene or the bacteria of strangers. He crams two in his mouth. "I was just telling Diana here that my good friend Sam took the photo with the polar bear. That's actually my camera he's peering through. We were shooting in the Arctic last year and I left it out while I grabbed a sandwich from the tent. I think the bear might actually be better at my job than I am."

I turn to "Diana," or whatever the hell she's calling herself these days.

A high-pitched-kettle scream fills my head.

"Cassandra." She glances at Will, then back at me, looking very nearly as disoriented as I feel. "I didn't realize that you and…" She hesitates. "We actually know each other already. From a long time ago."

"No way!" Will laughs and eats another quiche. "Small world! How?"

She looks at me. "We lived together, didn't we, Cass."

Her cheeks are pink and she's cautious and fine-boned, but her gray eyes are bright like twenty-pence coins and she looks very bloody pleased with herself for having finally hunted me down.

"Flatmates?" Will continues to chew, apparently oblivious to the prickly red rash spreading up my neck and across my chest. "In Walthamstow? That was your last flat before your current one, wasn't it, Cassie?"

I open my mouth and promptly shut it again.

"No, that definitely wasn't me. I'm not a Londoner." She laughs. "I was her first ever flat-share, as it happens." She is watching my face carefully, poised slightly on the balls of her ballet-pumped feet. "It's really good to finally see you again, Cass. How are you?"

I'm about to say *roughly the same as I was when I saw you a few days ago, you total psycho*, and then suddenly remember that she didn't see me, because I never went home. For me, it's been three days: for her, it's still been years.

Will's watching my face, so I carefully unstick my tongue.

"Fine," I reply curtly. "How are you?"

"Oh, you know." She grins. "Same old. Still making a mess. Still chaos incarnate. Although we both seem to be all over the place, because your address seems to be constantly shifting too. I guess neither of us are exactly easy to live with. Where is it you're based now?"

The absolute audacity of this woman.

"You know exactly where I live," I huff. She has successfully goaded me into non-scripted speech. "And I am *very* easy to live with, thank you. Most people barely even notice I'm there at all."

Her nostrils flare. That is not what I bloody meant.

"There was a little bit of *drama* last time we saw each other," she tells Will faux confidentially. "It was definitely my fault, but Cass is proving extraordinarily difficult to apologize to. I've tried, like—what?" She glances at me. "Fifteen times, now? She's having none of it. Let's just say we don't have very well matched cohabitation styles. I'm somewhat on the careless side, while Cassandra tends to like things neater and more organized than my personal preferences."

"*Somewhat on the careless side* is like saying Alpha Centauri is a bit of a pain to get to." I scratch at my arm with my fingernails; my leg is bouncing again. "You never once cleaned up after yourself. Not once. Literally. Not a single time."

"We had cleaners." She shrugs with laughing eyes.

"They weren't *cleaners*," I snap, then consciously lower my voice. ("Cassandra has a problem with volume control.") "I once found seven empty cans of beans, stored under your bed. By what logic? You'd have to literally eat out of a can with a fork and then get down on the floor and *place* it there intentionally, *seven times*."

"Not so." She shakes her head. "Sometimes you put it on the floor so it doesn't get on the bedding and eventually it just kind of *rolls* there and they collect."

I make an exasperated mewl. "There was a *cigarette butt* in one of them."

"There was not."

"There was! I saw it!"

She grins. "They weren't cigarettes, Sandy-pants."

I glare at her and her eyes sparkle at me, and Will clears his throat next to us; we both look at him with a faint air of surprise, having forgotten he's there. He's watching me a lot more closely. Now the quiches are gone, he's paying a bit more attention to his date.

"So…" He lifts his eyebrows. "A bit of a falling-out, I'm guessing?"

"You could say that," I confirm sharply. "Yes."

"I *wish*," she says, grimacing and running a hand through her short brown fringe. "For a *falling-out* there needs to be a fight, an argument, some kind of reckoning, and there wasn't one. Cass just legged it. Moved out the same day. The same *hour*. I've been trying to have it out with her ever since and she won't let me."

"Because I made it very clear I never want to see you again," I agree at the top of my voice, violence in my fingertips. "Yet here you are."

She visibly flinches, the exhibition goes quiet, and Will looks at me with that horrified Lamia expression again: the one I tried so hard to make go away. And I want to stop myself—I do. I just don't know how to. I'm like a train hurtling off the right track into a wall while everyone inside jumps out of the window.

Will frowns. "Cassie, why don't we—"

"Did you follow me?" I ignore the surprised tangerine color coming out of him and whip toward her again. "Is that what happened? I want the truth. Did you hunt me down and *stalk* me all the way here?"

When, though? Was she on the train behind me? In a different carriage? I was waiting outside for quite a while, but I did have my head buried in my phone. Maybe she somehow slipped in just ahead while I was googling *Interesting and Relevant Things to Say at a Photography Exhibition*.

"Yes," she admits reluctantly. "But before you get too mad—"

"Way too late for *mad*," I hiss. "*Mad* was three minutes ago. I'm moving rapidly through extremely irate and approaching incandescent."

She smiles, then tries to bite the smile with her teeth.

"Shit." An apologetic yet simultaneously flirty expression is aimed at Will. "This is so rude of us, fighting like this in front of you."

"We're not fighting," I clarify heatedly. "You don't get to fight with me."

"Yes, I've gathered that." She sighs and returns to Will. "I'm so sorry… What's your name, anyway? Who exactly are you?"

Will blinks. "Oh. I'm Will. I'm Cassie's…"

He never finishes the sentence, but I think his silence might be the loudest thing any of us has said so far.

I feel something inside me crumple into a sad, tired ball.

"Well." She glances at me with massive eyes. Why are her eyes that big? Nobody needs eyes that big. We're not owls. "Then I'm sure you know this already, Will, but Cass can be a little… black-and-white. It's just the way she is. Right or wrong, good or bad. Love or hate. She has this remarkable ability to classify and separate the world and everything and everyone in it. She's the Queen of Compartmentalization. Everything in tidy little Tupperware boxes, lined up straight, filed perfectly away in her brain with little laminated labels. That includes people."

I open my mouth to debate this, then shut it again.

Of *course* I compartmentalize. Of *course* I file memories and people and emotions away as neatly as possible. Emotions are confusing, people even more so, and I remember everything that has ever happened to me, in elaborate detail. If I *didn't* have an effective storage system, I'd go completely mad.

I also cannot believe she's using Will as a shield to have this conversation with me, just because I wouldn't have it with her by post.

"And if you screw up," she continues, her cheeks getting even rosier, "just *once*—just *a single time*—you're dead to her. It's over. Forever. There is no room for basic human error in the world of Cassandra Penelope Dankworth."

Why can't you just be normal.

My stomach hurts. It's one thing to follow me to a photography exhibition, and quite another to make wildly negative accusations about my character to the one man on earth who might be about to fall in love with me.

Even if they're 100 percent accurate.

"Pomegranates," I say suddenly, finally making the connection of why she's picked that specific scent. "Fruit of the dead. Hilarious."

"What can I say?" She grins. "I'm a creature of nuance and subtlety."

"No, you're not."

"Am."

"Subtle like a spear through the face."

"If it's sharp enough, I reckon you could barely see it from a distance." She laughs. "It's nice to meet you, Will. You seem lovely. Handsome, but not *too* handsome. Just the right amount of handsome. Enough to be secure but not enough to be a prick. And you're nice and relaxed too, which is good to see. I'm very glad that Cass has found someone who can balance her out."

She holds her hand out to Will; he takes it, and I stare at their hands.

Something bright pink flickers.

"Hi, Diana," he says, looking like he wishes he was in another room, in another building, on another planet. "In Cassie's defense, that doesn't seem a fair character analysis. I'm not sure when you last saw her, but she's been really cool and laid-back in the short time I've known her."

"Really?" She looks at me. "I guess time really does change everything."

That does it. Ugliness flares out of me with a *whoosh*.

"Her name isn't even Diana," I spit, losing all control now. "She's a liar."

I rotate back to her, lines of pure, hissing rage shooting out of my head like Medusa's snakes. If I wanted Will to know that I try to control *every single inch of my life and everything and every-*

one in it, I probably wouldn't have spent quite so much effort and literal time ensuring he didn't.

"And I might live in black and white," I say in a choked voice, "but *you* live in the gray area. No right, no wrong. No fact, no fiction. No good, no bad. No lies, no truth, no *consequences*. It's all just one big blurry mess to you, isn't it, where nothing means anything and you can do and say whatever you want, regardless of what it does to the people around you."

"Hey, I was just winding you up," she says in a small voice, reaching a hand out toward mine. "I'm really sorry. Old habit."

"Don't touch me," I say, whipping away.

"And I'm not *lying*," she objects desperately. "I could have been called Diana, couldn't I? It's not *that* different. It would have taken just the tiniest tweak. Just a nudge, somewhere in the past, and boom—a different story. So I'm not a *liar*. Sometimes I just enjoy living in all the narratives that never got a chance to happen."

"That's *the definition of pathological lying*," I hiss.

"Oh." She frowns, thinks about it. "Then, yeah. I might have a problem."

We stare at each other, breathing hard.

"Sam!" Will's cry of relief is so tangible it turns the air green. "Buddy! There you are! Where the *hell* have you been?"

With a quick, dutiful kiss on my cheek, he shoots away from us like a paintball and everything inside me abruptly hurts. She's done it again. She's ruined everything. This is exactly why I tried so hard to keep her away from me: I do not like who I become around her.

No, that's a lie.

I don't like being reminded of who I really am.

"Just stop," I say as my eyes fill. "Please."

I'm going to have to undo all of this, aren't I. Erase it from existence. I'm not sure when you're allowed to start shouting and swearing at a strange woman in the middle of an art exhibition, but I'm going to assume it's somewhere after date four; probably never.

"I'm sorry," she says in a tiny voice. "This has all gone wrong, Cassandra. I just wanted to run into you here, like it was a big old accident, catch you off guard, and then I got all preoccupied with showing off, trying to be funny, and I've gone ahead and screwed it all up again. Please can we just start again? I am so, so sorry. Truly. For literally everything."

Her gray eyes are so earnest and I can feel myself soften, begin to relent, and then—with a *crack*—one of my Tupperware boxes starts to leak again and I hear it as if it's still happening.

You're a monster you're a monster you're a monster you're a—

Something slams shut inside me.

Not because I don't believe that she's sorry—there have been enough letters over the years to understand that she is—but because, much like a curse from the gods, turning people into frogs and beetles and flowers and trees and then immediately regretting it, it doesn't really matter.

At some point, what is done cannot be undone.

But I know one thing that can.

"Sounds lovely." Sophie beams. "You can tell me all about it tomorrow!"

"Sure," I say distractedly, typing:

So sorry, can't make it—stuck at the office.

I press SEND, but all I'm thinking about is Greek Penelope.

Just like my other mythological namesake, it's starting to feel like every day I weave a complex tapestry, and every night—terrified of the consequences, of what will happen when I'm done—I simply unpick it again.

And nothing gets made at all.

26

THIS TIME, I GO straight home.

I return to the safety of my bedroom and throw myself into a loop of my own making: read a book I've already read, watch a TV show I've seen dozens of times, wear my Wednesday pajamas and eat my Wednesday dinner. I listen to a favorite song on repeat, dozens of times; bury myself in familiarity like a small, hurt animal in its den, turning in tiny circles until it can comfortably settle. I make the same small sounds to myself, over and over again. I curl up in a ball on my bed, rocking gently, losing myself in the comfort of a pattern.

I soothe myself with repetition until I feel calm.

Until I can finally fall asleep.

A bright blue light flash; a fraction later, the knock on the door like the thunder after the lightning.

"Mnnnnuh?" Disoriented, I sit up. "Will?"

Where am I this time? There's another knock, louder this time. Panicking, I try to process my environment: window outline, position of the door, the smell of my duvet, shape of my shelves. Relief settles gently like my old floating duvet: I'm at home.

A third knock outside my bedroom, and I now suspect it's not Will after all. Having woken up a little more, it seems unlikely that he left the exhibition and crossed London just to break into my house. Groggy and still confused, I turn the lamp on, grab my yellow dressing gown and unlock the door.

"Hey." Derek leans against the frame. "Were you asleep?"

Blinking, I glance at my wrist before realizing I took my watch off and put it on my bedside table as I do every night.

"What time is it?" I manage.

"Dunno. Midnight? Just after? The pub's kicked us out. Sal decided to go on with her mates, but I didn't feel up to it. Can I come in?"

Before I can say absolutely not, Derek slides past me.

Trying desperately to wake up properly now, I pull my dressing gown tight and warily watch my flatmate walk slowly around my bedroom like he's Dorothy in bloody Oz. He scans all my color-arranged clothes, walks over to my shelf and studies it, picks up my little gold peacock, turns it over and puts it back in totally the wrong place. What the hell is happening? I'm scanning my memories for this scene the first time round, but it isn't there. Although I worked so late in the original timeline, maybe I just slept through his incessant knocking.

Derek picks up my little silver deer figurine and hiccups, and oh my God, I've just realized: Is he drunk?

"Can you stop touching my stuff, please," I say sharply.

He puts the deer back in the wrong place and I wait until he's moved away before scurrying forward and pointedly moving it back again. I'm going to have to wash it with soap: it's got grubby, inebriated-Derek fingerprints all over it now.

"You've really made this space your own," he says, continuing to perambulate with a now noticeable wobble. "I've not been in here since you moved in. Which was...how long ago now? Five weeks?"

"Nine weeks," I say guardedly. "And two days."

"And two days." He flicks me a strange look and grins, then goes back to perusing my belongings as if this is a small station shop and he's got time before he catches his train. "It feels like you've only just moved in, Cassandra Wankworth."

My eyes widen. "*Dankworth*."

"That's what I meant. How are you finding it here?"

"Fine."

I feel invaded. Sullied. Like I need a six-hour hot shower and a power hose for my bedroom. There's something icky and khaki coming out of him in short, slimy waves: a really ugly color, but I have no idea what it means. I just know I want it out of my bedroom *right now* before it coats everything.

"Cool." Derek goes to my bookcase and begins scanning the contents with his fingers before pulling out a particularly brilliant story about Pandora. "Can I borrow this?"

"No. What are you doing in here, Derek?"

"Oh." He puts the book back in the wrong place and perches on the end of my bed; I have to stifle a roar. My bedding will need to be thrown out, possibly burned. "Sal is a bit worried about you. We don't really know much about you yet, you really keep yourself to yourself, so she asked me to check on you. See if you were okay."

I relax slightly. "She did? Really? That's so nice."

"Yeah. You're somewhat of an enigma, Cassandra." He looks around my room again. Burps. Teeth gritted, I immediately cross the room and open the window. "You're a bit of a mystery. It's hard to know what you're thinking. Your face never really moves, does it? And your voice is kind of flat. Like a robot. Hey." He picks up the paint chart next to my bed. "You can't paint in here. Sal's dad won't let us redecorate."

"I'm not painting," I say tightly.

"You're not painting?" Derek stares at it. "So…you've just got it here as, like, bedtime reading? Is that why there's one next to the bath, too?" He peers at me for a few seconds, then laughs. "You're a strange duck, Dankworth, that's for sure. Like, are you stunted in some way? Is something in here missing?" He taps his head. "Not being rude, but this doesn't look like the room of an adult woman."

I flush hot. "How is that not fucking rude?"

"Hey, don't get all prickly." He holds his hands out and drunkenly studies his own fingers for a few seconds, fascinated, then returns his focus to me. "I'm just trying to figure you out. I'm curious, that's all." Another hiccup. "You're kind of childish, but also a granny, with your frozen meals and your mad outfits and your cuddly toy and your dressing gown and your figurines and your hedgehog bowl. Don't think I didn't see the hedgehog bowl, Cassandra. What's that all about?"

I like to see his little friendly face when I eat breakfast—it cheers me up—but I do not think telling Derek this now is going to help my cause.

"It's just a bowl," I reply tersely.

"But you're hot too." He considers my face. "Very pretty. Rocking bod under all that fluff. I bet you're a bit of a surprise in the old bedroom department, actually. Efficient. Hardworking. Everything ticked off. Blow job—tick! Hand job—tick! Orgasm—tick tick tick! Marks out of ten, gold star, smiley-sticker sex."

My mouth drops open in shock.

Somehow, this is even worse than it was the first time round. Why does the universe keep trying to make me move? Why can't it just let me have a home? All I need is a room without a drunk man in it, waking me up at midnight to talk about my sexual prowess and crockery. Is it really too much to ask?

"Hey." He chuckles lightly as I attempt to pull the fluff of my dressing gown into the cells of my body. "I'm just joking,

Dankworth. Banter, you know? You don't need to look *quite* so appalled. I'm not a *predator* or anything. I'm just playing around."

A small wave of déjà vu, as if I'm on a boat.

"I'm very tired," I attempt, trying my best to stay friendly. "Can we have whatever this conversation is in the morning?"

"Do I make you nervous, Cassie?" Derek smiles at me.

"Yes," I admit this time.

"I don't mean to, you know. I just want you to be comfortable here, Cassandra. My *casa* is your *casa*, after all. Or, I should say, your *Casa*-ndra. Ha ha."

Oh, look, he obnoxiously extended it. I look desperately for an escape route, but there isn't one because this bedroom is supposed to be it.

"So, are you dating someone?" Derek reaches toward me and picks a ball of lint off my dressing gown; I flinch and jump away. "Do I know him? He's a lucky guy, whoever he is. You're quite the catch, if I do say so, Cassandra Dankworth."

My tongue finally unsticks.

"Leave," I say, holding the door open. "Now."

"Whoa." Derek blinks. "That's a bit rude. Why are you freaking out? I was just being friendly. You're reading it all wrong, taking it the wrong way. I didn't mean anything weird by it or anything."

I hesitate, studying him carefully. His colors and his words and his face don't match, and it's incredibly confusing. Last time he said I was *reading it all wrong, taking it the wrong way*, and I do it so often—destroy so many relationships, romantic and otherwise—that I believed him. I'm still not sure, it's all very confusing, but the inconsistency is suddenly making me doubt both of us.

"Sorry," I say uncertainly. "It's just… I'm tired, Derek. It's been a long evening. I really need to go back to bed."

"No worries." He looks at my bed, then stands up and sways slightly. "Look. Cards on the table. I know you have a bit of a crush on me, Cassie. It's really obvious. You can't meet my eyes, you talk nonsense when I'm around, go red constantly, scurry out of a room if I'm in it. It's really cute. Nothing to be embarrassed about. If I wasn't with Sal, then… Well, who knows?" He smiles, sadly. "But I *am* with Sal. I love Sal. That's the thing. It's a no-go between us. I came here tonight to tell you that."

Is that a thing people do? Come into other people's rooms at midnight to finger their belongings and declare love for someone else? It doesn't seem very logical, but people aren't very logical, so how the hell am I supposed to know?

"I can't meet anyone's eyes," I point out. "It doesn't *mean* anything."

"But you're looking at me now," Derek points out triumphantly, as if he's caught me out in a lie. "So that's clearly not true."

"Because now all I can feel is shock."

Hope blossoms abruptly. This might be my chance to set the narrative back on the right path. I just have to take it slowly, carefully: step through the crackling undergrowth one cautious foot at a time like a tiny animal evading a hungry tiger.

With all the energy I have left, I make unblinking eyeball contact.

"I am so sorry that I have given you the wrong impression," I say as clearly and as loudly as I can. "But there has been a bit of a miscommunication. I do not fancy you, Derek. I do not find you physically, mentally or emotionally attractive. If anything, you repulse me. Sexually, but also on a much deeper, more spiritual level. Even if Sal wasn't so nice, even if I didn't live with you both, I would never want to be involved with you in any way. Ever. Even with all the infinite chances that time might give me."

It's not very "friendly," admittedly, but it should at least clear the situation up. *A Bit of a Miscommunication* should be the title for my autobiography.

"Gotcha." Derek winks. "Loud and clear."

I stare at him. "Why did you just wink?"

"No reason." He grins at me. "I hear you. That's all I'm saying."

"It doesn't feel like you do hear me." I hesitate, frowning. "That wink feels like it's communicating something else entirely."

"Nope." Derek stretches. "You don't fancy me. I don't fancy you. We're on exactly the same page, Cassie. So we're all good."

He finally ambles out of my bedroom, then leans drunkenly on the door frame.

We stare at each other.

Derek is still grinning and it's nice that he's taken the rejection so well, but I can't help feeling that it's because he hasn't taken it at all. I'm not sure I can tell him he repulses me again, though: twice would feel a bit cruel.

"I looked you up," Derek says, apropos of nothing. "Did you know that Dankworth is one of the rarest surnames in the country? There's articles about it and everything. Dankworths are on the brink of extinction, apparently."

He's studying my face, inordinately pleased with himself.

"Yes," I say cautiously. "I know."

"And you are *surprisingly* absent online, Cassandra," he continues. "Like, nowhere to be found. No social media accounts. No online profiles. You work in public relations, yet you do not appear to exist on the internet. Which seems strange. As if you're hiding something. Or from *someone*."

I wait, then lose my patience. "Get to the point."

"I met the hot girl who came here the other day, looking for you," Derek concludes with yet *another* wink. "Very pretty. Supercute. So if you're a secret lesbian, Cassandra, that's something I could *totally* support. You know? Like, *really* get behind. If you catch my drift."

I have suddenly never been this tired.

Ever.

It would be so easy: to rewind time, hear the knock, not answer the door. But I suddenly don't want to. I'm getting sick of traveling through time. All it seems to do is carry me to places I don't want to be.

"Wrong conclusion," I say in exhaustion. "It's perfectly possible to fancy men and still not fancy you, Derek."

And I shut the door in his face.

27

EXCEPT—SOMETHING HAS GONE WRONG.

I'm not sure where it is or what has caused it, but I feel it the moment I wake up the next morning like a puncture in a bike tire. Just a tiny hole in time, yet somehow it's just enough to let all the air out and send everything wobbling in a completely different direction.

At first I think it's Derek, but when I bump into him in the hallway on the way to work, he eyes me sweatily over a glass of water and says: "Did we tête-à-tête last night, Cassie? It feels like maybe we talked, but I can't for the life of me—"

He ends the sentence by running to the bathroom and vomiting with the door open, so it's probably not him.

Then I worry that it's Sal—that somehow Derek may have said something to her when she got back last night—but she's in the kitchen, humming and fiddling with some pastry, and when I walk in she brightens.

"Morning! I am making croissants." She eyes them dubiously, unsure of this statement. "By *making*, I mean defrosting and twiddling them around, but I still feel quite French and sophisticated nonetheless. Would you like one, Cassie?"

So I'm guessing it's not her either.

I politely decline—it's a sweet offer but that's a lot of handling—and somehow make it to work, still trying to feel the shape of the day with my fingers. What is letting all the air out? But as the day careers forward, it doesn't seem to be Barry, or Sophie, or Anya, Miyuki or Anton. It's not Jack or Gareth or the SharkSkin campaign, which is taking an almost bewilderingly better direction.

And I'm not sure how I know it isn't them—given that the original timeline is rapidly becoming fainter, like a rubbed-out pencil line on a piece of paper—but I can feel it, in my gut: they're not the perforations I'm looking for.

At eleven thirty on the dot, I text Will:

Hey! So sorry about last night.
How was the exhibition?
I wish I could have made it! Cxx

It's the same text I sent the first time round, at exactly the same time.

Will doesn't reply.

I fake-phone a few more journalists and send some more copy-and-paste emails; Barry comments on the predictability of my pink Thursday jumpsuit, yet there's still no response from Will.

It's silence so solid I can squeeze it with my fingers.

And as the day hurtles toward an end, I can feel everything flattening, becoming unstable, as if time has leaked out. What has changed? I didn't go to the exhibition originally, right? I sent precisely the same text the next day. Will replied with No worries! It was great, you were missed! Dinner tomorrow night? xx

Except this time he doesn't, and the *only* difference I can find is that in the original timeline, Will and I hadn't had sex yet. For a brief moment, I worry that this is the difference and this is exactly why you're supposed to listen to the laws of the internet; then I remember it's Will and I'm being ridiculous.

He's a decent man; I do not think I have repelled him with my vagina.

But I still don't know how to fix it, or what to do to make it all return to its proper pattern, so while I'm walking home, I break yet another internet rule and double-text out of sheer desperation:

Everything OK? X

By the time my phone beeps at 10:00 p.m., I know.

Will is the hole, the puncture, the piece of glass. Something I have done has perforated us like a broken bottle.

All good! Shame you missed it!

Chewing my fingers, I stare at my phone.

No kiss. No missing me. No mention of dinner tomorrow night.

So what do I do now? I can't really *undo* anything just yet, because I'm not sure exactly where the mistake was made in the first place. What point would I aim for? Our first date? Second date? Yesterday? I can't do anything differently yesterday, because it'll land me in the same predicament again. If I go back to the beginning and start again, everything else I've done will be simultaneously unwound. My life might get even worse. I may get stuck. I may get chucked out of time and find myself unable to get back on, like a hamster from a spinning wheel.

Also, I just don't know if I have the energy to start this all over again.

Call me lazy, but time travel is absolutely exhausting.

Instead, I try to fix the situation with Will like a regular, chronologically inhibited human:

Next time, I hope! How about lunch
tomorrow? X

There's a long pause.

Far too long, frankly: Will obviously had his phone directly
in his hand thirty seconds ago.

Wish I could! But work right now is mad.
:(

I've long had the suspicion that being "too busy" means
people are just too busy for *you*, specifically, but this is the first
time I've ever had hard evidence.

Things were going so well. Which means that there's a point
where things broke between us again, and I just need to work
out *exactly what and when it was* so I can go back and fix it.

Unless...

("Cassandra tends to overthink everything.")

Unless I'm just *reading things wrong* again.

("Cassandra can be neurotic and obsessive.")

Unless I'm taking all the clues and piecing them together in-
correctly, like a jigsaw rammed together by an impatient child:
a nose where an eye should be, a tail on a forehead, a table in
the sky. It doesn't make sense because it's not supposed to. I'm
forcing a connection where there shouldn't be one; building a
picture that isn't on the front of the box, and then wondering
why it doesn't look right.

Not everyone is like me: that much is painfully clear.

Not everyone places this much emphasis on a four-month
relationship, or has no idea how to make a relationship go further than that. Not everyone hits thirty-one years old and has
zero serious romantic experience. Not everyone finds love confusing and surreal: mythical and unreachable, like a story told
a long time ago about other people.

Not everyone obsesses, analyzes, struggles to let go and move on.

Not everyone holds on to every single social interaction with their fingertips in terror, as if dangling off a cliff edge.

Maybe Will *is* just busy. He is a real adult with a real, grown-up life—with friends and a family and a job and hobbies and a part-time dog, apparently—whereas I am simply masquerading as one, like one of those spiders who holds its legs up so it looks like an ant and hopes nobody will notice.

There's a noise—a squeak outside my bedroom, like a mouse opening a door—so I instinctively freeze, phone held in the air.

When it doesn't happen again, I go back to scrambling:

What are you working on? Competing with another
polar bear? ;) x

A *beep*:

Ha, how did you know about the polar bear?!

Fuck.

You mentioned it at the pub! How about dinner on
Friday? x

Now I'm gaslighting the poor bastard on top of everything else and I'm a horrible, selfish person who deserves nothing but *Ha* texts and solo microwaved chili for the rest of my solitary life.

There's another squeak outside, and I stiffen.

Beep.

OK! That sounds good! Shall I come to you?
Brixton, right? x

And there we have it: I am a neurotic mess. I guess this is what happens when you live with a brain that treats every second of existence as if there's been an urgent crime that needs to be solved immediately.

Relaxing considerably, I type:

Yes! Brixton! Friday! Can't wait! x

Then I cautiously climb out of bed. Time to face the squeaking. If that noise is a lurking and drunk Derek again, I swear to God I will do things with my golden peacock that Hera would be appalled at.

"Hello?" I grab my dressing gown and open my door. "What do you—"

The hallway is empty.

With a growing sense of trepidation, I venture nervously into the corridor and pause with my head cocked like a spaniel. The squeak happens again, three times now, so I quietly trace it to Derek and Sal's bedroom on the other side of the house and promptly decide to leave it alone: it's almost definitely a weird sex thing, no need for further action.

I'm just creeping away when it happens again and I abruptly recognize it as crying. Now I can feel a dark blue-gray seeping out from under the door. And I'm ashamed to say my immediate reaction is no, thank you. No to crying. No to other people's strong emotions. They're too sticky, too dense. They fill me with too many colors until it feels like I'm drowning and I can't sense any of my own.

But the crying gets louder and something tugs through the middle of me: I step back and knock on the door.

"Hello? Sal? And-stroke-or Derek? Are you okay?"

There's a short silence—please don't be Derek, please don't be Derek, please don't be—and Sal opens the door, beautiful but puffy-eyed. "Did I wake you up?" She sniffs and gets back into an otherwise empty bed. "Sorry. I'll try to be quote, unquote 'worryingly unstable' with a little bit less volume next time."

Hesitating in the doorway, I attempt to work out the socially correct next move. I'm guessing society dictates that this is the point where I'm supposed to see her pain, sweep forward, wrap my arms around her and tell her everything is going to be okay, but I don't think I can physically do it.

("Cassandra lacks empathy.")

"You're sad," I guess tentatively.

"I am sad," Sal laughs with a liquidy snort into her wrist. "A bit. But mostly I'm furious and I'm going to have to do something with it. I've lined up things that aren't mine to break, just in case."

Sal points at a selection of aftershaves, electronic equipment and a bewildering quantity of hair products, all of which are clearly Derek's. I feel a little jealous. It must be lovely to know exactly how you feel at any given moment.

"Is this about Derek?" I venture in a step. "Are you…fighting?"

"Come in properly, Cassie." Sal taps the bed next to her. "Don't just hover in the doorway." Then her face crumples and she starts crying again. "Are we fighting? I don't even know. *I'm* certainly fighting. I don't know if he is. Derek just seems to think I'm constantly overreacting, and I worry he's right."

I hesitate, starting to feel incredibly anxious.

This is perilously close to what happened the first time round. They started arguing a lot, and when I finally accused Derek of hitting on me, he denied it, and somehow—I'm still uncertain how—the entire situation became my fault. One wrong move and it's going to blow up again. I just don't know what the *right* move is, because I still can't read the situation. What is going on? *Is* Derek hitting on me? Is he flirting, or being friendly? Is it inappropriate or am I overreacting? Are my social skills lacking again, or are his? How can I tell? And what would I even say to Salini? Your boyfriend has categorically told me he's not interested in me because he loves you? I'm no lawyer, but that doesn't seem like solid evidence against him.

Sal is still crying and I don't know what to do to make her feel better, but I desperately want to at least try.

I tentatively put a rigid finger on her shoulder.

"I'm thirty this year," Sal offers without prompting. "I'm nearly *thirty*, Cassie, and I live in a house my dad pays for, with no career and a boyfriend who keeps reluctantly telling me he's in it for 'the long haul' as if our life together is a battered cross-country lorry. I can't cook. I can't massage. I was thinking of maybe starting up a YouTube channel, but—"

"Don't," I say quickly, thinking of the lipstick video. "Bad idea."

"You're right, obviously." She starts crying again. "What the fuck is wrong with me? Honestly, I thought I'd know what I was doing with my life by my thirties, but I don't have a single clue. I don't know what I want. I don't know what I don't want. I don't know what's supposed to make me happy. In the meantime, the rest of the world seems to be just getting on with it. I look online and everyone I've ever met is having babies and getting engaged and getting promoted and buying a new kitchen. It feels like literally everyone I know is moving forward."

"I'm not," I offer helpfully. "I'm just going round and round."

She laughs. "It feels like that sometimes, right?"

"Yes." I nod emphatically. "It does."

"Maybe I should stop taking my existential crisis out on my poor boyfriend." Sal runs a hand through her waves and they inexplicably bounce perfectly back into place again. "That's what Derek says I'm doing, and he's probably right. I'm unhappy with my life generally, so I'm taking it out on him. I feel *crazy*. As if I can't work out what's real and what isn't real anymore. Derek can't do anything right. I accuse him of messaging other girls, and then it turns out she's his cousin or whatever. We go to a restaurant, and I accuse him of giving the twenty-year-old waitress his phone number, but he's just written down a recommendation for a wine they don't have on their menu. What the hell is wrong with me? He's right. I think I'm losing my bloody mind."

Sal looks at me with enormous, wet-lashed eyes, and I can feel her sadness, her fear, her embarrassment, her shame, all mixed up; I can feel her sense of self wobbling. And I don't want it to. With a sudden wave of conviction, I realize just how much I like her and have since the first day I moved in.

"You're not losing your mind," I say quietly.

Sal frowns. "I'm not?"

"Salini. Listen." I take a deep breath and plunge. "In thirteen days, I am going to tell you that Derek is hitting on me. He's going to deny it *so* emphatically, I apologize for reading the situation wrong. He is then going to accuse me of having a crush on *him* and hitting on *him*—in fact, he's going to say I'm making the living situation really uncomfortable for him—and I will get super confused at all the emotions and think maybe he's right and apologize for that too."

Sal frowns. "What?"

"And you'll get understandably upset about the situation and suggest that I find somewhere else to live."

"I..." Sal rubs her tired face. "What do you mean, *in thirteen days?*"

"It hasn't happened yet," I admit, realizing my finger is still perched on her shoulder and promptly removing it. "It's a... prophecy, I guess."

Sal studies my face carefully. "A prophecy? That my boyfriend is hitting on you? That my boyfriend is *going* to hit on you? In the future? I'm so confused. Has he hit on you or has he not?"

"I don't know," I admit. "I wanted to warn you, just in case."

Slowly, Sal leans away from me on the bed as if she needs to see me from a distance. "This is really weird, Cassandra. And hurtful. Derek has been saying you're a bit odd since you moved in and I've been defending you, but this is not really helping. So let me get this straight. Are you saying you can see the future?"

"No," I admit. "I can't see the future. Not properly. I hoped I'd be able to. I think that was the appeal of time travel, to see things coming. So I could prepare. But it's not working out the way I thought it would. Every time I go back, something changes. So, no, I can't see the future. I can just guess at it, based on what I've already experienced. I'm not a prophet, and I suppose that makes me the worst Cassandra ever."

I obviously mean Cassandra the Trojan priestess—not myself in the third person—but Sal doesn't give me time to explain.

She moves farther away. "Are you saying you're a *time traveler* now?"

I've read a few books about time travel now and they never really cover how to drop it into polite conversation.

"Yes." I nod. "Just kind of a…beta one. With minor powers."

Sal's eyes open wide and I obviously never expected her to believe me: if I've learned anything from Cassandra's original curse, it's that nobody ever will. But I needed to try anyway. Just once. Just so I don't feel quite so alone.

"Bloody hell," Sal says as I close my eyes. "And this is *exactly* why you don't find new flatmates on Gumtr—"

"What the hell is wrong with me?" Sal is staring at me again, soggy and shining. "He's right. I think I'm losing my bloody mind."

Clearly now is not the time to suspend her powers of disbelief further, though it was incredibly cathartic to get that all off my chest.

"You're not losing your mind," I say quietly.

Sal blinks. "I'm not?"

"No." I think about how to say this for a few seconds. "Trust your gut. Or…your kidneys, your earlobes, your ankles, wherever it is in you that feels the truth. There's a sensation, a kind of...solidness. A safe place. Somehow, it knows. If something feels off with Derek, then it probably is."

Frowning, Sal puts a hand on her stomach, then slowly pulls it upward and puts two fingers on the base of her throat.

"It's here," she says finally. "The sensation. It's here."

"Mine's in my shoulder blades and in the top of my spine." I smile faintly. "Also at the bottom of my stomach, but that could also be undigested veggie chili. Honestly, I'm terrible at listening to it too. I get caught up with trying to read all the music around me instead of one note inside myself."

We sit in companionable silence for a few minutes: Sal, with her hand on her throat, and me with my hand on the back of my neck.

"Thank you, Cassie," she says finally. "I feel a lot calmer."

"Me too," I say, standing up. I think that's quite enough emotional intimacy for one evening—no need to go overboard. "It's late. I should go."

We smile in embarrassment at each other, but somehow both our colors have shifted, as if we've run into each other like paints.

"You know," I add suddenly, pausing in the doorway with a wide yawn I'm too tired to cover with my hand. "Maybe we're both stuck for a reason, Sal. Maybe we're not supposed to move on until we know what it is."

"Maybe." Sal yawns too. "Night, Cassie."

"Night," I say.

And I take myself back to bed.

28

THE TRUTH ALWAYS HAS CONSEQUENCES.

My conversation with Sal stays with me the whole next day at work, drifting gently at the back of my head like a cobweb. It reminds me a little of Arachne, the talented Greek weaver who was challenged by a jealous Athena to a weaving competition. As Arachne wove her stories in silk, instead of telling the approved tales she was supposed to tell, she told the truth: of gods who abused mortals, tricked and assaulted women, punished us for their own misdemeanors and egocentricities.

When Athena saw what Arachne had woven—beautifully, accurately, honestly—she ripped the work to shreds in a fit of fury. After a distraught Arachne tragically hanged herself, Athena relented and turned her into a spider so she would spend forever weaving at the end of a rope.

The full truth is not easy or comfortable; it is often far safer to construct an alternative that keeps everyone happy instead. Especially when it's the story we're weaving for ourselves.

★ ★ ★

By Friday evening, I know I'm waiting for the end.

Will and I have been quiet and busy all day: him with editing animals, and me with trying to give the credit for the SharkSkin campaign to Sophie. She's convinced the entire thing was my idea, which is both frustrating and my own fault for forgetting to let her come up with it on this timeline. I've resorted to scribbling thoughts in her notepads while she's out at lunch and trying to convince her I stole them: a human notepad, carrying her plans from one reality to another.

Frowning, I glance again at my watch.

I'm waiting outside Brixton tube and Will is now—I quickly calculate—sixteen and a half minutes late. I feel a sudden glistening thread of truth, like finely woven silver silk: that this is not something I can live with for the rest of my life. That I'm not sure a constantly late person and a person highly distressed by any form of lateness are necessarily a perfect love match.

There's a tap on my shoulder and I jump half a foot in the air.

"Shit. Hi. Sorry. Didn't mean to scare you."

I whip round and soften: Will's face brings so much happiness with it, even if it's quarter of an hour after it was supposed to arrive.

"I'm so sorry," he says, softly kissing my cheek. "I couldn't find a cab, so I got a train and the platform was rammed. Have you been waiting long?"

"Yes." I smile faintly. "But don't worry about it too much."

Will strides down the pavement with his unbuttoned coat flaring slightly and I watch it with a faint pang. I'm trying to identify any colors coming out of him, but again there's nothing. Honestly, I wonder if there's a way of finding out how another human is really feeling. You'd think as a species we would have been clever enough to come up with something by now, but apparently not.

"How are you?" I ask, scurrying slightly to catch up.

"I'm good," Will says a little too quickly. "You?"

"Good," I echo in frustration: See what I mean? Useless. "Everything okay?"

Everything is not okay and I can feel it on the back of my neck like a cold, flat palm. He's moving extremely fast, for starters: I'm practically jogging now, but I still can't quite reach his hand to hold it. I've tried at least three times and it remains just out of my reach.

"I'm just ridiculously hungry," Will says, slowing down. "Sorry."

I finally manage to grab his hand; he squeezes mine, but it feels a little too hard and a little too quick, like a pat on the head.

"I'm hungry too," I admit with another flicker of impending doom. "Where are we going?"

"Huh?" Will doesn't look at me. "I thought we were trying out one of those cool new pop-up restaurants?"

"What?" I abruptly stop walking. *"Why?"*

"Oh." He stops walking, frowns. "I thought I texted you about it this morning, Cassie. Shit. I'm so sorry. Again. This week has been…confusing. You're vegetarian, aren't you? It's a new place a three-minute walk away from you, so I thought it might be fun to try it out." He smiles broadly. "A unique culinary experience."

Something cold flickers across my stomach.

"Okay. It's just…" I frown. "Never mind."

The sensation in my neck intensifies. No curry, no dramatic choking and drinking out of a vase. Something has definitely been thrown off course again. And sure, you could argue that it's a *positive* sign. That Will has chosen a venue he believes I'll enjoy, catered for my specific culinary tastes, which is objectively a sign of romantic effort. That's what the signs are telling me. Except it doesn't *feel* right, and I'm sick of trying to push that sensation away.

Together, we watch a white van speed past.

"I'm sorry I've been quiet this week," Will says as we cross the road, hands still linked but somehow locked as if nothing to do with each other. "Deadlines all seem to be hitting at once at the moment."

I nod. "Of course. I understand."

Brixton is bright and loud, but all I can think is: there were no deadlines the first time round, and now I just don't believe him.

We turn a familiar corner; I say, "So what is it exactly you're working o—"

Then I freeze.

"Are you okay?" Will frowns and follows the direction of my eyes toward the shipping container. "Do you not like egg, Cassie? Have I screwed up?"

Just an Oeuf is written in swirly yellow writing, exactly where If It Ain't Baroque was previously signposted. Or—if we're being specific—where it will be, in approximately three months' time. The antique lace drapes are now white muslin curtains covered in yellow spots, the corrugated walls are coated in shiny yellow plastic, and outside is a statue of a giant, ugly plastic chicken. The fact that I hate eggs with the passion of a thousand fiery suns seems the least of my problems.

I was right: something has spun off in the wrong direction.

I just don't quite understand *how*.

"Welcome to Just an Oeuf!" Lipstick and Lace Girl smiles at us from over her clipboard, except this time her lipstick is bright orange and her choker is made out of feathers. It's exactly the same girl as last time. Or next time. I'm losing track. "We hope to give you an *egg-cellent* alimentary experience tonight. Name?"

"Baker," Will says as the world starts to warp in and out.

Even in my shock, it's nice to hear the word *alimentary* casually thrown into my dining experience.

"Do you always work here?" We follow the chicken girl through to the exact same table with the exact same stools, except now they're covered in bright yellow fluff. "How long have you been here?"

"Sorry?"

"Does this place switch themes soon?"

"Oh." The girl frowns at me and places the menus in front of us. "Maybe. I think the owner is trying out a few ideas."

I study the restaurant carefully. Instead of flocked wallpaper, it's painted yellow, the duck heads are fake chicken heads, the carved gold chairs are fur-lined and white. It's a lot emptier than the next incarnation, and yet another courageously themed concept. Maybe they should just give up and try serving pizza.

"If It Ain't Baroque," I breathe.

"What was that?"

"If It Ain't Baroque," I repeat faintly, feeling a little sick. "That's what's coming next. It's eighteenth-century-themed food. You know, Fricassee, Goosed-berries, Beet Root Pan Cakes, four words."

"I like it!" The waitress laughs. "I'll let the owner know. He loves a culinary pun and he's looking for a new idea."

Piano fingers run down my spine: Did I just predict the future, or am I now actually *creating* it?

Will pours water from the jug and I stare at that too. "Is everything okay?"

"I don't know," I admit. "I feel a bit weird."

The waitress leaves and I pick up the menu and stare blankly at all the egg puns. Hard to Beat. What the hell is going on? Breggsit. We're here three months early. Practical Yolk. It's just a coincidence, right? Will picked the same restaurant, that's all. Eggstraterrestrial. It's no big deal. He saw a flyer and remembered I'm vegetarian. Eggspresso. I'm overthinking it all again, right?

Honestly, I'm getting to the point where I never want to see a pun again.

We're not haunted by them—we're *plagued*.

"This menu is *cracking* me up," Will observes, grinning at me.

I stare at him. "What?"

"Never mind." Will looks down at his menu again. "I think I'll go for the bacon and eggs. What are you going to have, Cassie?"

Maybe I'm not overthinking it. Maybe I've been told I'm *overthinking* it so often, by so many people, I've convinced myself it's all I'm capable of. But what if they're wrong? What if I'm thinking it exactly the right amount? What if everyone else is simply *underthinking* it, continuously, and the deficit is actually theirs? Because something tells me I'm not in the wrong here: my instincts are spot-on.

"Cassie?"

"Sorry?" Swallowing, I try to refocus on the menu: scanning for the least cloaca-originated option. Fried egg and chips: create a solid and impenetrable wall between them with some bread and hope it doesn't seep through. "Thank God It's Fry-Day?"

"That looks good." Will nods. "I think you should *whisk* it."

I stare at him. "Please stop with the egg jokes now."

"Okay." He smiles sheepishly. "Sorry."

The waitress brings a little basket of what appear to be bread rolls with melted Haribo eggs stuck on top, and I'm beginning to think whoever owns this place needs to focus less on novelty value and more on food.

"Are you ready for an *egg-streme* experience?" The waitress smiles and I recognize her white dress: & Other Stories, summer 2017. "Drinks? Can I suggest a couple of glasses of eggnog?"

"Just regular red wine, please," Will says, and I feel another shock of repetition combined with a flicker of relief. No custard masquerading as a beverage for us. "The Eggsplorer for me and the…"

They start chatting about how long the restaurant has been here, what the profits are like, so on and so forth, but I've stopped listening. I feel my stomach twist like a wet towel. This shouldn't be happening—it is nonsensical, illogical, irrational—but every single instinct in my body is now telling me that I have reached the end of my loop again, three and a half months early.

"Cassie," Will says quietly.

I look up. "Yes?"

"Is everything all right?" He frowns. "What's going on?"

I breathe out slowly. Oh, not much, Will. I just rewound time four months, exhausted myself trying to make this relationship work, and instead of improving the situation, it appears I just slammed my foot on the accelerator.

"I'm fine," I say with a smile. "Thank you for asking. How are you?"

"I'm *eggs*— Sorry. I'm awesome." Will looks up as our food arrives looking and smelling as disgusting as the cooked unfertilized embryo of another species always does. "Brilliant, actually. I just got some great news, but..."

He looks at his eggs, then back at me, then back at his eggs. I suddenly sense a torrent of colors, but yet again, I have no idea what they are, and I have to be honest: I'm getting so very tired of constantly guessing.

"So I just got offered an assignment in Mexico." Will reaches for his wine and takes a way-too-big mouthful. "To shoot a documentary on vaquitas. I'm leaving next Saturday, for two weeks."

What the hell is a vaquita, anyway?

"Except," I say, abruptly putting my fork down, "you didn't."

29

WILL DIDN'T GO TO MEXICO.

At no point in our original timeline did Will go to the Gulf of California to film whatever a vaquita is: I'm pretty sure I'd have noticed him disappearing at the start of our budding relationship for an entire fortnight. And now I know for sure: it's happening. The loop is over. We're at the end.

It's more than three months early, and our time is up.

"Cassie."

The restaurant is completely empty.

"Cassie."

Everything is silent.

"Cassie, please put your phone down. I'm trying to talk to you about something."

Blinking, I look up from the Wikipedia entry on vaquitas. Apparently they are a form of porpoise and the world's rarest marine mammal, and they're almost surreally cute: like a child tried to draw a dolphin, and then finished it with a little smiley face. Which I appreciate isn't really relevant right now, but I was hoping additional information might trigger some kind of memory and it doesn't.

"Hey." Will takes one of my hands and holds it. "Cassie, the thing is, I've had such a great time with you, I really have, but we've only just met…"

There are only logically two explanations I can see.

One: that Will wasn't offered the job in the first timeline, but something, somewhere, shifted that reality. Maybe he picked up the phone when he didn't originally; maybe something I did broke another cameraman's leg, and he's the replacement. Except *that* means the impact of my time hopping has spiraled out of control, and way, way out of my reach. In which case, what *else* could I be responsible for? What tiny decision have I made—to clean up a coffee spill, to rewind a TV show—that could have changed somebody else's life immeasurably? The scope of it is too massive: I can't even think about it.

The *other*, only slightly more reassuring explanation is that Will was offered exactly the same opportunity on our first run, but he turned it down to spend more time with me and didn't let me know.

Which is incredibly sweet and absolutely gutting in equal measure.

Mainly because this time he's decided not to bother.

"I don't feel very good," I say abruptly, standing up and knocking over the water jug for the third bloody time. "I think I'll go home now, please."

Lap dripping, I lurch abruptly from the table.

Except, now I don't know if I'm back in the old loop or if I'm creating a new, different one, and if it's me that's making it repeat. I just know that everything I've done over the last few weeks—every hop, every effort, every tiny tweak or edit—has been for literally nothing. Worse than nothing. All I've done is speed up my dumping.

"Okay." Will grabs a handful of sopping napkins. "Sure."

As I stagger outside, I can't help noticing that he didn't ask me to stay, didn't ask if we could finish our meal; he didn't seem particularly surprised or upset. Will can change. Will doesn't have a destiny, or a fate, or a predestined life already laid out for him. Will is capable of breaking the pattern and striking out on a different path.

It's only *me* who keeps constantly repeating.

Breathing hard, I stand outside the shipping container with my thumbs held tightly in my fists.

"Cassandra?" Will emerges behind me and I realize with a pang that he doesn't even know me well enough yet to call me *Cass*. "I've paid. I'm so sorry this has upset you so much. But this is only our fourth date, so I thought…"

This time his *only* is justified: it's only been thirty-one dates in *my* world.

"Can we go home?" Swallowing, I look up and down the street, scrabbling to gather my thoughts. I don't understand. This isn't how time works. It can't be. It doesn't have wormholes that just zoom you forward or backward like a giant, cosmic game of snakes and ladders.

"Home?" Will frowns. "To…your house?"

"Oh. Sorry." I shake my head in confusion, realizing I've accidentally slipped back into our old script and now it makes no narrative sense. "It's just… I live nearby. Unless you don't want to? That's fine too. Obviously."

Something gentle in Will's face shifts. "Of course I want to, Cassie."

A tiny flicker of hope lights inside me.

Maybe I'm "reading it all wrong" after all. Maybe I'm just jumping ahead again, making assumptions, preparing for my own heartbreak, planning for rejection. Creating a schedule for a future that isn't going to happen. Will hasn't actually broken up with me. He hasn't even hinted that he's going to. All he has done is take a job five thousand miles away that he didn't take the first time round.

"Are you sure?" I study his face, trying to read it. "Really?"

"Yes." Will nods, kisses my cheek. "Let's go back to yours. We can talk about it there."

We don't speak the whole way back and all I want is to loop time so we never actually get there, but I'm too scared to do it now in case I screw everything up even more than I have already. All the way home, something blue is arching out of him, and I know most people think blue is sadness, but this isn't.

It feels like Will is waiting for something.

"I'm sorry," I say, automatically taking off my white Friday jumpsuit and hanging it carefully on the hook. That was a mistake: now I'm randomly standing here in my underwear. "I don't know why I ran out like that. I'm not quite sure what is going on with me."

There's a silence as Will gazes around my bedroom. I frown—what on earth is he doing?—then realize with a sense of vertigo that he's never actually been here before: this is the first time Will has ever stayed with me.

"I like it in here," he says finally, studying my shelf. "It's cozy. Like a cocoon."

"Thank you." I throw on a T-shirt and perch warily on my bed.

With respect, touching nothing, Will continues to perambulate slowly, gazing with interest at my beautiful clothes, at my books, at my plants, at my collections. It's strange how it's almost exactly the same journey Derek took, just a couple of days ago, but I don't feel invaded or sullied this time: I feel seen.

With a small smile, Will picks up the color chart next to my bed.

He points at it. "Is this it?"

"Yes." I nod, embarrassed. "It's one of them, anyway. I have many."

Will sits quietly down on the bed next to me and opens it, staring at it for a few seconds, peering closely at each of the little rectangles. "I just see colors," he says finally. "I thought maybe I might see what you were talking about, but to me, it's just paint chips, something you pick up at a decorating shop."

"I know." Everything has gone very quiet. "I'm a bit odd sometimes."

"You're not odd." Will points at it, curious. "So this one, here. This...pale green. What does that feel like to you?"

I lean toward the color and feel a very specific wave of joy.

I'm not entirely sure what it is, though. That's the thing I've never really understood about emotions. We're given unhelpful words for them—*sad, happy, angry, scared, disgusted*—but they're not accurate and there never seems to be anywhere near enough of them. How could there be? Emotions aren't binary or finite: they change, shift, run into each other like colored water. They are layered, three-dimensional and twisted; they don't arrive in order, one by one, labeled neatly. They lie on top of each other, twisting like kaleidoscopes, like prisms, like spinning bird feathers lit with their own iridescence.

And then a therapist says *How do you feel, Cassandra?* and you're supposed to somehow know, just like that.

As if grappling for a rainbow you can feel in your hands.

"Well." I close my eyes and try to identify the feeling. "That particular pale green feels similar to the way I felt when I was about three years old and I got up in the morning before anyone else was awake, and I managed to open the back door for the first time on my own and it was cold and bright, but everything was whitened with frost and a wood pigeon was making that very particular sound and I walked into the grass and my feet got wet, I saw a frog, and then my mum said *Good morning, baby—how did you get outside on your own, you clever little monkey?*

from her bedroom window, and I realized she wasn't asleep, she was there, she had been watching me the whole time. That's what that green sort of feels like."

Will is watching my face. "You remember being three that clearly?"

"Three." I shrug. "Two, maybe. I remember pretty much everything, almost like it's all kind of happening now. It gets... confusing."

I suppose time doesn't mean anything when you remember everything.

My throat suddenly hurts and the lights flicker.

Carefully, I fold up the color card and put it back on my bedside table: all the colors are contained and organized so neatly in straight lines. I wish my colors were too. I try so hard to make them.

"Shit," Will says suddenly, rubbing his hand over the stubble on his face with a crackly sound. "I've screwed up, Cassie. I'm so sorry. I think...maybe I've been reading you wrong this entire time."

I blink at him, not understanding. Reading people wrong is my job.

"In what way?"

"I didn't quite...get you." He gazes around my room again. "I think I was measuring you by *me*. I was assuming we're the same, because that's what humans do, isn't it? Automatically. Without thinking. We see everyone through our own lens and assume it's the only possible way of being."

I blink. "Do we? I don't think I do."

"Well, I definitely do." Will smiles wryly. "I forget that it's not me looking through the lens, and sometimes it's actually... a polar bear."

Even more confused, I try to piece together what he's trying to say.

"I still don't think I understand," I admit finally. "What does this have to do with my paint chips? I'm so sorry. If you could just run it by me again, a little more slowly, I'll try harder. It takes me longer to process things than ideally I'd like it to."

"I thought you weren't interested in me, Cassie." Will turns to face me properly, legs bunched up on my bed. "At all. I saw things through my lens. In my eyes, we had a couple of really lovely dates, then we slept together."

"Yes." I nod. So far, so accurate. "True."

"I asked if you wanted sex again, and you said *absolutely not* and fell asleep." Will grimaces slightly. "So I was a bit hurt, my ego was bruised, but I thought *grow the hell up*, William, get over your ego, let the poor girl go to sleep. But when I woke up the next morning, you were gone. No note. No text. Nothing. You didn't text later in the morning, and I was too embarrassed to. But I swallowed my pride and texted again days later, and you seemed disinterested. A little cold, if anything. You didn't even remember discussing the exhibition date. Then you canceled it at the last minute, no mention of rearranging, and I thought, well. That's that, then."

I feel my mouth go suddenly dry. "But—"

My memories are landing on top of each other now: jumbled up, in a strange order. I remember every single thing that happened, but they all seem equally real, equally solid, happening simultaneously. Panicking, I scan my memories and try to piece the right timeline together. To undo screaming at Barry about my mug, I must have also deleted the text I sent after Will and I slept together, explaining that I had to leave early for work. I never sent it again—I was too humiliated by my behavior to remember—and I was too emotional and distracted to leave a proper excuse after running away from the exhibition, which made me look disinterested and cold.

Time is fragile; for every sweep of the broom, there are *consequences*.

"I left a coffee?" I finish lamely. "On your bedside table?"

"Look, it's okay." Will takes both my hands. "Honestly. This happens. You like someone, and they're not as into it. Nobody's fault. It's just… I'm starting to realize I may have read you wrong. You're…very difficult to read, Cassie. Your face is so beautiful, but a lot of the time you look far away. Detached. I make jokes, and you stare at me as if I'm the most irritating person you've ever met. A lot of the time when I'm talking, you look bored. I can see you thinking, assessing, judging, and I guess it just felt a bit like you were weighing me up and…finding me lacking. I mean, when you laugh—the entire room lights up. You make me feel like I've won the lottery. But in between…it's like you're somewhere else."

"People in shops always think I work there," I say abruptly.

Will blinks. "Sorry?"

"When I'm in shops. Any shop at all. Everyone always thinks I work there. Even if I'm not wearing anything that looks even faintly like a uniform, people will be like, excuse me, could you get me this in a size up, or could you tell me where the toilets are. Every single time I go into a shop."

Will frowns. "I'm not sure I…"

"There's something distant and frozen in my face," I conclude. "I don't look like a normal customer. A normal person. I look like I've worked somewhere for five decades and I'm about to hand in my notice. I look like I want to be somewhere else. Anywhere else. Even when I don't. Even when all my focus is matching the shade of a pair of red trousers to an orange shirt, and I'm enjoying it immensely. That's just my face."

"I see." Will nods. "Yes, I'm starting to realize that."

I've been so obsessed with chopping up time and stitching it back together, it didn't occur to me that the final version wouldn't be sewn together properly: that when I eventually tried it on, the hem would unravel, the collar peel away, the arms fall off. In trying so hard to *connect* with Will, I forgot to make sure that the narrative I left did too. All the mistakes, the

errors—the bits of myself I was too scared to leave behind—
were pulled out before they could do any damage.

Mistakes were flaws in my tapestry, so I ripped them all out.

"I'm never bored with you," I say, and my voice sounds so
calm and flat when my insides are ridged with storms. "I'm
amazed by you, Will. You are…spectacular to me. But I find
being around people so hard. Any people. There's all this noise
and light and color and sensation, all the time, and I don't know
how to read tone or emotions or jokes or sarcasm or flirting.
It's like all the things that everyone else can do automatically,
I have to do manually. And I get overwhelmed. Constantly.
That's the face you're seeing, Will. It's me, trying to process
everything at once."

It's true that I hate dirt and dog hair and lateness and mess
and loud noises and crowds and being wet or muddy—and,
truthfully, a lot of those things seem to come with Will—but
it's not a *judgment*. If I could choose, I'd roll around in mud
and laugh easily and be covered in puppies and take the world
in my stride, but I can't—I have never been able to—and the
judgment I feel about that has always been for *me*.

"Yes." Will looks around my bedroom. "That all makes more
sense to me now."

There's a long silence, and I can feel it: the end, like the knot
at the bottom of a piece of string.

"I thought this was done," Will says desperately. "She just…
We had this instant… We're just really similar, it was an immediate connection, and I think we want the same things. You're
spectacular to me too, Cassie, but when I'm honest with myself and I look into the future, I'm just not sure that we're—"

With the tip of my finger, I gently trace the circular face of
my old blue watch and wait for the world to collapse around
me. And—as I wait—I think about how time, as it grows old,
may teach all things, but that even when it doesn't get a chance
to, the lessons are probably there just the same.

"I love you," I say, because now I know there won't be another chance.

Then I close my eyes.

"You're spectacular to me too, Cassie, but when I'm honest with
myself and I look into the future, I'm just not sure that we're—"

"You met someone else," I say calmly.

"Yes." Will nods. "I met someone else."

30

"CASSANDRA."

I'm not time traveling again.

"Cassandra."

Ever.

"Cassandra," Barry says a third time. "Are you listening?"

Once Will had kissed my cheek and gone—taking both socks with him—I spent the entire weekend sobbing in a ball on my bed and realized I'm now very much done. It's too hard. Too painful. The experiment is over. Time travel is not for me. Thank you for the kind gift but please give it to someone else: I will not be navigating time and space any further.

Frankly, all I've done is make things considerably worse.

"Do you think she has a problem with her hearing? Like, physically? Do you think we should send her to get checked?"

Blinking, I attempt to drag myself back to the here and now.

"Sorry." My boss still appears to be waiting for an answer. "I missed all that. Are you firing me again?"

In Barry's defense, without time travel at least this time it'll stick.

"*Again?*" He lifts his eyebrows. "Cassandra, if I fire someone, they tend to stay fired. No, I'm not firing you. We called you into the office to *congratulate* you, if you could just pay attention for thirty consecutive seconds in a row."

"Synonyms," I murmur, now truly thrown. "Consecutive and row. You don't need to use both, Barry. Wait—you keep saying *we*. Who's *we*?"

Confused, I spin round and spot Jack: tucked in the corner with his fingertips propped on the arms of the armchair like a tanned spider. Has he been here the whole time? How long has he been *staring* at me like that? My ability to block the entire world out is truly extraordinary and may need to be studied by science.

"Hello, Jack," I say politely. "Why are you here?"

My emphasis accidentally goes on *you* instead of *here* and I watch his eyes narrow in familiar irritation.

"I won't make any bones about it, Cassandra," Jack says, standing up and walking to perch on the desk next to Barry like two head boys in a school office, getting ready to offer me a hallway monitor gig. "I originally arrived at the agency this morning to make an official complaint about you. It came to my attention over the weekend that the SharkSkin campaign looks absolutely nothing like the campaign I believe we agreed upon."

I nod. This is a fair assessment. "It doesn't."

"To say I was unhappy would be an understatement." Jack smiles widely and it looks absolutely nothing like a smile. "But Barry sat me down and explained that while my ideas were genius, they might need a *tweak* to hit a wider demographic. Just a *soupçon* of editing, if you will. And I could see, when he showed me the results and I checked the sales with Gareth, that a few adjustments could be—and indeed were—effectively made."

I stare at Jack, then at Barry, who immediately makes his

eyes go all round and strained—but I have no idea what that's supposed to be communicating, so I frown at him and look back at Jack again.

"But I told you that. Repeatedly. I said your ideas wouldn't work."

Barry coughs. "Sometimes it is less *what* you say, Cassandra, and more the *way* you say it. Anyway, I think the most important thing is that coverage has been good, sales have been strong, and everyone is happy. Well done."

"I quite like it." Jack nods thoughtfully. "Our skin care is so good you'll want to stop people stealing it. You should have come to me with that in the first place, Cassandra."

I stare at him, trying to work out if he's joking or not.

"And I admit I may have judged you too quickly," Jack continues, regarding me carefully. "First impressions are important, Cass, and you can be... What's the word I'm looking for? Aggressive. Rude. Arrogant and smug? Cold. Haughty and entitled. Uptight and superintense, for sure. I'm freaked out by the jumpsuit thing. But I'm a big enough man to confess that I may have been wrong about you."

Okay, that is so much more than one word: he scattergunned that approach.

"Cassandra," I say sharply.

Jack frowns. "Sorry?"

"Cassandra, not Cass." I stare him down. "That's reserved for people close to me. If you're going to call me names, Jack, please start with the correct one."

Is this how everyone exists, under a constant barrage of unasked-for observations? Reported on and narrated about endlessly, as if I'm listening to a looping David Attenborough documentary about myself?

Sometimes it feels like I am *drowning* in adjectives.

"Hey!" Jack holds up his hands and grins in what I assume is either a peacemaking gesture or an attempt to replicate the shrug emoji. "What can I say? We all jump to conclusions about others. I bet you had initial thoughts about me too!"

"Yes," I say tightly. "But I kept them to myself."

"Anyway," Barry says, clapping his hands and jumping up from the desk. "Good job, Cassandra. Water under the bridge and so forth. This is a lovely chance for us all to start fresh, isn't it? And, as a gesture of goodwill and gratitude, Jack was just talking to me about a charity ball you might quite like."

"Okay," I say in confusion, holding my hand out. "Thank you."

Barry and Jack both stare at me for a few seconds, then glance at each other and lift their eyebrows; men are so bloody weird sometimes.

"Is it bigger than that?" I hold out my other hand and cup them together. "Football size? I'm not going to have room in my handbag."

"Not a ball from a charity, Cassandra." Barry rubs his nose. "A charity ball. You know, black tie, pop music, round tables, dancing, tiny food on large plates, that kind of thing."

"You want to take me to a ball?" I turn to Jack with a sense of mounting confusion. "Like…Cinderella?"

"It's not a *ball*," my client says quickly, and now I can *feel* the horror pouring off him like a shower of blue icicles. "It's a *gala*, and I've bought a table for the entire SharkSkin team. Marketing, sales, development. Everyone involved. It's a way of saying thank you for the hard work running up to the launch. As a group. Not individual. Not just you."

I think about this offer carefully for a few seconds. Strangers, packed together in a loud, flashing room in scratchy clothes, making pointless small talk, eating food I don't like from plates that might not be properly clean, using cutlery with little bits of dried food still stuck to it. Intermittently dancing. Yeah: if Hades ever dragged me to the Underworld, that's exactly what I'd find there.

"No, thank you," I say as politely as I can. "That sounds horrible."

Barry and Jack lift their eyebrows at each other again.

"It's not voluntary, Cassandra," Barry says with a chuckle, and I stare at him in surprise: I'm not sure I've ever heard him laugh at something I've said before. "Jack is asking you to go to the gala as an official representative of SharkSkin and Fawcett PR, so you're going. Please just say thank you and go buy a nice dress."

"It's not a reward if I don't want to go, is it," I point out. "But thanks. I guess. You'll need to invite Sophie too because the entire campaign was her idea. She did all the hard work too. I just copy-and-pasted emails for her."

Brightening—at least Sophie might enjoy being tortured—I turn and rap briskly on the office window. She spins round, along with every other person in the office. Now I've got so much attention, I'm not quite sure what to do with it, so I wave like a member of the royal family until they go back to their computers.

Sophie waves jubilantly back—a phone trapped under her chin—and something about the scene makes me catch my breath.

"...a lot of notice," Jack continues behind me. "But you've got a few days, which should be enough to—"

I can feel my brain downloading something.

"Hello, Cassandra? Nope, she's gone again."

Come on, brain: just work out what the—

No.

No no no no no—

"Gotta go," Sophie says as I charge up to her desk and stand next to her, trying desperately not to interrupt her and knowing I'm going to fail. "Do *not* suggest pizza again, Darren." She puts the phone down. "Hello, Ca—"

"Someone called me. Last Wednesday evening, when I was

leaving work. You said you'd take a message, but there wasn't one."

"Oh!" Sophie frowns. "Did I? Hang on. Just trying to remember."

I am trying very hard to be patient, but it is *bewildering* how other people's memories seem to have giant holes in them. Where do all the memories go? Why haven't they filed them all away properly? Why is everything not tidy and immediately searchable, like a perfectly arranged larder? Why can't they pick and choose exactly when to open and replay a specific memory, and when to make sure the lid is kept on as tightly as physically possible?

"It's important," I prompt, starting to breathe loudly. "Please try."

"Right." Sophie nods obediently. "Yes. A phone call. It was a woman. I don't remember her name, but she said she knew you. Something about art. From art school? Did you go to art school, Cassandra? I did not know this about you. Where?"

"Focus, Sophie."

"Yes. Anyway. She said she was supposed to meet you, so I said you were already on the way to the exhibition."

The karate chop turns into two full fists directly in my windpipe.

"And what did she say?"

"She said, which exhibition again? I'm such a clutter-brain, I've forgotten the name. So I said it was something to do with animal photography in Shoreditch, just like you told me, and I could take a message. But she said not to worry, she'd just catch up with you there." Sophie pauses. "I guess that's why I didn't take a message. I thought she'd…you know. Caught up with you there."

"*FUCK!*" I yell at the ceiling, grabbing my bag.

Sophie's eyes widen. "Did I do something wrong?"

"When I get back we are going to have a little conversation

about information security," I say sharply. "Namely, not sharing my exact location with whoever casually asks for it over the phone. In the meantime, Sophie, please go into Barry's office to be congratulated and invited to a ball."

"Huh?" Sophie says. "Where are you going?"

My intestines are liquidizing, my cheeks are heating up; a rash is forming across my chest and so on and so forth. Dull pain begins to wrap itself around my neck, like a scarf pulled tight.

"Out," I say in exasperation, because here we go again.

I don't wait for the lift this time: I run down the stairs.

"Miss Dankworth? I—"

"Nope," I say, striding past the receptionist, pulling the door open, standing in the sunshine, and it's happening again: lights are flickering, exploding at the corners of my eyes like safety glass shattering. Reminding myself to breathe, I attempt to work out what to do next. Given that the entire universe is now falling apart around me, I'm going to need all the comfort and consistency I can get.

The blue café door tinkles and it makes me think of the bell at the end of class, which was so many years ago but also somehow still ringing now.

"Hello, Cassandra!" The old man smiles at me. "You're a little earlier than usual. Banana muffin?"

"Yes, please. Actually, I'll take all of them."

With a massive box held in front of me, I recommence charging: through Soho, around Tottenham Court Road station, past the Shaftesbury Theatre, down Bloomsbury and into Holborn. Everything is getting louder and brighter, but there's also a strange clarity I didn't have last time: a sharpness, like the edge of a piece of paper.

I know exactly where I'm going: I'm being tugged there, as if on a string.

That wasn't The End at all.

"Men have rights too!" I turn a corner and a leaflet gets thrust into my face by a man in a vest top; peanut breath, possibly honey-roasted. "Stop letting the feminazis control the narrative! Let men speak!"

I step around him—no, thank you—and continue to my destination.

Will's studio is in an enormous coworking space: exposed brick walls and black leather chairs and light bulbs hanging on cords from steel ceiling beams that have no structural purpose at all. It's nothing like my gold-leafed agency, but it's equally horrendous. Will says that people just turn up with their laptops and sit wherever they like, a different seat every day, like some kind of lawless *Lord of the Flies* with Ping-Pong and free coffee.

Spiraling now, I reach the outside of the downstairs coffee shop (neon signs, steel tables) and hesitate, unsure exactly what my next move should be. Do I text Will and wait for him to come down? Go up there? Accost him over lunch? All I know is that there are going to be many questions, and comprehensive answers will be required for all of them: repeated in extensive detail and ideally written down.

Questions like: What?

And: *What?*

And: Will, *what the actual fuck?*

I'm just trying to get my breathing back under control when I feel my hairline prickle again. As if there's a bolt of electricity from me to an unknown nearby source; a connection I can't see; the static sensation when you touch a cheap nylon jumper and there's an audible crackle.

And I know before I've even looked up: she's here.

Holding my breath, I lift my chin.

They're sitting in the middle of a huge steel window, as if held in a giant picture frame. Will is drinking a coffee with one hand, and she's got her hands wrapped around a large gray mug.

They're both chatting—animated, easy—and as they both laugh at the same time, I see something I've never seen before: the same color pouring out of them both, at the same time.

It's pink: simple, beautiful, smooth like a bright pebble.

And it finally hits me: I did this. I am the architect of my undoing, the weaver of my own story, and—much like Oedipus—everything I have done to avoid my doom is exactly what has brought it about. Which is funny, because—also much like Oedipus—now I'm going to have to rip my own bloody eyeballs out.

Frozen, I watch as the couple finally stop laughing.

Will drains his coffee, and I hold my breath as he stands up, leans over the table and kisses her smooth cheek. They exchange a few more lines, then he leaves through an internal door and I watch her sit for a minute or two: long neck stretched, head tilted back happily, absorbing the sun like an animal. And I knew she could be many things—impulsive, thoughtless, cruel—but I didn't think she would break my heart twice.

With my head dipped, I wait in the shade with damp eyes.

Finally, Artemis walks into the street, ramming most of a pastry into her mouth, and I feel an additional emotion: that she looks so pretty with her cheeks puffed up like a hamster. She pauses for a moment, examines the remaining bite, then frowns and abruptly looks up, as if she can finally feel me too.

And the world should be detonating, erupting, falling apart, but this isn't the first time I've seen her anymore and all I feel is…still.

"Oh." My sister smiles. "Hello."

31

SO...I HAVE A SISTER.

In my defense, I said I have no *close* family, which—to be fair—I've done my level best to ensure remains true. It's not my fault that Art has spent the last decade tracking me down like a hunting dog. She was the part of my story I ripped out, and I tried as hard as I could to make sure she stayed missing.

It's less of a lie, really, and more of a retelling.

"Artemis," I say, my jaw clenched. "What the actual fuck?"

"Cassandra," Artemis says in what seems to be genuine amazement, pastry poised. "Umm. That's an incredibly broad question. There's a lot of time to cover. Could you maybe ballpark it for me?"

It's been ten years and my sister has stayed almost exactly the same, as if she is, actually, immortal. She must be twenty-nine now, her cropped brown hair suits her—I will never tell her this—and there are a few lines around her mouth, but she still has the nimble, gray-eyed prettiness that led everyone to say our parents named her perfectly. *Artemis Helen Dankworth*. Artemis, goddess of the hunt; Helen, so beautiful she kicked off the Trojan War. Somehow I got a murdered prophetic priestess and an abandoned wife with a passion for embroidery—cheated on, somewhat ironically—and my sister got two of the most beautiful and powerful women in Greek mythology.

Artemis is also goddess of chastity, but clearly *that* didn't pan out.

"Stop being so obtuse." I gesture in frustration at the café window. "What are you playing at this time, Artemis? Is this some kind of new strategy? Sending smelly letters and stalking me across London didn't work out, so you've upgraded to casually destroying my entire life?"

"So you *did* get the letters!" Art beams, chocolate between her teeth. "I wasn't sure. Pomegranates! Which, if you remember from Mum, are fruit of the—"

"—dead," I finish for her. "Yes. I got it last time. Answer the question."

"I *would* answer it." Artemis frowns. "I'm ready and raring to answer whatever you want me to answer, Cass. But I'm not entirely sure how to, given that I haven't seen you for a decade. You look wonderful, by the way. I know that's not relevant, because you're clearly still super angry with me, but I feel I should bring it up anyway. You've gotten so stylish. Time suits you."

I open my mouth to yell at her, then shut it again. I've seen Artemis a lot over the last few weeks; I suppose it isn't her fault that she doesn't remember any of it.

"Tell you what." Art plops herself down on the curb, like a dismantled frog. "We have quite a lot to talk about, don't you think? So why don't you sit down and we can have this all out, finally."

I should have realized this would be her next move; it is so *very* Artemis. Once, when we were little, Art followed me around the house all day, begging me to play with her, and when I wouldn't, she went into my bedroom and smashed my favorite ceramic owl as punishment. Artemis will get my attention, one way or another—even if it means making a mess—and now she's done it again.

The story is starting to make sense, but pieces are still missing.

By my calculations, I undid seeing Artemis at the exhibition, but I *didn't* undo the phone call where Sophie told her exactly where I'd be. So Artemis went anyway, hit it off with Will—who was feeling rejected by me—and I didn't show up to prevent it. Which answers some questions, but not all of them. What happened in the original timeline? I didn't go to the exhibition then either. Did they meet the first time too? I was in the office the whole evening that time, so why didn't I get her phone call?

The Greek version of Artemis is famous for her aggressive nature—turning people into bears and deer, just so they get ripped apart in front of her—but stealing your estranged sister's boyfriend seems mean, even for her.

"Sit down, stalker," Artemis says, tugging on my trouser leg. "Come on, Cass. I think this has gone on long enough now, don't you? Ten years is enough. I don't know about you, but I'm bloody exhausted."

I stare at her, then realize she's right: I'm exhausted too.

I'm also going to need answers to all my questions, and frankly, I don't think it's possible for me to leave without them anymore. Finally defeated, I put the banana muffin box carefully on the pavement, then take off my jacket and place it neatly next to it so my emerald jumpsuit doesn't get covered in floor grime.

Then I lower myself slowly onto it like an old lady at a picnic.

"How am *I* the stalker?"

"You tell me." Art grins. "Only *one* of us followed the other one to a first date, Sandy-pants, and it wasn't me."

I narrow my eyes at her, ready to start snarling again—my pants haven't been sandy in a very long time—then stop. There's a strong color radiating out of my sister (golden, like a buttercup under the chin), but it doesn't fit the color I was expecting. There's guilt, definitely, but it's the wrong shade. The wrong intensity. She's hiding something, but it isn't anywhere near the color it should be. With Artemis, I could normally tell what she was thinking and feeling immediately, but—after a ten-year gap—I'm extremely out of practice.

Frowning, I lean a little closer so I can double-check.

"Are you still doing that?" Artemis laughs. "Sniffing people's colors, or whatever it is? How very unsubtle of you, Cassandra."

But I got close enough, and—as I glance back at the café window—I realize what it is: Artemis doesn't feel guilty about Will. She's nervous about seeing me—faking nonchalance so I'm not frightened away—but there isn't a trace of betrayal. My sister may be unpredictable, thoughtless, irresponsible, but she isn't evil. I know that. Which means she has no idea about the relationship between me and Will, and—by extension—Will doesn't know that she's related to me.

They are both completely oblivious to my connection to them.

My rage abruptly evaporates.

Logically, there's no point being angry when there's nobody left to be angry with: it's a waste of time and effort, and I've done plenty of that over the last few weeks.

Sighing, I open the box lid and survey my twelve beautifully organized banana muffins. I was planning to take them home and freeze them—stock up for future emergencies—but I think I might just eat them all right now. Nothing requires comfort quite like discovering you've traveled through time and space only to set your boyfriend up with your little sister.

I ram one in my mouth and wait for heartbreak to hit.

It could be any time: the really big and life-changing emotions tend to have extremely large delays, as if they're being sent via traditional mail, at Christmas, without the right postage.

"What?" I suddenly realize my sister is watching me eat. "What do you want from me now, Artemis? You're not having one."

"You still love nuffins." She smiles. "Such a creature of habit."

When I was a child, I refused to speak—everyone thought I couldn't, but I just didn't see the point until I could do it properly—but I did regularly demand *nana-nuffins*. Over time, that truncated to *na-nuffin* and finally *nuffin*. Obviously, I don't call them *nuffins* anymore: I call them banana muffins because I am thirty-one years old and can enunciate properly.

"People always say that as if it's a bad thing," I snap, taking another giant bite. "A character flaw. Nobody says, hey, look at that squirrel, climbing trees and burying nuts, what a creature of habit. They say, hey, look. There's a squirrel. Being a squirrel. I'm Cassandra. I do Cassandra things. Stop pointing them all out."

"It wasn't a criticism." Artemis shuffles toward me. "I've just really missed it, that's all."

A soft wave of warmth passes through me, pale lilac, and then I hear her again.

I hate you.

You're a monster.

Why can't you just be normal?

"Sure." I jump up. "And whose fault is that?"

There's nothing to be angry about anymore, but there's also nothing to stay here for. The man I love has decided he'd rather be with my closest blood relation—the person who has hurt me most—and there isn't a single thing I can do about it.

Except…where am I supposed to go now?

I could go back to work, but I don't know how long the Emotions are going to take to rock up: it could be hours, it could be weeks. I can't risk having them all turn up at once in the middle of a brainstorm, or the kitchen, or at the water-cooler. After all that effort, I'm not losing my job because of a meltdown in the office. I could go home, but Sal and Derek will almost definitely be there, and I'm not ready to pick that thread back up just yet. I could go to the museum, but if I implode there that'll be one more place I can't return to.

Obviously I could time travel—hop back and undo it all, prevent Artemis and Will from meeting—but that just seems petty. Anyway, I'm not touching time inappropriately again. My horological abilities were a gift from the gods and I should have realized that they come at a price: they always have done.

Also, Will has now dumped me in three different timelines; at some point, you've just got to let yourself stay dumped.

"You're not leaving?" Art jumps up after me. "We've barely talked at all."

"Exactly." I frown. "Artemis, how do you know where I work? Obviously you know where I live, hence the letters and doorstepping, but work? My name isn't on the Fawcett PR website. I made sure of it."

"I went to your house and your flatmate told me everything."

"Which one?"

"The handsome one that looks a bit like Apollo except his dick is right on his forehead instead of the floor."

I laugh loudly and immediately resent her for it. "Derek."

"Yeah. That's the one." Artemis looks chuffed at my laughter, which is extremely annoying. "Honestly, he seems like an asshole, Cass. He was hitting on me pretty much continuously. Speaking as your sister, albeit one you haven't spoken to in a decade, I hope you're not hooking up with him, because he's the human equivalent of the spit dregs at the bottom of a pint."

"Oh." I shake my head. "Don't worry. I'm not."

The final piece of the puzzle has now slotted into place: in the original timeline, Artemis must have waited on the door-

step for me as she did this time, but I didn't return home and
Derek simply left her sitting there on her own. Which means
she never spoke to him, didn't find out where I work, didn't
call my office, didn't speak to Sophie, didn't go to the exhibition and never met Will. It's such a tiny alteration, barely per-
ceptible, and I will probably never be certain of exactly what
caused it. Why did Derek decide to behave differently? Maybe
he was arguing with Sal and Artemis was his revenge. Maybe
I hadn't responded to his charm that day the way he hoped I
would; maybe he just felt particularly prickish.

Honestly, I can't believe my fate hinged on a man who regularly uses words from other languages with a full British accent.

I pick up my muffin box and make to leave.

"Wait." Artemis jumps in front of me with her arms out, as
if she's trying to herd me like sheep. "That can't be it. It's been
ten years, Cass. Ten *years*. Please. I need to apologize properly
for everything I said at the funeral. I was thinking maybe we
could go to the pub? There's also some really important stuff
I want to talk to you about. Stuff that wasn't in the letters."

"It's eleven in the morning, Artemis."

"Yes, but this is London." She gestures around as if this is
brand-new information to me. "Alcohol seeps from its pores,
twenty-four hours a day. Please? I don't need a very long time.
Just, like, an hour."

"You being drunk was part of the problem, if I recall accurately."

Which I do, and that is part of mine.

"So maybe me being drunk again is the solution?" Art cocks
her head to the side, wrinkles her tiny nose and twinkles at me
with her big bird eyes. "Just putting it out there. A hypothesis
we could test together, if you will."

I study my sister's colors carefully. They're nothing like my
colors, and they never have been. They're quick, fluid, running
through her like dye thrown into a river, blooming and leaving

again without a stain. With me, it's more like they've all been lobbed into a pond and now they're just sitting there, turning brown, while I try to work out where they came from, who put them there and what the hell colors they were supposed to be in the first place.

"I'm not talking about the funeral," I say firmly.

"But—"

"No. What's done is done. I don't want to discuss it. Are we clear?"

Her shade shifts, clouds, then visibly brightens again as the emotion runs away and is replaced with something else.

"Deal. Just two hours. That's all I need to make you love me again."

"You *just* said one hour," I sigh in frustration.

"I might need a bit longer than that." Art grins, hopping from foot to foot. "There's ten years of hate to erase, somehow. I'm not as cute as I used to be when I was a kid. I need all the time I can get."

Frustrated, I look at my watch and deliberate.

As we've already established, I can't go back to work quite yet, just in case I fall apart. I confess to being curious: I have no idea what Artemis has been doing for the last decade, and now she's finally worn me down, I sort of want to know. Something tells me that—much like her namesake—she won't stop chasing me, so it feels like an efficient next step to a quiet life. Plus, she's my sister: if the Big Emotions come while she's there, I have a lot of experience in just taking them all out on her.

"Fine," I say with a flash of what feels strangely like relief. "You have until 1:00 p.m., and then I'm going back to work. That's two hours and then we go our separate ways. I'm going to need your promise that once your slot is over you stop sending me letters, stop following me about, and the British Museum is *mine*, do you understand? I got it. In the sister divorce. It's mine and I want it back."

Artemis blinks. "Hey, I was there the other day."

"I know," I say tiredly. "Don't ask me how."

"Okay." Art jumps up and down again, clapping her dainty little hands together with a surprising amount of noise: her happiness is like a nuclear explosion. "I can agree to these terms and conditions. Three o'clock, Sandy-pants, and if you still hate me, you can go and that'll be that. Forever. I promise."

"Stop calling me Sandy-pants and stop adding on hours," I sigh as she links her arm through mine. "Don't think I haven't noticed."

Then I look down at the point where we touch.

It doesn't hurt, I can't feel her like an electric shock, it doesn't make me flinch and pull away. It feels like my sister is simply part of my own body, an extra limb, my largest organ. And even now, I can't quite believe that she doesn't get it. After all this time, Artemis still doesn't seem to understand that I do not set my life on fire and run away from somebody I hate.

Where would be the logic in that?

Hate is never what the matches are made of.

32

THUS THE ADVENTURES OF Artemis Dankworth.

According to my sister, once our parents' funeral was over she sobered up, tried to find me to apologize and discovered I'd already moved out and changed my phone number, so, after a fortnight of unsuccessful searching, she flew to India to seek forgiveness—"punishment, really"—in a silent monastery.

Eventually, she got thrown out for talking—no surprise to anybody—so she traveled to Peru and stumbled across an ayahuasca ceremony that involved some kind of psychedelic tea, talking to our dead parents and puking in a bucket. She progressed to a dark retreat, locking herself in a hut in complete darkness for an entire week—fed through a slot in the door only when blindfolded (which apparently "sent her a bit cuckoo")—so she then attempted a three-week "detox" in Thailand, which involved sticking a plastic tube up her bum twice a day, drinking bentonite clay and eating herbs that turned her shit bright green "like a duck."

Eventually—"about five billion dead brain cells later"—she returned to England and tried to contact me again.

There was no response, so she started a local acting course and bailed.

She started a comedy improv course and bailed.

There was an unnecessarily dramatic romance with another hopeful thespian—"he had a one-minute role in this really big historical drama and never shut up about it"—and they both ran away to an "aggressively naked" tantric sex camp in Germany, where they broke up within three hours.

Single again, Artemis backpacked through Europe—but "can't remember which bits, they mostly look the same, all cathedrals and cheese"—then returned to Cambridge, where she waitressed and rented out spare rooms in the family home "for pennies" to other impoverished artists—neither of which she was, as we both acknowledged—and got involved with yet another artistic man.

This one pawned three of her rings, so she burned his belongings in the back garden—"honestly, it was basically just a ukulele and some bead necklaces"—and escaped again: this time to the Himalayas, where she attempted and failed *another* silent retreat "and also a bit of mountain climbing, but they're bloody high, so I took inspiration and mostly sat in cafés, smoking weed."

Eventually, she returned, looked for me, found an address of a grubby flat-share in London and sent me a pleading letter, which returned unread with a note saying I had now moved to nobody knew where. Unsure what to do next, she worked in the uni library for a year, a vocation that "she struggled with immensely, mostly because I kept talking and the students kept *sssshhhhing* me."

Add six more jobs, eight awful boyfriends and one girlfriend—"I went with her to Australia for a bit, but she got annoyed with me, so I came back"—and eventually Artemis Helen Dankworth found herself back in Cambridge for the final time.

"And that's about it," she says with a wide grimace, finishing her second wine and wiping her lips on her crocheted jumper sleeve. "I'm a cliché, I know. But honestly, what else can you expect from a Sagittarius called Artemis? I'm the archer, squared. I'm unable to stop traveling and hunting. The stars proclaimed it, and then our parents decided to just double down."

"Actually," I say, sitting forward with a giddy rush of excitement, "did you know that Sagittarius is Chiron? He was the only centaur in Greek mythology who wasn't related to the other centaurs because he was the son of Chronus, so he was technically Zeus's half brother. When Heracles shot him with a poisoned arrow, he gave up his immortality and was turned into a constellation of stars known as Sagittarius. I'm a big fan of Chiron, personally. He always comes across as incredibly wise and brave, which makes Heracles even *more* of a raging dick, in my opinion. I hate him."

My sister's eyes widen slightly. "Huh."

I flush, as I always do when I've downloaded something fascinating to me and not to anybody else. "What's 'huh' supposed to mean?"

"I didn't realize you'd taken over from Mum, that's all." Artemis smiles at me. "That's lovely. You inherited the Greeks."

"It's just a vague interest." I shrug, then swig from my wine.

"What about you, though?" Art leans forward. "I've told you all about *me*, Cass, but what have you done for the last ten years? What's your story?"

I blink into my glass, thinking about it carefully.

Honestly, I'm now two glasses of red wine down and I'm still trying to work out how a decade for Artemis is supposed to be the same as a decade for me. We've had the same amount of hours—give or take the few hundred I've pinched over the last couple of weeks—yet somehow my sister has crammed in several lifetimes and you could argue I haven't even managed one.

I know the original Artemis is immortal, but this one isn't meant to be.

"You can't time travel, can you?" I ask, just in case it's genetic.

"Not last time I checked," Art sighs. "There *was* a moment during the ayahuasca ceremony where I thought I might have, but it turned out I was just hanging upside down from a tree. But seriously, Cass. Don't change the subject. After you walked out of the funeral, what happened? Where did you go?"

I consider my answer, but it's all incredibly vague.

If I'm being totally honest, I don't remember much. It's the one giant gap in my memory: a black hole of nothing at all. Somehow I ended up in London, where I had the Mother of All Meltdowns: one that lasted nearly six entire months. I have a faint recollection that I may have started and then quit smoking. I ate a lot of Wagon Wheels. Eventually, I emerged, got a job in public relations and moved in with some strangers. Then I got another job in public relations and moved in with some more strangers. And I did that a few more times until I ended up here.

In Greek mythology terms, I'm less a heroine or goddess and more the unnamed herald who comes on for thirty seconds, blows a trumpet and walks off again.

"Wait." I stare at my sister. "What did you do with all my stuff?"

It has only just hit me that Artemis kept our family home in Cambridge: I'd assumed she'd exchanged it for three magic beans and a gerbil.

"I put it all in boxes." Art grins, standing up. "Although I reckon there's a statue of limitations on how many years someone has to store shit for you when you live in another part of the country."

"Statute," I say automatically.

"What?"

"It's a statute of limitations, Artemis. Not a statue."

"Really? Are you sure?" Artemis signals for another drink, even though I'm pretty sure there isn't table service. "That doesn't seem right. There should be a statue of limitations too. Like, a naked woman crouching under a glass ceiling with a man balanced on top—how poetic would that be?"

I can't quite believe my home is still there. The garden, the stream, the oak trees; the specific clunking of the radiator; the cupboard I used to hide in when the world got too big. Flickering memories of Mum and Dad, listening to the radio, yelling up the stairs for dinner, arguing over who didn't lock the front gate. Gone but still there, unchanged and unchanging. My home is the same as it always was, a constant, and there's a sudden, overwhelming tugging sensation under my ribs.

"My bedroom." I look up with a pulse of alarm. "You didn't let strangers sleep in it, Artemis. Not in my bed."

"No, I turned the entire thing into a giant Cassandra shrine." She sits down and smiles sweetly up at the barman, who has inexplicably brought us more drinks. "I painted a life-size portrait of you on the walls and set up candles, and every day at 3:00 p.m. I would ring a bell and call your name, and whoever was in the house would come upstairs and pray to it with me. Sometimes we sang. Sometimes we cried. It was beautiful."

I narrow my eyes. "That seems dramatic, even for you."

"Of course people slept in your bed," Artemis laughs brightly as I take a swig of my new wine. "It's a room, not a bloody mausoleum. And you didn't *die*, by the way, Cass. You got on a Megabus in a mega strop."

My wine goes straight up the back of my nose.

I choke until I can swallow again.

"See." Art beams at me, clearly delighted. "I can still make you laugh. *That* hasn't changed, at least."

"I wasn't laughing," I lie in irritation, wiping wine off my chin. "I just forgot I can't breathe and swallow simultaneously because I'm not a dolphin."

Now it's Art's turn to laugh loudly and chuck a coaster at my head.

When the noise fades, we look at our drinks.

"Did you think about me at all, Cass?" Art's colors shift again. "Because I thought about you constantly. Everything reminded me of you. I still go into paint shops and collect all the color chips, just to bring them home for you."

Pain flickers. "No, I didn't think about you."

"Oh." She looks down and now there's a translucent shade of jade. "Fair enough. Of course. What I did was truly awful. I understand."

The width of her sadness knocks the wind out of me.

"That's not true," I say a lot more gently. "Of course I thought about you, but I had to try and…compartmentalize you. It was too painful not to. You know what I'm like, Art. It's exactly like you said at the exhib—" Nope. That didn't happen in this timeline. "I have to put everything in my head into Tupperware boxes, keep my feelings and my memories neat and tidy and stored away. I have to control when I access them. Otherwise…it's just too much."

She nods, and her sadness ebbs slightly. "You're a human filing cabinet."

"Yes," I admit softly. "Although it doesn't always work."

Even now, I can feel the containers in me starting to rupture: everything threatening to spill everywhere. Too many emotions and memories. Too much mess. I can feel my brain responding by preparing to close down. Getting scared; ready to cut the pain away at the base. Because all this time, I allowed myself to believe that I was the victim and my sister was the villain—black and white, good and bad—but what if that was never true? What if she was just a drunk nineteen-year-old girl, screwing up? What if I made a decision in unbearable pain and heartbreak and didn't know how to undo it? What if I became so rigid, so focused, so unyielding that I made a plan and couldn't bring myself to change it?

What if the biggest mistake was actually mine?

And suddenly I understand why Athena felt the need to destroy Arachne's tapestries in a fit of rage: anger is one of the simpler colors, and the truth in its complex entirety can be overwhelming.

"Ooooh!" Artemis hiccups. "Shall we get cheesy chips?"

"Art—" I begin, just as my phone starts ringing. I stare at it for a few seconds, but I'm unable to not answer it. If texts make my bag feel heavy, a phone call feels like its own gravitational force field.

"Cassandra," someone says as I hit the right button after three attempts. "I can't help but notice that you abruptly left our meeting and have not returned. Sophie says you're unwell and had to leave. Is everything okay?"

I hold my phone away from my face and stare at it, momentarily stunned into silence. Admittedly, I think I've drunk two-thirds of a bottle of wine now, but I'm not sure I'm drunk enough to be hallucinating quite yet.

I put the phone back to my ear. "Barry?"

"Yes, Cassandra."

Artemis mouths *who is it?*, so I mouth back *my boss, I think* and then stifle a hiccup against my hand.

"Hi, Barry. I had a…family emergency." I glance at my little sister. "But thank you for asking if everything is okay, because people say *how are you* and the scripted reply is *I'm fine, thank you, and how are you*, and they say *I'm fine, thank you* or *not bad, what about this weather we're having* and you're not allowed to be honest because it's this weird social interaction that's a token question, not a real one, but now you've asked, Barry, I am not sure I'm okay at all."

There's a pause. "Cassandra, it's lunchtime. Are you drunk?"

"Oh." I look around the pub: everything glows and wobbles slightly. "Very."

"Okay." There's a sigh. "Let's have a chat tomorrow."

I glance at my sister again.

"I'm not okay, Barry," I continue, more firmly now. "And I don't think I have been okay for quite a while. So I'd like to take a few days off while I work out what I need to be okay again, if that's okay with you." I hiccup. "I'm saying *okay* a lot, but I'm okay with that. Also, *may* I just add that I like bulldogs. You have nothing to be ashamed of."

Another pause, then Barry says: "Cassandra, take all the time you need."

"Thank you," I say in surprise. "Although, while we're being candid, Barry, that's exactly what I've already been doing."

Beaming, I aim for the right button until the call ends. Maybe that's all Barry needed too: the whole truth, instead of tiny dribbles of it.

"Hey." Artemis is tipsily studying her palms. "Do you think sheep know they're fluffy? They don't have hands to feel their own fluff, right? Do you think they look at *other* sheep and say *wow, I wish I was fluffy like him*?"

I watch my sister for a few seconds: the tiny broken baby hairs around her hairline that she's always had, since she was little. The dark freckles on the end of her faintly turned-up nose, exactly like every single summer holiday. The slightly pointed ears that give her an ethereal, graceful quality even as she's burping loudly and at length, which is exactly what she's just done.

Time is strange: it moves so quickly and so quietly that sometimes it feels like it hasn't moved at all.

"It's three minutes to one," I announce, glancing at my watch.

"Oh." Artemis visibly flattens. "Bollocks. That came around fast, didn't it? I kind of wish I'd spent a little bit less time talking about sticking straws up my bum now."

My nostrils flare. "Me and you both."

My sister's colors have shifted and bloomed into an orange panic now, and she glances around the pub, desperately looking for something to hold me here: as if she's casting a net and hoping I'll stay caught in it.

"Quiz machine!" Her eyes widen. "We could do a quiz machine! You *love* quizzes, Cass. Remember? Any opportunity to get something right and for other people to get it wrong and for you to win. It's, like, your favorite thing in the world."

She's correct: it very much is.

"I said two hours. I'm afraid time is up." Pointedly, I take off my watch and put it on the table between us. With my fingers, I gently pull out the stiff little gold stem on the side of it. Then, carefully, I wind it back two hours and click it back in again. There's more than one way to time travel, after all. "So now it's eleven o'clock again."

Artemis hesitates, works out what it is I'm saying, then lights up; I feel her colors in all of me.

"Cheesy chips?"

"Yes," I agree. "But only if you eat all the creepy ones."

33

THERE ARE INFINITE THINGS you can do with time.

You can save it, spend it, stitch it, kill it.

You can beat it, steal it and watch it fly.

You can do time and set it; you can waste it and keep it; it can be good or bad, on your side or against you. You can have a whale of it; be in the nick of it or behind it; you can have it on your hands.

Memories are time travel, and so are regrets, hopes and day-dreams. When we die, the people we love carry us forward into it. So if we're all just moving forward and backward, living all the times at once—if time is an arbitrary concept that we can bend to our will—then what does 11:00 p.m. last orders mean, anyway?

If time belongs to all of us, how can you possibly *close* it?

And it's saying this kind of drunk shit that gets both me and Artemis thrown out of the pub.

"Have you ever wondered," Art hiccups as I rummage through my bag, "what the innards of a toilet roll are called? Like, it's not a toilet roll anymore. Because the bit that *rolls* is gone. But it doesn't have its own name, right? Which is *tragic*, because it works so hard and unites so many of us."

"Thassa vey, very good point," I agree, pulling out my key card and holding it up to the square thing with the lights. "In old Greece, they had ceramic pieces called *possois*, and they scraped their poo off with that instead."

I slap the key card again: it hits the side of the door.

We're both completely hammered, despite my insistence on sensible breaks for some soft drinks and food. I guess that's what happens when you pretend it's lunchtime in a pub for fourteen straight hours: drunk carnage.

"Amazing," Artemis burps enthusiastically. "How sustainable. How environmental. Ahead of their time, those classicals were."

Focusing, I slap the card: a light finally goes green and the door clicks.

"Hurrah!" I am triumphant. "We're in!"

The normally buzzing reception is bizarrely silent, like a mythical beast that is sleeping but with twinkling security lights on its face.

"So what are we doing in here, anyway?" Artemis follows me jubilantly up the stairs, two at a time. "How did we get in? Did we *break* in? Oh my God, are we *criminals*? This is so fun. I always knew I'd go to jail one day, but I didn't think it would be for robbing an office block in Soho."

"We didn't break in. You literally *just* watched me use a key card."

"Oh, yeah." Art trips up a stair. "My bad. Forgot."

"Our boss likes to encourage *flexible working*," I explain as we enter the office itself. "He thinks it cultivates a work hard, play hard environment."

Swaying slightly, we both stare at the empty room. I guess nearly midnight on a Monday falls into the *play* category. The only thing that can be heard is the dripping watercooler, which should be an inspiration to us all because it never seems to take a bloody break.

With determination, I head straight to my desk, then hesitate. I had a reason for coming here at this time of night. A very important reason. I'm just way too drunk now to remember what it was.

"Oooh!" Art kneels at the gold reception. "Pretty."

"There's a climbing wall in the meeting room," I say as I peruse my desk, still trying to work out what I'm doing here. "If you feel like entertaining yourself like a baby monkey."

"I sure do," my sister says, disappearing straight into it. "No way! Swings! Balls! Jelly beans! So fun! Bet these have sweat and urine all over them." A pause, then: "Mmm...tangy."

I smile faintly, then remember what I'm doing here. Glancing up, I check the coaster is clear—ha ha—then open my drawer and pull out my mug. I haven't gone more than two days without drinking out of this mug in the last decade, and it's my holiday: I'm not starting now.

"Whatcha doing?" Artemis says from directly behind me. "Oh. My. Gods. Is that what I think it is?"

"Huh?" I tuck the mug into my bag. "No."

"It is." She leans over and pulls it out of my hands. "That's my mug. The one I sent you years and years ago for your birthday."

"No," I lie pathetically. "It isn't."

"I got it made for you in Thailand in my gap year, Sandy-pants. I know my own bloody joke when I see it. Look, see, it's a deer, because the deer is my special animal, and the joke is *Did You Myth Me?* You know, because you're Cassandra, the tragic mortal, and I'm Artemis, the Greek goddess, and it's a play on the word *miss* because the arrow didn't hit the deer and also because it's short for *Artemis* and also because I hadn't seen you in so long. It's multifaceted comedy and goddamn hilarious."

"You don't need to explain the joke." I snatch it out of her hands. "I got it. And it's just a mug. I like the shape of it, that's all. It holds a good amount of coffee."

Artemis sits on Ronald's desk and grins at me.

"Stop it," I say.

She continues grinning.

"Stop it," I say again. "Or I'll punch you in the face."

"You *did* myth me." She swings her trainers back and forth. "You mythed me so hard. This is so embarrassing for you, Cassandra. I'd be mortified right now if I were you. Wow."

Nostrils flaring, I put the mug safely back in my bag. Honestly, I just couldn't bear the thought of the cleaner moving it again and Barry breaking it: I don't think he could handle the violence in me it would unwittingly provoke.

"What do you do again?" Artemis gazes around the office. "Advertising?"

"Public relations," I say, making sure my desk is perfect before I leave it on its own for the first time. "And you know that, because I've told you, and also I'm assuming when you rang Sophie said *Force It PR, how can I help you?*"

"Oh." My sister nods. "Yeah. That was funny. Do you like it here?"

"Of course I don't like it," I say, using one of my wet wipes. "I don't like relating publicly. I don't even like relating privately, most of the time. Ideally, I'd be paid money to sit in a dimly lit room, reading and talking to nobody. Apart from maybe on the rare occasion where I'm wheeled out to talk *at* someone about something I'm interested in, and everybody is forced to listen but not allowed to respond."

"So, exactly like Mum, then," Artemis laughs.

"Yeah." I smile slightly and suddenly see our mother, sitting on the desk chair opposite us, tucked into a pretzel exactly as Artemis always sits. She was so beautiful. So full of joy and brilliance. It would have been an honor to have turned out like her. "Except, unlike Mum, I don't have a doctorate in Classics, so I guess it's communication and anxious pooping for me."

"Speaking of shit and the classics, I have a bit of a problem."

"Yeah?" I think I'm done with cleaning an already spotless work environment now: let the holiday fun commence. "What is it?"

"Will sort of thinks my name is Diana."

I look up so quickly that my eyes spin. "Sorry?"

"Oh. Right." Art picks up a squidgy toy off Ronald's desk and squeezes it experimentally. "Will's the guy you saw me with, in the café. It's brand-new. We only met last week, at this exhibition thingy. Honestly, I was only there because I thought you'd be, but you never turned up, so I guess I got my venue muddled."

I breathe out steadily: I'd totally forgotten about Will.

Carefully, I search myself for an emotion—scan my body, go through each limb separately—but there isn't much there. The slightest hint of pale lavender, maybe, but I'm not sure what it means or what is causing it. Maybe the emotion is there and I'm just too drunk to acknowledge it properly; like when you suddenly realize the pain in your abdomen isn't anxiety, you just really need a pee.

"Anyway." Artemis puts the ball back. "I told him I was called Diana. You know, my Roman equivalent. Not sure why, really. At the time I told myself it was in case you turned up. I didn't want you to get wind of me too quickly and bolt, but I think actually I just quite like…making things up."

"You enjoy living in all the narratives that never got a chance to happen."

"Yes!" Artemis widens her eyes. "You get it! You're so clever."

"I am not," I decide firmly.

"So this guy…" Her face softens. "He's *amazing*, Cass. So sweet, so chilled. So adventurous and thoughtful and *hot*. His smile is… It's one of those smiles that just *spreads*, you know?

Makes everyone else smile too. We really hit it off. Spent ages chatting about all these places we'd been, all the places we want to go, how we want, like, seven billion dogs all in one go, so they're climbing all over each other. I even told him about the silent retreat and he said *he* tried to do one years ago but couldn't manage it either. We decided they're stupid and we want to set up a retreat where you can talk *all the time* because we think that would be better for mental health generally."

My eyes widen: I did not know this fact about Will.

I knew about the smile, obviously.

"But then I lied, so I think I've buggered it up already." Artemis blows her fringe upward, like a mermaid. "Which is *gutting* because he might be the first nice guy I've ever liked. Dad was so lovely, so calm, it feels like after he died I couldn't be with men who reminded me of him. But this is different. Will just feels *safe*, you know? *Good*. I'm even convinced he wouldn't sell my belongings or dump me while I'm stranded in a foreign country."

I smile faintly. "I don't think he would do either of those things."

"So what do I do?" Art bites the end of her fingers. "Tell him I'm a liar or change my name by deed poll? I'm leaning toward the latter. I've looked it up and it costs forty pounds, so it might be worth just reinventing myself again."

Quickly, I scan myself for emotions a second time.

There's still nothing like what I was expecting. There's a shimmering yellow, a little pink, the same lilac—marbled, like a sky at sunset—but none of them feel like heartbreak. None of them feel like grief or loss or intense sadness. More importantly, there's no sign at all of *jealousy*, which is the emotion I'd assumed would be blazing right at the front. Frankly, it makes no sense at all. Use my mug and I'll kick the hell off, but take the boyfriend I love and I'll be miffed for ten minutes?

"Just tell Will the truth," I say, sitting abruptly down on my spinning chair and rubbing my neck. "I think he'll understand."

Greek mythology is chockablock full of monsters.

Some of them were born. Typhon, with the torso of a man but a hundred dragon heads; Echidna, half woman and half snake; Cetus, with its slimy face and giant tentacles. Some of the monsters were made: Medusa, who was once a beautiful woman but was raped by Poseidon and transformed into a gorgon; Scylla, once a sea nymph but gifted by Circe with shark teeth and dog heads attached to her body. And some of them stayed human but slowly changed—often with good reason—until everyone simply saw them as monsters, like Medea or Clytemnestra.

As I sit on my swivel chair and search for the emotions I'm supposed to feel now but cannot seem to find, I can't help wondering: *Am* I a monster?

And—if so—was I born or was I made?

"What about you?" Artemis kicks at my chair. "Are you seeing anyone, Cass? I hope they're nice. I hope they're as nice as Will."

I shake my head. "No. I'm mostly on my own."

And the complete truth of this statement shocks me, because I *am* mostly on my own. I am so permanently alone that I can feel it in my bones, in my eyeballs, in the roots of my hair. I feel loneliness like a physical presence, as if someone heavy is sitting on my chest. I feel it when I wake up and I feel it when I walk down the street. I feel it when I eat and when I dance; I feel it when I'm with people, and I feel it when I'm not. I feel loneliness inside me, all of the time, but I also like to be alone and I don't really like other humans much either, so where the hell does that leave me?

No wonder I spent so much time and effort trying to make Will stay with me, just so I could breathe.

"Artemis?" I exhale abruptly. "I can time travel."

"Cool!" She gets a stolen red jelly bean out of her pocket. "I love that for you."

"No." I clear my throat. "I mean it. I can time travel. I don't have a clue how, but I just sort of…can. It just *happened*, a couple of weeks ago, so that's…a thing I can do now, I guess. Which makes me a time traveler. A shit one, admittedly, but a time traveler nonetheless."

Artemis stares at me for a few seconds and I close my eyes.

Not to time travel; just so I can't see her.

"Okay," she says after a few seconds. "So walk me through it."

I open my eyes. "Huh?"

"More details, please. You can't just lob time travel out there and then not give me the juicy bits. I want to know literally everything."

I stare at my sister. "You believe me?"

"Of course I believe you, Cassandra. You're the most honest person I've ever known. Also, I don't even know how time works generally, so I'm not going to argue with you about the technicalities. *Although*—" Artemis gets a green jelly bean out this time "—I *did* lose quite a lot of brain cells in South America and Asia, so you're not exactly talking to a physicist here."

My brain is now rotating.

I did it.

I broke the Cassandra curse: my sister broke it, just by believing me.

"Well." The relief is so great I feel a little queasy. "I can't go back very far. Only to a specific day and time a couple of weeks ago. I tried to go back to, you know, undo Mum and Dad…" I pause and Art nods, so I crash on. "But I couldn't, I wasn't strong enough, so I've mostly been using it to…not get dumped by my ex-boyfriend."

Artemis stares at me. "Say that again?"

"It didn't work," I explain quickly, embarrassed. "Even with endless time on my side, it turns out I'm still extremely dump-able."

My sister continues to stare at me, no longer chewing.

"Not *just* that, though," I add again, slightly desperate now. "I did *other* things too. I avoided getting fired at work. My flat-mates don't seem to hate me so much, so maybe I won't end up moving house again. I went to a museum on a weekday, which was so cool. But…mainly I used it in tiny amounts to undo things I didn't like and redo the things I did. You know, kind of like a cosmic remote control."

Artemis spits her jelly bean into the bin.

"Cassandra Penelope Dankworth," she says in an appalled voice, "are you telling me that you have been given the epic, extraordinary, *magical* ability to commandeer the rules of time and space and see into the future, and you've been using it to get a boy back and avoid awkward social situations?"

I look at the floor. "Yes."

"Oh my God, you could have won the lottery." She jumps off the desk and stands in front of me. "You could have bet on all the right horses, forever. You could have started up your own television show where you predict things that will hap-pen. Called it *The Cassandra Conundrum* or something. Become famous and rich in, like, thirty days."

"But that would be cheating," I object, cheeks flaring.

"*That* would be cheating?" My sister's eyes open wide. "You could have saved so many lives, Cassie. How cinematic and dramatic would that story have been? Imagine. You, diving in front of buses and pulling people out of rivers. Please tell me you saved at least *one* life?"

"But…" I frown. "How, though?"

"I don't know, you could have checked the internet or local newspapers for tragic accidents over the last few weeks and gone round making sure they didn't happen." She holds her hands up. "That's just your *basic* time-travel narrative. Then there are all the *other* ones. Stopping wars and saving the world or whatever. Are you seriously telling me you did *none* of this?"

"No." I scratch my head. "It seemed a bit complicated."

"This is brilliant." Artemis is squealing with laughter now. "Cass, you are the worst time traveler *ever*."

"Also the worst prophet." I nod sheepishly. "I know. Although I *did* stop someone from losing some important computer files, so…"

Okay, I'm starting to feel ashamed of myself now. Art is totally right: I could have approached all of this on a much *bigger*, more cinematic scale. It just didn't really occur to me. All I can say in my defense is that if you give the power of time travel to a woman who eats banana muffins every day for three decades, you can't go expecting her to be someone else with it.

"Wait." Art stops laughing. "Have you time traveled *me*?"

"Yes," I admit sheepishly. "Not today. I gave it up for good recently. But yeah. We've had several run-ins over the last couple of weeks and I deleted them. A few fights. A bit of me running away. Once I did it right in front of you. Sorry about that."

"Shit." My sister shakes her head. "That's so crazy. What are all the alternative-universe versions of me like?"

"Exactly the same. Not much happens in that kind of time."

"Disappointing."

"Right?"

We sit in sobering silence for a few minutes, and I think about the day her letter arrived and the time our postman tends to deliver our mail, just after lunch. About 1:02 p.m., as it happens. And I think about how maybe it's less about where a story *starts*—or even the sand it's drawn in—and more about the person who's telling it.

"I'm sorry it didn't work out with the boy," Artemis says finally.

"That's okay," I say, standing up. "I don't think that was the relationship the universe was telling me to fix anyway."

34

I SPEND THE REST of my time off with my sister.

It's only three days, so we don't get carried away: I suggest the British Museum again, but Artemis insists that it isn't a holiday if you're still in London, doing all the same things you always do, so we get on a train to Cornwall and spend it eating chips, drinking cider and arguing about going in the sea. I don't want to get my trousers wet; Art walks in fully clothed.

Which is probably the essential difference between us.

Together, we take long strolls along the coastline—watching the turquoise-and-green seas break alabaster, white houses cling like Lego, birds swoop down and steal lunches, little children squeak, wrapped in red towels, tiny as fire ants—and energetically debate the difference between a "walk," a "hike" and a "trek" and exactly what it is we think we're doing. I say trekking—given the exercise levels required—and Artemis says walking, given that we keep sitting down on the edge to look at the sea, so we argue again and I stomp off for a bit to watch the waves on my own.

She sits down next to me and we debate how far France probably is and argue about that until I google it and win.

We dispute places to eat, every single time we need to eat.

I get angry that she's made a mess of our last-minute rented studio apartment within thirty seconds of arriving and construct a line down the middle of the room with paraphernalia out of the kitchen: cups, cushions, plates.

Artemis keeps moving the line, shifting it slowly until I'm barricaded in.

I shout at her to stop being childish.

She shouts at me to stop being childish about her being childish about me being childish, and we agree to remove the crockery from the floor and never tell anyone how we're still behaving at twenty-nine and thirty-one years old. Artemis leaves her wet sea clothes in a bag until it starts to smell like a teenage boy, so I hang them outside in the hallway and she tells me I'm being "totally ridiculous," so I hang them on her headboard while she's sleeping and she changes her mind.

I wake up one morning with her giggling face three inches from mine and her finger up my nostril, so I smack her.

She wakes up with her empty suitcase balanced on top of her; she smacks me.

We get a little bored when we're in our little adjoining double beds, so we play What Am I Pinging?, a traditional game we developed as prepubescents—fascinated with our developing bodies—that involved snapping your knicker elastic or the elastic in your brand-new bra and challenging each other to accurately guess which one it was. I win because adult bras sound nothing like teenage bras: they're an entirely different noise, it's not even a real test.

It's like no time has passed between us at all.

As if we've found a way to time travel without going anywhere, simply by being sisters. Ten years evaporate, and then they just keep disappearing: twelve years, fifteen years, twenty years, twenty-nine years, and I clearly remember Artemis being brought back from the hospital, standing in front of her cot and declaring her *mine*. *My* sister. *My* baby. *My* best friend.

Mine, like a cartoon mug that nobody else can drink out of.

Every few hours, Artemis gets a text or a phone call from Will and I watch her glimmer like an opal: first taking them out of sight or earshot—sensitive to my "recently singled status"—and eventually just falling in love in front of me.

For three whole days, I watch as my sister's ears go pink, her feet grow lighter and bouncier; as she smiles with her whole body and bends down to talk to every single bloody dog that ventures onto our path. Every single one. Sometimes she crosses the road, specifically so she can cuddle a canine. She ends up with hair all over her, saliva coating her face, and a small wet nostril in her ear, and all she does is laugh and look for another one to be assaulted by.

"Can you stop," I say eventually. "They keep touching me too."

"I want one." She beams, scanning the road for a new one. "I want *loads*. And pigs. Chickens. Kids. The human kind, not the baby goat kind. Although maybe some of the baby goat kind too. I want kids just *everywhere*. Climbing up the walls and up the trees and up on kitchen cabinets, like I used to. Remember? I want laughter and shouting and sleeping bags and tents in the garden and a house that's just full, *all* of the time. Doesn't it sound like bliss?"

"No," I decide firmly. "It sounds loud and dirty. It *was* loud and dirty, and there were only four of us."

"Exactly." Artemis smiles.

On our last night, just before we head back to London, I catch her watching me with a peculiar expression over an early dinner. It's so weird: I can read her without trying again. And I suddenly realize that she's the only person I have ever been able to do that with. It's a magical, heady power, and if this is how other people feel all the time, I don't know how they ever take it for granted.

"I haven't time traveled," I say when I've finally swallowed. She frowns. "Are you *sure*?"

"I told you, Artemis, I'm not doing it anymore. It's exhausting. And confusing. I'm terrible at it. All I do is screw up and forget what I've done and what I've undone. Also, let us be reminded of what happened to Trojan Cassandra when she kept telling everyone what was going to happen to them next."

"From what you've told me, she pissed everyone off."

"Exactly." I nod, satisfied that she was listening. "Nobody liked her. She was super unpopular. So unpopular that Agamemnon kidnapped her, and his wife, Clytemnestra, murdered her. Cassandra spends all of Greek mythology standing outside gates, yelling warnings and being told to bugger off because she's crazy, and then the Trojan War happens *anyway*. History does not treat prophets well, or know-it-alls, or people who really like being right. Even if, like me, they can't see the future but only sort of guess at it for the next three months."

Artemis nods. "What's happening right now? Just out of interest."

I glance at my watch. "The agency is stuck in an overrunning brainstorm about home composting. Everyone is fuming about being kept so late, the pizzas aren't well received and there's going to be a load of complaints to HR tomorrow. It's riveting stuff."

Art pretends to deliberate. "And on a national scale?"

"I'm not telling you the lottery numbers, Artemis."

"Oh, come on." She makes her gray eyes even bigger. "I've got the numbers right here—just rewind enough and we'll go get tickets."

"No."

"Just *five* of them? And a bonus ball?"

"No, Artemis. It's unethical."

"Ugh." She sighs and cuts her steak. "I wonder if it's even the same numbers. Like, if it's a different timeline, does it mean different balls? Maybe something happens and there's just a *second* of delay? And it changes everything? It's an interesting hypothetical question. Philosophers have been pondering this for thousands of years. You know how we could find out for sure?"

"No, Artemis. I'm not time hopping so you can win the lottery."

"Fine." She shoves the carcass in her mouth. "In that case, *you* are paying for dinner, you magical tightwad."

Art's phone rings and the air turns bright pink.

"It's Will." She studies my face. "Can I get this? I won't get it if it'll make you sad, Sandy-pants. It sucks, going through a breakup. I don't want to rub it in."

"My pants are only a bit sandy," I say with a small smile. "Take it."

For the last few days I've waited patiently for Romantic Heartbreak to arrive, and I don't think it has. I could be wrong, obviously, but from all the books I've read and films I've seen and songs I've heard, real heartbreak feels a bit worse than a blue fluttery sensation, similar to indigestion. From what I can tell from my colors, I'm a little sad, a bit lonely. I'm going to miss Will. I'm very worried I won't be having good sex again for a very long time. But I'm mostly okay. Maybe that means I'm broken, or a monster; maybe there's something fundamentally wrong with the way I'm wired.

But hey: this time my weirdness kind of worked in my favor.

"Hello, you!" Artemis hits the button. "Are you all packed and ready to go?"

I continue eating my pasta, listening to Will's warm voice bouncing off the side of her face. He has such a lovely voice. Thoughtful. Interested. I'm so glad he's being kind and warm to my sister. And I appreciate that might sound like sarcasm or bitterness, but it genuinely isn't.

"I looked up vaquitas, by the way." Art winks elaborately at me. "They are *super*cute. Like dolphins with smiley faces. Please can you bring one back—I promise I will take such good care of it."

She did not look up vaquitas: I looked them up for her.

Will says something else.

"Yes!" Art bounces in her seat. "I'd love that! I'm just having dinner with my sister. I got the steak, chips, spinach, which I picked off, and Cass got the…" She looks up. "What did you get, Cassandra? Some kind of mushroom tagliatelle."

I freeze with fungi still dangling off my fork.

"Huh?" Artemis frowns. "Cassandra. I told you about her! I did! My big sister. We haven't spoken for years, but I think she's very close to forgiving me." She winks at me, then frowns again. "Her last name? Dankworth, obviously, same as me." A short pause. "What do you mean I've never told you my surname? I'm sure I did. Or maybe it just never came up. We've only just met. Why are you being weird?"

Unable to move, I watch as Art's face changes.

Her colors have shifted into something dark, tangled, horrified, confused: an unwound ball of gray and green string.

Okay, I probably didn't need the powers of prophecy to predict a point in the near future where Will might ask for Art's incredibly rare surname. Or for the name of her sister. Or somehow put those two extremely obvious points together and reach an accurate conclusion. I'm just not very good at multitasking and I was having such a nice time arguing with my sister again, I totally forgot about it.

"I'll call you back," Artemis says flatly, putting the phone down.

She stares at me in horror.

I close my eyes.

"Don't you dare," she breathes. "Don't you *bloody dare*, Cassandra Dankworth. I swear to God, if you time travel right now, I am going to—"

"It's Will." Artemis studies my face. "Can I get this? I won't get it if it'll make you sad, Sandy-pants. It sucks, going through a breakup. I don't want to rub it in."

Desperate, I scrabble for my only available option.

"It's still so raw," I say, putting down my mushroom and trying to look distressed, which involves biting my lip and staring at the ceiling. "So much pain. So much...aching." I tentatively place my hand on my chest. "Here." Then on my head. "And here." Where else could romantic heartbreak go? "Also, a little bit in my nose."

"Oh my God." My sister cancels Will's call and tosses her phone into her bag. "Of course. Shit, I'm being so insensitive. Just flaunting my happiness in your face, like a complete brute. The evening is yours. No more texting or phone calls. I didn't realize it was still so painful. You haven't talked about him at all, but I forgot that's what you do when you really care."

I nod in relief, but I'm going to need a new plan.

That was a temporary measure, but what do I do about a long-term solution? Now I've had time to adjust, I just want to give Artemis and Will a little more time together before I reveal this relationship-shattering news. Just a few weeks, that's all. They've only had one coffee together so far. It's still so brand-new. Fragile. Maybe if they've really bonded, the fact that her new boyfriend is my ex and his ex-girlfriend is her only sibling won't be quite so bloody weird.

Who am I kidding: it's always going to be weird.

We're not sisters Ariadne and Phaedra, sharing the hero Theseus. There will be very few people in the world—apart from me—who aren't grossed out by this complicated new dynamic.

"I think," I say slowly, scrabbling for a stopgap idea, "maybe you should hold off telling him your real name for a little while, Art. Stay Diana until you see Will again. You've only just met him. I'm pretty sure he'll react well, he sounds so nice, but it'll probably be easier when he gets back from his trip."

"Yeah." Artemis thinks about it. "Admitting to lying about who you are is more of an in-person confession, isn't it. Fake names tend to make you sound mad." She coughs. "I'd imagine. Not that I've done it before or anything."

"You've done it before, haven't you?"

"Just a couple of times," she admits, laughing brightly with no shame at all. "But, in my defense, those times I was working in a theater and *everybody* has a stage name, so it doesn't really count."

My brain is desperately searching for the next logical step.

Will leaves for his work trip to Mexico soon, and he gets back in two weeks. I suspect Artemis is going to keep referring to me as *Sandy-pants* between now and then, even though I've repeatedly asked her not to. That gives me time. I should have worked out how to gently break this awful information to them by then. Maybe buy them a drink—buy them a *lot* of drinks—sit them down and explain that they're not *related*, it might just feel for a minute like they are.

"Don't tell him your surname," I add quickly, just in case. "Or he might google you and realize you're lying before you speak to him."

"I didn't even think of that." Artemis rolls her eyes. "Thank God for you, Cass. You always think things through properly."

I swallow what feels like a tidal wave of guilt. For someone who finds lying so physically painful, I sure seem to be capable of doing it quite effectively. Except I'm not doing it for me, right? I'm not manipulating them for my gain this time; I'm manipulating them for theirs.

Somehow that does not make me feel any better.

"Do you want to talk about him?" Artemis leans across the

table and puts one finger on top of my hand. It's what she's done ever since we were little because she knows I don't love being touched: it's our version of a hug. "The breakup? We can get into the nitty-gritty. Make a list. Rip him apart. Talk about *all* the worst things about him, then emphasize them, then *exaggerate* them, until we conclude that you've officially made a lucky escape and you can do *so* much better. I'll start. From the absolutely nothing you've told me, he sounds like a total *tosspot*."

I laugh and feel a flicker of what might be real sadness.

Then I get excited about feeling sad—*Sadness! A little splash of heartbreak! I'm human!*—and the excitement at feeling an appropriate emotion wipes it out and I'm back to square one again.

"He's not a tosspot." I shrug. "It just didn't work."

"But maybe it *could*," Artemis points out. "You're a time traveler, remember? I know I mocked you, but are you *sure* you don't want to try again?"

I think about everything I'd have to give up to do it.

And I suddenly realize that my life no longer feels paper-plate disposable; I can't just throw it away or undo it. I don't want to discard it because it's not perfect, or because there are flaws in my tapestry. It's not quite there yet—there's still a long way to go—but I want my life to eventually become ceramic: one I can wash and keep, even when it chips. A life I can use every day; one I smile at because it makes me happy, like a picture of a cute hedgehog.

"I don't want to try again," I say with a bolt of surprise. "I think I do love him, in my own way, but I'm not sure I love him in the way I want to love someone. Not in the way I'm waiting to love someone."

While her sister married Theseus, Ariadne ultimately ended up with the god Dionysus, although I suspect she would have been equally happy on her own; sometimes things just work out the way they're supposed to.

Art nods. "You're so wise. So grown-up."

"Right?" I laugh. "Pudding?"

"Shall we share?"

And another fight kicks off immediately.

By the time we return to London, I'm ready to be alone again. My insides don't ache anymore, my bones aren't hollow with loneliness; I'm craving silence and the contentment of my own company. Artemis is enormous fun, but she doesn't have a pause button, or a volume button, or a standby button, and her batteries seem to be constantly charged, whereas mine appear to have run out.

"I probably need to head back to Cambridge," Art says reluctantly as we get off the train at Paddington. "I'd imagine my boss is going to be a bit mad at me for skipping out."

I stare at her. "You have a job?"

"I *did*." She grins. "I'm a waitress. Or I was. I'm sure it'll be fine. But if it's not, I'll just go be a waitress somewhere else. Priorities, and all that."

We stand in silence for a few seconds.

"There's still stuff I need to say," Artemis starts tentatively. "Important stuff, Cass. It was just so lovely seeing you again, I didn't want to disrupt our holiday by bringing it all up."

I think about everything she said, all those years ago, at the funeral.

I think about all the things we haven't said since.

And I suddenly wonder why we put so much store in words, when they can mean so incredibly little.

"You don't need to," I tell her, kissing her forehead. "I love you too."

35

BY THE TIME I REACH HOME, I'm a human firework.

I'm so exhausted that every cell in me is exploding: fizzing and screaming in a painful mess of sound and color and light. My body crackles, and every time I breathe, the sound sets off a brand-new detonation. With my eyes open, the world flashes and lurches like a boat in a storm, but with my eyes shut, it's like being locked inside a black box while Guy Fawkes goes hell to leather with my very own private display. From decades of experience, there's absolutely nothing I can do: all of this noise and light is coming from inside me.

Shaking, I close my bedroom curtains, ram earplugs into my ears, climb under my duvet and wait patiently for the storm to pass. Eventually, it starts to slow down, so I'm extremely irritated when there's a faint beep, accompanied by another shooting pain and a new, blinding flare of electric green.

Emerging like a disgruntled tortoise, I grab my phone.

Hey! What are you wearing? ;) x

I stare at the unknown number.

I've briefly dated a *lot* of men over the last few years, so once they've evaporated, I delete their numbers to keep my phone book nice and tidy. Whoever it is, this feels like an inappropriate question regardless.

Frowning, I type:

Pajamas. Why?

A *beep*.

LOL! You can do better than that! ;)

This is now almost definitely a sex thing and I am so not in the mood.

Scowling, I type:

Pale blue pajamas with flying horses on them.
Who is this?

A *beep*.

It's Sophie! They sound amazing! But you can't wear
them to the party can you? Isn't it black tie? <3 Xxx

I stare at my screen. Sophie from work? How did she get my number? Are we on texting terms now? We need to discuss our work privacy policy. More importantly, *party*? Why would I ever agree to go to a—

Shit. I hoped that was an alternative timeline.

The gala is tonight?

The three flashing dots seem to last forever.

Yes! I forgot you've been on holiday! Was it fun?

Where did you go? Are you tanned? Did you get
the email with all the deets? If you didn't, it's 7 pm in
Holborn! I've attached a link! What are you going to
wear? I'm SO excited. I've got this floor-length coral
number, it's got kind of appliqué flowers all around
the top and it's SO fancy. Lol. Will you wear heels?
Do you think there'll be dancing? I love dancing. Do
you like dancing? This is my first ever work gala!
Eeeeeeeeekkkk! Are you excited?

That's an awful lot of questions to answer in one go.

Honestly, I wish people would just keep their communication to the essentials and leave The Irrelevants until they're at
least standing in front of you, or—in an ideal world—never.

Frustrated already, I type:

Yes. Cornwall. No. Haven't looked. Thanks.
Don't know. Don't know. Maybe. No. Not really.
See you there.
Cassie.

Then I look at my watch and winch myself painfully out of
bed.

I know I promised I wouldn't fiddle with time anymore—
a promise I've broken once already—but for a few seconds, I
genuinely consider erasing the entire last month of my life just
to get out of this one social event.

Increasingly irked, I go to my open rack and stare at it.

Nobody at work knows about all my vintage clothes, or that
I'm a diligent collector of color and texture and shape and fabric. My hoard makes me so very happy. There's a ruffled primrose dress and a pair of soft, pink balloon-silk trousers and a
red corduroy jacket with a gold silk lining so gorgeous it makes
my womb hurt. There's velvet and cashmere, damask and linen
and muslin; plums and indigos and creams and aquas and cel-

adon and apricot and lavender. All things bright and beautiful. Anything that brings me happiness gets carried home, and
then I wear my five allocated jumpsuits Monday to Friday so
all the joy doesn't get ruined at work.

Sighing, I run my fingertips over the rack, but I'm so tired
now everything suddenly feels scratchy and unwearable. Also,
I don't want the bad memories of a work gala to seep into an
outfit I otherwise love and ruin it forever.

Frustrated, I tug on my chicken dressing gown and walk into
the kitchen. Sal is perched in the breakfast nook, surrounded
by what looks like seven dismantled jumpers. Something I said
must have stuck: she has clearly eschewed the YouTube channel
for what I assume is an attempt at either knitting or whatever
it's called when you take it all apart again.

"Hello, Cassie!" Sal glances up and looks genuinely happy to
see me. Something in my stomach feels warm. "You're back!
Did you go somewhere nice? You look well—you're *glowing*.
I wanted to say thank you again for the other night. I've been
trying to listen to my gut, or my throat, or whatever it is, and
I've decided to start my own knitwear range! I've got little labels made up and everything."

She gestures at tiny black fabric tags with *Salini Sews* embroi-
dered on them. Now is probably not the right time to point out
that she's not sewing anything; she seems happy and inspired,
and that's what matters.

"Sal?" I hover awkwardly by the table, unable to meet her
eyes. "Do you think I could have my dress back?"

She frowns. "Sorry?"

"The big blue tulle dress I gave you a couple of weeks ago.
I don't need it *back* back, but I've got this party ball gala thing
tonight and I want to wear something I already hate so it doesn't
make me hate something new."

Sal stares at me, eyes narrowed, and I think I may have broken an unspoken social rule about gifts: beware the Trojans,

etc., and also asking for them back so you can sweat profusely in them in public.

"Oh," she says with a frown. "No. I don't think so."

I flush hot. "Please."

"No." Sal assesses me carefully. "You can't go to a ball wearing something you already hate, Cassie. It'll be no fun at all. Why don't I lend you something? That way you can just give it back when you've turned against it and I'll make sure you never have to see or touch it again. Something supersoft, right? Wait there."

Sal jumps up, bounces up the stairs and disappears into her bedroom.

My throat abruptly tightens.

Sal somehow understood what I needed without making me feel weird about it first, and now I think I might be about to cry. Desperate to show my gratitude, I swallow and look at the labels again. Maybe I can sew them all in for her, to say thank you. I cut out all the labels in my own clothes, obviously, but it's a thing other people enjoy: they seem to put such great store in whatever they say.

The kitchen door opens again and I brighten. "Sal—"

"Well, *hello*." Derek swaggers in and grins at me. "Where have you been, you dirty little stop-out?"

I freeze and look at the table. "On holiday."

"With a new guy? Must have been a good few days." Derek opens a cupboard, assessing me as he selects a plate. "I didn't know you had it in you, Cassandra. Although it looks like you did. More than once, judging by the state of your hair."

If Will is a man with a myriad of destinies and futures contained inside him, I think Derek might be the opposite: he has just the one, and he's going to goddamn fulfill it in the same way if it kills him.

Dismayed, I try to inhale deeply and realize I can't.

"Hey." He opens the fridge and leans his body into it. "I'm

just joking, Dankworth. Banter, you know? You don't need to look *quite* so appalled. I'm not a *predator* or anything. I'm just playing around."

Terror mounting, I pick up a label and stare at it.

"Do I make you nervous, Cassie?" Derek picks out a container of fried rice and struts over to the dinner table. "I don't mean to, you know. I just want you to be comfortable here, Cassandra. My *casa* is your *casa*, after all. Or, I should say, your *Casa*-ndra. Ha ha."

With a fork, he picks out a green pea and pops it in his mouth.

Rigid, I glance at the kitchen door and wait for Sal to come back. It's about to happen. I can feel the end of the loop coming again, like the end of a roll of toilet paper, and it's way, way sooner than it should be. Yet again, everything I've done to avoid my fate has only brought it to me faster. *Derek keeps hitting on me*, I'll say. And Sal will say, *What the fuck, Derek?* And Derek will open his eyes wide and say, *I cannot believe you would say that, Cassandra. I'm incredibly hurt. I was just trying to make you feel welcome in your new home*, and next thing I know, I'm apologizing profusely and they're yelling at each other and laptops are being left with "Rooms to Rent" already opened for me.

With shallow breaths, I watch the door and pray for Sal to come back or not come back: I can't work out which.

"So who's the lucky guy?" Derek grins and takes a small step toward me. "Because you're quite the catch, if I do say so, Cassandra Dankworth."

He leans over for the salt and I feel his hand rest gently, just for two seconds, on my waist.

Pain shoots through me, and that does it: every tiny bit of doubt and hesitation evaporates. I cannot believe he convinced me I was imagining this. I cannot believe I *apologized*. His creepiness is now as clear as those bloody teeth-whitening strips he leaves stuck to the floor of the bathroom every week.

"Derek." With a flash of bright purple, I stand up. "Keep your *fucking hands* away from me, you *rampaging dickface*."

He blinks. "Huh?"

"You will not touch me *ever again*." I take a step toward him, so our noses are almost touching. My rage feels like a bolt of lightning I can throw across the room. "You will not enter my bedroom. You will not make inappropriate comments. You will not gaslight me *ever again*. The next time you do, I am going to rip your fucking fingers off and ram them, one by one, down your throat. And then I'll go back in time and do it again. And again. And again. Do you understand, Derek? I can *literally* turn back time to torture you and I will, happily, so consider this my *only* warning."

He opens his mouth. "I was just trying to be fr—"

"No," I hiss, finally certain. "You were not."

"What's going on?" Sal says in a carefully light voice behind me. "What's with all the shouting, guys? That's normally a job I take very seriously. You're going to make me fully redundant."

Cheeks flaring, I spin round to face my flatmate. Sal has an armful of beautiful evening gowns skimming the floor, and I'm so touched and simultaneously so ready for this to be over now. I'm done with the looping. I'm done with the prophecies. I'm done with inching through time as if on a Battleship board, trying to remember all the places I've already exploded.

"Derek keeps hitting on me," I say firmly.

Sal's eyes widen. "What the fuck. Derek?"

"Oh my God, I cannot *believe* you would say that, Cassandra." Derek's eyes grow round, and honestly, it's so convincing he nearly fools me again. "I'm *incredibly* hurt. I was just trying to make you feel welcome in your new home. You always seem to be on your own, and we felt sorry for you. Didn't we, Sal?"

Sal turns to me and gently rests her hand on her throat.

"Didn't we, Sal?" Derek says again when she doesn't answer. "Come on, we've *talked* about this. There's obviously something wrong with her. She's pretty clearly on the spectrum or whatever, and I knew someone at school like that, so I *think* I know what I'm talking about. It's not her fault. She just doesn't really understand what's going on, that's all. She's, like, fundamentally incapable of it."

I close my eyes briefly: it never gets old, being told that you're broken.

"Red or green?" Sal says quietly.

I open my eyes again, unsure if she's talking to me or Derek. "Huh?"

"Red or green?" She lifts two silk dresses: both bright and floor-length, soft and so slinky they look like fresh fruit skin. "Green would look stunning on your coloring, Cassie, but the red is a showstopper. Do you want to try them on so we can see?"

Disoriented, I blink at the dresses, then at Sal, then at Derek. Then at Sal. Then at Derek, just for good measure. Did I accidentally erase time again? I think I must have done, because none of this dialogue seems to fit together properly.

"I..." I frown, looking for the segue. "Derek hit on me."

Maybe it needs saying again, just in case.

"Yes," Sal says in a low voice, and I suddenly realize her colors are simmering close to her skin and reflecting, like the bubbles on top of oily water. "And I am so incredibly sorry, Cassie. You shouldn't have to deal with that kind of shit in your own house. I'm just about to go into the bedroom and throw Derek's belongings out of the window, but I thought before I did that we should probably decide on your outfit. It's about to get really loud and really messy and there might be some small fires set, so I don't want to make you late for your gala. Red or green?"

My eyes suddenly fill. "You believe me?"

She smiles. "Of course I do."

"Wait." Derek situates himself between us and holds his

hands out like a matador. "You believe *her*? The crazy girl who moved in two months ago versus the man you've been living with for *five years*?"

"Completely." Sal nods, her dark eyes glittering. "Without a single second of hesitation. Get your shit out of my father's flat, Derek. You now have thirty seconds to save everything you want to keep before it gets smashed, flushed down the loo or shoved up your perfect little tanned ass. Twenty-nine."

"But—"

"Twenty-eight, twenty-seven…"

"This is ridiculous."

"Twenty-six, twenty-five, twenty-four…"

"I *barely* touched her."

"Twenty-three, twenty-two, twenty…"

"I was just trying to *stabilize myself* while I *reached for the salt*."

"By the time I've finished with you," Sal says calmly, and her bubbles glow purple, green and pink, "the salt will be somewhere you will never be able to reach again, darling. Twenty-one…"

Derek yells "FUUUCCCKKKK" and runs to the bedroom.

Sal turns to me and grins; I feel myself slowly grin back, our colors reaching across the kitchen and swirling into each other.

"Hey!" She holds a hand up, so I obediently tap it. "So I think I worked out why I'm stuck, huh?"

I'm still trying to work out what changed between us. What exactly shifted the narrative? Was it the dress I gave her? Was it the chili Sal brought me? Was it a finger on her shoulder when she was crying, or the offered raw croissant I never ate? Was it sharing the truth with each other? Or did every tiny connection— every word, every gesture, every kindness—simply nudge us in a brand-new direction?

"Green," I say with a sudden lump in my throat.

"Good choice." Sal holds out the dress and I stare at it for a few seconds and immediately change my mind.

"Red." I take it. "No, green. Wait. Red. Green? Do you have blue?"

"Take them all," Sal laughs, shoving the slippery heap into my arms simultaneously. "See which one feels right when you put it on. You know, in your shoulder blades or wherever."

We smile at each other and I suddenly realize I have a new friend.

The room turns yellow.

"Have all the fun tonight, Cassie." Sal begins to limber up as if she's about to run a marathon: stretching her neck and pulling her arms above her head. "Tomorrow, if you want to, we can reallocate all the kitchen cupboard space and go for a drink to celebrate our freedom?"

I nod formally. "I'd like that very much."

"Me too." Sal cracks her knuckles. "Now, please excuse me while I go *overreact* just as much as I bloody want to."

36

THE GREEK DEITIES LOVE a good dramatic reveal.

They're regularly disguising themselves as peasants or old women or young boys, before abruptly discarding their human bodies as the ultimate *fuck you* to anyone who underestimates them. Dionysus does it (before transforming those who wronged him into dolphins); Zeus and Hermes do it together as a bro-team effort to Philemon and Baucis; Athena does it to Arachne just before her moment of cruel triumph. It's a classic moment, and so instinctively appealing it has been wound through fairy tales and Disney films and brightly colored '90s rom-coms ever since.

Thought you knew what I was capable of? Think again, bitches.

And I confess there's a moment—while I'm waiting for Sophie outside Holborn station in Sal's long, silky red dress and orange sky-high heels that I'm already regretting—where I briefly imagine striding into the gala and everyone I work with falling to their knees, cowering in awe and regret. Subdued by my lack of scheduled jumpsuit and the realization that I am not who they thought I was. I am more than they could ever have possibly imagined.

I am Cassandra Dankworth: goddess of time travel.

Okay, technically Chronos was the god of time—hence the word *chronology*—but they didn't have horological *travel* as a concept in ancient Greece, so you could argue that there's a neat little opening, ready to be filled.

Either way, I am so very ready for my moment.

Then Jack appears behind me and says, "Hi, Cassandra, do you need the toilet? Why are you jiggling up and down like that?" So I guess that's my big reveal ruined already.

"A little bit," I admit, watching the road. "There's Sophie."

My colleague is swishing very self-consciously down the road toward us in an elaborate peach ball gown—as pleased with herself as a cat—and I feel a sudden rush of fondness toward her. It's not just me. We're all just one excellent outfit from becoming Aphrodite in *The Iliad*, getting ready to drop the weird old-lady syntax and blast everyone away with our glory.

"Isn't this the most exciting thing that's ever happened to any of us?!" Sophie beams at us. "Doesn't everyone look beautiful? I wish we all dressed like this all the time. Look at what happens to my dress when I spin!"

Sophie rotates like a kebab and Jack lifts his eyebrows at me.

"Is she with us?" he asks sharply. "Or did the poor girl get lost on her way to a local art school prom?"

"This is Sophie." I lock eyeballs with him and try to send the pain straight back to him, telepathically. "She's the new junior account executive on your account, a public relations genius and *entirely* responsible for the SharkSkin campaign, so I believe that this is the person we're all here to celebrate."

"I did almost nothing." Sophie beams. "It was Cassie's idea. Also, it *is* my prom dress, Mr. Burbank! How did you know that? I wore it when I graduated last year with a first-class honors degree in mathematics and physics. Although I confess my degree hasn't been that useful yet on your account. Maybe I'll do more adding up and subtracting when I'm the CEO of my own company, just like you?"

Jack's face twitches in shock and I laugh loudly: looks like the Big Reveal this evening belongs to Sophie.

"Well." He assesses her with a brand-new expression. "Glad to have you on our little team. Let's go."

Jack strides off toward the historic Lincoln's Inn with irritated shoulders and Sophie links her arm through mine and beams at me.

"I *love* being underestimated," she whispers. "It's my superpower. Nobody ever sees me coming."

"They do not," I admit, feeling a sudden swell of pride.

Arm in arm, Sophie and I walk toward the gala with colors starting to ripple through me in waves. Even from across the road, I can hear it: music, chattering, laughter. People in black tie are gravitating toward the elegant redbrick building as if magnetized by medieval architecture. From the research I did on the way here, I am fully prepared for a Great Hall, complete with Striking Fresco and Minstrels' Gallery and a ceiling of Beautifully Worked Oak. I am prepared for Natural Daylight (even though it's dark) and Modern and Traditional Spaces. Most importantly, I am prepared for a capacity of up to 450 guests, with dining spaces for up to 250.

I'm sorry, but that's just way too many humans in one place; we're not camping outside the gates of Troy for the next ten years.

Heart rate increasing, I rummage through my handbag until I find a set of neon-yellow earplugs. Nope. Rummaging again, I find a pair of pink ones. They clash unpleasantly with my dress, so I keep rummaging until I find the little gold pair I keep for particularly fancy kinds of noise.

Relieved, I pop them in and feel my breathing slow.

I can still hear, but everything is muffled, far away, as if everyone has had their volume buttons turned down.

Entering through the front doors, I stand at the entrance and feel reluctantly impressed: the room is dim, lit by candles, beautiful, and the fresco is magnificent. Underneath are long, thin tables—crammed with glittering people, mostly in black— and at some point, I have a horrible suspicion they're going to clear them all away and expand the dance floor into something truly horrifying.

"Oh my gosh!" Sophie grabs my hand and pulls me across the room, waving her hand so frantically I worry she's about to sprain her wrist. "We've got just the *best* table! Right in the middle of all the action! Hi, guys!"

In my muted bubble, I get tugged behind her like a tiny boat tied to a ship.

Strangers stand up and greet Sophie with kisses.

She beams, kissing them all back. "John, you dashing fellow, how's the sprained ankle? Much better? I'm so glad! Gareth, your hair looks amazing! What mousse are you using? Jada, you absolute sweetheart, did you save me the seat next to you? That's exactly where I wanted to be! Gabby, can I just say how *stunning* that color is on you? And Elaine! We've not met yet, but I have heard *all* about you. How's your son? Is he settling into uni better now? Remind me to give you a list of all the best party venues in that area. It should help him acclimatize more easily."

Stunned, I stare at Sophie as she makes her way around the circle, not an ounce of fakeness or sarcasm in sight. Who are all these people? I'm assuming they work at SharkSkin, which is ridiculous. I had *all of time* at my disposal, yet while I was on holiday Sophie managed to connect with the rest of the in-house team more than I managed in literally all of eternity.

When Prometheus made us, he clearly used very different clay.

"Oh!" Sophie takes her seat and jubilantly gestures at the spare seat space next to her until I sit down. "Cassie, this is everyone! I got to know them while you were gone and they're awesome. Everyone, this is our amazing PR account manager and good friend of mine, Cassandra Dankworth!"

"Hello," I murmur, staring at the table until everyone has gone back to whatever conversation they were having before we arrived. At Sophie's last few words, a pleased bolt of orange has leaped through me—neon and warm—so I sit and wait for the glow to dissipate.

I guess I'm adding Sophie to my new-friend list too.

My shoulder prickles slightly, so I swivel to stare curiously at the man sitting directly to my right. He's in a tux, just like every other man in here, which gives him a strange, homogeneous, penguin quality. For a moment, we're both so out of context, I can't work out who he is. He's both familiar and strange, like seeing your dentist buying a loo roll next to you in a supermarket. Thrown, I frown at his chest—something is missing—and then realize what it is: a navy cashmere jumper.

"Ronald!" I say in amazement. "It's you!"

He frowns. "Hi—"

"What are you doing here?" I'm so ridiculously pleased to see him. After the chaos of the last month, he feels deliciously known. Even though we've never really spoken. It's quite strange: everything else has reached its conclusion now, and Ronald feels like the final piece of my time puzzle. "Of course, you must have started now! I sit next to you at work."

Ronald is staring at me with the regular old expression on his face—I still have absolutely no idea what it is—and I feel a wave of pleasure at the sheer familiarity of it. It's identical and so incredibly comforting. Although I have to be honest: this particular timeline must suit him, because I don't remember him ever being *this* attractive before. He has a little dimple in his cheek and everything.

"Oh my God!" Sophie leans in front of me toward him. "Cassie, this is Cameron. Cameron, this is Cassie. You're going to love her. You haven't even seen the Weekday Jumpsuits yet! They're a wonder! Ron started at Fawcett PR this week, but I *begged* Barry to put him on the SharkSkin account with us and it worked, so he's here at the ball to get to know everybody properly!"

"Not a *ball*," Jack sighs in frustration across the table. "A *charity gala*."

Introduction done, Sophie returns to laughing with Elaine.

"Hi there." Definitely-not-Ronald smiles.

I stare at him in blank silence while I wait for this horrifying new information to process. Either something I have done over the last few weeks has altered Ronald's entire identity from birth—which seems unlikely—or, in an effort to be more polite and formal, I have been calling this poor man by the wrong name since he started.

At least I finally know what that bloody expression means.

"Cameron," I say, putting my hand over my mouth. "Fuck. I'm so sorry, I just assumed… And I've been calling you *Ronald* for *months*." I kick myself yet again. "By which I mean days, obviously. Because you only just started and we've never met before, so that would be chronologically impossible. Time is a bit weird. Sorry."

"Just Ron is fine." Ron laughs and leans slightly toward me. He really *does* smell lovely: like vanilla and doughnut and a hint of something blue. Have his eyelashes always been this long? "I actually feel much more like a Ronald than a Cameron, if I'm being honest. And time *is* weird. For instance, I'm not a big fan of stuff like this and my watch is saying I only arrived fifteen minutes ago, but I'm pretty sure it's been years."

"Decades," I laugh, knowing exactly what he means.

"When I got here," he whispers, "there were still bloody Tudors."

We both chuckle like coconspirators who hate socializing, and was his smile always this wide? Were his eyes always this warm and friendly? Were his cheekbones always so high, and his shoulders so very—

Fuck.

I drop my gaze to the tablecloth, suddenly unable to look at him.

"Wow, I like your earrings." I can feel his dark brown pupils on the side of my face. "Are they earrings? I've never seen the kind that goes *inside* your ear before. It's cool. You look like a glamorous spaceman."

I flush with pleasure and risk another quick glance at him. There's still a strange expression on Ron's face—still incalculable, still unreadable, like a book written in a language I can't understand—but there's a beautiful shade of peach coming out of him now, warm like a nectarine in the sun. Except, if his facial expression wasn't entirely me getting his name wrong, then what else could it be? Unless...

Oh.

"They're earplugs," I admit as the space between us crackles bright magenta. "I find everything a little bit too loud."

"Me too." He nods and passes me the bread. "I have noise-canceling headphones permanently attached for the same reason."

"Me *too*," I say in amazement, finally meeting his pupils with mine.

There's an almost audible explosion.

Something in me leaps like a little yellow fish, there's a flicker of something neon orange, then Jack stands up and aggressively tinkles his glass with his fork, thus immediately ruining everything.

"Speaking of unnecessary noise..." Ron chuckles quietly.

"Before the official event begins," Jack announces, surveying our table with distaste as if he's just inadvertently found himself in the servants' quarters, "I would like to thank the entire SharkSkin team for—"

I can feel myself starting to beam at everyone, in no particular direction. The room is shimmering; with the volume turned down, I can feel and see the soft colors seeping from everyone, and it's so incredibly beautiful.

"Cassandra."

Raspberry and mint and cornflower and crimson and jade.

"Cassandra."

Ruby and flax and flamingo and azure; cream and bronze and cyan and lavender and coral; tangerine, charcoal and mustard. And as the brightness melts and spirals, I feel an abrupt shudder of happiness so overwhelming—so three-dimensional—I have to bounce up and down and wriggle and flex as it moves through me: channeling the excess joy through the soles of my feet.

I did it.

I used time travel to take me to a happier place, and I'm so *incredibly* grateful for it—so thankful to the universe for this extraordinary gift—but now I simply don't need it anymore. It's something I have but will never use, like one of those gadgets that turn zucchini into spaghetti.

"Cassandra Dankworth," Jack says loudly as Ron gently leans to the side and nudges me with his shoulder. I turn to stare at him briefly, amazed that I haven't instinctively lurched away. Then I look back at Jack, staring at me over his champagne. "Okay, she's back. I would like to raise a toast to Cassandra. It's certainly true that I *may* have had my misgivings about you in the beginning."

Stifling a sigh, I wait for the onslaught of adjectives to begin.

"*But*—" Jack holds his glass in the air "—I'm delighted to say that you have proven me wrong. You may not work as most people do, or indeed probably should, but you are an asset to the SharkSkin team. So I'd like to say thank you, from all of us, and congratulations on a fantastic launch. To Cassandra!"

"Speech!" Sophie claps loudly next to me. "Speech!"

Everyone raises a glass in my direction, so I tentatively pick up my glass and stand. The candles are flaring and the colors are bleeding and I can feel the safe cocoon of my breath, wrapped around me like a roaring blanket. A solid sensation settles on my shoulder blades, and suddenly I feel transformed: dropping my disguise and holding up my imaginary sword like Athena.

With a smile, I lift my glass. "I quit."

My colleagues are staring at me with slightly open mouths, but I have never felt this calm, steady or powerful. I feel solid, whole, unbroken, as if all my colors have finally settled into the right place.

"I hate this job," I clarify helpfully. "So I quit."

My speech is obviously over—that's all I have to say—so I sit back down, but everyone is staring at me in silence, so I reluctantly stand up again.

"I shouldn't be here," I explain, staring fixedly at a napkin on the table. "I've been fired from this job about nineteen times over the last month, and I think I was supposed to stay fired. We are entirely incompatible. I don't like the public, I don't like relating, I don't like SharkSkin moisturizer and I also don't need time travel to undo this mistake. So I'd like to quit, please. And, Sophie—" I flash a shy smile at her "—thank you for being so kind to me. I know this version of you won't remember a lot of it, but the impact you have had on all my timelines has been... enormous."

Done, I sit down again and briefly study Jack's face.

He looks...shocked. Unimpressed. Irritated?

Ah. Mad as hell.

"Can I wait to eat my dinner before I leave?" I glance around the still gobsmacked table. "No, you're right. I think I'm probably supposed to make a big dramatic exit now, aren't I."

With a wave of something that feels surprisingly like sadness, I stand up, take out my earplugs and hold them out toward Ron. I really was looking forward to getting to know him properly.

"It was very nice to meet you, Ron. Would you like these? You might want to clean them first, obviously."

"Thanks." Ron takes them and grins up at me. My stomach flips again. "Good luck, Cassie. I really hope I catch you around sometime."

I smile at him. Some time. Who knows? There's so much of it.

"I really hope so too."

Feeling triumphant and glorious, I clear my throat and push my seat noisily back just as a master of ceremonies starts slapping a microphone at the front of the room. I've actually done it. I've made a change. Altered my own path. Time travel aside, I've been stuck in a loop of my own making for a very long time now, just going round and round.

"I haven't even made my first joke yet," the compere laughs loudly. "And already someone is leaving!"

Every person in the room turns to stare at me in one smooth motion.

But all I can think about now is the biggest reveal story of all: that of the poor mortal Semele. Zeus visited her in human form, and the two fell madly in love with each other. When his wife, Hera, discovered yet another flagrant infidelity, she visited Semele in the disguised form of an old lady and convinced her that she was a fool, because it couldn't possibly be the king of the gods she loved. The only way to find out for sure was to demand that Zeus show himself to her in his real form.

Convinced, Semele begged Zeus to show himself to her as he really was.

Reluctantly, Zeus did exactly that.

Within seconds, the sheer reality of Zeus caused Semele to explode: pop like a blood blister and burst into flames. As I stand in the middle of the gala and feel 398 eyes on me, I realize that's how it sometimes feels to be me.

As if I have to hide who I am, all of the time.

As if I have to pretend to be like everyone else, just so people will love me.

As if I'm constantly being asked to *share*, to *reveal* myself, to *open up*, and when I do—when I finally show people who I truly am—it's not what anyone wanted and they explode right in front of me.

I am so fucking *done* with making myself smaller.

Without a word, I pick up my handbag, grin at Sophie, Ron and Gareth, and walk toward the exit with my head held high, eyes burning holes into my back. Because I am not a monster or a goddess; I am not a prophet or a princess, a gorgon or a priestess. I am not Aphrodite or Athena, Arachne or Medusa. I did not emerge from a seashell, or the inside of a head; I do not have to weave my story, over and over again, and it is not—and never should be—told by other people.

My fate is not written in time, or sand, or stars, or in a tapestry, or a spider's web, and it never actually was.

I am Cassandra: the future was always in me.

As I walk calmly out of the building, I feel the earth settle.

A rumble, now flattening.

And when I see my sister, sitting impatiently on the steps outside the gala, I finally realize why I couldn't time travel back to that moment, ten years ago: the moment my life exploded and took me with it.

I couldn't travel there because I didn't need to.

In one way or another, a part of me has been stuck there all along.

37

TEN YEARS AGO

"Thank you for another touching speech, Cassandra."

The vicar patiently waits for me to return to my seat at the front of the congregation, hands folded neatly in my lap. My black dress is damp and tight. "All Things Bright and Beautiful" is being played loudly on the organ, which seems a bit ironic, given how clearly nothing will be bright or beautiful ever again.

"Is it my turn now?" Art staggers to her feet. "I have something to say."

"Artemis." The vicar smiles patiently. "Your turn is *after* the end of the second hymn, if you look at the schedule."

"Bugger the schedule," my sister slurs, adjusting her hat.

Everyone watches as my nineteen-year-old sister sways to the front of the church, red wine bottle gripped firmly in her right hand. She's dripping in black lace with a little perched pillbox hat and veil, and everyone thinks she's grieving in style, but I know she's mocking it: dressing up in sadness like a kid raiding their mother's wardrobe.

"Wow." Art stands behind the pulpit and takes a flask out of a lacy cape sleeve. She takes a swig and pops it on top of the hymnbook, then follows it with a swig of red wine. "This is a proper party, isn't it? So many people." She whips round to glitter furiously at the poor little organ boy. "Could you shut the hell up, please? Who chose that song, anyway? It's not a school assembly. What are you going to play next—'Cauliflower's Fluffy'? Jesus fucking Christ."

The entire congregation inhales in one go, like synchronized swimmers.

"Oh, *please*," she sighs. "It's just words. And we're not even religious. We're only doing this in a church because it's close to the house. Where was I?"

Artemis sways slightly and I abruptly realize why she turned up late.

Also why she sat at the back of the church.

"Oh, yeah." Art hiccups and holds her hands out, and I have a sudden image of her at six years old, preparing me for a dramatic two-person performance of a play about unicorns. "Ladies and gentlemen, welcome to the Death of My Parents. It's a show we weren't prepared for, isn't it, Cassie? No rehearsal for this one. One moment you're on your gap year, lying on a beach in Costa Rica, and the next you're being told to come home because your parents just exploded in a ball of flames at the same sodding time, very typically efficient of them."

Art's mouth is stained bright red all the way around and her colors are the saddest I've ever seen: grays, silvers, blacks, all spiky and sharpened.

I can feel my body temperature start to drop steadily.

"We've talked a lot so far about *the loveliness* of my parents." Art hiccups and grips the pulpit with both hands. "And they were. They were *lovely*. Susan Dankworth, genius, oddball and world-renowned Classics professor at Cambridge University. A lot of you are here for her, which is nice. And Gordon Dankworth, the nicest man that ever walked the earth, gardener and a big fan of what are they called? Begonias. Some of you are here for him, which is nice too."

My eyes are starting to close; the darkness is coming.

"I mean," Artemis continues, audibly slurring, "I don't feel like we talked enough about how terrible they were at driving, clearly, but time and place, right?"

Art's eyes intensify, and as I lift mine to meet them, pain shoots through me like a single flying arrow.

Sleep cascades in another wave.

"But for a show about their death," Artemis says, leaning forward on the pulpit with her elbows propped and her chin in her hands as if she's a tiny child posing for a picture, "nobody yet has brought up the *cause* of it. I mean, it feels like a key part of the narrative is missing, is it not? Don't bury the lede before you bury the leads, so to speak."

Art laughs wildly and takes another huge swig of wine.

My head is starting to bob, my chin drifting toward my chest; everything feels distant and muffled, as if it's being slowly tugged away.

"Wake up, Cassandra," my sister snaps. "Don't worry. This bit is about you."

Desperately, I try to lift my chin, but I'm slipping into unconsciousness as if it's a big empty hole and there's nothing around the edges left to grab on to.

"My sister, ladies and gentlemen." From a few meters away, I feel Artemis gesture toward me. "Cassandra Penelope Dankworth. Let me tell you about Cassie. She's not what you call a *People Person*. No, Cassandra is allll about Cassandra. You want to go play outside with her? Nope, it's dirty. Keen on a birthday party? You can't, because Cassie won't be able to handle the noise or mess. Would love a dog? Or a cat, or even a sodding gerbil? No, sorry, Cassie doesn't like animal hair or being licked or climbed on. Want to go to a new restaurant as a family? Bad luck, Cassie can only go to the same bloody restaurant and eat the same bloody meal, so that's where we're going. Again. And school? Let me tell you about *school*."

My eyes close briefly; the church is slipping away.

"You try to make friends, but everyone is like *oh, is that your big sister, hiding in bushes again? Rocking and clawing at her legs? What the hell is wrong with her, anyway?* So you say *nothing is wrong with her* and punch someone in the stomach, and next thing you know, you're the one with 'behavioral problems.'"

I try to sit up, but time is shifting away like sand in an egg timer.

"But there *is* something wrong with her," Artemis slurs fiercely, and suddenly her voice is choked, blocked, a sink full of debris. "Cassandra is broken and it's ruined my goddamn life. Her rules, her restrictions, her schedules, her rigidity. *Everything* has been about her, and now *she's* the reason our parents are dead."

Somehow, I get to my feet and stand, frozen.

"You *are*, Cassandra." She's started crying loudly. "You're the reason they're gone. They were *five minutes late* for your graduation ceremony, but you couldn't handle it, so you rang them. And rang them. And rang them. And rang them. You told me you rang them *fifteen times*, and somewhere in all that obsessive, relentless, batshit crazy ringing, they got distracted and crashed the bloody car."

Her sobs are filling the church, bouncing off the stained-glass windows.

"I hate you, Cassandra. If I could choose, I would pick somebody else for a sister. I just wanted a normal life, like everyone else, and I couldn't have one because of *you*."

She takes a large step off the podium and stumbles into the aisle.

"And you don't care." Hiccups, makes herself vertical again. "It's our parents' funeral and you haven't even *cried*. Look at you, standing there, dry-eyed and sleepy, like you're bored already. Like it doesn't matter. Like you're somewhere else. You're a monster." Hiccups. "Why can't you just be *normal*." Hiccups. "Be *human* for, like, *one minute*." Hiccups. "This bottle is empty," she concludes, holding it upside down. "Vicar, do your water-into-wine thing for me, pronto. Or is that Jesus. Or Moses. Who the hell cares anymore, I am here to *party*."

Slowly, I lift my chin and turn around.

Everything is still and everything is calm, and as everything I have ever known and loved crumbles around me, I stand in the wreckage with my face still and my eyes still dry and rubble in my hair.

"Thank you for coming," I say quietly to the hushed congregation. "There are cucumber sandwiches back at the house. And more wine, although you may want to get there before Artemis does."

Shoulders straight, I walk slowly down the aisle like a bride.

I open the church door.

I hold my hand up against the light and feel the scaffolding inside me dismantle, fall inward like a building that can't stand up anymore.

Then I close the door gently behind me.

38

NOW

"I couldn't go home," Artemis says.

"Yes." I sit down on the step next to her. "I can see that."

"I got all the way back to our house and all I could see was you, everywhere. The house is full of you. So I needed to come back." My little sister stares at me with wet eyes like a pavement after it's been raining. "Your flatmate told me where you were. The girl one. Not the dick one. She seems really nice."

"Sal," I say. "She is."

"And I know you don't want to talk about it, Cass, but I think we need to."

I nod. "Yes."

There's a long silence as we both listen to the laughter pouring out of the thick door behind us. I do not think the Tudors had much noise insulation; they should think about putting that in.

"I didn't mean it," Artemis says eventually. "Any of it. I was crazy with grief. I was in so much pain, and I just needed you to hurt like I was hurting. Also, I was very, very drunk. Like, so drunk that I think I puked on a member of the choir."

"Yes." I nod. "That sounds likely."

"I think I lost my mind that day. You've always been able to control your emotions, contain them somehow, but mine just get so...big. Too big to fit me. And it's not an excuse—there isn't an excuse—but I didn't know where to put them. You were all I had left in the world. So I put them on you."

I nod, looking at my hands.

"And I've spent the last ten years hating myself for it." Artemis is crying again. "I am so sorry, Cass. I am so, so sorry. It wasn't even your fault—you know that? I found out afterward. I mean, even if it had been your phone calls that... It still wouldn't have been your fault. But it *really* wasn't your fault. They found Mum's phone on silent in her handbag, at the back of the car, where she always put it. It was just an accident. A horrible, tragic accident, and you had nothing to do with it."

"I know," I say. "I checked."

It was the first thing I did when I got to London: just before I went into a meltdown that obliterated half a year and all of my memories. Perhaps it shouldn't be that surprising that I'm not very keen on *sharing* after a heartbroken confession was used to destroy me in front of everyone I've ever met.

"And I don't know how to fix it." Artemis rubs her jumper sleeve across her face. "I thought time would help, but that just came between us too. I sent letters, I sent gifts. I tried to call you, and you kept changing your number. Every time I found you, you disappeared again. You kept avoiding me, so I kept running away. I feel like somehow I wrecked both of us."

"You didn't," I say quietly. "I've always known that—"

My face crumples, so I wait until I can speak again.

"In early Greek mythology, Zeus fell in love with Metis, the goddess of prudence. When she was pregnant with his child,

Metis outwitted him. She turned herself into a fly, so Zeus turned himself into a lizard and swallowed her, whole."

Artemis frowns and opens her mouth. "I'm not sure what—"

"Eventually Zeus got a massive headache, and in agony he demanded that Hephaestus cut open his head, which he did. Out popped a fully formed Athena, the goddess of wisdom. But Metis stayed inside his head, and she whispered words to him. It tempered everything Zeus did and everything he thought from that point on, for the rest of time. Metis became a part of him."

I look at the step I'm sitting on and wonder when it was last scrubbed.

"I have my own Metis, Artemis. Ever since I was tiny, I have been surrounded by words. Adjectives. Observations, about me. At first it was discussions over my head, as if I couldn't hear them, but the older I got, the more they were simply directed at me. Until I absorbed them and they turned into a kind of... Greek chorus. A constant voice, inside my head. Other people's words about me became how *I* saw me too. But *home*. That was where that voice was gone. Because there were three people in the world who didn't see me as a list of adjectives. They saw me as me."

Artemis opens her mouth. "But I do—"

"I'm talking," I sigh sharply. "You wanted to talk, Artemis, so now we're talking. Don't bloody interrupt me."

"You're right." My sister smiles sheepishly. "Please continue."

"They saw me as me and they loved me for everything I was instead of everything I couldn't be," I say. "So when the world was hostile and unkind and loud and bright, when the whispering voice became so loud I couldn't breathe, it didn't matter, because I was always safe with you."

Art wells up and I roll my eyes.

"Are you going to cry again, because I really feel like this is not the appropriate time for you to do that and you should control yourself, Artemis."

She wipes her face. "I'm not going to cry."

"You're already crying."

"I'm just a very watery person. Continue."

"That day, I lost everything," I say, and there it is: not a splash of truth, but gallons and gallons and gallons of it. "You weren't safe anymore, Artemis. Metis was everywhere. You judged me too, so I had nowhere left to go."

"Don't say that." Artemis is properly crying now, zero self-control at all. "I know you always say what you mean, Cass, but not everybody is like that. Sometimes people just *say* things. Because they're bored. Or angry. Or hurt. Or sad. Or hammered and in need of attention. I didn't *mean* what I said, but you took it so literally. I resented you for, like, minutes, every now and then. You know, like a regular pissy younger sibling who isn't allowed a dog. The rest of the time you were just my sweet, smart, beautiful big sister who I loved more than anyone else in the world."

"Yes." I nod. "I'm starting to realize that."

Because the whole truth is overwhelming, but sometimes you have to be brave enough to look it straight in the eye. Artemis has spent the last ten years apologizing, but I was the one who couldn't forgive, who ran away, who cut her off without giving her a chance to make things better. Who tucked my pain and memories neatly away where they could never be accessed, never be processed, never be given the room to breathe or grow old. Who trapped the past in a time capsule, sealed it up and buried it deep inside me where nobody could reach it.

Artemis keeps saying sorry, but this has *never* been all her fault.

"I'm so sorry too," I say quietly. "And, for the record, I never said you couldn't have a dog. Or a birthday party, or a new restaurant. I'd have just gone upstairs and looked at my paint chips with my headphones on, or ordered a bowl of chips and picked out all the black bits."

"Yeah," Artemis sighs. "I'm realizing that, now I'm older. I think they were Mum's rules, not yours."

There's a silence, or as much of a silence as can be had with people tripping down the stairs around us and lighting cigarettes directly in front of us. You'd think they'd realize we were having a moment, but apparently not.

"You're safe with me, Cassandra," Art says finally.

My throat abruptly closes in its entirety like a Venus flytrap, which is named after the Roman goddess of love, who was named after Aphrodite, so really it should be the Aphrodite flytrap and the Romans just stole it, as per usual.

Artemis holds out a finger; I touch it with my fingertip.

"Why did you suddenly come back?" I say abruptly, because this has been bugging me for ages. "I know you tried to contact me over the years, but you *really* amped it up this time. Following me about, sitting on my doorstep. You went full throttle with the stalking. You'd never done that before, had you?"

Maybe I'd missed it. Let's be honest: it wouldn't be the first time I've missed something painfully obvious.

"A bit," Artemis admits. "But not as much, no. I…"

She hesitates, then bites her lip and reaches into her bag.

"I've been thinking of finally selling the house, so I was going through the attic and looking through some old boxes." There's a plastic folder in her hands. "I'd not been up there in all this time. I was shocked by how organized it was. Everything is labeled and tidied into perfectly arranged stacks. It's absolute madness."

I smile, remembering Dad's constant grumbling over our mother's anally retentive obsession with storage solutions: even the toilet roll had its own designated compartment.

"Anyway." Artemis opens it. "I found this."

She hands the folder over to me and I stare at it blankly, flicking through the pages, trying to work out what it is and what it means.

"I don't understand," I admit finally.

"It's a clinical report," Artemis explains, pointing at the front page. "Mum was diagnosed as autistic six months before the accident. I guess she was getting ready to tell us, because there are all these notes scribbled all over it. She corrected a lot of the psychologist's grammar too, but that's probably to be expected."

I stare at the paper again, then at Artemis. "Oh."

"Yeah." My sister smiles, shrugs. "I mean, we should probably have worked it out for ourselves, what with the lifelong obsession with Greek mythology and the rules and regulations and the need for quiet, dark rooms and the same restaurant and food over and over again and the sensory issues and the repetitive movements and the massive meltdowns, but we all just thought she was your bog-standard academic."

I blink. "Wow. That's…"

"I know." Artemis studies me. "Are you okay?"

"I mean." My eyes well up properly now, and I realize I'm scratching at my legs again. I really need to start keeping my nails short. "Yeah. It's a lot. I just wish she'd told us, so we could have supported her better. Poor Mum."

Artemis is still watching me.

"What?"

Artemis continues to watch me.

"What is it?"

She's still watching me.

"Have I got something on my face?" I rub it with the palm of my hand. "What are you staring at me like that for?"

"Look," Art says gently, pointing at the file.

On the back page, scrawled in our mother's beautiful handwriting, is written:

And Cassandra.

There's no question mark. No doubt. This is not a debate.

"And Cassandra what?" I say automatically, then jolt backward. "I'm not autistic. Don't be ridiculous. I'd know if I was. You don't live thirty-one years without realizing something like that. Somebody would have said something."

"From the sounds of it," Art says quietly, "they did."

My brain feels as if it's folding into tiny pieces, like a note in school you can switch into different shapes to read different things, although I wouldn't know for sure because nobody ever passed them to me. Is this why everyone keeps asking if I'm *on the spectrum*? I thought maybe they just meant I was inordinately colorful.

"I'm on the spectrum," I say with a jolt. "Derek and Jack were right."

"They were not." Artemis scowls. "That's a euphemism. They don't want to say *autistic* because they think it's rude. It is not rude."

"It's not?" I say distantly, observing my brain shift again.

"Nope. People think autism is some kind of *error*, and it's not. You're not broken or 'disordered,' or whatever they say on their little bits of paper. That just means 'not exactly like me.' Which—" Artemis points at the folder "—I think you'll see is one of the many things Mum wrote in the margins, along with the words *go to hell*, highlighted in pink. Autism is just a different wiring. You're built in alternative neurological software, from the ground up. Every single part of you. And it's…"

"Colorful and loud?" I guess, and Artemis laughs.

"I was going to say *brilliant*," she says. "But, yeah, I'd imagine that too. Although I don't know why anyone is surprised at how the world treats you. This has never really been a planet that embraces difference."

The new solidness inside me shifts and settles, consolidates a little further. I should be more surprised. I should be reeling. But isn't this exactly how I've always felt? That I'm not quite made the same? That I'm some kind of alien, trying to learn how to be a human from scratch every day? That I constantly need to translate the world around me to myself, and then my-self back to the world again, like speaking two completely dif-ferent languages simultaneously?

Wow. No wonder I'm always so bloody exhausted.

"What I'm saying," Art continues, and I can feel her eyes roaming my face gently like fingertips, "is that you've been taught to hate yourself, Cass. From the beginning you've been told you're broken, over and over again, and forced to try and be like everyone else. Then I did it to you too. I'm your sister and I called you a *monster*. How could I blame you for shutting me out? I'd have got up and smashed my head into the pulpit, if I were you."

"A good thing I'm not, then," I observe lightly. "They don't like that kind of behavior in churches."

"They certainly do not." Artemis laughs. "I don't want you to be *normal*, Cass. I never have. Honestly, if the world was built for your wiring, it would be a much better place. There'd be a lot less overhead lighting, for starters."

I stare at the floor as the world and everything in it tilts, then straightens.

"I'm like Mum," I say softly.

"Yes." Artemis nudges my shoulder with the end of her nose, like a puppy. "But you're yourself too, Cassie. Never be ashamed of that. You have always been unquestionably, unde-niably, unmistakably you."

I sit still and wait for the Big Emotions to come steaming in. They don't.

Nothing comes, and I know at some point in the future they'll probably all arrive at the same time—clogging up my doorway exactly like after a postal strike—and it will be over-whelming and beautiful and painful and lovely and I won't be able to pull them apart or name them, just point at all the colors and guess. But for the first time ever, it feels like maybe that's okay. Maybe they'll take their own sweet time. Maybe they'll turn up when they bloody want to turn up, in any shade they like, and when they do, I will deal with it the way I always deal with it: noisily, in a ball, on the floor.

"Don't sell the house," I say finally.

"I thought you might say that." Artemis nods.

"I'm moving home," I say, now with even more clarity. "To Cambridge. And I'm going to go back to uni to study Greek mythology, just like Mum."

"Yeah." Artemis smiles. "I'd already worked that out too."

This must be why my love of Greek mythology has never felt like a hobby, or a way to pass the time. It's how I make sense of the world and everything in it. It's what grounds me, makes me feel solid, gives me something constant to return to. It's a home inside me: a safe place that never changes, never fades, never grows boring, never tells me I'm not good enough, never asks me to leave.

Most importantly, mythology makes me so ridiculously *happy*. This is the path I would have taken, if I had only known myself a little better.

No—if I had just allowed myself to be me.

Calmly, I stand up, brush down Sal's red dress and wonder vaguely if I'll be different, now that I know who I am and how I'm made. I doubt it. I haven't changed one iota in thirty-one years: I don't plan on starting now.

"Have we had this conversation before?" Artemis stands up next to me and surveys my outfit with clear appreciation. "Have you time traveled back to it from the future, Cass, or is it all brand-new?"

"Oh my God." I think about it briefly. "I'd forgotten I can time travel."

"Sure." Art laughs loudly, kisses her finger and touches the end of my nose. "I forget I can travel through time and space just by closing my eyes all the time too. Totally slips my mind."

I stare at her, assessing her face. "Sarcasm?"

"Sarcasm," she confirms.

I look at the infinite colors spinning out of me, and the infinite colors spinning out of Artemis—at the colors shooting out of strangers, standing on the pavement, spiraling over our heads—and my sister is right: it doesn't feel like I'm *on* a spectrum so much as the spectrum feels like it's tucked neatly inside me.

I suddenly feel an incredibly strong emotion, overwhelming in its intensity.

Here it comes. Prepare. Galvanize, Cassandra.

Then I realize what it is.

"I'm hungry," I say abruptly. "Did you bring anything to eat?"

WHERE DOES A STORY END?

It's a lie, the last page of a book, because it masquerades as a conclusion. A *real* conclusion—the culmination of something—when what you're being offered is an arbitrary line in the sand. *This story ends here.* Pick a random event. Ignore whatever comes after it, or write a sequel. Pretend the world stops when the book closes, or that a final chapter isn't simply another random moment on a curated timeline.

But life isn't like that, so books are dishonest.

Maybe that's why humans like them.

And it's saying that kind of shit that will—one day, possibly—get me chucked out of the Cambridge Undergraduate Book Club.

So I draw my line here.

This is where I choose to end my story: arbitrarily, in a quiet Soho pub, carefully selected for its low lights, scented candles and nonsticky tables. I choose to end it surrounded by more people than I have ever had in my life.

On the seat opposite me sits Sal, lining up vodka shots with zero precision but impressive vigor, despite being told repeatedly that nobody wants one yet because it's 5:00 p.m. on a Tuesday. Next to her, Sophie splits open a pack of crisps—which promptly go everywhere—at which point Barry sighs and goes to the bar to get more. Nobody quite knows why he's here, but apparently he wanted to "say my goodbyes too," as if I'm dying, which—to clarify—I'm not.

Luckily Jack didn't feel the same compunction, but Gareth has joined the festivities, and so has Ron. The latter keeps glancing my way, and every time our eyeballs meet it's like paintballs exploding: yellows and pinks and oranges, splashed across the back of my brain. He's also back in his navy cashmere jumper, which I'm extremely happy about. Apparently he has nine identical versions, and frankly, I've never heard anything so sensible and clever and sexy in my entire life.

Artemis is next to me, which is where she has been since the gala.

She was next to me when I painstakingly filled out an application to Cambridge University, and googled *How to Survive University as a Mature Autistic Student*. She was next to me when I packed up my Brixton bedroom, when I moved it all to Cambridge in the back of her car—she can actually drive, kind of—and she said nothing at all when I played the same song, over and over again, in an attempt to calm myself down. She was next to me when I walked into our family house for the first time in ten years and started crying, and then when I kicked off and cried again because someone had repainted the bathroom blue.

Artemis was next to me when I settled in; found my new patterns.

Refound my old ones, like friends.

And for the first time in years, I don't feel loneliness like a constant seagull cry inside me: screeching and shitting over everything, eating my happiness as soon as I hold it in my hands.

Honestly, I'm kind of ready for Artemis not to be next to me all the time.

I need my space and she has taken to sitting *way* too close.

"Have you got everything ready?" Art leans toward me and nudges my arm with her nose. "You're all packed?"

Finally free of my loop, I realized where I wanted to go: Athens. Only for a long weekend—that's enough change for now—but I've broken it into hour-long intervals and made a plan, and then I used my last day in the office to laminate it. Barry didn't say anything, so I think we've finally reached a kind of mutual understanding.

"Yes," I say. "Have you?"

"Ha," Art says loudly. "Have I packed? Of course I bloody haven't. When I move, it will be a last-minute swear-fest of chaos and plastic bags that break under the sheer weight of all my jewelry and dream catchers."

My sister is temporarily taking my old box room in Sal's house while she works out what she wants to do next, which—knowing her—will never conclusively happen. I'm fighting the urge to make a plan for her. Some people are weird like that, and just prefer not to have one.

"Anyway," I say, looking at my watch, "I think I should probably be—"

"Speech!" Sophie jumps up. "Speech!"

"No," I say tiredly. "Please stop saying *speech* constantly."

"Okay, then *I* will make one." Artemis stands up and holds her glass of beer in the air. It's filthy. I should have picked a different venue. "As we know, my sister, Cass, is extraordinary. Only *I* know quite *how* extraordinary, obviously, and if I don't win the lottery in the near future, I'd like everyone to know it's her fault."

Art winks at me and I scowl back at her.

"So out of respect for her hatred of speeches and unnecessary attention, I will keep this brief." My sister laughs brightly. "To my big sister. Thank you for always being so *very* Cassandra."

"For always being so *very* Cassandra." Everyone beams while I stare at the table. I glance up just in time to catch Ron's eyes, flush happily and look back down again. Remind me not to ever leave anywhere ever again: if this is what happens every time, I think I'd prefer to stay where I am.

"*Speech!*" Sophie shouts again, and seriously, I give up: I might as well be talking to one of my plants.

"Well," I say, standing up. "There isn't much to—"

"Oh my God!" Artemis bounces up again, cheeks flaming. "Oh my God, oh my God, what are *you* doing here?"

"You invited me," I say in surprise. "It's my Leaving Do."

Then I watch in amazement as my sister clambers over my lap and runs toward the door of the pub. And as she bounces across the floor, I feel my brain freeze again. In my defense, I didn't *forget*. Not exactly. I've done a lot of research about my personal neurology over the last ten days—with many more fascinating years still to come—and it turns out I am very, very good at hyperfocusing on things I'm interested in, and not so good at noticing anything else.

Which is why, when I see Will's face light up, it takes a while to adjust.

It's Will.

Will is here, with both of us, and I'm pretty sure that there was something I was supposed to—

"Fuck," I say loudly, slipping under the table.

"What are you *doing* here?" Artemis has somehow thrown herself through the air and stuck herself to the front of my exboyfriend like one of those little sticky men you chuck at windows. "You're not supposed to be back for another three days!" She kisses his nose. "You didn't tell me!" She kisses his ear. "I can't believe you didn't tell me!" She kisses his eyebrow. "I mean, I know we've only met twice and I'm being a bit clingy, but this is bloody *outrageous*."

Will is laughing. "I thought you liked surprises?"

"I *love* surprises." Art grabs his head with both her hands, as if she's going to eat it, and they both look so happy to see each other. I can feel their neon-blue joy spilling over like one of Sal's poorly organized vodka shots. "How did you know? Oh. I told you. Okay, that makes sense. How was it? Tell me *everything*."

"I will." His eyes are captivated by her beautiful face, like Paris meeting Helen for the first time. "Turns out there are only seven vaquitas left in the world, so we've had to make another plan to find the poor little buggers."

"That is *far* too sad," Artemis announces. "Just pretend you got kidnapped by pirates or something. Keep the tone celebratory."

Laughing, they both lean in for their very first kiss. It's surreal, how I can feel their clear connection from all the way under this tiny wooden table where I'm currently crouched in a ball.

"Come with me." Art grabs Will's hand. "You have *got* to meet my sister. You're going to love her. If you don't love her, I can't love you. It's as simple as that. So you'd *better* love her, that's all I'm saying. No pressure, but literally all the pressure."

"I'm sure I will love her," Will laughs. "Can I please get a drink first?"

"No." Artemis tugs him toward us. "You can have a drink after. Then we can celebrate your return and her imminent departure at the same time. You're kind of swapping over. William Baker, meet— Cass? Cassandra, why are you under the table? She hates meeting new people. I should have done it a little bit at a time, like introducing a recently acquired kitten. Can someone please go under and get her?"

Closing my eyes briefly, I take a deep breath.

Then I clamber out awkwardly and stand in the middle of the pub, with the rest of our party watching me curiously. In fairness, I asked for this. It serves me right for spending a hundred hours googling maps of Athens and facts about the Acropolis and Temple of Poseidon instead of remembering the small yet arguably more important point that I currently share an ex-partner with my own bloody sister.

"I couldn't find my phone." I realize it's in my hand. "Oh. There it is."

"Cassandra?" Will says.

"Hello, Will," I reply stiffly. "It's nice to see you. How was Mexico?"

Will opens his mouth, shuts it, opens it again. He glances from me to Artemis, then back to me again. "What the bloody hell is going on?"

"Wait." Artemis is also visibly spiraling. "You know each other already? How do you know each other? Through work? Cass?"

There's an awful lot of truth, but I'm not sure how much they're asking for.

"I can't tell *exactly* what is happening," Sophie narrates chirpily to Sal, "but it looks like they've had a bit of boyfriend swapsies. This is *very* exciting. Like a reality-TV show, except everyone is quite a lot older."

Will kindly decides to step in and elucidate further.

"So what's going on is I dated Cassie." He frowns. "Briefly. We went on three dates, just before I met you, Diana. Which is why I'm a bit thrown. You're sisters? Is this some kind of... joke? A setup? Am I being recorded?" He looks around the pub. "Am I missing something that makes this situation less weird?"

"Artemis," Art says abruptly, her face suddenly pale.

"I'm sorry?"

"My name is Artemis. Not Diana. I lied."

"Now?" I sigh in frustration as Will's colors shift yet again. "Of all the possible times, you decided to tell him that *now*?"

"It just came out," Art says in desperation, then frowns.

"Wait. *This* is your ex? Will is the guy you've been traveling through time for? Cassandra?"

"I…" I swallow. "A little bit."

"A little bit?"

"Yes."

"Oh my *God*." Artemis crumbles. "Cassandra, how did this happen? Do I already know this? Have I found out already?" She studies my face and freezes. "So that's a yes. How many times have I found out?"

"This is the second," I say in a small voice.

"You cannot *do* this to me," she shouts, picking up crisps and throwing them at my head one by one. "I am *so* cross with you, Cassandra Dankworth! *So cross*."

I duck the crisps and we both turn toward Will.

The poor guy looks like he might be about to be sick, and I can't blame him. It takes a certain kind of man to happily date two sisters—one of whom is apparently a secret time traveler— and I'm not sure it's one either of us would want. I think the time for breaking this news gently might now have passed.

"I…" Will starts, then shakes his head and takes a step back. "This is too much. I don't know how to… I can't… I'm so sorry, but nope."

Looking wild-eyed, like a captured Pegasus, Will slings his backpack over his shoulder and leaves the pub even faster than he arrived in it, which is—I think about it—yup, exactly what I logically assumed would happen.

Artemis sinks back into her pub chair. "Shit."

Nobody moves.

"Wow," Sal observes approvingly, looking at me with an expression I haven't seen before. "What an incredibly dramatic family this is. I love it. I'm buying a subscription. Does this sort of thing happen a lot?"

"Let's give the poor girls some space," Barry says firmly. "Drinks are on me. Everyone. Bar. Now."

"SHIT," Artemis yells much louder as our party scuttles away from the table. "This is *so typical.* You finally meet a great guy and he's already been in an on-again, off-again relationship through time and space with your closest blood relation. There's always something, isn't there. How did this even happen? Cassandra Penelope Dankworth, you have got a *lot* of explaining to do."

Desperately, I scan through my phone.

"Cass."

I hit Google and read the results.

"Cass."

Memorize the contents as fast as I can.

"Cassandra, put your bloody phone down and talk to me." Artemis rips it out of my hands and stares at it. "What is this?"

I shuffle away. "Nothing."

"You just googled a list of local accidents over the last month. Do you think I'm stupid? You're not doing it."

"I am."

"No, you're not."

"But I am, though."

I take my phone back off her and stare at it again. I can do this. I know I can. And while I'm there, I might as well branch out a bit. Put my time to good use. There you go: there's another expression about time to add to the list. You can own time and put it anywhere you like—you just have to decide where.

"No." Artemis chucks the phone on the floor—it smashes, no big deal, I'm about to undo that too—and grabs my hands. "I am not letting you do this. You will lose *everything.* Do you understand, Cassandra? Everything you've done, all the things you've achieved, it'll all disappear. All these people who care about you. Poof. Gone. You'll be alone again. It'll be like it never happened."

"Yes." I roll my eyes. "I do grasp the general concept of time."

"Then at least do it for *you.*" Artemis has started crying again, and I swear to all the gods and their cupbearers, she needs to get a grip on her emotions. She lives *way* too near the water-works. It's like building houses three inches from the ocean. "Just go back and get Will, Cassie. I'll never know."

"There's no point." I realize it's true as soon as I say it. "It wouldn't work. Will and I are completely incompatible. I don't need to see the future to know we'd eventually make each other miserable. I could try again and it would end again. And again. And again. We're very different people."

"But—"

"I love Will," I say calmly. "But we don't want the same life. I don't want children and noise and travel and mess and dogs and *tents*. You do. So have it, Artemis. Let me be the cool aunt with the amazing clothes and the quiet house full of books and peace and beautiful things that nobody ever touches. Let me have the life I'm supposed to have. Let me love you both, the best way I can. Please."

Artemis hiccups, her sweet little face all soggy.

And here they come: all the Emotions.

Every color turns up—together, in one go—and I feel them in their infinity, their breadth, their overwhelming spectrum.

I close my eyes.

"Not yet," Artemis says urgently, tugging at my sleeve until I open them again. "You're not thinking this through properly, Cass. We won't be talking. Remember? Everything we've shared will disappear too."

"It won't." I smile faintly, fiddling with the watch our parents gave me: the parents who are still here, still exactly as they were, held tightly in a past I always carry with me. "I will remember it all."

It will all be so very neat and tidy.

I won't go into the café. I won't order my banana muffin, and I won't talk to the handsome man sitting opposite me. Instead, I will go to the British Museum, I will see my sister standing by the naked centaur, and I will tell her I love her. That I have always loved her; that I will never worry again that I cannot love, that I cannot feel a connection, because she is the living proof that I can, that I do, that I will.

That all the love I have is right here, stored inside me.

I'd imagine she'll be quite surprised.

Then I'll casually suggest that we go see an animal photography exhibition in Shoreditch, and I'll simply let fate take its course from there. And if fate decides not to—if it decides to be a little bugger, as per usual—then I'll keep giving fate a nudge until it finally gets the message.

Whether their love works out is up to them.

I can only do so much; I'm not Eros.

As for the rest of my story... There's just no way of knowing what will happen to it. I'd imagine it will change. I'd imagine I will want it to. Maybe it will have different characters. Different emotions. Different social events I have to avoid. Maybe my story will be better, maybe it will be worse. Maybe it'll be bigger, maybe it'll be smaller. Maybe I'll be a hero, maybe I'll be a monster. I'd imagine ultimately I'll hover somewhere in between, the way most of us non-goddesses tend to.

Only time will tell, and now I'll be listening just as hard as I can.

"Cassandra," Artemis says. "Open your eyes."

I open my eyes.

"Six." She leans forward to kiss my cheek and I can feel the love pouring out of her into me and mine straight back into her, primrose yellow. "Twenty-nine. Eighteen. Forty-three. Nine."

"I'm not winning the lottery for you too," I laugh, wiping her face. "Stop being so greedy. I'll see you next time, okay?"

"Bye." Artemis nods, taking a deep breath.

"Bye." I smile.

And I close my eyes to go back to the beginning.

★ ★ ★ ★ ★

ACKNOWLEDGMENTS

Writing often seems a solitary endeavor. In truth, all books require a brilliant team behind them, and I have been incredibly lucky with this one.

Massive thanks to my wonderful UK agent, Kate Shaw, who has been with me from the beginning, and my brilliant US agent, Allison Hellegers, who is always a joy and a pleasure to have on side and worked tirelessly to find Cassie the right home. Thanks to my incredible US editor, April Osborn at MIRA Books: your insight, encouragement and eagle eye have been invaluable and have made the book infinitely stronger and more powerful.

Publishing a story about an autistic character is one thing—making sure that the autistic author is listened to and given additional support when necessary is quite another, and my team at MIRA have absolutely smashed both. Leah Morse, Heather Connor, Ashley MacDonald, Puja Lad, Ana Luxton, Colleen Simpson, Ariana Sinclair, Brieana Garcia, Nora Rawn—you have done an amazing job at championing both Cassie and me, and my gratitude is extensive. Thank you. The cover is incredible, so an enormously special thanks to Alexandra Niit, Elita Sidiropoulou and Erin Craig for absolutely smashing it out of the park.

To my wonderful film agent, Rebecca Watson at Valerie Hoskins Associates, and my foreign language agents, Nicki Kennedy, Jenny Robson, Katherine West and Alix Shaw at ILA: thank you, always, for your continued support, hard work and vision in getting this book out to the wide world and into exactly the right hands.

Mum, all of these books are because of you. Thank you for reading to me every night, for saving all my first attempts at writing, for making stories an inherent part of me. Dad, my unofficial Creative Consultant, your generosity, energy and sense of humor are constantly inspirational, and I will continue to steal them whenever I can. To my little sister, Tara: you are the bravest half of me, and one day I'll have to stop writing about how much I love you. To my niece, Autumn—you're the smartest, funniest, weirdest little nugget in the world, and I adore you. To the rest of my family—Grandma, Lesley, Judith, Caro, Vero, Louise, Adrien, Charlie, Suzie, Victoire, Vincent, Simon, Ellen, Freya, Robin, Lorraine, Romaine, Dixie, Chelsea—thanks for the support and love, as always. A shout-out to my North American buds too, Ashley, Jeff and Patrick. This is just another excellent reason to visit you.

I lost my beloved granddad just before I finished writing this book, so this book is for him. He was (and will always be) my favorite person, and not just because he read every word I ever wrote. He was also the kindest, most gentle, most curious and most compassionate person I have ever known, and I miss him daily. Thank you, My Granddad. I hope you're enjoying this story now, wherever you are.

Finally, this book does not represent autism, and neither I nor

Cassie represent autistic people. We are simply individual voices in a choir of millions of amazing neurodivergent people, all with our own experiences, our own ways of seeing the world, our own ways of existing. I cannot speak for anyone but myself, and I would not want to try. So, whether you enjoyed this book or not, whether you see yourself represented in this story or not, I urge you to seek out other autistic voices.

We are beautiful, we are unique, and we are legion.